Only Ever You

Only Ever You

HALEY WARREN

This book is a work of fiction. Any references to historical events, real people, or real places are used fictitiously. Other names, characters, places, and events are products of the author's imagination, and any resemblance to actual events or places or persons, living or dead, is entirely coincidental.

Copyright © 2025 by Haley Warren

Cover Illustration and Design: Summer Grove

Editing: Briana Ozor

First paperback edition November 2025

ISBN 978-1-0697501-0-5 (Paperback)

To my brain—I don't always like you, and I don't think you always like me. Some days, you've made loving me and being loved by me hard, even though the climb has always been worth it in the end.

You're not always kind, but you're mine.

Thank you for making me, me.

Author's Note

Dear Reader,

Thank you so much for picking up Only Ever You.

We've got another absolutely stunning, beautiful and smart cover by Summer Grove on the outside (very heavy on the yearning vibes), and another emotional romance by me on the inside—who would have thought!

Before you start reading, there are some things about Only Ever You that I want to share. A second-chance romance full of yearning, pining and tension, it's also a story about healing and finding happiness. It's a book about what it means to love someone when you don't love yourself. It's a love letter to people with unkind brains and heavy hearts that are so capable and so full of love, even when they don't have any left for themselves. It's a love letter to the sensitive girlies, and anyone who's ever thought their big feelings were a hinderance, not a superpower.

They are a superpower, by the way. But that doesn't mean we don't struggle with them. For most of my life, I've lived in a world that was so big and so loud and it was a world where everyone said I felt way too much—and I gave that world to Sloan. I gave her the parts of myself that I still don't like, even though I'm trying to understand them. I gave her my insecurity, my sensitivity, my reassurance seeking—but I also gave her someone who sees all those things, and at the end of the day, still thinks she's the best person on the planet. I gave Bohdan the utter despair I've felt when I was trying to understand who I was and where I fit, but just like with Sloan, I gave him someone whose heart fits with his just like the pieces of a puzzle.

Sloan moves through a world where she feels like she just doesn't fit, unmoored and unanchored, with big feelings that don't seem to match her surroundings, a mind that races and doesn't really let her rest and repeats itself. I don't mention her diagnosis on page because I wanted to capture what that felt like for me, and for so many other people out there, to be so uncertain and so unsure while you're just trying to understand who you are and how you work. I hope, if you see yourself in her, or in Bohdan, you find something healing in them too.

Content Warnings:

- Discussions of head trauma and injury (Accident occurs on-page from a different POV and is loosely described)

- Exploration of the impacts of trauma and loss

- Anxiety, depression, and intrusive thoughts (Described, and on-page)

- Migraines (On-page and loosely described)

- Compulsions, both mental (Checking, reassurance) and counting (physical)

- Therapy, mentioned off-page and experienced on-page

- Substance use on-page (consuming alcohol and prescription medication, including anxiety medication/sedatives)

- A relationship in crisis

As much as I hope you read Only Ever You, you matter more.
All my love,
Haley

Only Ever You

Prologue

Sloan

I loved a boy once. With my whole heart.

For a very long time, actually.

So much that I would have died for him. Even though that's not what he wanted. He wanted me to live and breathe and feel. And once upon a time, he wanted to do all those things with me.

Sometimes I think about taking out a pen, scratching out all the words of our life together, and trying to rewrite a story where he's a villain. But it's just not true.

He loved me with his whole heart, too. And I think that's what makes it so hard. Because even though I gave, and gave, and gave—it wasn't enough. And in the end, a part of me withered away; maybe it died, or maybe it just went to sleep for a long, long nap when he left.

I can't be certain, but I've never been quite the same, and I don't think I ever will be.

But I do know love isn't a mistake I'll be making again.

Prologue

Bohdan

Somewhere in the multiverse, if you believe in that sort of thing, twenty-year-old me sees eighteen-year-old her for the first time.

He sees her through the scratched-up glass surrounding the ice when he's supposed to be focused on a million other things.

She smiles quietly, nodding along with her friends, blinking beautiful blue eyes a bit too much, like maybe she's trying not to cry, with these wisps of raven hair tumbling around her face.

Dark all over, except for those shining eyes.

All of her shines under the shitty lighting, actually.

Zlatíčko, *little gold*, he thinks when he skates by.

I imagine the story shakes out more or less the same in those endless, rolling universes.

He bangs on the glass for her attention before the half, and tries to shout over the music and noise of the crowd that he wants her number.

She figures it out eventually, and she does wipe a shaky hand across her cheeks, tears glistening on her fingertips. He finds out later that sometimes that just happens, even though she wishes it didn't.

But that night, she hands him what turns out to be a Polaroid picture of her, taken by one of her friends minutes earlier, her number scribbled across the back.

I bet he calls her before he's even changed out of his equipment after the game.

But I'd like to think in at least one of those universes, even though the years probably go on more or less the same in all of them, and as much as I hope some things turn out differently for him, I mostly hope that in at least one, he goes to sleep beside her. He wakes up beside her. That he sees her every day in all the ways you see a person when you make a life with them, and he doesn't have to resort to pulling that ancient, peeling, fraying photograph out of his wallet each day to get a glimpse of her.

It couldn't be this one. But the idea that maybe it's happening for some version of me out there somewhere makes it feel a bit easier to breathe in this one when that hidden picture is all I've got.

Bohdan

Of all the home remedies for a migraine, the combination of lavender and peppermint oils on my neck and temples is usually my favourite.

But they aren't doing shit right now.

I think the opponent might have been too great—five hours of live on-air commentary under blinding studio lights after a night of next to no sleep.

I'm not thinking when I press my fingers to my temples, like the pressure might will the oil to sink further into my skin and fix my broken brain.

It doesn't work.

I'm certainly not thinking when I take those same fingers and press them against my eyes, groaning in frustration and leaning back in the chair I sat in for two hours this morning while someone flipped the waves of my hair to the left, and then to the right, tugging on them so they curled over my ears just so.

The oil doesn't fix whatever the fuck is going on in my head—but it does come off my fingertips and somehow get all over my eyeballs.

By the way it burns, I'm guessing it's the peppermint.

"Kurva." *Fuck.*

"That doesn't sound good."

I blink, eyes still stinging, the figure leaning in the doorway recognizable because he's the only asshole who could get away with wearing a brown suit and still be taken seriously when he's commenting on plays during the biggest hockey games of the week.

That happens when you're AJ Stone and you have a perfectly respectable, perfectly long career with two Stanley Cups, and no one's seen you splayed out on the ice before they have to cut to commercial because everyone thinks you might be dead.

I squint, shrugging. "It's not."

AJ tips his chin towards my fingers, back digging in at my right temple. "You alright?"

I nod, pressing my fingers down again before running them through my hair, trying to flatten it. Like a wave might rest on top of the scar in the exact trajectory it snakes across my skin and hide it from him, even though I know he knows it's there.

Everyone in North America who watches professional hockey knows it's there.

"Lights bugging you?" he tries again.

"Nah." I give a noncommittal jerk of my chin and stand, grabbing my suit jacket from the back of the makeup chair. "No sleep last night."

I've already lost the only two things I loved because of this. The last thing I need is for everyone in broadcasting to know I can't hack it under bright lights, and I'll lose the last thing I have a modicum of fondness for.

He nods, but there's a flash of sympathy behind his eyes; they darken for a moment, like he doesn't quite believe me.

He shouldn't.

A crease scores between his brows, and he nods again, thoughtful. "You were great tonight. And those one-to-one segments did huge numbers."

Before I can answer, he pulls a rolled-up magazine from the back pocket of his suit and points it at me, grinning. "Probably helps with numbers when you look like that."

"Weren't you just in a cologne commercial with not one, not two, but three unnecessary shirtless scenes?" I offer him a wry look, shrugging my suit jacket on before rolling my shoulders.

My specialist tells me I clench my jaw too much when a migraine starts—referred me to another psychiatrist because he said it seemed psychological—something about misplaced frustration. I never went, and he was probably right. You could flick a quarter off the muscles in my neck, and my traps always start to ache around hour three.

AJ smiles, pushes off the door, and hits the magazine against his abdomen. "Airbrushing. I'm thirty-seven now, Novotnak. Not fresh off the ice like you."

A brow lifts. "Sounds like a washboard to me."

He crosses the room with this easy grace—one hand still tucked into the pants of his suit, the other wrapped around the magazine—and it's not because of the general superiority of whatever makes up the muscles of a generational athlete, it's the type of ease you see in someone content.

Happy with life and their lot in it.

Tossing the magazine onto the desk in front of us, he tips his chin. "One of the techs dug this up."

I don't have to look to know what it is.

But I do anyway.

I even reach forward and pick it up—like I don't have a copy in a frame stashed in the back of a closet somewhere at home. Like it isn't framed in my parents' sad, abandoned shrine to me that's just a closed-off room now. Like a copy doesn't sit somewhere in my grandparents' place in Brno, even though they can't read it.

Like she didn't make me a collage of the thing when she was nineteen and I was twenty-one.

There I am.

Twenty-one-year-old Bohdan Novotnak. Gloved hands wrapped around the top of a championship-winning stick. We were superstitious back then—said we wouldn't pose with anything but the ones we'd actually played with, even though they were covered in ugly, frayed, stained tape we just kept wrapping over.

Golden-brown hair a bit more wild, styled to look like it was fresh from a postgame shower.

Top scorer in the entire NCAA standing between his two linemates and best friends.

Smiling. Happy.

No scar.

Girl of his dreams waiting for him back in that shitty apartment she shared with her best friend.

"You still talk to them?" AJ gestures towards the two people flanking me, pointing at each of them in turn. "Valdez and Choi?"

"Every day." I swallow, roll my shoulders out, and toss the magazine back onto the desk. It skids across the lacquered surface until it knocks into a bottle of hairspray and rests just under the mirror, the reflection of that old me staring up mockingly.

AJ cocks his head, considering the me standing in front of him and the me immortalized on that glossy piece of paper that somehow hasn't lost its shine in the last nine years. "Valdez, Novotnak, and Choi. Once-in-a-generation kind of thing. Lightning in a bottle. You and Choi went—"

"First and second in the draft."

"And Valdez?"

I grin, despite the whole fucked-up, heavy thing. Talon's been the same since the day I met him. "He skipped the whole thing and took a lot of money to go play in Sweden. He just decided to retire, actually"

"Retire? He's, what, thirty? He get injured or something?"

Shaking my head, I fish my phone from my suit jacket and thumb through my texts until I find the gaudy invite he sent around. It only went to four people: his sister Tia, Jay, me, and Sloan.

Talon's Retirement River Cruise
You are cordially invited to the party of the century
Meet me in Barcelona and help me celebrate my retirement in style!

I didn't answer.

Neither did she.

I hold the phone out for AJ and watch his eyes move across the screen, the corners of brown skin crinkling before he cracks a grin and looks up at me, eyes wide. "Retirement river cruise?"

"That's Talon. The only thing he ever really took seriously was that"—I point my chin towards the magazine—"and it's only because of me and Jay. He wanted it for us. Not for him."

"You're telling me that an NCAA-calibre athlete, part of probably the best line collegiate hockey's ever seen, two-time Frozen Four champion didn't want to win? Hard to believe." Doubt creeps across his brows when they come together.

"Then you haven't met Talon Valdez. He's one of a kind." I shrug again, glancing towards the unanswered invite before pocketing my phone again.

AJ clears his throat, eyes flicking back to the magazine before they land back on me. "You going?"

I can feel my pulse behind my eyes now, and I take a slow blink. AJ didn't come here to show me an old magazine or to ask me about my best friend's penchant for theatrics, and I wish he'd cut to the chase so I can go home and lie in the dark with a stupid ice wrap on my head. "Undecided. Trying to figure out my next move with my agent."

I've been joining panels and shows as a guest analyst while I've floated about unmoored in the world over the last year.

When I think about what I planned for my life, it certainly wasn't a forced retirement from professional hockey before I turned thirty.

I definitely wasn't sitting behind an analyst's desk, lights that made me uncomfortable beaming away over top of me while my thirtieth birthday came and went with no consequence.

I wanted to be the man standing in front of me—to play and play and play until I felt my body start to slow just the slightest bit so I could leave on top.

"That's actually why I came to chat. I was just talking to Zane, I know this was just an as-needed, part-time thing for you. Working as an analyst is usually a gig for retirement, but ah—"

"I'm retired, AJ, you can say it. It's not a bad word," I mutter, even though it is a bad word. It's the worst word, and I've spent too much time in therapy trying to get used to the sound of it on my tongue.

Something like sympathy flashes behind his eyes, and he raises his palms in concession. "Alright. You're retired at the ripe old age of thirty, still probably one of the best centres to grace the ice, and you happen to be great on television. With social media, it's a whole new landscape for networks. They're constantly trying to appeal to younger audiences. You poll great with men and women ages eighteen to twenty-nine."

"Fascinating."

AJ snorts before continuing. "Just a fact, Bohdan. Zane is going to offer to make you a regular at the desk. But just so you know, he's going to ask for something else, too. Those one-to-one segments you did with the team fresh off the world juniors, he wants a new show with different coverage. Something short, clippable. Where you'd—I don't know, skate around with other players, kick a ball down a field, and talk about . . ." He swallows, an apologetic shrug to his shoulders. "Injury. Recovery. Expectations. Mental health."

It's a psychosomatic, a figment of my imagination, but the scar along my temple feels like it's pulsing with the beat of my heart, and a sharp pain stabs at my brain behind it. I feel my lips curl backward and I give a jerk of my head. "Zane wants me to . . . what? Be some sort of pseudo talk show host? About mental health in sports?" My nostrils flare with an exhale and I reach down, snatching my duffel bag from where I left it beside the makeup desk. I need this conversation to be over. "Am I supposed to be some sort of example? Don't worry, you might lose it all, but there's light at the end of the tunnel?"

AJ's mouth tugs to the side, and he gives a weary shake of his head, hands finding the pockets of his suit again. "I'm just the messenger. You can't do that anymore"—he angles his elbow towards the magazine, still askew on the desk—"but you are good at this. You've got too much talent to let it all go to waste."

"Bit late for that," I say flatly, pointedly walking past him towards the door.

I'm being difficult. I'm being rude. This isn't the version of myself I want to be—the one I've been stuck with for a little over a year.

Not the me I used to be.

But she's not here to remind me, and she's not here to stop me, so I brush past AJ without a backward glance.

His voice stops me when I reach the doorway.

"You could be, you know. An example. That injuries should be taken seriously. That your brain matters. That there's life waiting after sport."

I do turn back, about to tell him that I pissed away the only life waiting for me after hockey, but he grabs the magazine from the desk and hands it to me. "Go on the cruise, Bohdan. Celebrate your friend. Think it over. Decide who you want to be now."

He leaves me standing there, half in, half out of not just the doorway but probably my life, lights beating down on my throbbing head and a brain that feels a bit like it's bleeding, holding an old magazine with the only version of myself I was ever interested in being immortalized on the cover.

The me who had his whole life ahead of him.

The me who knew with absolute certainty what he was supposed to do.

The me who had her.

I fish my phone from my suit pocket and open the text thread. It's been named the same thing since college.

The Only Line to Ever Exist—Talon's doing.

It's full of mostly unanswered texts from Talon, with the occasional begrudging response from Jay.

> **Talon:** Bohdan, please. I can't celebrate my retirement without you.

> **Talon:** You're Czech. You'll love the cruise. Back to your roots.

> **Jay:** Is the boat even going by there?

> **Jay:** And leave him alone, he's on-air.

> **Jay:** You know, his job. He has actual responsibilities, Talon.

> **Talon:** Says the guy who's probably sitting on his couch because he didn't make the playoffs. Unfortunate run, Jay.

> **Talon:** Novo? Bohdie? Bohder? Please say yes. I need you.

I don't know who I want to be—certainly not any of those unfortunate fucking nicknames—but I know I don't want to stand in this doorway any longer.

> **Bohdan:** If it'll shut you up—you can count me in.

Sloan

"Professor Joseph!"

I don't hear the shout the first time. It's a bit hard, over the music and the drunk graduate students standing huddled around sticky, worn tables and the clink of glasses, beer frothing and foaming over the rims.

"Professor Joseph!"

I hear it the second time, though. I glance over my shoulder when I shrug on my coat and spot not one, not two, but three of my grad students, who, judging by the rosy hue on all their cheeks and shining eyes, have had a few too many of the three-dollar beers.

"Do you have to leave?" Salome, the one in the middle, whines. On a good day, she can make a convincing argument to counter just about anything, but today, her words tumble together into one long, almost intelligible string.

"Right now? Yes. I need to get home." I give her a flat smile.

I don't mind the conversation—but I'm trying to spare her. I know what I'd feel like if I woke up the morning after a night at the Grad Club, realizing I'd drunkenly spoken to one of my professors for too long.

But not everyone's brains are as mean as mine.

"No," she pouts, tipping her head back before levelling me with wide, unfocused puppy dog eyes. "Leave the program! We're going to miss you."

"Adjunct Professor." I lift my palm, moving it up and down in space like I'm holding the merit of position—all my worth there—before raising my other, sending it skyrocketing past. "Assistant Professor. I think you know which is better."

But my palm holding up my current role has all this other baggage they can't see.

It's weighed down by these impossibly heavy things, anchoring it to the floor and making just about anything in the entire world better than staying here for a moment longer.

A boy with golden-brown hair and grey eyes who used to love me.

A girl who loved him back and wanted a life with him so desperately she'd have followed him to the ends of the earth.

One hand holds a life marred by Bohdan Novotnak.

The other holds a fresh start.

"Boo!" Salome shouts, gesturing downwards with her thumb before knocking her beer over and sending the entire group of them jumping back so their boots don't get splashed.

Holding my hand up, I wrinkle my nose with a small smile and take the opportunity to duck out while they try to mop up the deluge.

All the music and all the shouts fade, nothing more than the muffled thump of dull bass once the door closes behind me.

The University of Washington campus is about to be beautiful, objectively speaking—we're right on the precipice of spring, which means the cherry trees are about to blossom.

Twisted branches with their peeling bark are about to be hidden behind clouds of white and pale pink.

This was never where I wanted to be—I'd always planned on moving back home to Toronto after I graduated from Michigan State.

But I ended up here all the same, and it felt a bit like something out of a movie—how beautiful the campus was, blossoms pluming along the trees, with ancient brick buildings peeking out from behind them. Bohdan's hand in mind, eyes on me and nodding quietly, sunlight hitting the planes of his face, studying me in that funny sort of stoic way only he ever did while I showed him around.

I thought it was the most wonderful thing I'd ever seen back then.

I can't really stand the sight of it now. I keep my eyes down, firmly on the toes of my worn leather boots. Each step is one step closer to leaving this place, this godforsaken city where it gets harder and harder to breathe each day because Bohdan took all the oxygen with him when he left.

Alone. Left behind. Disposable.

Each word echoes alongside the sound of my heels hitting the stone.

I stop abruptly, wincing when I reach into my pocket for my headphones.

"Shut up," I whisper, but it's not quite loud enough and the melody continues, with colourful new notes.

Abandoned. Awful. Not enough and too much all at the same time.

My phone rings before I can find something else to listen to.

"Tia." I smile into the phone, thankful, not for the first time and certainly not for the last, that my best friend called me.

"Sloan," she croons, and I can just make out the resounding tap of her heels against marble. "What are you doing?"

"Leaving campus. What are you doing?"

"Leaving work." The symphony of her heels is joined by car horns and inaudible conversation. Enough to tell me she just stepped out of her office, right by that stupid golden bull on Wall Street. "Thought I'd give one last shot at convincing you to come on my brother's sad little Peter Pan–esque, 'I'll never grow up' cruise before I catch the subway."

I snort, starting my walk across campus again, the nefarious sounds of my footsteps chased away by the sound of my best friend. "It's a good thing you went into accounting, not advertising. Your pitch needs a bit of work."

"I do believe in faeries, I do, I do!" Tia shouts into the phone, the lilt of her laughter warm before she tries again. "You don't want to board the ship, hit the second star to the right, and head straight on till morning?"

"Not only does the idea of a cruise in general sound unappealing, but the guest list really isn't doing it for me." I pause, the phantom ache from that empty place where Bohdan used to live making it hard to breathe, but I take a shaky inhale and keep talking before Tia can interrupt. "And it's like you forget, I'm moving. It's a lot to move from one apartment to another, let alone to an entirely new city in a different country. I can't just call a moving company."

"And what does our therapist think about this big move?"

I roll my eyes. "Lu isn't *our* therapist, she's mine. And I'll have you know that she thinks it's a great idea." She doesn't, not really. It kind of goes against the basic tenets of Exposure and Response Prevention therapy, and it's a bit more like avoidance for me to run away to a place Bohdan never touched.

Tia snorts, all laced with disbeliefs and the truths she knows about me and my brain. "Well, she's always felt like my therapist. I've gained so many insights second hand. Lu is your third-longest relationship, you know. Are you going to keep doing video or . . . ?"

"We've severed ties. She's sent me on my way with a list of practitioners she knows in Toronto, and when I get settled, I'll find someone." I tip my chin up in a swallow, cross my arms, and ready for the inevitable.

"Does a break in therapy seem like the best idea?" Tia asks softly. I picture her lips twisting to the side, eyes clouding in concern.

I blink. Tipping my chin up further even though she can't see it. "It's only temporary. I'm perfectly capable of managing on my own for awhile. I'm *fine*."

I hope the emphasis on the word that certainly doesn't describe anything about me is enough to get her to drop it.

It is.

Tia changes tune, her voice rising again. "You know, I'd have made a bigger fuss about this move had your relocating to Toronto not brought you closer to me. Despite the short flight time between New York and Toronto, I can't believe you're leaving. You loved Seattle."

Loved. The tense being operative and entirely telling of why it doesn't bother me at all to leave.

I don't tell Tia that, I try to deflect instead. "You forget I'm Canadian. It's where I'm from. It's where I grew up. It's not shocking. It's where I wanted to be before I was . . . brought here."

It doesn't work. She gets right back to the heart of the matter anyway.

"Sloan. Don't rewrite history." I don't have to see her to know she's tugging a curl in exasperation, that she's shaking her head slowly, something that looks like pity painted across her face. "Bohdan didn't drag you by a leashed backpack to Seattle."

I've stopped walking again, feet silent against the cobblestones. But I hear what those footsteps would tell me all the same.

No. You followed him, nothing but a little puppy. And in the end, it still wasn't enough.

"What is love if not a leashed backpack?" I raise a hand, trying to be laissez-faire for once in my life.

"You're my best friend. I love you. Is that a leashed backpack?"

Sometimes the words *I love you* sound a bit like someone dragging an axe along a whetstone, sharpening it, readying it to take another piece of me.

Bohdan didn't take my ability to feel love when he left—even though I wish he did. It might have made things easier.

I love Tia. I love my parents. I love my grandparents. I love Talon and Jay, even though we don't talk as much because they were his to begin with.

I still love him, even though I like to pretend I don't.

He didn't take any of that.

But the pieces of me that he watered and grew and cherished—those pieces of me that believed I were worthy of love—they left with him.

I stay silent, and it hangs there, heavy and taking all the air out of this phone call with my best friend.

I think some of the cherry blossoms even furl their petals inward.

Tia sighs—all sad and weary and like someone so much older than she is. "It'll be good for you. He's not coming, Sloan. He never answered. You can deal with Talon and Jay for a week. I'll ban them from uttering his name. I'll go as far as banning them from even using words that start with the letter *B*."

My eyes prickle and I scrunch up my nose. I wish it didn't hurt me, but it does.

Because the only version of Bohdan I know who wouldn't answer his best friends is the Bohdan from a year and a half ago—this impossibly sad, impossibly hurt boy who felt like a shell of the man he used to be.

I swallow. "Shouldn't Jay be—I don't know? Skating? Scoring goals?"

"Season ended." I can picture Tia shrugging one shoulder, full lips tugging into a resigned line. "They didn't make the playoffs. Which you'd know if you turned on the TV. Bohdan actually commented on the—"

"I don't watch TV." A lie. I watch so much reality TV. I know everything there is to know about the so-called hottest bartenders in LA in the early aughts, every housewife who has ever graced the screens, and all there is to know about what happens below the deck of a ship. It keeps my brain quiet. "And if I did, I certainly would not watch my former boyfriend watch a bunch of grown men chase a tiny rubber puck around a rink."

Tia scoffs. "Funny, you used to love watching anything to do with that boy and rubber pucks and rinks."

"New year, new me," I say, forcing myself to start down the path again. I've started and stopped abruptly so many times someone's probably about to call campus security.

"Alright. If it's really a new year, a new you, then you should have no problem coming with me. Don't make me beg—I'm about to go onto the subway. I'm not above calling you back as soon as I get to my stop." Her voice turns pleading.

And if there's one thing I've never been able to do, it's tell Tia Valdez no.

"Fine," I concede, and her answering shriek does make me smile for real.

Tia talks for longer than she should, excitement rising in her voice, not a care in the world that she's probably blocking the entrance to the subway, that she's taking up all this space, but she can't seem to help it because she just has so much to look forward to, and her life is so wonderful, so good—that she won't apologize for it.

And she shouldn't have to.

It's always been like that. I can picture an eighteen-year-old Tia smiling at me when I opened the door to our shared dorm room at Michigan State—happy, exuberant, and inviting me into a world that, despite what it would look like to an outsider, felt a lot quieter than the one I occupied.

It's a stupid thing to think about, us back then. Because the memories of Tia, Talon, and Jay are all tied up in my memories of Bohdan.

Those memories are sort of like those cherry blossoms, stubborn and desperate to poke through and find the sunlight.

But they're beautiful and wonderful, and all the things I thought were beautiful and wonderful aren't.

And I wish they'd stay in the dark.

Fortunately for me, I don't remember the exact moment I fell in love with Bohdan.

I just know that I did—quickly and all at once, in that big, giant way you do when you're young.

But I do remember the moment I prayed and prayed and prayed to whoever might be listening to please, please, *please* make it stop.

Sloan

Then – College

"I can't believe you're going out with one of my brother's teammates." Tia makes a face behind me in the mirror, nose scrunching with disgust. She shakes her head with an exhale before taking a too-long sip of her terribly mixed vodka cranberry.

I pause, pulling the eyeliner away from my face before I accidentally stab myself. "You guys told me to give him my number!"

"I didn't think he'd actually call!" She holds her hands up in the air, drink splashing over the rim of one of the plastic cups we've had since frosh week, our dorm name stamped and peeling across the neon. "He's friends with Talon. I figured he'd be the same—you know, gross."

She gives another exaggerated shudder before scooting forward so she can see herself in the mirror that sits between our two beds in our dorm room. I watch as she tips her face back and forth, like she's admiring the pink flush on her cheeks from the alcohol.

"Should I—" My grip loosens on the pencil, and I swallow, blinking. "Should I not go? Do you think it's a mistake?"

Tia swings her head to me, curls flying around her face. "What?"

"Do you think it was a mistake?" I repeat, mouth drying out and the onslaught of my brain starting in. "You say he's . . . gross, like your brother. Maybe I shouldn't go."

She studies me, cheeks softening, brown eyes blinking at me, like she's trying to figure something out, before she takes a final sip of her drink, sets it down, and somehow scoots closer to me, so our heads are pressed together. "I think my brother is gross, but I also think he's one of the best people on the planet. If Talon thinks Bohdan is worth his time, I think he's worth yours."

There's a different question I want to ask, and she knows me enough now to know. I can see it as she tilts her head, temple pressing against mine, eyebrows rising with an encouraging lift.

"Do you think he'll like me?" My voice cracks, and all those things I think about myself peer through the gaping wound of me, and they dig their claws in and they try to force the crack larger so Tia will see them, too.

I give my head a tiny shake and close my eyes, but I think a tear escapes anyway.

Her thumb finds my cheek, brushing the tear away before she grips my chin. "Hey. Sloan. Look at me."

I press my eyes closed harder.

"Sloan." Her voice has an edge this time, and I blink my eyes open. "If he doesn't like you, sounds like maybe he's taken one-too-many hits into the boards. Now give me your eyeliner, you smudged it."

And he does seem to like me.

At least I think he does.

He doesn't look disappointed or left wanting when I walk down the dorm stairs to meet him at the bottom.

He stands there, hands shoved into the pockets of a black jacket, the hood of a grey sweater peeking out, amber hair damp and curling against it at the nape of his neck, jaw set in a firm line as he watches me walk down the steps.

But it's the way his voice lowers and catches on a rough note when his eyes pass over me and he says hi, and I hear my name on Bohdan Novotnak's lips for the first time.

"Hello, Sloan."

The sound traipses across my skin, my shoulders, down my spine until I shiver, and I think my heart starts beating for the first time in my entire life.

I raise a hand when I stop on the stair at the bottom, eye level with him. "Hi, Bohdan. It's nice to meet you . . . in person, I guess. I'm not sure the Polaroid exchange counted."

"Can you skate?"

He doesn't say thank you for coming, that it's nice to see me, he doesn't even ask me how I am or what I might want to do. It's something I learn quickly about him—he doesn't always say much, but he says what he means.

"Not well." I blink, wrinkling my nose with a smile. "Are you asking me that because I'm Canadian?"

"No. I'm Canadian, too." He gives me a sideways grin, pointing his chin towards the other end of campus, where the faint glow of the lights from the Munn Ice Arena are visible against the dusk.

He waits, holding his hand out expectantly, and I nod, warmth flushing across my cheeks when my palm meets his.

Our skin touches for the first time as he helps me step down, and I raise my chin to keep my eyes on his.

It's just a brush, two palms touching for the first time, old skin that's already living on both of our bodies, but I think I'm new all the same.

Bohdan looks down at me, too serious for a boy his age, and his fingers curl against the back of my hand for a too-brief moment, before he tips his elbow in the direction of the rink again and shoves his hands in his jacket pockets.

The lamps lining campus flicker on over us, but all that does is illuminate the carved line of Bohdan's jaw, the planes of his cheekbones cutting across his face, and make the grey of his eyes look like an early morning.

"I didn't know you were Canadian. Where are you from?" I fold my arms across my chest, falling into step beside him as we weave through the groups of students spilling out from dorms, linked arms and laughter echoing up to the sky.

Bohdan nods once, eyebrows raising and chin tipping up in acknowledgement as people stop and point at him, some students going as far as to scream his name like they're watching him on the ice. "Yeah. Recruitment landed me here. I grew up in Ottawa, but my parents are originally from the Czech Republic. We immigrated when I was two."

He sidesteps a student who stumbles backward from a group, looking like they've had far too much to drink for seven p.m. on a Thursday, shoulder bumping mine before his hands reach out with reflexes faster than your average person to keep me from rolling my ankle off the sidewalk.

"Oh," I say, straightening my shoulders when his hands leave them. "Do you still have family there?"

He nods, stepping closer to me as we walk, and I think it's probably just to avoid all the students, but a small part of me hopes he wants our shoulders to accidentally brush the way I do.

"My grandparents. Aunts and uncles. Cousins. They mostly live in Brno." He glances at me. "Where are you from? How'd you end up coming to school here?"

"I'm from Toronto. But my grandparents had a cottage on this side of Lake Huron and . . . I don't know." I shrug, giving him a small smile. I'm not quite sure how to tell a boy I just met that the only time I ever really remember my mind being quiet and kind was when I was that little, that small, and nothing could touch me when I was there every summer. "Sentimentality won out in the end, I guess."

He looks at me, and there's something in the way one eyebrow rises, the curve of his mouth not quite a smile, that tells me he doesn't believe me.

Bohdan doesn't say anything as we walk the last block towards the arena, and neither do I.

Usually, I'd feel so guilty, like the whole weight of carrying the conversation, of making him happy, of entertaining him, of generally being enough would be sitting on my shoulders, but I can feel his eyes on me with each step we take, and he doesn't seem to mind.

I think I can even see the slant of a smile on his lips.

They're great lips, actually. Full, bowing slightly in the middle where they part. They might be the only soft thing about him, offset by the sharp lines of his jaw, shadows of stubble peeking through golden skin.

Tia would call them sensuous.

I call them beautiful. Fascinating, even.

"What's your major?" he asks, voice low, practically drowned out by the loud squeak of hinges when he yanks the arena door open.

"Oh." I blink. "Anthropology."

Bohdan pushes the door back, hand splayed wide across the glass, arm raised so I have to duck under it to get inside.

Out of habit, I try to shrink myself, shoulders curving inward, but I brush against the planes of his chest, hard even beneath his jacket and sweater.

His breath whispers across my ear. "What do you want to do with that?"

It could be a rude question, but somehow, coming from him, I know it's not.

I pause, halfway inside and halfway out, turning my head to look at him.

He's studying me, striations in his eyes alight with interest, head cocked slightly to the left, and those lips parted just so in the middle.

I inhale, expecting the telltale scent of the arena, whatever it is they use to make them all smell the same way, but it's just him invading my lungs—pine and snow and quiet nights.

That might be why I give him the real answer.

"Understand people. Maybe understand me."

He nods once, considering, thoughtful, and I think we might stare at each other all night, me half pressed against him, his eyes nowhere else, but he jerks his chin towards the inside of the arena.

"What about you?" I step out from under him, looking back over my shoulder when he closes the door.

"Geological science." Bohdan shoves his hands back in his pockets, crossing the concourse of the arena with purpose, like this is where he belongs, and I guess, in so many ways, it is.

I follow, watching, and maybe a bit envious he has a place where he knows he's meant to be, where he feels so at home. Smiling, I repeat his question. "What do you want to do with that?"

He grins at me, left side of his mouth quirking up just a bit higher than the right—a little piece of him I categorize and file away in my brain under things that make my heart stumble and all the air leave my lungs.

"I won't do anything with it. I just like it." He says it simply, and I follow him through a narrow hallway that doesn't seem to belong to the general public, until we come out beside the small skate rental shop by the left entrance to the ice. It's hardly ever open, and none of the skates stacked neatly in the cupboards along the boards look used.

"This is what you want to do?" I point towards the sheet of ice, stretching and illuminated under soft lights.

"Since I first set foot on the ice." Bohdan nods before pointing to a small bench. "Sit, I'll fit you for skates."

"You're actually taking me skating? Isn't that a bit cliché? Us alone in this empty rink?" I ask, folding myself down on the bench, arms still wrapped around my chest, like maybe I need protection—it's an old habit—but I look at him, sharp features thrown into contrast by the arena lights, and I think I might be safe in here with him.

"Probably." Bohdan gives me a wry shrug before rifling through the cupboard, searching for two skates in the same size. He runs his finger across the blades of a few different pairs before continuing. "I'm not good at much, but I know I'm good at this. Maybe I want to impress you."

"Why do you want to impress me?" I tip my chin up, smiling.

He looks back over his shoulder, thumb pressed into the spur of a skate, cheekbones carving across his face and grey eyes honest. "Because you're beautiful."

"No, I'm not." I give a small, stubborn shake of my head.

I don't really think about the way I look—I see myself in the mirror, and I think, objectively, I'm just fine. But my brain spends so much time telling me how horrible and ugly and terrible the inside of me is, and it's hard to imagine it doesn't bleed through and paint the outside of me, too.

"Okay, Sloan," he laughs, eyes rolling before he pushes to stand, two seemingly acceptable skates held in his hands. "You're right. You're hideous. You remind me of that ogre. What's his name? Starts with an S."

"Shrek? You aren't even going to say Fiona?" My mouth parts, incredulous, but my cheeks have that faint bit of hurt starting from a smile that might go on too long. One of Bohdan's brows lifts, and he drops into a crouch in front of me, sliding off each of my boots in turn, his fingers skating across the arches of my feet.

It's colder in here than it is outside—but I feel heat flame across my cheeks.

He doesn't say anything when he slides each of my feet into the skates, fingers moving around my ankles like he's testing for something, before moving to the laces.

"At least give me Shrek from *Shrek 2*. It's the—" I start.

"Best one," Bohdan finishes for me, eyes lifting with one corner of his mouth when he tugs the laces of the skate tighter.

"Yes," I whisper, and we stare for a bit too long before he smiles, eyes flicking back down to my skates. I watch him lace them, fingers traipsing over the cotton, tugging and tying with a practiced dexterity that makes my skin hot. "Maybe we can watch it sometime."

"Whatever you want, Sloan." He says it softly and with a quiet smile, stretching with promise.

It's only the third time he's said my name, and I think I like it more and more each time. That there's a part of me who might like being Sloan, if she's someone whose name gets to sit on Bohdan Novotnak's lips.

I watch him finish with my laces, his gaze meeting mine when he's seemingly done. "They feel okay? Tight enough?"

Twirling each of my ankles around, I nod. "I think so. It doesn't feel like I'm going to roll my ankle and fall or anything."

"I won't let you fall." Bohdan pushes to stand, turning back to the cupboard, grabbing a pair of skates seemingly at random.

"Are those yours?"

He shakes his head, sitting beside me and tying the skates with less care than he did mine. "I don't wear my skates outside of games."

"Superstition?" I ask when he stands, pushing open the door to the ice.

"Something like that." He tips his chin towards the stretching ice pad, sparkling and waiting to be carved up by the likes of him. "You ready?"

I nod softly, and he waits for me to step out first, one hand hovering just above the small of my back, but I don't fall.

It's quiet. So quiet out here on this ice with him, and I look around at the empty arena, probably a bit in wonder, eyes wide because I think my brain might be tired, asleep for the first time in a very long time, while

I stumble like a baby animal alongside Bohdan's practiced, purposeful strokes.

"I can pull you," he offers, voice low, and when I nod, he turns with quicker precision than I've ever achieved at anything in my life, skating backward in front of me, warm hands wrapping around my wrists.

I watch the world go by, utterly transfixed by empty seats, glowing lights, a boy with watchful grey eyes and safe hands, because the whole thing really feels a bit like a movie.

"Why were you crying?" Bohdan cocks his head, and I wrinkle my nose, confused, before he points his chin in the general direction of the stands. "At the game. I saw you."

"Oh." I sniff, considering, but Bohdan keeps skating backward slowly, his pace almost lazy while he waits for my answer. "My parents say I'm too sensitive. But my therapist says I get overstimulated."

"What's that like?" he asks, and he looks at me like he really wants to know.

"Loud," I tell him truthfully.

"I'm not loud."

"No," I say with a small smile, "you're not."

We skate for three hours.

Maybe it's more accurate to say Bohdan skates for three hours, backward the entire time, hands journeying from my wrists to my palms, until his fingers laced with mine.

I'd say it was to keep me from falling, but after a few minutes my legs weren't wobbling as much, my movements steadier.

I just don't think he wanted to let go.

And he didn't.

Even when he skated as fast as he could, the entire arena a quiet, wonderful blur.

But never as beautiful and wonderful as the boy pulling me along—face alight, grin wide and somehow the loveliest thing I'd ever seen.

He doesn't even let go of my hand the entire way back to my dorm. Not until we walk up the steps, the entire campus somehow still, just a shadow of what it was earlier.

We pause in front of the door, a cracked light flickering above us, sharpening the lines of his jaw.

His hand moves from mine, finding the side of my face, rough palm cupping it gently. He stares at me before he drops his voice to a low whisper. "Good night, Sloan."

I inhale, and I think the sound of him saying my name fills up my lungs the way oxygen does. "Aren't you going to kiss me?"

"No," he says with a shake of his head, followed by rough, quiet words that make my breath hitch. "Not tonight."

His thumb grazes my bottom lip, pausing in the centre before he scores a line down to my chin, across my jawbone, to the skin where it meets my ear—skin I've never really thought of as being terribly important or sensitive before, but it is, it's on fire.

I'm on fire.

Burning up here while the snow falls and Bohdan's fingers trace my cheek, moving to tuck errant hair behind my ear.

His mouth curves into a grin, and he murmurs something I don't understand. It sounds like it starts with a Z.

"What does that mean?" I whisper, so quiet because I'm afraid someone might hear us and whatever bubble we're existing in might burst.

His palm cups my cheek again, grey eyes rove over my face, categorizing or memorizing or something that seems beyond the capacity of most twenty-year-old boys, and he takes a measured step back, hand finding its way to his pocket.

The absence of him touching me feels a bit jarring, and I blink too much, watching him walk backward down the dorm steps, like he doesn't have a care in the world.

He grins when he gets to the bottom, calling up to me, "I'll tell you what it means if you go out with me again."

I do go out with him again.

And again.

And again.

Bohdan

Then – College

I try to wait to kiss her.

To show her that it's not some fleeting, dumb college thing.

That I don't think a single girl has ever really existed to me before I saw her—certainly not since—and never again.

But I don't make it that long.

Three days after I took her skating and all I could see when I closed my eyes was her smile and all I could feel were her fingers slotting into mine, I realized I needed her more than I needed most things—so I made Talon and Jay fake a stupid reason to throw a party to have an excuse to invite her over.

They didn't need much convincing. They were more than happy to oblige, saying I hadn't shut up about her since the date, and they'd do anything to go back to the relative silence of the house.

The only thing I said to them was that the date was great, and that Sloan was entirely inconceivable—because she was absolutely none of their business—but they claimed that was a ringing endorsement and the fact that I was more glued to my phone than I'd ever been, hoping she'd text me or call, was reason enough for celebration.

She comes to the party, hand in hand with Tia Valdez—who watches me like a hawk—but she doesn't need to.

I've never been more interested in anything than making Sloan Joseph comfortable enough to smile.

She does smile. I even make her laugh.

I'm pretty high on myself over that one.

She sits with me in the corner of the living room, away from Talon and Jay and all the noise of the party, talking softly about things she likes and things she doesn't—ancient civilizations rank pretty high, olives rank pretty low—and she listens more than anyone I've ever met when I tell her about hockey, but she's more interested in asking me about geology.

She stays all night, until I notice her press her eyes closed, rubbing her palm across her chest, and when I come back from the kitchen, she's not in the living room anymore.

She's outside in the backyard.

"What are you doing out here?" The door clicks shut behind me, and Sloan whirls around when I walk down the worn wooden steps into the yard.

"Oh." Sloan's fingers tighten on her red cup, and a faint blush paints her cheeks. "It's just . . . quieter out here. And the snow—" She gestures to the giant flakes, drifting lazily down from the sky, illuminated by the light hanging above the back deck. "It's my favourite when it snows at night like this."

"It's nice." I reach forward, taking her cup, crouching down to set it on the frozen ground.

She blinks up at me when I stand again, closer to her than before, eyes brighter than all the stars in the sky, snowflakes catching in her hair and melting on her cheeks. "Are you going to kiss me now?"

I nod, eyes tracing the pout of her lips. "Yeah, Zlatíčko. I think I will."

She looks almost puzzled—a fleeting crease between her eyebrows and a wrinkle across her nose—but I cup her cheek, thumb sweeping under her left eye over a snowflake obscuring these three freckles that I think I'll count to go to sleep.

She takes a tiny inhale, then my lips are on hers, and I think my life as I know it is over.

Now, she comes to my place at least twice a week.

I hate going longer than that without seeing her.

But we don't share a single class. I have practice at least once a day, usually more, so my evenings are rarely free. Our schedule has us away for games more than we're home.

I don't mind going to her dorm. Tia has more sense than her brother and usually leaves to study so we can be alone—but practice runs late more often than not, and by the time I'm out of the shower, sometimes she's just here.

Sitting cross-legged on my bed, usually in an oversized sweater, jeans or leggings, and a pair of my socks, with her textbooks spread around her and music playing softly on her phone.

Talon and Jay cut her a key the day after the party, when I couldn't stop swiping my thumb across my bottom lip—right where hers had been.

Tonight, she's got stacks of brochures and pamphlets spread out around her.

"What are these?" I point my chin towards the mess she's got going before toweling off my still-damp hair.

"I went to that anthropology program open house tonight. They had a bunch of different booths with field study and internship opportunities," she says, and I catch her shrugging when I toss the towel onto my desk chair.

"Oh yeah? Anything you're interested in?" I drop down on the bed beside her, picking one up at random.

"Oh! That's for the field study in Northern BC!" Sloan lights up, reaching forward to grab it from me. I circle her wrist, but she switches hands, holding it up.

Tugging her towards me instead—I've been thinking about her in my bed for the entire day—she holds up another pamphlet, eyes and smile bright. "Last year at this field school, someone found an entire pot!"

"A pot?" I grin, thumb stroking across the inside of her wrist. "What's so special about a pot?"

Sloan purses her lips. "What's so special about an igneous rock?"

"Well, they are formed when magma or lava solidify, so some might say that's significantly more interesting than a plain old pot."

She lifts her chin. "Who says it's a plain old pot? It could have been used for any number of things."

"Was it?"

Her eyes narrow. "They haven't been able to determine its exact function yet."

"Fascinating." I raise a brow and tug on her wrist again.

Sloan glances at the pamphlet before dropping it onto my bed beside all the other scattered pieces of paper. "I've been talking a lot," she says softly, a wrinkle cutting across her nose I'd like to smooth away with my mouth. "I'm sorry."

"I'm not," I tell her.

"Are you sure?" she asks with a sniff, eyes getting bright in the way they only do when she's going to cry. "It seems like you're trying to get me to lay down so maybe I'll shut up and stop talking about these stupid digs."

"I have been trying to get you to lay down. But it's not because I want you to stop talking, Sloan." I press my thumb down, and I can feel the faint beat of her heart in her pulse. "And I'm certainly not interested in making you shut up. I'd actually like you to make quite a bit of noise."

She blinks, full lips parting while a pink blush rises on her cheeks. But she tips her chin up again, that funny streak of stubbornness shining through. "How lewd."

I grin, bringing her wrist to my mouth, pressing a kiss there. "I'm twenty and you're the most beautiful person I'll probably ever see in real life. I can get lewder."

She gives me a flat look this time. "Talon and Jay could come home."

"Talon and Jay fucked off to the movies," I say against her skin.

She blinks again with a tiny swallow.

She looks a bit nervous. Not because of me. We've got a rule about boundaries. She's clear about them—best day of my life when she took her clothes off in front of me for the first time and we didn't do anything but lie there.

She's beautiful, radiant, probably made from the sun and the stars, but it wasn't because of that.

It was the way her eyelashes fluttered softly, her lips curved into this little shy smile and her shoulders relaxed. How she blinked slowly. How her hands painted these patterns across my chest, arms, and back when we lay there, alone in the dark except for the moon peeking through the window, whispering quietly, doing nothing more than laughing and kissing.

It was the way she was entirely, utterly relaxed. Comfortable. Quiet and at ease.

I don't think I've ever felt more worthy of anything—more like a man—than I did that night and I probably never will again.

I always ask Sloan permission to do anything, and when she says stop, I stop and take ten steps back. But I know her enough now to be able to read these different subtleties in her, the way the font of her changes in the shifts of her body language.

She's nervous about something her brain just told her.

I hold my hands up in submission and jerk my chin towards the brochure again. "How long are these field schools?"

"Uhm. It depends. This one was two weeks. But some of the European ones are a month." She chews on her bottom lip, glancing towards the stacks strewn across my bed.

"A month?" I echo. "What's so interesting you're digging through the dirt for that long?"

She folds her arms, sitting up straighter. "Says the guy who goes to school to study rocks."

"I'd miss you," I tell her, voice low.

"It's been like, two months." She rolls her eyes, but she glances back up at me, and there's this tiny bloom of hopefulness there, like when the sky turns blue first thing in the morning and you've got no idea what's coming for you—a day that could be anything at all.

"I can't miss you after two months?" I ask, leaning forward with a grin and plucking the brochure from her hand.

Sloan purses her lips, straightening the rest of the pamphlets on my bed before stacking them together. "Well, you can, I guess. Just—why would you?"

"Zlatíčko, come on."

She pauses, the stack of pamphlets still between her fingers. "What does it mean?"

"It's killing you, isn't it?" I laugh.

"No." She shakes her head, hair tumbling around her shoulders, trying to look resolute.

My brow lifts. "You could just Google it, you know."

"No," she repeats, stubborn. "I'd rather you tell me."

I groan, scrubbing my face, like it's this old, tired thing, when really, it's one of my favourite games to play with her.

I say something in Czech. She pretends not to care what it means, looks befuddled for a minute before she moves right on in conversation, and she spends too much time trying to trick me into telling her instead of just using the computer she carries around in her pocket.

I hope I spend my whole life playing games with Sloan Joseph.

But this one needs to end—because I think she needs to know how precious she is.

"Sweetheart," I say, before I tell her what it really means to me. What she really means to me. "Or 'little gold.'"

"Oh." She breathes softly, looking down when a crease of apprehension sketches between her eyebrows.

I reach forward, tilting her chin up. "You looked—golden. Under those arena lights."

She shakes her head. "Nothing about me is gold. I have brown hair."

"Let me compliment you." I press my thumb to the pout of her bottom lip. She blinks a bit too much, and I see a solitary tear slip over and slide down her cheek. Wiping it away, I ask quietly, "What's going on in there?"

"Nothing good," she says, shaking her head again with a sad, wet laugh.

"Can I kiss it better?"

She nods, softly this time, her fingers fluttering around my wrist.

I do kiss her. I hope I make it better.

She doesn't seem to mind that I lose track of time, sitting up on my bed, surrounded by all these brochures, thumb still gripping her chin, her hand around my wrist, lips on mine.

The outside world could implode. Stars could die and the sun could burn out and maybe the rest of civilization is just dust.

All I know is that I've got her, that I've never wanted to kiss someone like this, that I don't think I ever will again, that it's stupid and makes no sense because she's eighteen and I'm twenty but I think she's it for me because she's quiet and shy and soft and stubborn all at the same time and no one's ever taken my breath away quite like she has.

That I would stay here kissing her, because even if the world did end, it wouldn't, not really, not as long as she was still living and breathing, but Sloan pulls away, tucking her hair behind her ears, lips parted and swollen when she asks softly, "Can we lay down?"

"Yeah, Zlatíčko, we can do whatever you want."

Whatever she wants turns out to be the lights off, music she likes but seems sort of sad to me, all of our clothes gone, and her hair fanning out across the pillow, big blue eyes fluttering up at me suspended over her with one hand gripping the sheets and the other holding up a condom, asking her if she's sure.

She says yes.

But it's not all she says.

"Yes. It's not my first time and I know it's not yours but . . . it feels a bit . . . like maybe it is?" She bites down on her bottom lip, eyes wide like she's worried I won't understand. "Do you know what I mean?"

"I do." I brush a thumb across her cheek.

It does feel like the first time.

I try to be careful with her, and the funny thing is—she tries to be careful with me. Her teeth graze my bottom lip, my shoulders, my arms, but she never bites down. She stops herself before her nails dig too deep into my back.

But I'd let her break me apart, if she wanted.

I'm gone the second she is, and something in me does shatter when she comes, my name on her lips—but not in a bad way.

In this way that tells me my heart was only ever supposed to be pieces she could hold in those tiny hands, anyway.

Not the first time, but she kisses me afterwards, tentative, like it's new, and I think every single kiss with her is. Later, her laughter echoes into the dark room, her fingers trace portraits on my skin, and I think I'd be more than happy for my last everything to belong to her.

Bohdan

I've lived a few different lives in my thirty years on earth, but the most important ones were the ones I lived at night.

On the ice and under all those lights in college, skating with Talon and Jay. Somehow the best on the entire planet at the thing I loved the most, but then loved second after I saw her through the glass one time.

Sneaking into Sloan's dorm room after games, suit still on and half askew because I never bothered to put it back on properly—I was too focused on getting to her.

Other nights playing under other lights with a different jersey, that same girl still watching me from behind different glass, still the best according to everyone else, but the only thing I wanted to be best at was Sloan.

Coming home to her in that apartment with the floor-to-ceiling windows, the view of the Sound and the Olympics and all that Seattle had to offer. But what that apartment really had to offer me was nights with that girl—usually on the couch, textbooks all around, music on low, her socked feet kicking in the air, chin propped up in one hand, dark hair fanning around her face, and blue eyes more beautiful than any body of water anywhere in the world.

Her face softening when she'd tilt her lips up to brush mine, smiling, loving me in this quiet way that somehow felt louder and more all-encompassing than anything I'd ever experienced, and ever would again.

Now I live this life, in an objectively nice apartment in Brooklyn, because I refuse to live near the studio headquarters in Secaucus, but nothing particularly important happens at night anymore.

Drinking ginseng or turmeric tea because my mom read somewhere it was good for brain health, and now I can't go a month without new kinds showing up at my door.

Practicing mindfulness.

Taking my antidepressants, and sometimes a sedative if I've had a particularly rough day.

Trying all sorts of migraine-prevention techniques that probably don't work.

But it is the one time a day I let myself open my wallet and pull out the picture of Sloan.

My therapist says I need to stop doing that. Can't move on if I'm staring at the past each night before bed.

I think he'd probably sing a different tune if his past was Sloan Joseph.

It's also the one time a day I let myself take an active stroll down memory lane. It's pretty hard to avoid Sloan in all things because she is all things—at least all the things that matter.

Talon and Jay would tell me it's pathetic. It is. I know it is.

But tonight, it doesn't stop me from dropping my bag, yanking off my tie, grabbing a beer I shouldn't have, and climbing the wrought-iron stairs to the rooftop so I can sit out there under all the stars and look at the brightest one that lives in my wallet.

A breeze lifts my hair from my face, cool against my skin, and it feels for a second like it might be a nice reprieve from the pounding starting along my hairline, but nothing's ever hurt more than looking at all the things I used to have.

I take a swig of beer before dropping into the lounge chair in the middle of the rooftop. Stretching my legs out, I inhale before fishing out my wallet, finding the picture right behind my ID, where it always stays safe.

I could keep it anywhere, really. But there's something about the fact that all I have left of her lives alongside this stupid piece of plastic that's supposed to tell people who I am.

She forged me, after all.

The edges of the Polaroid are worn, starting to peel, not from lack of care on my part—this picture with her old number scrawled across the back is probably my most prized possession—but from time.

Funny thing, time.

It hurts the same way it always does, along the scar first—a pulsing pain every doctor and psychologist I've ever had has told me is firmly in my imagination, that there's no physiological basis for a hurt like that to be caused by nothing more than memory, because that's what Sloan is now, memory.

It moves along my scalp, the way her fingers used to. It twirls in my hair before it slides down my face, almost lovingly. Reverently. Before it scrapes down my neck and digs into my shoulders, finding its way down to the place I'm told my heart still beats because doctors can hear it, where it lives and makes a home.

Exhaling, I swallow another sip of beer, eyes roving over the picture, this deep, hard-to-explain pain pushing against my chest when I look at her.

Hair tumbling around her shoulders, eyes even more blue because they're sparkling with unshed tears, and those painful arena lights shining down on her.

I flip it over, twirling it between my fingers, and there it is. Her name and her old number in that beautiful, loopy writing of hers.

Sloan Joseph
555-6718

A smile twitches the corners of my mouth, and I press the bottle to my lips.

It used to strike me as funny that she'd written her last name down, too. Like she wanted to make sure I knew who she was and give me some piece of truly identifying information so I'd never forget her.

There was never a risk of that.

I don't know how long I'm staring, but my phone rings when I take the last swallow of beer.

A picture of my mom lights up the screen, and I'm not sure I feel like answering, but I don't want her to get the wrong idea, thinking I've died of migraine-induced heart failure or something else she's made up in her head, and call the police for a wellness check when it's not needed, because I didn't answer.

It wouldn't be the first time.

Discarding the empty bottle beside me, I place Sloan back where she belongs, right beside me in my wallet, and my mother's voice croons through the speaker.

"Broučku." *Little bug.*

Her voice sounds the way it always does, warm and loving, before it turns serious with the edge of a reprimand. "It's late."

"You called me."

"It's early here." She's visiting my grandparents in Brno, but I can hear her smile all the way over here in Brooklyn. I can imagine the whole thing pretty clearly, actually. Where she's sitting in the apartment, window thrown open and cool, spring air filtering in while she watches the square with her morning coffee. "How are you feeling?"

My eyes pinch closed and out of habit, I press my fingers to my temple. It might seem innocuous, but it's a frustrating question.

The only one I ever get asked anymore.

Never how I am, just as me, the person—but how I'm feeling.

Like the entirety of my being disappeared the moment my head cracked against the ice.

Maybe it did.

"Fine. I just got home. I was at the studio, sorting some stuff out." I stretch my legs out along the chair, wincing when my right quad cramps. I swallow, pressing my eyes closed again. "Went out on the ice for a bit this afternoon with a friend who still plays here."

I toss the words out before I can regret it, because I know it'd only be worse if I kept it secret and she finds out.

It's met with silence.

Heavy, all-encompassing, and somehow choking me from an entirely different continent.

"Were you careful?" she asks, just like her words.

Pounding my fist into my quad, I push against the muscle spasm and try to take my frustration out on the shitty, underused, probably equally-as-frustrated tissue instead of my mother.

My therapist says I need to be better about that sort of thing.

It already cost me the world. I don't need it to cost me my mom, too.

"I can still skate, Mom." I try to sound light, but the words slice through whatever the silence wrapped around us anyway.

It's another question I get asked all the time with good intentions. Was I careful?

But it's not just the ice, I rarely skate anymore. This was the first time in months.

It's "Did I remember my prescription sunglasses?" because it was a sunny day. It's "Did I remember my meds?" It's "Did I take extra care walking down the street to the subway, because you never know—someone might accidentally bump into me and send me careening to the ground where I'll smash my head against the pavement?"

She forgets I'm a grown man who lost more than his ability to get through a week without a pounding headache.

He lost his career. His dreams. His entire life.

Himself, probably.

The silence carries again, and for one stupid minute, I let myself hope that she'll ask me the question I wish someone would.

How did it feel? Am I okay?

I'd tell her the truth—that it was the first time I've felt free in months. That it was just as incredible as I remember. That I'd do anything to be able to get it back. Would she please help me?

But she doesn't.

She changes the subject.

"Of course you can, Bohdan." I can practically see her forced smile from here—the way her eyes, just like mine, collapse a bit before she scrunches her nose and gives her head a tiny shake. "Why don't you come out here? Join me for a few weeks? Playoffs are just about done; you won't have many other commentating spots. Your grandparents would love to see you."

She's not wrong. Cup final is this week, and then I'm as free as someone like me could be.

I don't know what I'm going to do next. Zane's offer is still there, hanging over my head. My agent, Shay, thinks I should take it. Says it would be groundbreaking. The opportunity to make a difference.

My therapist says I should only do what I'm ready for.

The only thing I know for certain is that I'm booked on a flight next week for Talon's stupid cruise.

Eyes cutting to the empty beer, I wish I'd thought to bring up another. "I'd love to. But I can't. I'm actually heading to Barcelona next week to meet Talon and Jay. Talon's retiring and he roped us into a cruise to celebrate. You know him, I'm sure he wants to—"

"Start his retirement in style?" My mother's fond laughter spills through the phone, and I think I feel it in my chest, cracking the thing open and lightening it all, just a bit. "That sounds fun. Who's going?"

That sends the whole thing crashing to the ground, and whatever modicum of happiness I felt before dissipates, and my chest seals itself shut again.

"Me, Talon, Jay, and Tia." I tell her the whole guest list, minus the one name she wants to hear the most.

Silence again.

But heavier this time, because it's weighed down by a woman with brilliant eyes and an even more brilliant brain.

"Oh," my mom starts, and I can feel her debating her next words from here. "I thought maybe Sloan would go. Talon is one of her best friends, too."

"Sloan doesn't want anything to do with me," I cut out, words harsh. "I wouldn't want anything to do with me either. She didn't even answer the fucking text."

"Bohdan, if you'd just call her—"

"No," I interrupt, a throb aching in my temple.

My mom thinks I'm being stubborn—a display of wounded male pride.

She doesn't know I'd drop to my knees and beg for Sloan in the middle of Times Square and let everyone in the world record it if it meant a second chance with her.

I just won't put her through it again.

She swallows, voice shaky with tears. "Are you sure? If you just explained, she'd understand. She loved—"

"Enough."

I sound harsher than I mean to because it's a plea, really.

I don't want to be reminded of the fact I had the heart of this spectacular, wonderful, effervescent, brilliant person in my hands—this person who never really felt worthy of love because their brain was so cruel—took the edge of a dull skate blade, and systematically carved it up until there was nothing left of either of us.

That I'm the villain in her story, and I should be. I'm the villain in mine.

But every time I made Sloan bleed, I bled, too.

Bohdan

Then – College

"One, two, three, four, five, six," Sloan whispers softly with each step of her feet on the library staircase, before she starts again. "One, two, three, four, five, six."

"Are you counting?" I cut her a sideways look, laughing, and she stops, startled almost, left foot poised above the final step—six, according to her.

She does these funny things sometimes without realizing it—counting, tracing certain patterns, and tapping with her fingers.

I usually think it's cute, but I get a good look at her in the low light of the library stairwell, and today, it seems like it might be bothering her.

Sloan blinks, column of her throat moving with a slow swallow, full lips parting at the Cupid's bow. She shakes her head, hair tumbling around her shoulders. "No."

"Sloan." I start to laugh again and tip my chin towards her mouth. "I heard you."

"It's just a pattern," she says quietly, hand fidgeting with the strap of her backpack before she turns away and starts up the rest of the stairs.

"There's more than six steps," I call after her, louder than I should because it's early and we're on a quiet floor.

I take two steps at a time, my quads still twinging from morning skate. I should have stayed and rolled out my muscles, but Sloan on a Saturday morning, the sunlight streaming in on her through the old paned windows of the library, isn't something I like to miss.

We've spent almost every Saturday morning here after practice, unless I have an away game, for the last three months.

I'm supposed to study the way she does, nose wrinkled in concentration, eyes tracking the pages of her notes, different colours of pens and highlighters all strewn about beside her—different colours for different things—but I usually just watch her.

She always catches me with a roll of her eyes, cheeks turning pink, and she walks around the table, flips open my textbooks before pulling up my notes on my computer, because she has my passwords for everything—they're all something to do with her—and reminds me how much I allegedly love the rocks I'm studying about.

We make deals some days.

A certain number of uninterrupted minutes of studying and she'll let me kiss her in public.

If I'm really lucky, it's a day her roommate's gone, we go back to her dorm, and she lets me do all sorts of things that I can't in a library.

"There's more than six steps," I repeat when I catch up to her. She's sitting in her favourite chair, making a big show of straightening her pens. "Sloan, what were you counting?"

"I know."

It's all she says.

"Sloan—" I start, pulling out my chair and dropping my backpack on the floor beside the table.

She doesn't look back up at me, and her voice wavers. "Study, Bohdan."

"Will you let me come back to your room if I do?" I try grinning at her, dropping my voice the way she likes and leaning forward on the table.

"Tia's home." She starts to blink rapidly, staring determinedly down at her textbook, but her eyes cloud over in a way that tells me she's not really reading anything.

I swallow, tossing out a desperate attempt to get her to even look at me. "You can come to my place. Talon and Jay are—"

"I'm trying to study, Bohdan." Her words are soft, and I can see a tear start to track down her cheek.

"Sloan." I push my chair back, the legs scraping against the floor.

She closes her eyes at the sound, like it's hurting her.

The idea of that hurts me.

I go to stand, but she beats me to it.

"I don't feel well." Sloan slams her textbook shut; her chair screeches against the tile, somehow so much more jarring than mine sounded.

I reach for her when she storms by, and for an NCAA athlete, one of the quickest wrist shots ever seen, a top-five skater in the entire country, I'm somehow too slow.

I sit there, stunned and stupid, unsure what the hell just happened.

She had a decent head start, and I have to wait outside her building until someone lets me into the main entrance because she's not answering her phone, so I don't catch up to her at all until I'm pounding on the door of her dorm room.

"Sloan!" I slam my palm against the peeling wood laminate.
Nothing.

There's no way Tia's actually home like she said—Tia wouldn't be able to mind her business if she tried. She's like her brother that way.

"Sloan!" I try again, dropping my ear to the door, beside my palm, trying to hear anything at all. "Sloan! At least tell me if you're okay."

I'm about to shout again when the door across the hall creaks open.

"Dude, can you—" He cuts himself off when I whirl around, muscles in my jaw ticking.

"Oh. Shit." He blinks, stupid, looking a bit like he smoked too much weed. "Aren't you Bohdan Novotnak?"

I don't answer, turning back to Sloan's door, pressing my palm against it like maybe she'll feel my arm straining against the wood, as if I could break the thing down and get to her.

"Can I have your autograph?"

"No." I don't bother looking back at him, about to actually try my hand at breaking down her door when it swings open.

My reflexes finally decide to show up and I catch myself before I fall forward.

But it's not Sloan standing in the doorway.

It's Tia Valdez, and she looks decidedly unhappy to see me.

"Quite a scene you're causing out here, Novotnak." She purses her lips, arms crossed firmly over her chest before she peers over my shoulder. "Krish, mind your business."

He does, and fortunately, he does so quietly, his door clicking shut behind me.

Tia's eyes snap back to me, flashing with displeasure. "What do you want?"

I give her a flat look. "What do you think I want?"

"She came back here from the library crying, but she wouldn't say what happened. What did you do?"

Splaying my arms wide, my voice rises again. "I don't know. I fucking sprinted across campus after her to find out."

"Hmm." One eyebrow flicks up.

"Tia, please just let me in." I rub a hand across my jaw, not against begging. My voice sounds a bit like I feel—split wide open, cracked and bleeding out at the thought that I've somehow done something to hurt the person who's quickly becoming the most important thing in my life.

Tia angles her head, eyes narrowed and assessing. One finger taps against her sweater, right above her bicep, like she's considering.

Her mouth parts, but before she can utter whatever line she's come up with, I hear Sloan's voice, and my knees might actually buckle with relief.

"Tia. He can come in."

Tia glances over her shoulder before holding up a single finger. "One moment please."

She takes a step back and I think she's about to let me in before the door starts to shut.

"Oh, come on!" I groan, entirely to Tia's delight. Her eyebrows lift, this look I could only describe as devious scrawls across her features, and she looks so much like her brother, I debate pushing past her into the room.

But the door pulls open, and I get eyes on Sloan for the first time since she somehow evaded me in the library.

She doesn't look any worse for the wear. I catalogue every inch of her, and I think I bleed a bit more when I see the dried tears streaking down her face.

But she looks the same otherwise, hair down, falling over the shoulders of her grey sweater, leggings tucked into big, slouchy white socks that used to belong to me before she stole them.

"Are you okay? Are you sick?" I ask, words all strangled and desperate.

She cuts Tia a look. "Don't you have somewhere to be?"

"Do I?" Tia glances back and forth between us, chin resolutely pointed in the air.

"Yes," Sloan and I both answer at the same time.

Tia rolls her eyes, raising her hands before turning and stalking back into their shared room, making a big show of packing her bag and grabbing the textbooks strewn across her rumpled bedding.

Sloan waits, arms wrapped around her middle, blinking while Hurricane Tia spins around the room.

She doesn't make any moves to come closer to me, or to do anything at all really, until Tia pulls open the door again with a dramatic flourish, pointing a bony finger at me in a gesture that's probably supposed to be menacing.

I'm not sure the desired effect is achieved, but I can't really say because the only thing I care about is the girl who just dropped to the edge of her bed to sit, feet dangling off because both she and Tia added these risers under them to create more storage.

The white bedding pools around her, and she looks beautiful despite the whole thing, with the lights strewn along the wall behind her twinkling, interspersed with different Polaroids and photos.

"Can I sit?" I grip my jaw again before pointing towards the empty space beside her on the bed.

A small shrug, and I take that as a yes.

My quad twinges uncomfortably when I drop beside her, and I dig a fist into it before glancing sideways at her, helpless.

"What did I do?" I ask, words rough.

Sloan stares determinedly ahead, and a new, fresh tear rolls down her cheek, and before I can reach forward, she bats it away with her hand.

"You laughed," she whispers, voice impossibly small.

I give my head a shake, brow furrowed, and I shift so I can face her. She doesn't recoil or shy away, so I take that as an invitation to lean closer, reaching out and swiping a thumb across her cheek.

She doesn't elaborate, but she does angle her head so she can rest against my palm.

I think there'd be a lot of people who might press, say the whole thing was ridiculous and preposterous, tell her she was being dramatic because nothing really happened.

It's been three months, and maybe it's a drop in the proverbial bucket of time—but it's been enough to learn a few things about Sloan.

She knows exactly who she is, and she wants to take up space, but she does it in this quiet, tentative way like she isn't sure how.

She spends a disproportionate amount of time worrying about whether she's good or bad, and if whatever she is, is enough for other people.

And I don't think she's very nice to herself.

"When did I laugh?" I press my thumb into her skin.

Sloan blinks, letting her eyes stay closed. Her voice breaks when she speaks, I feel tears splash against my hand, and she bats at her other cheek. "When I was counting on the stairs."

"I like when you count," I tell her.

It's true. I like everything about her.

She opens her eyes, rolls them like she doesn't quite believe me, before giving a small shake of her head. "It's weird."

"It's not weird." I try to grin at her, angling my head down so my mouth can brush the shell of her ear. "Do you think the Sumerian's thought it was weird when they invented the abacus back in 2700 BC?"

She pulls away, but I think the corners of her mouth tilt with a smile. "There's archaeological evidence for the abacus in more than one civilization, you know."

"I do now." I give her a wry look, and she does try to smile, but those beautiful full lips can't quite pull themselves into a straight line. "What's this about, Sloan?"

Shoulders curve inward, and she shrinks. I hate when Sloan shrinks. I want her to take up the same amount of space in every room that she takes up in me.

She taps her fingers together in quick succession. I count this time. Two sets of three. She shakes her head before stretching out her hands, finally turning to face me. She blinks, blue eyes wide, tears glittering, frozen on the surface and ready to fall.

They start when she finally speaks.

"I don't know why I do it. It's just . . . comforting, sometimes."

"I don't really care why you do it." I give a jerk of my chin, reaching forward and tucking her hair behind her ear. "Does it matter?"

It doesn't matter to me. If it's something she takes comfort in, something she needs for whatever reason, I'll count with her everyday for the rest of my life.

I'll learn new languages, and I'll tell her all the numbers in those, too.

She swallows, fingers rolling over each other, twisting into knots before she drops them on her thighs and takes an inhale, like she's bracing for some deep truth. "My therapist . . . they think I have undiagnosed . . . something."

"Who doesn't?" I try to make her smile, but it falls flat, and I think a spurt of blood from the open wound I tore in my own chest when I laughed earlier splatters all over her pristine bedding.

"I guess it makes sense," she says, shrugging and turning inward again, like she's trying to offer herself acceptance but she can't really figure out how it fits. "I've never really liked my brain. It makes sense that it's . . . off."

"I like your brain." I lean forward, wrapping my hands around her wrists and pulling her to my lap. She folds in easily, arms twining around my back like she wanted to be there the whole time. "I like you," I whisper into the crook of her neck, mouth brushing along her skin.

"That makes one of us."

I fucking hate that.

I want her to see herself the way I see her.

The way I saw her that first night—entirely alight in that arena. More beautiful than anything I'd ever seen.

The way I see her now. Smarter—softer—funnier than most people, with this weird stubborn streak cutting through it all.

Little gold.

My arms tighten around her, and I inhale. "Is there a particular way you like to count?"

"I guess groups of three are the most common?" Her fingers paint across my shoulder blades, her face nestles into my chest. "One, two, three. One, two, three. Or sometimes it's all the way to six."

I pull back, one hand coming up to cup her cheek before my thumb traces a pattern towards the tiny constellation of freckles just below her eye, and I punctuate each word. "Jedna. Dvě. Tři."

She blinks, softer and slower, like she's finally relaxing. "What does that mean?"

"One, two, three."

Sloan inhales, sharp and sudden, her eyes water, but I think they're good tears this time.

"Jedna. Dvě. Tři," she repeats.

"Slower," I encourage, grinning now. It's a harsh language, but it sounds beautiful when it's coming from her.

She says it again, and it's closer this time and I'm about to tell her, but she asks another question, words soft, tentative, and maybe she's able to peer into that open wound and see what's written on the inside of me.

Her name. Golden and bright.

"How do you say I love you?"

My thumb twitches against her cheek. "There are a few different ways, and it's not usually said like that, but . . . literally, you'd say miluju tě."

"Miluju tě," she repeats, bringing a palm to press against my chest, right over my heart.

I smile, my thumb dragging along the curve of her mouth. "Better."

Sloan tips her head, hair falling over her shoulder, cheeks soft, words even more so. "Have you ever been in love?"

I debate lying, but the bleeding seems to have stopped, the wound in my chest stitching itself back together each time she smiles, and I decide I don't want to hurt her again for the rest of my life; I don't think I'd survive it.

Brushing my thumb across her lip, I pull back and count each freckle smattering her cheek again, and tell her the truth.

"Only ever you."

Bohdan

There's something a bit cathartic about sitting at a worn table on a too-crowded port street in a too-crowded city, teeming with tourists spilling onto the pedestrian-only cobblestone streets, while you drink too much beer with your two best friends you don't usually let yourself see.

I've avoided everyone for the better part of the last year and a half since it ended with Sloan, and I wouldn't let them come see me the year and a half before that after I got injured, but maybe my mom and my therapist were onto something about not trying to heal alone.

It's been refreshing. Haven't even had a single migraine.

But that's about to come to a screeching halt.

"That doesn't look like a fucking boat that's going to take us down rivers for a week." Jay tugs on the gold chain hanging against his neck, visible through the too-many open buttons of his white linen shirt, before pointing a finger towards the port, the array of patchwork tattoos on his arm stark under the sunlight.

"River cruise rhymed better with retirement." Talon's grin splits wide when he kicks back in his chair, the legs teetering precariously on the uneven cobblestone. One hand flexes, and he stretches out his arm, like maybe he's admiring the stack of rope bracelets sitting around his wrist, or the deeper-than-usual bronze of his skin from the last few days we've spent following him all over Barcelona.

Jay groans into his hand before draining the rest of his beer. "Talon, is it a river cruise or not? I was told river cruise. You know, a significantly smaller boat traversing significantly smaller bodies of water with significantly smaller numbers of guests. I didn't sign up to get on a floating mall." He drops the empty pint glass on the table where it wobbles precariously before settling beside the steadily growing collection. We've been sitting here all afternoon because Talon wanted to "watch the ship come in."

I can see why now.

"What's an ocean if not a really big river?" Talon holds up a hand before smacking his giant luggage where it sits beside him.

"One's a vast body of saltwater encircling a continent, and the other is flowing fresh water that empties into said vast bodies of saltwater," I answer dryly, eyeing the ship behind Jay, distaste curling my lip upwards.

It's huge. You could probably fit four riverboats onto the deck alone.

"Rock boy." Talon grins again, folding his arms and rocking back and forth in his chair. I imagine his eyes light up behind his Ray-Bans at the use of yet another dumb nickname he came up with in college.

"No," I tell him, draining the rest of my beer. "Not a rock fact. You don't need a degree in geological science to know the difference between a river and an ocean."

Jay leans forward, banging his head on the sticky surface of the table. "Don't tell me there's skydiving on board."

Talon pulls back, like it's the most preposterous thing he's ever heard, but I think I see three different waterparks dotting the deck of the ship from here. "No, but there is a skating rink."

Jay lifts his head, making a show of rolling his eyes before he drinks the rest of Talon's beer and slumps in his chair. "Oh, great. The thing we're"—he gestures between us sharply, gold rings on his fingers glinting under the sun—"paid to do. That you just retired from, that we're supposed to be—"

He cuts himself off before he can go any further, tossing me what's supposed to be an apologetic look but really just makes him look uncomfortable.

"Shit." He scrubs his face before pushing his sunglasses up, taking the strands of black hair hanging across his forehead with them. "Sorry, Bohdan. I wasn't thinking."

"It's fine," I tell him, trying to force a smile, but I think it snags on something. Probably the shitty taste and heavy weight of the stupid word—retirement—hanging heavy in the air around us.

Talon retired because he wanted to.

I retired because my bleeding brain said I had to.

Talon smacks both hands against the table. "No. No. That's not how we're starting the Retirement River Cruise."

"Not a river cruise," I correct.

"It sounded better—" He pushes into the table, standing so he can lean closer, the rims of all the empty pint glasses brushing against the pale blue of his button-up shirt, but he doesn't seem to care, because he shifts forward again, pointing at us. "You know what? It's becoming abundantly clear neither of you read the itinerary I sent you, and you just told me to book your travel for you. If you had, you'd know, or at least Rock Boy with his infinite wisdom and knowledge of all things Mother Earth would know, that we weren't going to places joined by rivers."

I shrug. "Well, some of them might be joined by rivers. I wouldn't know, because as you've pointed out, I clearly didn't read the itinerary."

Talon says nothing, but his fingers tap against the table before a grin stretches across his face. Who knows what he's about to say, but his phone starts buzzing against the table. His mouth moves as he reads whatever text lights up his screen.

Looking back up to Jay and me, he practically jumps backward, grabbing the handle of his luggage. "My sister just got here, and she says she has a surprise for me. We can go meet her down at the gangway."

Jay pulls his wallet from the pocket of his shorts, tossing a stack of euros down on the table before standing and grabbing our bags from where they sat beside Talon's. "What could possibly be a bigger surprise than an upgrade from a small boat to a giant-ass ship?"

Talon doesn't bother to answer, and he doesn't bother to wait for us, his eyes glued to his phone as he navigates his way to his sister.

"What's the big deal? Worried someone in the significantly larger passenger count will recognize you?" I hoist my bag over my shoulder and pull my sunglasses from the neck of my shirt. "Maybe comment on Philadelphia's abysmal run this year?"

Jay cuts me a sideways look, tipping his own sunglasses down before we start weaving after Talon through the throngs of photograph-taking tourists. He's practically at the ship already.

"Yes." Jay shakes his head, tugging on his chain again like it's a nervous habit he's developed since I last saw him. "Philly fans can be mean, man.

Passionate, sure, and that feels great when we're winning. But when we're having a bad season . . . someone told me I sucked in the grocery store the other day, and then their fucking ten-year-old kid repeated it."

"No one ever told me I sucked."

He gives me a flat look. "That's because Seattle fans are a bunch of New Age, crunchy hippies."

"Maybe it's because I didn't suck."

"Ha-ha." Jay rolls his eyes before he stops to look at me—really look at me—and I know what he's going to say next when his gaze flicks up to my temple, to the scar I've purposely tried to hide by letting my hair grow a bit longer. "Aren't you worried? That someone might recognize you? It hasn't been that long."

I give a noncommittal shrug, raising a hand in the air to let Talon know we see him where he's standing by the gangway, like he's the first kid in line waiting to be let onto a rollercoaster.

It's a painful thought, that someone might recognize me for the person I used to be—who I was supposed to be—when it's been nice to just try being the person I am now, whoever that is, for the last few days with Talon and Jay.

But it's not as painful as it is to see Sloan again for the first time.

Sloan

Talon spins me in the air, arms wrapped around my stomach, the crowd of people just a blur, and it's on the second whirl around that I see him.

I still feel a bit like I'm spinning when Talon sets me on the ground.

And it's not from the centripetal motion of being spun around by a freshly retired professional athlete still in his prime with more power in his quads than some cars.

It's Bohdan, stepping out of the parting crowd, like he's some sort of hero, coming to rescue everyone and bring them to safety.

Except it's just me here, and I'm not safe.

Not with him.

Not when he looks like that.

Hair almost bronze under the sun, a bit longer than usual, casually windswept in this way he knows I love, and I wish I didn't but I know exactly what it would feel like under my fingertips. Striped linen shorts cuffed and sitting a few inches above his knees, ridges of muscle popping in his thighs, more defined than they have any right to be, glowing with a new tan settling against his skin.

Eyes that used to be warm but cooled off significantly as the years went on, hidden behind tortoiseshell Ray-Bans.

A white linen shirt rolled up on his forearms, revealing valleys of muscle I could navigate with my eyes closed. And I see it there—stark against his newly tanned skin. The looping *S*, in my handwriting, tattooed at the precipice of his left elbow.

I slap my hand over the tiny *B* inked on the front of my shoulder, like I can pretend it's not still there and not on display for everyone to see.

"No," I whisper, taking a tumbling step backward. "No. No. No." I whirl on Tia, a shaking finger pointing towards her. "You said he wasn't coming."

I'd like to try and sound strong, menacing even.

But I don't. My voice is this tiny, infinitesimally small thing, drowning in the tears already running down my cheeks.

It's just like me.

Not enough. Not enough. Not enough.

Tia frowns with a tiny shake of her head, curls immobilized under a giant sun hat but doing their best to escape, before she flicks a manicured finger towards her brother. "I never said he wasn't coming. Why wouldn't he be coming? It's his cruise! I was, however, under the impression this was a river cruise. Talon, have you hit your head one too many times? This is not a boat. It's a ship. See *boat*: a vessel built for navigation of rivers or inland bodies of water. And see *ship*: a large, ocean-faring vessel propelled by multiple sails or engines."

Talon throws his hands up, one raking through freshly styled curls, but I don't give him the chance to speak.

"Not him." I enunciate each word before wiping at my cheeks and pointing towards the crowd. I'm not looking anymore—I can't—but I know exactly where he's standing in the way you're aware of your own heart, the way it sits in your chest, suspended and beating and keeping you alive.

The way a magnet knows just where to pull.

"Him," I say, pointing but not looking, my finger quivering in midair and my voice shaking with a sob that's going to make itself known sooner than I'd like.

Tia turns, slowly, like it's a horror movie and she's just realized there's something in the room with her.

There's something in the room with me, and there has been since he left. He's always there, right under my skin, festering and living there in me, stealing all my oxygen and all my air, and I can't dig him out no matter how hard I try.

"Talon." Tia takes a measured pause, and she blinks slowly, her nostrils flaring before her mouth pulls into a firm line. "You said he didn't answer. You said he wasn't coming."

I think Talon's hands are still in the air, something more like surrender now, but I'm shrinking, arms wrapped around my chest, trying to hold together the open wound Bohdan carved there before what's left of me spills out onto the dock and everyone sees exactly how not enough I am.

"He hadn't. He wasn't. He"—Talon hikes a thumb over his shoulder before swinging it back around to his sister—"was a surprise for you! You've barely seen him in like three years! No one has!"

"Don't you think there's a reason for that?" Tia jabs her finger towards Bohdan, and I feel a bit like sitting down with my head between my knees because I know exactly what he looks like, head angled to the side, grey eyes impassive, steadfast—and somehow it hurts even more to know he's somehow exactly the same, even though he's a stranger now.

75

Tia waves a hand between the two of them, voice rising to a shocking octave. "I have no interest in seeing him. And as a matter of fact, I have no interest in seeing you." She turns on her heel, smiling tightly at Jay, who stands there looking decidedly uncomfortable. "Jay, I'm not talking about you. Why don't you come and spend the week with me and Sloan? Away from these two—one can't tell the difference between a ship and a boat, and the other one—" Her hand waves in the air again, but it's missing some of its former grandeur, and I think she means to sound cruel, harsh even, but she just sounds sad. "Might as well be a ghost."

He is a ghost, I think.

I don't think there's been a single day since he left that I haven't been haunted by Bohdan Novotnak.

I dig the heels of my palms into my eyes, and I try counting to three over and over again. I try all the things my therapist suggests to interrupt the cycle and the spiral, but I hear the words anyway.

Not enough, not enough, not enough.

I don't want him to see it all over me, the way he marked an already rotten body, a rotten heart, and an even more rotten brain. I don't want him to hear me. He always knew when I was counting, even when it was quiet, so I do what I do best, and I try to pretend I hate him.

One more shaky inhale, and I blink, lift my chin, and finally, finally look at him.

As beautiful as ever.

As lovely as ever.

As horrible as ever.

"Oh look, it's the smallest man who ever lived." I try not to blink.

It's a lie. He's huge. All-encompassing. The whole world, the whole universe.

My whole life, for a too-short time.

Bohdan angles his head, appraising, studying, before he slowly takes off his sunglasses, hanging them on the neck of his shirt. The corners of his lips pull into a slow, lazy grin. "Oh look, it's the most beautiful girl on the planet."

"No." I shake my head, and I try to stand taller than I feel. "No. You don't get to call me that."

"I don't?" he asks, like it's a simple thing.

"This might have been a bad idea." Talon presses a fist to his mouth.

"Bit awkward." Jay nods, adjusting the chain around his neck. "But you do look beautiful, Sloan. And so do you, Tia."

"Shut the fuck up," Tia hisses, rolling her eyes.

I take a step forward, closer than I ever would have dared to get to him again. But my heart, this organ that I think went to sleep in some sad attempt at self-preservation blinks sleepy eyes, and it slowly wakes up, and it starts to beat again—sluggish, measured, taking its time—but entirely resuscitated because his voice was the compressions on my chest.

"No. You don't." I narrow my eyes, nostrils flaring. "You don't leave the most beautiful girl in the world. You don't turn your fucking back on her."

I'm pointing at him now, and he takes a slow step towards me, hands finding their way into the pockets of his shorts and I'm hyper-aware of the way the material tenses against the muscles of his thighs.

"Do those two things negate the fact that she's still the most beautiful girl in the world?" His voice drops, his words rough. "Because I don't think they do."

"Forgot what it was like with you two. Fireworks. Poof." Talon mimes an explosion with his hands. "But I think this might be a more dangerous, life-limiting kind than we were used to back in college."

Bohdan takes another deliberate step, like he might walk right up to me, might push his chest against my still-extended finger. Like maybe our skin might touch for the first time in too long.

My heart beats a bit funny at the thought, living and breathing again on his voice, not blood flow, not oxygen.

But I hear Talon's words, and there's a terribly sad sort of truth to them.

"Life-limiting is a good word for it," I whisper, vision blurring at the edges, and I can barely make out anything but Bohdan's silhouette when I turn to walk down the dock, far away from him.

I hope that turning my back on him, walking away the way he did—that it might give me some sort of terrible sense of satisfaction.

I know it won't.

But I do it anyway. I turn to walk down the dock, to board the giant ship I'm suddenly thankful isn't a boat, so I can be far, far away from him.

I think he might reach for me, but it doesn't matter. It's too late.

Sloan

Then – College

Bohdan doesn't flinch when the needle of the tattoo gun whirs to life, dancing over the skin of his inner bicep.

I do. I hate the idea of anything hurting him.

I've seen him in pain too much for my liking over the last two years. I've seen him with too many cuts to count: a thin slice along his jaw that didn't end up needing stitches, but left a faint scar you can only really see when he's clean-shaven and there's no stubble dusting it. A gash through his eyebrow that had to be taped, but if you look closely, you can see a tiny bump of raised skin that sits above the left brow; and more than one concussion.

None so severe he was out for more than a week, but I don't actively enjoy seeing him hit the boards at all, let alone when his head makes contact with anything.

I think he might be a little too high above it all right now for anything to bother him.

A graduating senior who holds more on-ice records than he cares to remember, the best centre in MSU history with not one, but now two Frozen Four titles.

First overall in the draft, and so many bright, lovely things waiting for him in his future.

A big, beautiful life on the West Coast, where he says he'll wait for me, too.

It's not just Bohdan I've seen win and lose and get hurt and get back up over the last two years; I've seen Jay and Talon do the same and get hurt right beside him. But even though they're just as high in the stratosphere as he is, and Jay's no stranger to ink—tiny tattoos dot his arms in patchwork sleeves—they both wince when the needles pierce their skin.

Bohdan's eyes cut to the tattoo gun as it presses down, but they don't stay there long. They're back on me, perched beside Tia on the end of Jay's neatly made king bed, watching the three of them stretched out across Jay's room—the biggest in the house, a point of pride for him over the last two years. Bohdan has one leg kicked up, lying back on a padded table, his left arm extended out into space, with a tattoo artist hunched over his bicep, making tiny, precise strokes with the needle.

Talon and Jay sit on either end of another table, opposite legs stretched out with artists hovering over the pop of muscle above each of their knees.

"This doesn't feel sterile. Shouldn't we have gone to the tattoo parlour?" Tia frowns, apprehensive.

Jay glances up from the tattoo artist, hunched over his thigh where she moves the gun up and down in a way that tells me she's drawing the twenty-two for Talon. His mouth pulls tight and his nostrils flare, but he shakes his head at Tia. "My dads gave me money as a present for winning the Frozen Four twice. Said I could do whatever I wanted with it."

A brow flicks up on her forehead. "So you called a mobile tattoo truck and thought that permanently scarring your body with all your respective numbers from the 'only line to ever exist'"—she pauses so we can all give appropriate deference to her exaggerated air quotes—"was a good use of their hard-earned money?"

Jay grins before he exhales sharply when the gun carves above his kneecap. "I'll pay them back. I'm about to have a lot of my own hard-earned money."

"The only line to ever exist." Talon's smile splits across his face. He holds a palm up, and Jay looks like he might reach out for it, but the artist working on Talon moves to the second number, seventeen for Bohdan, and her eyes don't leave his quad when she cuts in, "Do not move."

Talon flashes his other palm in apology, but he's still smiling. "Tell Mr. Choi and Mr. Solorzano thank you very much."

The corners of Bohdan's mouth twitch, like he's vaguely amused, the left corner just a bit higher, and he winks at me before looking back towards the needle. "You okay over there, Zlatíčko?"

"I'm fine, thank you." I roll my eyes, but my hands curl around the edge of the mattress and I lean forward to get a closer look. "Does it hurt?"

Bohdan gives a jerk of his chin at the same time Jay says, "Yes," and Talon inhales with a hiss.

"You can come watch, baby." He gives another jerk of his head, but this one in invitation.

Talon jumps backward in age by about ten years and starts making high-pitched kissing noises when Jay snorts and lifts his brows at Tia. "You can come watch, too, baby."

I can practically hear Tia's eye roll when I stand, head tilting as I cross the room, watching the needle whir across the stretch of Bohdan's muscle. The artist just finished with his number, and she's moving to the next one—twenty for Jay—when Bohdan's hand finds mine.

He laces our fingers together, pressing his lips to the back of my hand, and he does the whole thing in these sharp, precise movements—the way he does everything. Careful, thoughtful, measured. So much so that the tattoo artist doesn't look up, she doesn't reprimand him or warn him not to move.

His skin touches mine and it always feels like the first time.

It's been two years—but it's never really stopped. Not with us.

I smile softly, tightening my grip on his hand.

I've been afraid of so many things in my life.

My own mind usually contends for first place. But now, I think the thing that scares me most in the entire world is the idea that one day, my hands won't know his.

Bohdan cocks his head. "Do you want one?"

"Pardon me?" I blink.

"A tattoo." His hand tenses in mine, and he points a finger towards the shining, black ink stretching across his bicep. "Do you want one?"

"Oh." I nod, like he's asking me if I want something simple and mundane. "I've never really thought about it."

"You should get one, Sloany," Talon calls, and I imagine him nodding exuberantly, eyes coming alive and a deep brown curl flopping over his forehead. "Mr. Choi and Mr. Solorzano already paid."

"Yeah, go nuts." I glance over my shoulder at Jay, who nods along and stretches his leg out to admire the artist's handiwork. "I paid for the time. Not for the three pieces."

Tia purses her lips, pointing at Jay. "Another colossal waste of your fathers' hard-earned money."

"Do you want one?" Bohdan's voice, low and rough and still the most wonderful thing I've ever heard two years later, cuts across everything else.

I flick my eyes back to him with a small shake of my head and pout of my lips. "I honestly wouldn't know what to get."

He nods, thoughtful, before offering me a gentle smile. "That's fine, Zlatíčko. Just thought I'd ask."

"What would you get? If you were going to get a second one?" I tip my head back and forth, examining the new piece of him, this thing about his body I'm not intimately familiar with, blurred slightly now under a clear plastic bandage.

Bohdan's eyes rove across my face, a crease scores between his brows, and he never looks away from me when he says, "Get Sloan a pen and a piece of paper."

"Why?" I frown, but his hand squeezes mine.

Tia does get me a black marker and piece of paper, clearly ripped out of the first notebook she could find on Jay's desk, and she shoves them at me, brown eyes wide and sparkling with interest, flicking back and forth between Bohdan and me.

"Draw an *S*," he says, words firm and quiet.

"Why?" I ask, even though I do it anyway, and I'm a bit nervous now because there are all these horrible, worst-case scenarios running through my head.

He's leaving me. It's something to remember me by.

He's dying, actually. A terminal illness and you didn't see the signs and now it's much too late.

It's not for you, idiot. It's an S for Seattle.

I almost breathe a sigh of relief when that particularly rude thought strolls across the expanse of my brain, but Bohdan sits up, legs swinging over the edge of the table, and he stretches his left arm out again. He takes the piece of paper between two fingers, hands it to the artist, and without looking away from me, he taps his left forearm, right where the muscle sits, just beyond the precipice of his elbow. "I'd get you. On me forever. Where you belong."

Everything goes so, so quiet. It's wonderful and it reminds me so much of this one night when I was in Lake Huron with my grandparents and it snowed. These giant, fluffy flakes floating down from the sky, all cloudy and grey, and everything was so still when I watched them fall to the earth under the glow of a streetlight.

Talon mutters somewhere behind me, "I think I could have pulled off a better line. Bit cheesy."

"Tracks. This makes more sense for him than the numbers." Jay would be nodding, I think.

"You can't pull anything off, Talon. Shut up." Tia rolls her eyes again I'm sure, folding her arms across her chest.

But I don't see any of that when I drop down beside Bohdan on the table, and ask softly—maybe as quiet as my world is right now—but our best friends hear me anyway, because I do think they're always listening, "Can someone get Bohdan a piece of paper, too?"

Sloan

My wish to be far, far away from Bohdan doesn't come true.

"I hate it here," I hiss, watching Tia file her nails in the reflection of the mirror that stretches the entire length of the bathroom, propped up on the edge of a freestanding clawfoot tub.

Brown eyes flick up, meeting mine in the mirror. She pauses, pointing the file around the bathroom. "Here?" She waves it in the air. "Or here, as in, this giant suite we're all staying in together that my brother booked and didn't tell anyone about on this ship that's definitely not a riverboat?"

"No. Here. In the figurative sense. Where he is." I widen my eyes towards the door, fingers gripping tighter on the porcelain of the sink. "Do you think we could get another room?"

She ignores me, before her features soften with an exhale. "Once upon a time, you loved being where he was."

"That was . . . before."

The truth is—I don't know why he did it. I have no idea why he left.

Bohdan's never been a particularly talkative person. It was one of the first things I learned about him.

He doesn't say a lot, but he says what he means.

And he said he was leaving.

So he must have meant it.

The only conclusion I can find, after turning it over and over and over in my head, is that my brain must have been right all along, since I had my first conscious thought that there was something wrong, just . . . off about me, and little four-year-old Sloan tottered off to preschool with worries in her backpack beside her crayons.

It wasn't that the life he had wasn't enough anymore.

It was me. I wasn't enough, and I never was.

"Maybe this is a good thing." Tia leans forward, nodding softly like she's trying to be encouraging. "You could talk. You haven't spoken to him since. I can't imagine how hard that is."

"It's not hard," I bite out, but the tears welling in my eyes say otherwise.

It's one of the hardest things I've ever done, becoming someone who doesn't know him.

Tia taps the nail file against her fingers before she gently sets it down on the edge of the tub and comes to stand beside me. She drops her chin against my shoulder. "What do you want to do?"

"I'm going to ignore him," I say, faking conviction and a smile that doesn't meet my eyes.

She wrinkles her nose, looking half tempted to moan in exasperation. "For a whole week? I don't think that's the solution, Sloan."

"What do you propose I do, Tia?" I wipe at my cheeks, watching in the mirror as I turn inward, all that fake confidence shrinking in real time. "I mean it," I continue, words all small and sad. "What would you do?"

"What if we gave you two some space? You guys skip this private tour of the ship Talon arranged"—she rolls her eyes, and a tiny smile fights against my tears, peeking through like sunshine on an otherwise grey day—"we'll go, and you talk? Just . . . say what you need and put it to rest. I'll catch you up. God knows there's nothing so important you can't miss."

I blink and give a shake of my head. "I don't want to talk to him."

It's a lie. I do.

I've wanted to talk to him every minute of every day since he left. It's a visceral ache, really.

This empty spot in me that just rings endlessly because the person who used to occupy it packed up and moved out.

I could move on; I should move on eventually. But he carved out this home that I don't think anyone could ever touch.

He built it from scratch. With rough hands that were soft with me, all the framing made of wood grown from his love and the foundation poured from understanding no one else could ever come close to offering. The drywall and flooring and paint and decorations and all those lovely things were put there by those hands, too. All the furniture the colour of his eyes and in the shape of his mouth, with lights dotting the ceilings like the freckles dotting my face.

Who'd ever want to try and live there?

"Why not?" Tia drums her fingertips along my arms, tapping at the tattoo still inked there.

I watch her finger touch the letter, and I wish she had a magic eraser. Bohdan lives in me, and I don't need a reminder painted on my skin for the whole world to see.

It's like wearing around my thoughts, a little sign strapped around my neck like a name tag:

Sloan Joseph
Once loved by Bohdan Novotnak
But not enough, as it would turn out
Just like her

I don't know how to tell Tia that Bohdan leaving was all the proof my brain needed to launch a new campaign against me.

So, I try to shrug, and say something else. "He's tricky. Manipulative. He'll start speaking Czech halfway through the conversation, his voice will get all rough, and he's just got an unfair advantage, walking around and looking like that, don't you think?"

One hand leaves my shoulder, and she taps my nose. "Some might say the advantage is yours. All that dark hair, eyes that blue, and that cute little triangle of freckles he loved to trace with his thumb?"

"I'd prefer not to test the theory."

Tia exhales, lips tumbling into a sad smile before she squeezes my shoulders and takes a step back.

She's running out of things to try and say to me, I can see it in the way she angles her head back and forth, studying me in the mirror.

Bohdan always said I was stubborn, and maybe he was right.

But it doesn't matter what else she's going to say because there's a pounding on the door that could only belong to Talon.

He organized this whole thing with much more structure and thought than any of us could have ever imagined he had in him. The royal suite with the two stories of rooms, the sprawling, modern marble staircase in the middle, the monochrome cream furnishings set off with gold adornments, and the sweeping balcony with a view of the stretching ocean.

An excursion each day at each port, theme nights, and even designated downtime.

It all starts in fifteen minutes with a private tour of the ship.

All these small, minute details accounted for.

Tia throws open the door with a loud huff of breath. "We wouldn't miss your little tour, Talon. I know how badly you want to see the captain's quarters."

What I don't think he accounted for—he can be a bit obtuse like that—even though we were both on the invite list, was what it would mean for Bohdan and me to see each other again.

I see Bohdan now, one leg kicked up against the back of the giant sectional spanning the middle of the room. All that does is draw attention to the carved muscles of his thighs, and it *is* unfair. Arms crossed over his chest, face impassive and head angled in a way that makes him look like someone carved him from a marble statue, hair a shade of golden-brown in the sunlight shining through the floor-to-ceiling windows that I don't think a painter could ever swirl the right colours to replicate, and grey eyes wholly on me.

His jaw flexes, and his hand tightens on his bicep when I walk by, and I think he might want to say something.

But it wouldn't matter. I can't hear him over my brain anyway.

Bad. Worthless. Insignificant.

Those words were always there. It's funny how he spent the better part of a decade trying to get them to quiet down, to soften their edges, and to keep them from stabbing me from the inside out, but in the end, it was him who made them the loudest they'd ever been.

Bohdan

I watch Sloan tug either side of the brim of Tia's giant hat down over her face, like she can hide from everyone on the ship.

It might work to keep strangers from noticing her, but she's never be able to hide from me, and something about the way her knuckles turn white, fingers ramrod straight as she holds the ugly hat like it's a buoy in the ocean, tells me she's trying not to tap against it and count.

So, I do it for her, and hope her brain hears me and stops whatever it's saying that makes her think she needs to atone through numbers. "Jedna. Dvě. Tři."

"Pay attention." Talon cuts me a sideways look, elbow finding my shoulder as he walks along behind the suite concierge—Aron, a much too-friendly, too-passionate employee who definitely couldn't read the tension in the room at all—on this little private tour of this giant ship he arranged for us. "What are you even saying?"

"I'm counting."

"Counting what?" he prods, promptly forgetting his own demands to pay attention, eyes on me instead of watching this makeshift tour we're being given.

"How long it's going to take before my restraint snaps and I fucking clock you for doing this." I jerk my chin towards Sloan where she walks side by side with Tia, nodding along like she's so interested in the activities schedule and the water aerobics offerings. "How could you do this to her?"

I wait for him to repeat everything he said earlier. That he expected us to read the itinerary, that the booking was clearly for a suite, not individual rooms, that he never believed we'd both come.

But he stops, cocks his head back, eyes sharpening with something like disappointment, and asks me in this uncharacteristically quiet voice, "How could you?"

"Don't tell me this was some shitty attempt at getting us back together." I shake my head, pressing my fingers between my eyes before they find my temple. "It's not going to work."

Talon glances over his shoulder, waiting until Tia and Sloan are further down the hall with Aron before whistling through his teeth at Jay.

Jay tips his head back, cheeks puffing out in exasperation before jogging back towards us, hands shoved firmly in his pockets.

"Hypothetically," Talon starts, waving a hand between me and Sloan's retreating figure, "if it would work, would you want it to?"

Jay pinches the bridge of his nose and swipes a hand through his hair. "Would he want what to work? Don't tell me this was some sort of setup, Talon. Jesus."

Talon's lip curls up and he waves his hand at Jay. "Give me some fucking credit, Choi."

"I don't know, man, last time I visited you, there were a surprising number of romance books on your shelves. Thought you might have picked up a thing or two and wanted to see if you could put it to the test, help your friend out at the same time." Jay holds his palms up.

"Men can read romance, Jay. In fact, I think they should. Might learn a thing or two." Talon clicks his tongue before turning to me. "Big thing the books talk about—communication." He starts walking backward, pointing. "Maybe you should try it some time."

"Solid advice, man." Jay widens his eyes, giving Talon's retreating back a sarcastic thumbs-up when he turns around.

I dig the heels of my palms into my eyes before tugging on the ends of my hair. My hand grazes the raised edge of my scar, and I feel a bit like recoiling.

"You okay?" Jay asks, quieter now, hands back in his pockets, and he points with one elbow towards the end of the hall, where Aron has them stopped, pointing at the golden crown moulding and the wall sconces with a bit too much enthusiasm. "Head bothering you?"

Talon's the only one who looks remotely interested.

"My head's always bothering me," I mutter, pinching the bridge of my nose.

"Do you want to, I don't know, go somewhere else? We can grab a drink. I counted at least eight bars on the way in." He jerks his head in the opposite direction of Talon.

Of Sloan.

"Nah. It's fine." He looks at me like he doesn't quite believe me, and he shouldn't, but I start walking down the hall anyway. "Don't worry, I've got a whole pharmacy back in the room if I need it. You ever tried medication in the form of a nasal spray?"

He laughs, I think in spite of himself, but I'll count it anyway. "Can't say I have."

We catch up just in time to hear Aron talking about the passenger capacity of the ship in mind-numbing detail.

One of the things I loved first about Sloan was how herself she is.

She's always known exactly who she is.

But it was also one of the first things to break my heart, because she might be herself, but she's always been apologetic about it.

Case in point: Aron won't shut up about the capacity of the ship, the sheer size of it, how we'll probably never see the same passengers twice on any given day.

And so quietly—not like she doesn't want anyone to hear her, but like she's afraid they might—Sloan taps a finger against her thumb and whispers, "No wonder cruise ships are a central hub for human trafficking activity."

Tia turns to her just as she's rounding the corner. "Did you say something?"

"No." Sloan shakes her head, full lower lip pouting.

They all follow. It's just us here in the hallway with the stupid golden sconces and the ostentatious crown moulding, and I decide to try and take Talon's advice.

"Louder. Take up space," I murmur, pressing a knuckle between her shoulder blades where her tank top hangs loose, giving me a glimpse at the expanse of skin stretching down her back that makes me want to die a bit.

Sloan jerks away, one hand swatting at her back where I sort of hope she can still feel me, and she narrows her eyes before taking a measured swallow. "Don't. Don't say things like that, and don't touch me."

"Sloan, I just—"

"No," she says, pressing her palms together to point them at me, and there's conviction in her voice, but I can see the damage I did strewn all over her. "This whole thing will be much better if you and I just don't speak."

"You think we're going to spend a week together—staying in the same suite—and we're going to be able to just . . . not talk to each other?"

"I've had a year and a half worth of practice, Bohdan."

It's the first time I've heard her say my name, and there's no fucking way anyone could say the pain lancing across my forehead is psychological. She might as well have ripped the whole thing open again.

It gets worse.

She keeps talking. "I've gotten pretty good at it."

I grip my jaw, shake my head, and I'm about to say something—I don't know what, but I'd do anything to be able to fix this.

I'd go back in time to when they stitched up my head, and I'd ask them to take the string and save it to tie her back together.

But she holds up a hand.

"You made your bed, Bohdan. And it was, unfortunately, one without me." Her voice cracks, her eyes cloud over, a solitary tear slips out, tracking down over her freckles, and I reach out to wipe it away, but I catch my hand right when she jerks backward.

I don't think I could say anything even if I tried.

I've hated a lot of things over the last year and a half I've been without her.

I've hated even more things in the year before that, and they all started on the day I got hurt.

I've hated my brain for failing me in more ways than one.

I've hated my body for not being able to catch back up.

I've hated my lungs for depleting faster.

I've hated that fucking equipment company.

I've hated my former equipment manager for the sole fact that I ended up with a bad helmet.

I've hated the guy who hit me.

I've even hated the guy who made the play that had me close to the boards.

I've tried my hand at hating my two best friends, because they still get to skate.

But I don't think I've ever hated myself. At least, not the way I do right now.

She gets the last word.

"Now lie in it."

Sloan

Then – Seattle

Years can go by in the blink of an eye.

A boy can see you through scratched-up glass and change the trajectory of your whole life.

You can spend so many nights wrapped up in each other, and you can miss out on things you thought were important to you but seem entirely insignificant because they aren't him.

If you're lucky, you might get to watch him turn into a man: planes of his face drawing harsher lines and stubble spreading slowly across his jaw, darkening angles that only seem soft to you. Hands widening with the stretching topography of new veins, his shoulders and chest even more so, more than enough to hold you just right.

You change, too.

Your cheekbones lift, your body moves through more than one phase and it goes back again, your hair grows, but you get to grow into yourself, too.

It's all still there—the general rot of my brain and maybe who I am underneath it all.

When I started college I told my therapist if I went down to the cadaver lab for study, they'd be horrified at what they found if they peeled back my skin.

But I think if you stripped me back now, maybe you'd see some of that. The inherent badness of Sloan Joseph and all the worries and all the wonders about conversations of years past and whether she really did embarrass herself that one night or if she's done something awful she can't remember. Maybe you'd see the dig I didn't go on that one summer and some habits I formed that I shouldn't have.

I think though, mostly, you'd see Tia. Talon. Jay.

Nights hand in hand, screaming their names under bright arena lights, and the feeling of my shoes against the sticky floors of their house at endless parties afterwards.

Dinners and away games and trips and jumping from rooftops into pools and all sorts of things you'd be horrified your parents found out you did in college.

You'd see Bohdan, sharp grey eyes that blink in time with the beat of my heart, and instead of ribs, I think you'd find his hands, suspended there in me, holding everything important in place.

You wouldn't see the different types of failed therapy and medications that made me sick and lose all sense of who I was. You wouldn't see my parents, a supportive omnipresence who just can't understand why their daughter is so sensitive.

But Bohdan does and he always has, and when my life changed and crashed into his, this beautiful gift came along too: I got to watch him achieve his dreams, and even though it meant he had to move across the country, he's always there to pick me up at the airport.

He leans against a pillar in the arrivals lounge, head resting against the cement, damp hair spilling around his ears from a post-practice shower, a faint shadow of stubble inching along his jaw, and I light up from the inside out as the too-serious lines of his face split into a grin when he spots me at the top of the escalator.

People stop and stare, a few children point at him—he did score his first hat trick this week—but he only has eyes for me.

I feel my ribs—his fingers—strum against my heart. The chords they pluck and what they say. *Hi, I missed you. I hate being apart like this.*

His lips say it, too, writing symphonies with mine when he kisses me in front of the crowded airport.

He's quiet in the car, the way he usually is—leaned back in the driver's seat, one hand loose on the wheel, thumb tapping against the leather, and the other, stretched out against the back of my headrest, tugging on loose strands of my hair, tucking them behind my ear, thumb tracing the curve before it sends shivers down my spine.

Dropping my head back, I watch him drive, silhouetted against the backdrop of trees—evergreen and firs, some shedding their leaves, the colours faded by their time spent under the last of the fall sun.

The sun dips, and it might signal the end of the day, but to me, it signals the start. One whole week of Thanksgiving break, and even though we're well into our second calendar year of long distance, it's the first time I get to stay here for more than a long weekend during the semester.

The idea of us both being Canadian was somehow a funny joke for our friends, but it worked out when this week became something just for us.

"I brought you a present," I say, sitting up to rifle through my backpack.

"It's not you?" The corner of his mouth slants up.

"No. It's a housewarming gift." Pulling the cardboard box out of my backpack, I hold it up, triumphant.

His eyes cut to me, and he presses a thumb to his lips. "Candy Land?"

Frowning, I glance back at the board game, still encased in plastic, the jarring, bright colours juxtaposed against the muted landscape of Seattle surrounding us. "The Gumdrop King was very persuasive. It was the only thing they had at the gift shop."

"They sell Candy Land at airport gift shops?" He cracks a real grin, amused, before his eyes are back on the road.

"It was this or a singing fish mounted to a Michigan license plate. Did you really want that in your new home?"

"Our new home," he corrects, firmly and quietly.

I roll my eyes, tossing the game back down beside my bag. "Your new home."

"Ours," he repeats.

It's a constant tug-of-war between us. He's here in Seattle because it's where he was drafted, and he bought us this apartment, meant to be our new home, but maybe not, because I can't guarantee I'll get into UW for grad school, and entirely not because I haven't paid a single cent for it.

I didn't bother applying back home after he was drafted.

UW makes the most sense because it's where he is, but WSU makes the most sense because of the research streams I want to study: psychological and medical anthropology. It was a bit more of a reach to try and align my research interests with someone at UW. That's not to say they don't or won't fit, and it's not as good of a choice—it just doesn't fit as well as WSU would.

But WSU is in Pullman.

Bohdan isn't in Pullman.

And I don't think anything will ever fit the way Bohdan does.

It's hard to explain to someone who didn't fall stupidly in love when they were stupidly young how it changes you, on a cellular level, I think.

We're both restricted in these funny ways. He's in Seattle because he has to be, and I'm at the mercy of the admissions committees at graduate schools with anthropology programs that have concentrations in anything remotely related to health, and maybe those missed opportunities live inside me—but it doesn't feel limiting.

The whole thing really feels like the possibility of a beautiful life with someone I love who loves me in a way I think people go their whole lives without being loved.

I step into this new home he bought, and it's not restricting or limiting, it's wonderful and lovely.

But it feels a bit wrong, to claim it as mine.

"Do you like it?" he asks, almost hesitant, while I run my fingers along the floor-to-ceiling windows, really just a mirror to the Sound, sparkling in the distance.

I glance back over my shoulder. "It doesn't matter if I like it. It's yours."

"That's not how this works." Bohdan shakes his head, a hand tracking through his still-damp hair when he crosses the empty apartment towards me. "It's ours."

"How about this? It's yours, but you've given me free reign on artistic privileges until I start making money and can contribute to the financial security of the household?"

"Too late. I already hung the only piece of art I'll ever give a shit about on the fridge." He points a thumb over his shoulder. I peer past him, and I see it there on the fridge—that old, worn Polaroid of an eighteen-year-old me.

I try to smile, but my heart stumbles against my rib cage, where it's caught by Bohdan's hands. I blink away tears, but one slips out anyway. "Why do you still have that?"

"Forget my date of birth. Told you before, my life started that night." He looks at me, impassive and stoic and serious as always.

"Well." I roll my shoulders back to rest against the window. My voice gets quiet. "It can be your house for now, then. Until I move next year. Almost ours, if you will."

"I will." He nods, eyes going dark when he angles his head, looking down at me. One palm presses against the glass, right beside my head, the other finds my waist, and the heat of him radiates through the cotton of my T-shirt. "I missed you."

I give him a small smile, bringing a hand to his chest. "Are you sure? Not too busy scoring goals to miss me? You should have seen everyone watching the game at FieldHouse. People go nuts when you score. Bohdan Novotnak, the pride and joy of MSU."

"Yeah?" He gives me a wry look, drumming his fingers at my waist. "They were for you. Did you tell everyone you were my girlfriend?"

"Really?" I ask with a tiny roll of my eyes. "Your first professional hat trick was all for me?"

Bohdan grins, tipping his head down so his mouth rests against mine. "Most things I do are for you, Sloan." He lingers there, lips moving slowly, tongue brushing against the seam of my mouth, searching for permission.

He kisses me, thoroughly, unhurried—we've got a whole week, after all, where we could stay here, pressed up against this window. My hands scramble across his back. They tangle in his hair, pulling on the wayward waves, and I'm arching into his chest and starting to move against his leg when he slides it in between mine.

His teeth catch my bottom lip with a tug, his words a rough groan. "You didn't answer me. Did you tell everyone you were my girlfriend?"

"People know I'm your girlfriend, trust me. I get stopped on campus and asked for your autograph at least once a month." My nails dig into his shoulders with a tiny intake of breath when his mouth moves across my jaw and down the side of my neck.

I feel him smile, teeth scraping my skin before his tongue brushes away the slight hurt. "You could sign for me, if you wanted. I'll teach you to forge my signature."

"I can't imagine your agent would approve of that." I bite down on my lip when his teeth find my earlobe.

"No different than me signing it, really." He breathes against my ear, fingers bruising my waist, and his other hand finally comes off the window to tip my chin up. He looks down at me, grey eyes impossibly dark and his already full lips swollen from mine. "Pretty sure you're what I'm made of."

Another tiny inhale because I think my heart might stop. Not in a bad way. In the best way really.

I swallow, blinking up at him. "That's quite the line."

"Yeah. I guess it is." He presses his thumb to my chin. "Got it from Talon. Says it has a pretty high success rate."

"As much as I hate for Talon Valdez to be right about anything . . ."

A grin splits across his face. He leans down, hands gripping the backs of my legs, and he hoists me up.

He finishes the tour of the apartment like that: me in his arms, legs wrapped around his waist, one of his strong hands pressed against my back.

He shows me our bedroom—it's just a mattress in the middle of the floor, he still technically lives with the team captain, and he will until I move—but it might be the most beautiful thing I've ever seen.

A mattress with crisp navy sheets and a haphazardly pulled-up duvet.

It's where he lays me down.

It's where he undresses me with a sort of kind, gentle precision that could only ever belong to him.

It's where he makes my body react and makes me feel things that I've never felt before and I don't think I ever will again.

It's where we sit, wrapped up in sheets and eating Chinese takeout from containers.

It's where we play Candy Land all night.

It's where we say I love you long after the sun sets, casting shadows through all those giant windows, and even though it's not even close to the first time we've said the only three words that really matter, it feels a bit like it is.

When looking back, I'd say it's also where we start the rest of our lives.

Bohdan

To no one's surprise, the tour ended in the helm of the ship so we could see the control room.

But to Talon's surprise, the wheel of the ship was for show, not to steer.

He insisted on taking photos with it anyway. He posted one of the three of us online, him stretched out along the floor in the front, pointing up at it, Jay crouching down and ruffling his hair, and me leaning against the control board, foot kicked up, and looking at Talon, generally displeased.

The caption— *"the only line to ever exist" made it out of the group chat*—seemed to be an annoying hit with the sports fans of the internet.

People still talk about us, and they still love us all these years later.

There hasn't been a line like us since, and the competitive part of me hopes there never will be. That there's this one, glowing thing on the sunset of my career.

I had to mute my phone because the constant vibrating from the onslaught of notifications and texts as the cell service went in and out was starting to grate on me, including another text from Shay, asking if I'd given any thought to the offer.

I told her before we boarded that I wasn't buying the Wi-Fi package and to expect to hear from me only sparingly. But her tenacity was one of the reasons having her in my corner as my agent had gotten me all sorts of deals other rookies and players could only dream of. But now she was asking me if I'd given any more thought to doing this thing that felt like going on live television, digging my own hands through my chest, and peeling back my rib cage for the world to get a look at all my failures up close.

The answer was probably no before I stepped on this ship, and it's leaning even more that way since I laid eyes on Sloan and had a face-to-face reminder of what my inability to be candid about my own mental health cost me.

But it's not like the notifications were keeping me from riveting conversation.

Sloan hid back under her sun hat, linked arms with Tia, and didn't say a word until we reached activity number two on the itinerary: drinks and sunbathing on the entertainment deck.

"Oh. No. Sorry." Sloan gives a tiny shake of her head. "We can't sit here."

"And why not?" Talon asks, swinging his legs over the edge of a lounge chair he spotted from across the deck of the ship and sprinted towards, practically shoving more than one child with floaties strapped around their waist out of the way, somehow avoiding spilling any of his drink.

"Sun exposure."

Talon pushes his glasses down his nose, lip pulling back. "You're half Italian, Sloan. Isn't your dad from Sicily?"

Her grandfather. But I don't correct him.

She waves a hand in the air. "Skin cancer is a threat to us all."

But her eyes flick to me, and they land on the wave of hair I tugged down over my forehead to hide the scar.

She doesn't want me to be out in the sun.

"I'm not moving. Do you know how many photos of this ship I looked at to scope out the best possible seats? I've been living in Sweden since I was twenty-two. I need the sun." Talon points to his chest.

Tia lifts her sunglasses to roll her eyes at his already dark skin before she drops down on her chair, stretching out.

Sloan says nothing, but a furrow pulls across her brow. I watch her bite down on the inside of her cheek, eyes swinging between the chairs and the sun umbrellas pushed to the side.

She's not wrong.

Sun this bright would usually hurt me. Maybe not right away. But later tonight or tomorrow morning.

I'm not sure I really care when she stands there like that. More beautiful than anything and worth every second of pain it's going to cause.

Hair shining impossibly bright, spilling over her shoulders, that *B* inked on her skin, sitting right beside the strap of her linen tank top. Lines of her legs tensing and shifting when she taps her foot in time with her finger against her bicep, denim shorts brushing against her thighs.

Her eyes find me again, she swallows, and then she's bending over, arms wrapped around the cement base of one of the sun umbrellas, trying to drag it across the deck into the centre of our chairs.

"Jesus Christ, someone help her," Talon mutters, brow lifting behind his drink.

I start forward, but Sloan's eyes flick up to me, tracing over the scar half hidden under my hair, before she tugs harder on the cement base of the umbrella.

"Someone else then." Talon holds his hands up, frozen daiquiri sloshing over the sides of his glass.

Jay cringes. "I've got it."

"Thanks," I mutter, and I don't watch him drag the umbrella into the centre of the chairs, but I sit in the one that's going to get the most shade.

Sloan exhales, soft, just a tiny flare of her nostrils and slump of her shoulders.

Her eyes sweep over me, tracking every inch of my body that might get exposed to the sun, but when she sees it's just my legs and my left arm when I shift, she glances towards the scar again before sitting in the chair furthest away from mine, puts her headphones in, and doesn't look at me for the rest of the afternoon.

Bohdan

I thought seeing Sloan again was painful.

That spending a day in such close proximity, sneaking glances at her sitting there, book propped up on her knees, chin in her hand, and headphones firmly in her ears while she ignored the rest of us was hard.

That it was torture, really, to be so close to her brain—the one she hates but I know is beautiful, wonderful, endlessly fascinating—and not be able to lean over, take one of those headphones out, press my mouth to the spot where her neck meets her collarbone, and ask her what she's thinking.

I thought the last year and a half of my life was objectively brutal without her.

But I guess it was all just preparing me for this.

For her walking into the dining room of this godforsaken ship. For her hair lifting off her exposed shoulders in a phantom breeze, eyes bright and maybe happy for the first time since she saw me again. For her head tipped back in laughter, showing me the lines of her neck I used to sink my teeth into while she laughs at something Tia says. For her skin glowing from the sun and her legs stretching out from underneath this yellow silk dress that hits her mid-thigh. The *B* on her shoulder tucked away under its thin straps.

"Fuck," I mutter, absentmindedly rubbing at my chest.

I don't think there's ever been a more beautiful person on the planet.

Jay tips his wineglass towards her with a low whistle. "Think she wore that dress on purpose?"

I give him a flat look and grab my beer, swishing it around before taking a too-large swallow.

Talon cranes his head, eyes sweeping over Sloan before he lets out a bark of laughter. "You're so fucked."

"Thanks to you." I empty the glass, wishing I'd had the foresight to ask the server for more than one.

I debate reaching across the table and taking the rest of Jay's wine and draining that when Sloan and Tia reach the table.

Tia smiles warmly at me, looking like she might feel a bit sorry for me. Sloan pointedly ignores me, even though Tia took the only other open chair, beside Jay, and now she has to sit next to me.

Talon glances back and forth between us, eyes pinched and smile strained, while Sloan grabs the edges of her chair and tries to shift it further away from me.

He waits, like he's expecting one of us to give in, turn and drop to our knees and declare our still undying love for each other.

My love is undying, but judging by the way she's trying to get every single millimetre of distance from me she can, I'd say hers is well and dead.

I press my fingers to my temple and try to pretend I'm not bleeding out in the dining room on a fucking Mediterranean cruise.

"Well." Talon clears his throat, clapping once before raising his glass of scotch. "A toast to me and my retirement then. I'd say it was a pretty successful career."

Sloan raises her glass, arm twisted at an awkward angle to avoid brushing her skin against mine.

It's for the best. I don't know what I'd do if we touched.

I still love her, and she looks like that.

Our glasses meet, the clink barely audible over the noise of the dining room, and Sloan breaks away quicker than anyone else, snatching her drink back to her chest like she's risking contamination by it being so close to mine.

Tia cringes, nose wrinkling. Jay looks anywhere but at us, and Talon carries on like nothing's wrong.

"You know," Talon starts, leaning forward, waving his glass around. "I only have one regret. No cup."

Jay's eyes finally snap back to the table. "That's on you, Talon. You're the one who got the great idea to go play in Sweden after college. You had interest. And now I have two cup rings, Bohdan has one, and you have none."

"Where do you keep your cup ring?" Talon angles his scotch glass towards my hand, like I'd be wearing it right now, splayed against the table—the only place it's safe from acting on my shitty impulse control and trying to play with the hem of Sloan's dress under the table.

"Lost it." I shrug a shoulder and try to pretend I don't care.

I couldn't find it after I left Seattle, and it felt like a fitting punishment, so I tried my best to forget that I lost the only relic of my prematurely ended career that mattered.

Jay pulls his head back. "How'd you lose your fucking cup ring? I don't even let anyone touch mine. They're in my trophy room."

"Jay's got a shrine to himself." Talon grins. "That tracks."

I'm about to make up an excuse—something that doesn't have to do with me leaving the love of my life behind with my failed dreams in a post-concussion-induced mental breakdown and not really being able to keep track of my own mind, let alone my personal belongings—when yellow silk flashes in my periphery.

Angling my head, I watch Sloan shift in her seat, tugging at the hem of her dress before rolling her shoulders back and sitting up straighter than necessary.

I almost laugh, but I tip my chin towards her. "You have it."

Sloan pulls her head back, giving it a shake and rolling her eyes before reaching for her wine. "No, I don't."

"Yes, you do, you little shit." I shift in my seat to face her, and I press my fist to my mouth before a smile splits across my face. I feel a bit torn, sort of like throttling her for being so stubborn and petulant; but the girl I've loved since I was twenty sits beside me, acting just like she used to before she hated me, looking like something that walked right out of the recesses of my imagination.

The yellow silk dress wrapped around her, just enough skin on display to drive me insane: the lines of her shoulders, the jut of her collarbone, legs stretching out underneath the table. The tiny constellation of freckles under her eye on her left cheek more vibrant from the sun.

One shoulder rises, the thin strap of her dress brushing against her skin. "A baseless assumption."

"No. Not baseless." I raise my eyebrows, point at her. "You're shifting in your seat. You've blinked a few too many times."

"You don't know anything about my body language." Sloan scoffs, taking a sip of wine, but I catch the way her lips pause against the glass, the way her cheeks start to heat.

"Oh really?" I do grin now, leaning forward and closer to her than I probably should, but it's always been like this. She's the sun, and I'll be in her orbit forever. I lower my voice, and I don't mean for it to be, but it's rough. "I think I do. I know everything about you, Sloan. I know what you look like when you're mad. When you're sad. When you're frustrated. When you're happy. When you're lying. When you're coming—"

"That's indecent." Sloan inhales, nostrils flaring, and her eyes go wide.

"This feels like a private conversation." Jay gestures between us, mouth tugging to the side behind his wineglass.

"I'm starting to regret this." Talon nods, but his eyes move back and forth between us like he doesn't want to miss a single second.

Tia leans across the table, snatching the open bottle of wine and pouring a too-full glass. "It doesn't exactly feel like normal dinnertime conversation. Should we talk about the time Jay and I had sex?"

Talon drops his glass, scotch splashing on the formerly pristine white tablecloth. "You had sex with my sister?"

"Jesus." Jay scrubs his face, groaning into his hands. "No, Talon. She's joking."

"You don't remember?" Tia slaps a manicured hand to her chest, smile visible over the curved crystal edge of her wineglass, eyes glinting. "I'm hurt, Jay."

I think Talon shouts something about Jay having not only the audacity to have sex with his sister, but the audacity to not remember it. Jay might lean back in his chair, tugging on the ends of his hair while Tia bats her eyelashes at both of them like she didn't just cause a shitstorm.

But I know why she did it.

She did it for her best friend.

For Sloan, who sits, back ramrod straight, blinking too much, eyes too blue, and her grip on the stem of her wineglass too tight, breathing in and out.

"Sloan." I can't help myself and I reach forward, tugging on the ends of her hair. "Why do you have my ring?"

I'm hoping for an answer I'm not going to get and one that I don't deserve—that it means something more than it does.

That it means she doesn't hate me.

I'll learn to live without her, because it's what's best—but I don't think I can live knowing she hates me as much as it seems like she does.

She jerks away from my hand, and I raise it in surrender.

"In your"—she inhales again, teeth coming down on the inside of her cheek, and I know what she's about to say hurts her—"haste to leave me, you left quite a bit behind."

I wasn't in a hurry to leave her. I dragged my feet for months even though I knew she deserved better and always had.

She takes a small sip of wine, straightens her shoulders, and starts ticking things off on her fingers. "Clothes. Shoes. Books. Your cup ring, sitting on the nightstand on what was once your side of the bed."

Her words trail off with a tiny crack of her voice, and she wipes a knuckle along her lash line before the tears start to fall.

I know what else I left behind. The word she won't say.

Me.

It hangs heavy in the air, unsaid, and that fake fucking pain lances across my temple.

I press my fist into my thigh, kneading against the muscle so I don't reach forward and try to smooth out the frown wrinkling her brow, kiss away the tears sitting on those freckles.

Sloan waves a hand, like we're speaking about an errant nuisance in our past, not the destruction of our relationship by my hands, before she keeps talking. "And seeing as I had no means to contact you—"

"No means to contact me?" I cut in, incredulous. "My number didn't change."

I kept it the same—because I'm unhealed and selfish and a pathetic part of me hoped she'd call.

She tips her chin up. "I deleted your number. And then I deleted it from my brain."

"That's not how numbers work with you."

She finally turns to look at me, slowly, entirely controlled, and she blinks those blue eyes, frozen now and all of her looking cold. "Well maybe something broke when you left, Bohdan."

It's not silent in the dining room, but it is at our table. Tia, Talon, and Jay staring at the broken pieces of a girl who deserved to be whole, and I can hear the phantom crack of my chest and spurt of blood across the white tablecloth.

I left because I didn't want to hurt her anymore—I couldn't do it for another second of another minute of another day.

I couldn't let her watch me drown, couldn't let her try to keep me above water while she sank, too.

I pinch my eyes closed and shake my head. "Tia has my number."

"We don't talk much." Sloan shrugs.

"We talk every day." Tia drums her fingers across her cheek.

Sloan exhales, lips tugging into a taut line. "Not helping."

It's silent again, but not for long because Talon can't keep his mouth shut.

He knocks a fist against the table, grinning, like the carnage I created doesn't sit across from him. "You ready for your big move, Sloany? Back to the old Great White North."

The idea that she's going to leave the place we made a life together makes me feel like tossing myself overboard. "You're moving?"

"Yes. Back home." Sloan whispers the last word, barely audible, and I think it's more for her than it is for anyone else. "Finally."

"What are you going to do with the ring?" Talon asks, nodding as he considers. "Seattle's only cup run. Never been close since Bohdan. Might be worth something."

"Pawn it for gas money." Jay leans back in his chair, and I know they're trying to deflect, to carry some of the weight for me.

But she looks at me and I can see her a bit like I did all those years ago—little gold, under those arena lights.

The way she looked after I got the stupid ring—back in the hotel with me, tangled up in sheets and the stars painting her skin under the moonlight.

I think she sees it, too, can hear it the way I can.

Our favourite three words whispered over and over again. I love you. I love you. I love you. The only count of three that mattered.

Tears pool along her lash line, one slips down her cheek, and I wish they'd drown me. It's what I'd deserve.

So I whisper something, just for her, and I hope she knows I'm talking about more than just the ring. "Keep it."

—ele—

Even though there are twelve bars on this ship, Sloan finds me right away.

You could write it off as coincidence, and if it were Talon, Jay, or Tia pulling out the chair across from me, I'd say you might be right.

But it's Sloan, still in that fucking yellow dress, who carefully climbs up, the breeze from the ocean lifting her hair, heels sitting neatly on the rung of the chair.

She doesn't say anything, but she tilts her head, studying me, and there's a tiny scrunch of her nose that looks something like confirmation, and I wonder if she's thinking what I'm thinking.

That she found me right away because she still knows me. She knows I don't like crowded rooms, and that being on this ship would already be suffocating—that I'd pick the one bar stretching out across the deck, and I'd pick the table furthest away, closest to the open air and the ocean.

That we'd never be able to carve the other out of our own bodies because we met when we were too young and fell too in love and even though we aren't together, I'll always be hers and she'll always be mine because when my twenty-year-old hands were busy sculpting her, her eighteen-year-old hands were busy sculpting me.

"You trying to kill me?" I jerk my chin towards her and the yellow silk dress wrapping around her, clavicle and collarbone dusted with something that shimmers, on display under the setting sun.

"Maybe," she says simply. "It's what you'd deserve."

I exhale a laugh, raise a brow, and take a sip of scotch. "You look beautiful, Sloan."

She says nothing, but her eyes find my hairline, her features soften, and she closes her eyes for a bit too long before she speaks. "Should you be drinking?"

My fingers tense on the glass. "I'm okay. My head feels okay. I've got my meds, everything I need back in the room. Besides, someone made sure I kept out of the sun today."

She doesn't bite.

I drop the glass to the table with a shake of my head. "Sloan . . . if you're not going to speak to me . . . if you're uncomfortable around me . . . I can't be here, this close to you, without being able to . . ."

My words fall into nothing because I'm not even sure what I'd say.

I gave up my right to anything with Sloan when I walked out.

I might have done it for her, but it doesn't make it any less true.

"Without being able to what?" She reaches across the table, and I let myself imagine, for one stupid second, that she's going to wrap one of those perfect hands around my forearm, but she grabs the glass of scotch instead.

She sits taller in her chair, swirls the scotch, and sends the ice cube knocking against the sides of the crystal.

"It's a special kind of hell, being this close to you and not even being able to talk to you."

"Not to beat a dead horse, but . . ." She quirks a brow with her shoulder lifted, taking a small sip.

I almost laugh, even though there's nothing funny. "I know. It's my fault." I press my fingers to my temple, out of habit more than anything, and I catch the way her eyes widen, almost imperceptibly, like maybe she's worried. "I'll get off at the next port, if you don't want me here, Sloan. Talon'll get over it."

I watch her set the glass down, careful, measured movements, before she slides her clutch off her arm, where it was resting in the crook of her elbow.

She unzips it, hand fishing around for a minute before she drops something on the table beside the glass.

My cup ring.

The giant turquoise *S* inlaid with diamonds, and the words spelled in gold.

"Why'd you bring that?" My words lift, buoyed with hope—and it's stupid, because it's not like she brought it to make some grand gesture with it. She didn't even know I was going to be here.

Sloan taps her finger against the edge of the ring.

Six times.

I press my eyes closed, feeling a bit like each tap was a cut.

"It didn't feel right . . ." she starts, shaking her head before she turns and stares out at the ocean, watching the last rays of the sun disappear beyond the horizon.

Sloan tips her chin up towards the sky before she turns back to me, lips tugging to the side in a sad, rueful line. "I wasn't going to leave it in a box, sitting in a storage unit until I got around to unpacking it. It felt sort of like it . . . wouldn't be safe there or something. I just wanted to make sure . . . it was the most important thing in the world to you."

"It wasn't the most important thing."

Her nostrils flare with a dry laugh, and she closes her eyes.

"Sloan—" I start, but she cuts me off with the flash of her palm.

"I'll make you a deal." She puts her finger into the centre of the ring, lifting it and twirling it around before dropping it back into her open clutch. "When I walk away from this table, we call a truce. For the rest of the cruise. We can speak, but we don't fight. You don't get to touch me, not even a helping hand on my back when I'm going up the stairs, and you certainly don't get to talk to me like you have a right to know what's going on in my brain anymore. No counting for me. No telling me to take up space. And certainly nothing like what you said at dinner."

Her cheeks pink, and I know she's talking about what I said—how I knew everything about her body. I scrub my jaw. I hate myself more than I ever have right now. "I didn't mean to make you uncomfortable."

"You didn't. What you said wasn't a lie. We were . . . good together."

A colossal understatement.

I don't think a man has ever been lit on fire the way I was with her in the entire history of our sorry civilization.

"You do know me, in all the ways you can know a person." She looks down, picking at the leather strap hanging around her wrist, and when she flicks her gaze back up, tears pool in her eyes. "And I know you, but I won't survive knowing you twice."

Confused, I jerk my chin. "So you want to pretend we don't know each other? That we're fucking strangers?"

"However you need to make sense of it. If you can follow the rules, you can have the ring back at the end of the week." Sloan shrugs, tapping her clutch, before she looks up at me, full lips parting and her words dropping into a whisper. "But I want something in exchange."

I'd scale the side of the ship and try to jump to the fucking moon if she asked. I swallow. "Whatever you want, Sloan."

But she asks for the one thing I can't, won't, don't want to give her.

The two things, actually.

"I want the Polaroid back." Her voice splinters, and she shrinks, in real life, in real time, right in front of me.

Small again, the way I made her.

"And I want to know why."

My eyes close, my scar throbs, and I feel like I'm going to be fucking sick.

But she mistakes my silence for something else—not the confrontation of the worst thing I've ever done that I'll never be able to justify.

"Unless . . . unless you don't have it?"

Her voice rises, and I can hear the sob caught there.

She thinks I threw it away.

I open my eyes, and there they are—escaped tears, streaming down her cheeks. Beautiful under the empty sky.

I shake my head. "Of course I still have it."

Sloan blinks away her tears, nodding once before she pushes to stand. "Great. It's decided then. I look forward to seeing you for the first time this week tomorrow morning at breakfast. The itinerary says we're getting off in Mallorca for a cooking class."

She gives me what she might think is a bright smile—but she's forgotten already, no matter how much she might want to pretend otherwise, I know her the exact way she knows me.

I can see her brain whirring to life, and I can almost hear it, whispering cruel things in her ear when she turns on her heel and leaves me with one last view of that stupid yellow dress.

Fishing my wallet out of my pocket, I raise a hand to the bartender and tip my chin towards my empty glass. I'd ask for the bottle if that wouldn't fuck up my brain even more than usual.

I lay the picture flat against the table, eyes roving over eighteen-year-old Sloan—trapped in time before she meets me and the ruination of her life immortalized with her, a decade in the making.

The only thing I have left of her and the only thing I really care about. The one thing I would never willingly offer up for anything.

But if she wants it back, I'll hand it over, because it's the only thing she asked for that I can give her.

Sloan

Then – College

The pounding on the door starts when the clock on the stove says 10:37 p.m.

I can see it from where I'm sitting, back against the cupboards, the green light mocking me as shadows from the kitchen window slink across the floor, closer and closer to me.

I sort of hope they'll eat me alive.

It makes sense. The game was at seven, and then they had a postgame press conference because it was the qualifier for Frozen Four—they won and Bohdan scored twice—and I didn't show up for either.

Not because I didn't want to.

I wanted to quite badly.

I press the heels of my palms into my eyes. I'm trying to work up the courage to stand, but I hear a key turn in the lock of the door, and then I hear his voice.

"Sloan?" He sounds panicked, and I don't get up from my spot on the floor, but I can imagine him—suit jacket undone, tie haphazard around his neck, wide hands gripping the doorframe as he leans into the apartment I share with Tia, one wave curling over his forehead, caramel hair almost ebony from the shower. "Are you in here?"

I take a shaky inhale, and I try to steady my voice. "In the kitchen."

It doesn't work. I'm crying again.

And they're these really loud, pathetic, guttural sobs that echo throughout the apartment.

Bohdan's frame fills the doorway, and then he's crouched down in front of me. He's a bit of a blur, but I think he cocks his head to the side, that his mouth pulls into a frown, that his fingers flex before they tip my chin up. "Baby, why are you on the floor?"

"It's comfy down here." I try to smile at him, but it feels all wrong. I squeeze my eyes shut, and another horrible sob sounds from my throat.

I hear him exhale, and he waits until I'm blinking away the tears before he asks, gently, like the way his fingers hold my chin, "What happened? I looked for you before the game, and again after."

I happened.

Me, and the brain I was born with.

I don't say that though. It's not that Bohdan isn't a safe space—he's the safest. But one day, he might wake up and realize he doesn't want to be my safe space. That he wants a nice, normal girlfriend who doesn't count and doesn't cry when her clothes feel weird on her skin and doesn't think about what a colossal loser she is on a regular basis.

He'll want someone just right.

Not me.

Not someone too much and not enough.

I jerk back, away from his hands, holding my own in the air before trying to wipe away the tears. "I'm sorry. It was an important game and I missed it. You must be so disappointed."

Bohdan interrupts me with a thumb brushing across my mouth. "I'm disappointed, Sloan, but not in you."

"That can't be true," I whisper with a shake of my head.

He gives me a resigned smile before shrugging out of his suit jacket and tugging off his tie. He tosses them haphazardly onto the kitchen floor and settles beside me against the cupboards. One leg stretched out—he winces when he does it—and the other raised, his hand drumming against his knee before he flips his palm up for me. "Were you here the whole time?"

"Not the whole time." I sniff, setting my hand gently in his.

His fingers close over mine, and he turns to me, waiting.

I throw my other hand in the air. "I didn't know what to wear and then there was part of one of those plastic tags stuck in the sleeve of my sweater, and I could feel it against my skin. Nothing fit right. Nothing looked right and I tried to call my mom and she said she didn't understand and to just pick something and then it was after seven and I'd missed the start of the game and—"

"That's okay," he says, like it's a simple thing and it's fine that I missed one of the most important games of his collegiate career.

"No, it's not! How is it okay?" I try to tug my hand away, but his fingers stay firm in mine. "I'm so proud of you and I wanted to be there shouting for you like everyone else, but I missed one of your most important games of the season because of my stupid brain."

"Your brain isn't stupid." Bohdan brings the back of my hand to his mouth, shrugging one shoulder. "And it wasn't that important of a game."

"Yes it was!"

"No," he says firmly, turning to face me. "It wasn't. It was a qualifier. It won't even be my first time in the Frozen Four."

"But it'll be your last," I murmur. "You're a senior, and next year you'll—"

"Be playing significantly more important hockey games on a regular basis." He leans forward, pressing his mouth to the tears on my cheeks.

I start to shake my head. "I let you down."

"You couldn't let me down if you tried, Sloan," he says against my skin. "Do you want to talk about it?"

My eyes flutter, and I think my breathing starts to even out for the first time all night. "I don't know what to say. It's nothing new. Just me and all the things wrong with me that I'm stuck with and one day you're going to wake up and realize you don't want to be shackled to."

"Impossible." His lips skate across the apple of my cheek, down the side of my jaw, until they find mine. "There's nothing wrong with you."

"Bohdan. My brain doesn't fucking work."

"No. It works *differently*." He pulls back and emphasizes the word, like it's somehow special and wonderful, lovely and effervescent, and not the thing that's made me feel alone in rooms full of people and haunted me when I was a child, peeking out of my backpack to whisper to me like some sort of monster that lived under the bed, always there to remind me of the ways I was wrong.

I start to roll my eyes, but he grips my chin again. He shakes his head, one wayward piece of hair curling over his ears, left side of his mouth lifting just so, sharp planes of his face and stubble peppering his jaw.

He's special and wonderful, lovely and effervescent.

I'm none of those things.

"Sloan. Zlatíčko. Listen to me," he states, like he's ready to make a declaration. "I'm not going to get sick of you, or the way your brain works."

"You probably should." I sniff. "You're what—the top-ranked hockey player in the world? And you look like that?" He grins when I gesture wildly at him, his smile splitting me open, shining a light and chasing away the shadows in this dark kitchen, and maybe, some of the ones that live in me. "You should be with someone who has cute, curated outfits and knows exactly what she's going to wear to all your games and coordinates with the other partners. A blonde, maybe."

Bohdan lifts a brow. "I don't like blondes."

I do roll my eyes this time. But my words don't have the same bravado. They're small and sad. "Someone who can show up for you, the way you show up for them. You're always doing things like this—rushing into the kitchen of my apartment or helping me count and learning new languages. What do you get out of it?"

"You," he says simply. "You, and all the things about you that you don't see. How curious you are. How thoughtful. How intentional in your actions you are. How funny you are. The way you snort sometimes when you laugh too much. The way you get excited when you flip through pictures of artefacts, and how that excitement brightens everything it touches. How your brain might be mean to you, but it actually makes you more understanding and lets you offer kindness to people who might not otherwise deserve it."

"Those sound made up," I whisper.

Bohdan's mouth tugs to the side in a rueful line. "I imagine they would to you. But they're real to me."

"What if it's always like this?" I ask quietly, afraid of the answer. "You giving more than you get?"

"It won't be. I can hold you up now, you can hold me up later." He presses his thumb to each of my freckles. "We're a team."

"A team?" I wrinkle my nose. "What position do I play?"

"Left wing, like Talon, but I'll probably make you ride the bench during the important games. I've seen you try to skate and shoot a puck at the same time." He gives me a wry grin.

I shove at his shoulder, and he grabs my wrist, brushing his mouth across the sensitive skin before he tucks me into the crook of his neck, and drops his head back against the cupboard.

"How'd you get so mature for your age?" I place a hand across his chest, moving it around until I can feel his heartbeat against my palm.

"Slavic stoicism," he deadpans, pressing his lips to the crown of my head. "Do you want to leave the kitchen? We can go to your room, or I'll take you back to my place. But I think Talon and Jay were planning on throwing a party."

"No." I sniff a laugh. "I live down here now."

"I guess I'll have to move in, too." I feel him grin into my hair. "Good thing because I don't think I'll be able to move my fucking legs."

"Should we start decorating then? You've got a good eye." I pull back, smiling softly up at him.

He nods, eyes sweeping across the kitchen like he's being thoughtful about the whole thing. He points to the fridge. "That's too empty. I've got the perfect thing we can hang there." Reaching into the back pocket of his suit pants, he pulls out his wallet, flicks through the bills and plastic cards, until he pulls out something from behind his ID, and holds it out to me between two fingers.

I take it, hesitant, running my fingers over the softened edges, and the black ink with my name and number scrawled on the back that's starting to smudge. The picture of eighteen-year-old me, frozen in time with tears in her eyes and absolutely no idea how lucky she really was that day. I take a tiny inhale, glancing back up and blinking at him, another tear slipping down my cheek. "You kept the Polaroid?"

"Yeah, Zlatíčko. I did. Start of the rest of my life, the night I got that."

Bohdan might be the special, wonderful, lovely, effervescent one.

But he's never, not for a single second, made me feel alone.

Sloan

Colourful buildings peek out from behind towering trees along the coastline, visible and brighter in the morning sun, where it sits heavy in the blue sky, wisps of cloud tumbling along.

I keep my eye on the horizon, the ocean sparkling, water churning into whitecaps as the ship moves closer to the port.

The door to the suite slides open, and Tia steps out, frayed denim shorts brushing against her thighs, one arm angled in the air, holding up her cellphone. Her eyes narrow and she moans in frustration before practically throwing herself down in the lounge chair beside me.

She chucks her phone to the end of the chair, dropping her head back dramatically before she rolls to face me, smiling. "You know, it was nice of my brother to get us this shared, family suite—"

"Was it?" I interrupt wryly.

Tia purses her lips. "Yes, it was. The private balcony? Hello!" She waves a hand towards the empty balcony, dotted with lounge chairs like the ones were sitting on, the unused Jacuzzi in the corner, the dining table, and the vast stretch of ocean. "But the Wi-Fi still sucks. I was trying to connect to Slack."

"What could you possibly need to check in on at work?"

"The accounts won't account themselves, you know." She flashes me a bright smile before she wrinkles her nose and leans forward, plucking at the front cover of my book. "And what are you doing? This looks like work to me. Something for the new job? Wait, I'm sorry—*A cultural analysis of cruise ships?* Feeling inspired by my brother? Don't tell me you're going to start exploring the phenomenon that is a cruise ship in your studies? Do we need an intervention? I've got Lu on speed dial."

She holds up her phone, eyes big and wide like she's about to press call.

"Why do you have my ex-therapist on speed dial?" I roll my eyes and jerk the book away from her. "I just thought it was interesting."

"Ex-therapist. Still not sure that's the best idea given the recent developments . . ." When I don't respond, Tia clicks her tongue, dropping her elbows to her knees and her chin to her palm. "When we . . . 'go ashore'"—she rolls her eyes, air quotes around her brother's itinerary descriptors—"I thought we could skip the cooking class? Go find a rooftop somewhere out in the open air, ask for bottomless alcohol, and not get stuck inside with the fumes of whatever Talon fails to cook properly and . . . *him.*"

"No." I sit up straighter, wanting so desperately to be relieved of all the weight of Bohdan I carry around on my shoulders, but it's still there, and I think it will be until I understand. "It's fine. We made a deal."

"A deal," Tia repeats, skeptical.

"Yes, a deal. We're going to be civil, and we're going to achieve such civility by pretending like we don't know each other."

She blinks, once, and then two more times before she bursts out laughing. "You're going to act like you don't know him? I'm sorry, you expect him to act like he doesn't know you?" Tia pulls back, incredulous, before she shakes her head at me. "The man who couldn't keep his hands off you for the better part of a decade? Who quite literally saw you once through shitty, scratched-up glass when he was on the ice and banged on it until you gave him your number like we were in a Hallmark film? Who once ran across campus and almost knocked down our door until you let him in? Who didn't go home after games and road trips, but went straight to you? Who learned to count to six in five languages to distract you?" She almost looks sympathetic before she scrunches her nose, bringing her thumb and forefinger together to form an OK. "Sure. Yeah. Bohdan can pretend he doesn't know you."

"I didn't mean it literally, but he has incentive." I shrug, sticking my hands under my legs. "I have his cup ring, and I said he could have it back."

Tia cocks her head, a smile splitting her cheeks. She looks radiant all the time, but particularly when she's vindictive. She flicks a manicured finger at me. "You are a little shit. So what, he follows the rules and you give him the ring back?" Tia widens her eyes. "What do you get in return? A peaceful week cruising the Mediterranean with my brother? Sorry, I don't think such a thing exists."

"No. I get . . . to move on." I don't look at her when I say it, because I know she won't understand.

No one does.

Why he's still all over me, why the weight of being loved by him sits so heavy on my shoulders it buckles my knees and some days I don't think I'll be able to walk, let alone get out of bed.

She hasn't lived in my brain, or one really like it at all, and she'll never understand what it means to have your worst fears come true—the things you've obsessed over, tried to cure and tried to absolve yourself of since you were little and painting patterns in watercolour on an easel.

Not enough, not enough, not enough.

My eyes pinch closed and I feel the tears pressing at the back of them, warm and ready to slice me open. A cut for each failure I've ever had.

But my best friend speaks, soft and lovely, and even though she'll never understand, I know she's trying.

"You think entering into some sort of deal with rules that, I'm sorry, neither of you are ever going to be able to achieve, is going to help you finally move on? You've got this new job, and this exciting new move ahead of you ... Sloan, it's been a year and a half. This isn't going to change how you're feeling."

I blink, pressing my hand to my chest, counting the beats of my heart and trying not to remember what it was like to lie in the dark in a different life, with Bohdan's hand spread over my chest, fingertips tapping out the counts when I couldn't.

"No." I shake my head, tears making the ocean seem even brighter. "But I'll finally know why."

"Sloan ... what difference does it make?" Tia angles her head, full lips curving down. She drops her elbows to her knees, her chin to her palm. She looks so beautiful out here, sparkling under the sun, but her words don't feel beautiful. They just remind me that there was one person who understood me, my brain, and he still left. "People don't always have good reasons for the things they do. He'd lost his career. He could barely walk into a room with the lights on. His dreams ... he was on three different antidepressants. Sloan ... you do research about human behaviour and culture for a living. Quite literally, you explore social and cultural representations of mental health and illness . . . use your head."

He knew. He knew I loved him. That I would have died for him, happily. I gave up so much for him. Hopes, dreams. So he could chase his.

None of me was enough, and I never will be.

I dig my hands into the side of the lounge chair, fingers gripping the curved edge. She doesn't understand.

It's not a want. It's not a curiosity. It's a deep, visceral need that lives in me and swims through my bloodstream, permeating through every inch of my body because living this last year and a half without knowing why, and only being left to wonder with my brain for horrible, cruel company, revisiting every single thing I've ever done and ruminating on all the ways they might not have been enough—I told Bohdan I wouldn't survive knowing him again.

But the truth is, I'm not sure I can survive another minute of knowing this version of me.

I can't tell her that, I can't tell anyone that. The only person I could tell all of the horrible, depraved things that my brain tells me left. So I settle on telling her a different kind of truth, a more palatable one. "Well, your brain doesn't work like mine, Tia."

"I know. I know." Her words are soft. She holds her palms up in surrender before slowly prying mine off the chair and interlacing our fingers. "I just don't want you to get hurt."

"A little late for that, no?" I ask dryly.

Tia gives me a watery smile, blinking away her own tears, shining under the early-morning sun. "She's still got jokes."

I don't have time to answer, because the door to the suite gets thrown open by Talon, who steps out, arms wide. The sleeves of his blue striped linen button-up bunch against the muscles of his arms, and the matching shorts ride up his thighs. He slides his Ray-Bans down over his eyes. "Who's ready to cook?"

Tia raises her hand with a half-hearted "Me," and I watch Jay step out after him, cuffed denim shorts that only he could pull off straining against his quads, oversized white T-shirt hanging down with the gold of the chain around his neck glinting under the morning light.

"Why are we going to a cooking class? You're thirty years old, Talon." Jay slides his sunglasses up his head, but wisps of ebony hair still escape when he shakes it at Talon, who looks like he's testing the length of his wingspan as he stretches his arms and shoulders against the glass railing surrounding the balcony.

Talon glances over his shoulder, leaning to his left and inching his hand further across the glass. "Team had a nutritionist. We had one in college. I've barely cooked for myself my entire life. I can't lose my physique now."

Tia rolls her eyes, mouthing the words *my physique* before flopping back on the lounge chair, stretching out her legs, and lifting her tank top to tan her stomach.

"You're thirty." Jay holds his arms open. "Why'd you even retire? You probably had—" He eyes Talon, like he's assessing the athletic prowess still living in his legs as he lunges in front of the glass. "Four or five years left, especially in a European league."

"Especially in a European league," Talon parrots, his middle finger flicking up when he inches his feet back together. He raises each knee to his chest in turn before seemingly deciding he's done. He shrugs, considering. "I dunno. I was bored of it, I guess. Time for the next great adventure and all that."

It's not a bad thing to say. Talon's always known who he is, even when he didn't know what he was doing.

But it's ill-timed, because he says it right as Bohdan steps out onto the deck. Another white linen shirt lifting, pushing against his chest and abdomen in the breeze, doing nothing to conceal the ridges of muscle stretching across his stomach. Tan linen shorts practically moulded to the muscles of his thighs, golden-brown hair tousled just so, eyes hidden behind impossibly dark black sunglasses that look like they're prescription, and the *S* scrawled across the cords of his forearm muscle stark against his skin.

Talon pales, one shoulder lifting and a cringe settling on his face. "Sorry, Novo."

Bohdan shrugs, but a muscle ticks in his cheek, dusted with stubble, cutting down his jawline and making him look like one of those statues you'd probably find in any museum just beyond the port.

"Bohds? You okay?" Tia sits up, frowning and tugging on a loose curl before she points at his sunglasses. "Those are your prescription ones."

I can't see his eyes, the frames are practically opaque to block out as much of the sun as possible, but there's a small, hopeful part of me that imagines his eyes flick to me before he answers.

It's squashed, trampled on, and tilled into the earth by my brain reciting the only fact it knows when he speaks, the shrug of one shoulder, like it's all nothing. "Yeah. Just didn't sleep, that's all."

Not enough, not enough, not enough.

Bright red tomatoes spill out from vines tumbling along the garden path, winding along crumbled stones that line the hillside giving way to the ocean. I'm careful not to step on any as I trail behind Talon, Tia, and Jay, the skin splitting open on some, tiny seeds visible just underneath.

Dishes and glassware rattle from the open kitchen in the restaurant behind me. The hosts sent us out here to collect our own ingredients from the garden, and Talon, the self-proclaimed vegetable expert, ran ahead.

Tia followed, because she's nothing if not competitive, and probably didn't want to be bested by a pepper picked by her brother. Jay seemed more interested in whatever he was doing on his phone, following them without much care to notice the garden path.

Bohdan seemed more inclined to spend his afternoon studying the rocks jutting out of the restaurant wall, one thumb trailing over the rough edges with a reverence I recognized all too well.

But I know his footsteps without having to look.

He's always had this way of shortening his strides to match mine that never made me feel like he was slowing down so I could keep up, but like that's just how it was supposed to be my whole life: him and me, side by side forever.

I do look, because I can't help it.

He's beautiful, sunlight sketching across the sharp planes of his face, full lips set in this serious line that makes you want to know what he's thinking.

It turns out I don't have to ask because he takes one handout of his pocket, and he extends it, the ropes of muscle stretching down his forearms tensing when he does.

"Hi," Bohdan says, voice low and one side of his mouth kicking up like the ghost of a grin sits ready and waiting. "I'm Bohdan."

I stop, the edge of my sandal catching on a stray rock lining the dirt path of the garden. "What are you doing?"

"Introducing myself."

"Why?" I ask, wrapping my arms around myself more out of habit than anything.

"You seem like someone I'd want to get to know." He does smile now, a slow, lazy thing that stretches across his face, stealing all the sharpness painted there by time and by the shining sun, and he almost looks like the boy I used to know.

I give him a flat look and pretend my heart, still half asleep, doesn't stir in my chest.

One brow lifts with the shrug of a shoulder. "You said to act like we didn't know each other."

I blink, before a scoff sounds from the back of my throat, and I stab my finger towards his still outstretched hand. "This is not what I meant. In fact, I actually think this is in violation of one of the other rules: no touching."

"You count a handshake as touching? It's our palms, Sloan."

"With you?" I narrow my eyes, jabbing my finger at the offending appendage again. "Yes. Trust me, any contact counts."

The smile shifts into a grin, and Bohdan shifts with it. Back to the person he was before that scar I can barely bring myself to look at stole from him. This too-serious, stoic boy who became this driven, endlessly patient, steadfast, obstinate man with this secret playful side, who wanted nothing more than to be the best at the only things that mattered to him: hockey, and me.

And when that scar became a thief, it took his first love, and it made him forget about his second.

I forget that, though, that he forgot how to love me, because he angles his head down, one wave of hair flops forward onto his forehead, and those lips form rough words that skitter down my spine and make me shiver under the sunlight.

"How do you know? We don't know each other." He still has his sunglasses on, but I can feel his eyes all over me. "If you want to test out what contact with me feels like, I can think of a few more interesting things we could do other than shake hands."

"Indecent." I tip my chin up, but my stomach twists and I feel the blush on my cheeks.

The Bohdan I knew loved when I blushed. He said it made the three freckles—the only constellation he cared about—stand out even more.

I press my palms to my cheeks, not because I'm flushing, but because I'm not sure he deserves to see those freckles anymore.

"You used to like that," he says, words heavy with far too much meaning than appropriate for the public garden at a family-owned restaurant.

"How do you know?" I shriek, waving a hand between us. "We don't know each other!"

Bohdan leans forward, full mouth curving into a different kind of smile—one that tells me he wants to devour me, the way he used to.

But he doesn't. Whatever he's about to say—or do—gets interrupted by a shout from Talon.

"Look at this tomato!"

I glance sideways towards Talon, standing probably right where he shouldn't—in the middle of the vines tangled across the ground, holding what's objectively a giant tomato in his palm.

Tia stands to the side with Jay—who looks like he's a second from dropping to his knees and begging whatever God might be listening to please, please save him from this—and she widens her eyes at me, tapping her fingers against her bicep. "Hurry up. It's time to make the dough for pasta."

Talon holds his tomato up in the air.

Bohdan doesn't look away from me. "Cool."

I give a tiny shake of my head, and I'm about to step around him, to take the path back to the restaurant, when he tips his chin towards his hand, still there, still waiting for me. "I'll wait all day, Sloan."

"Fine." I roll my eyes, meeting his hand with mine.

He's right, by technicality. It's just our palms touching. Not even particularly sensitive skin.

But it is.

Because he's him and I'm me, and my heart might have gone to sleep when he left, but it's wide-awake when he touches me.

His hand in mine—not the way he used to hold me, but holding me for the first time in too long, out here in this garden. And if I didn't know any better, I'd think the vines were conspiring with the earth, twisting around our feet, ready to tie us back together because even after all this time, I think we're still two halves of one whole.

Bohdan breaks away first, and it's a kindness really.

I blink away the tears that snuck up on me like he did all those years ago, and he presses a fist to his mouth, a bit like he's in pain, before he jerks his head towards the restaurant.

"Come on. I'll make your dough for you."

"Why?" I ask, my voice so much smaller and sadder than it should be. We're just talking about pasta, after all.

But we're not, not really.

Because Bohdan looks at me, this sad smile tugging at his lips, and he shrugs before he says, "You seem like the type of person who wouldn't like the feeling of the flour all over their hands."

The only thing I've ever really liked all over me was him.

I sniff. "You can guess a person's sensory issues just by looking at them? What a talent."

"Only ever really worked with one girl. I knew enough about her to fix just about anything. But it went where all my other talents ended up going: to waste." He says it with this awful sort of finality, and he turns, walking back towards the restaurant, leaving me surrounded by split tomatoes and the ghost of someone I used to love.

Bohdan

Then – Seattle

I'd always thought the only thing I wanted in the world was to play.

It was the only dream I had.

But then I met her and somehow we made this life together, and it's beyond anything I think I could have ever imagined.

My bag hits the floor beside me, and I drop a shoulder against the frame of our open bedroom door.

It was worth taking the early flight back to be here, to watch Sloan, one hand tucked under my pillow where she sleeps on my side of the bed, gilded by the fading moonlight still reflecting off Puget Sound through our windows, textbooks and markers and her computer spread out over the duvet on her side.

The TV's still on—ESPN—and I catch a replay of the game earlier.

I played well. I always do.

I've already seen the clip, and they're talking about how I'm the best. Making bets on all the records I'm going to set and titles I'm going to take.

I work hard. But I don't work hard to be good. Hockey comes naturally to me, and I know that's lucky—talent that a good chunk of people all over the world would die for.

But the only thing I'd die for is her. Life with Sloan is the only thing I really care about being good at.

It's hard to explain to someone—how it changes you, probably deep down in your bones, to fall in love young like we did and to get to stay in love because we were lucky to grow together, and we had the same dream at the end of the day: each other.

She's still asleep, taking faint little inhales, her cheeks pillowy and soft when I sit beside her on the bed.

"Zlatíčko." I tuck her hair behind her ear, brushing a knuckle over her cheek. "Sloan, I'm going to shower, okay?"

Her eyelashes flutter before she blinks, sleepy, and opens my favourite eyes on the planet.

I press a kiss to her temple, and I think she's still half asleep, but her fingers wrap around my wrist. "Bohdan. You're supposed to be in Tampa until tomorrow."

Smiling against her skin, I move my mouth to her ear. "Caught an earlier flight."

"Won't you be in trouble?" she whispers, and I can feel the shiver run across her shoulders.

"Maybe." Yes.

But it'll be worth it.

Her arms wrap around me, hands playing in the hair at the nape of my neck, and I pull her up, gently, so we're sitting together on the edge of the bed.

She buries her head in my neck, murmuring against my skin. "Six-game road trips are too long. What if you came back and I was an entirely different person? What then?"

"Are you?" I ask, grinning and running my hands along her shoulder blades before moving to the curve of her waist.

"No. But I could have taken up a new hobby."

Her fingers tug gently on my hair, and a groan catches in my throat. "Did you?"

"Yes." I can hear the petulance in her voice. "Rabbit husbandry."

"Then I guess I'm making room for some rabbits."

Sloan pulls back, smiling softly with a sleepy shake of her head. "Why'd you come back early? I'm okay without you, you know. I miss you, but I promise I don't sit here every night watching you on TV, pining for you."

I do worry about her when I'm gone. That something might hurt her, and I won't be there. That texts with three facts I love about her won't be enough from a distance. That it'll get too much and too big, and she'll wish she never followed me to Seattle, that she went to school in Toronto like she wanted.

But I know her better than I think I know myself, and I think even from across the entire universe, I'd be able to spot the subtle shifts in her that tell me when she's lying, and she's not. "Couldn't go another day without seeing you in your—" I pull the sheet down to see what she's wearing before flicking my eyes up. "Raccoon shirt. Sexy."

Her lips purse and her chin tips up. "Tia got me this."

"Thank her for me, will you?" I give her a dry grin. "Just couldn't get the idea of you in this shirt, on my side of the bed out of my head. Had to book the first flight out or I wouldn't have made it. I dream about you and this raccoon shirt on a constant fucking loop. Thought about getting you some fresh rose petals to, you know, sprinkle them all over the bed before I made love to you in this shirt—"

"Made love to me?" she cuts in, nose wrinkling.

I nod. "Sex, but make it romantic."

"Make love to me, Bohdan," she laughs, her voice taking on this stupid, exaggerated breathy quality, and she flops back against the pillow, her hair fanning out everywhere before she rolls her head dramatically from side to side.

"Shut up." I smile, shaking my head, grabbing her chin to stop her before she gets carried away and knocks us both off the bed.

But all it does is show me how her eyes look under an early-morning sky. How her cheeks are soft, still sleepy, her mouth parted just so, and the swell of her chest just under the navy sheet covering her.

I trace my thumb over her lips, pausing in the full pout of the bottom one. She blinks up at me before she takes my hand, interlaces our fingers, and pulls me down towards her, mouth hovering just below mine when she says, "Well, you came all this way."

It's one of my favourite times to be with her—early morning, hazy sky, ocean sparkling as the sun rises, her hands all over me when she strips me out of my suit, nails digging into my shoulders when I spend time between her legs.

Mine all over her, angling her hips the way I know she likes when I'm inside her.

Just us while the stars go to sleep.

The only person who matters.

"I can't imagine not knowing you." I move my mouth against her collarbone, teeth scraping her skin, marking her even though I don't have to.

She's mine and she always will be.

Her fingers paint down my back, probably the most beautiful portrait in the world because it was done by her hands, and she arches into me, hips meeting mine, her words just a whisper in the dark. "And you'll never have to."

Bohdan

"Thank you all for joining me." Talon waves his arm with an unnecessary flourish, gesturing to the balcony of our suite where we're all spread out, a beer bottled angling from his fingertips a bit too precariously.

"We had no choice." Tia smiles tightly at the same time Jay nods, one hand tugging on the chain around his neck.

"I was already here when you came out."

Talon waves his hands again, but I'm looking past him to Sloan, where she sits on one of the lounge chairs. Her legs folded under her, arms wrapped around her chest, and her hooded sweater falling down over her knees. With her hair tied back into a ponytail, it gives me a clearer view of her mouth, lips just parted, the freckles on her cheek under her left eye that seemingly glow under the moon.

Fuck the endless, stretching ocean.

She's the most beautiful thing out here.

I think she might feel my eyes on her, because hers flick to mine, and she swallows, blinking, before she looks away again.

She hardly spoke to me all afternoon, other than a quiet thank-you and soft smile when I made her pasta dough for her.

Tia folded her ravioli. I would have offered the second I saw her try—hands extended, prodding the dough, covered in white flour before she stretched out her fingers with a rough shake of her head.

But her best friend beat me to it.

I should probably be grateful for that—but the only thing it did was make me hate my useless fucking brain more.

It should have been me—standing beside her, close enough to bend down, brush my mouth across her temple, down to her ear where I could whisper to her about things that might make her smile. Like why Talon picked an Italian cooking class on a Spanish island, the rock formations we stood on, and the historical and cultural uses of flour.

She'd know more about those last ones than me, but I'd make something up, spin an entire story if it would make her smile.

But that's for one of the Bohdans living out there in another universe. In this one, I was just the guy she hardly looked at all day.

"Why are we here, Talon?" Tia gestures to the stretching balcony. "I'm tired."

"Seeing as no one bothered to read it, I'd like to discuss the itinerary." Talon tips his bottle of beer towards his sister before he jerks his chin to the table closest to Sloan. "I had the suite concierge print off some physical copies. Sloany, if you'd be so kind as to distribute them."

One brow arches, and she almost looks amused. But she grabs the stack of paper, and when she does, her sweater falls down her shoulder, and I can see it there under the thin strap of her tank top.

The *B* from all those years ago when we were young and dumb and thought we were invincible.

It disappears again when the sweater shifts as she takes one sheet from the top and sets it beside her on the chair.

She stands, and I can't help it, but I watch her. Every little movement. Her fingers tugging the hem of her sweater down, smoothing it out before she brushes her palm down her thigh. The way those same hands clutch either side of the stack of papers.

Ordinary movements I've missed out on over the last year and a half, and maybe longer because my brain was broken. Things I took for granted because I thought they were mine to catalogue forever.

She looks up at me through her lashes when she hands me my paper, careful our fingers don't accidentally brush.

It doesn't matter that our skin didn't meet.

Sloan Joseph looked at me, my heart still stopped in my chest, and I might as well be dead.

The look lingers.

But this time, she breaks away first.

It feels a bit like a string pulled too taut in my heart and snapped. I roll my shoulders back, rub my hand across my chest and the phantom ache that lives there now because she doesn't.

Jay's eyes track the page before he looks up at Talon. "This feels like school."

"Well, you weren't very good at that, were you?" Talon leans back against the glass railing.

"Hey!" Jay throws his hands in the air, gold rings glinting under the starlight.

Talon shrugs, angling the bottle towards me and Sloan. "Not everyone can be Rock Boy and Mrs. Worldwide."

It's one of those things that happens when you've known someone the way we knew each other. When you've known so many different versions of each other, grown together and intertwined a bit like the roots of two trees that were planted too close together.

There's this certain language you share. It can be words, it can be laughter, it can be just a look.

In this case, it's just a look.

Sloan's eyes rise, meeting mine, lighter and happier than they've looked the entire time, her nose wrinkles, and her teeth come down on her bottom lip.

I grin, the muscles in my cheeks aching because I don't think I've smiled like this since long before I left her.

But it's not *just* a look. Her eyes on mine opens this door we both sealed shut, and we watch the years go by through the glass surrounding that rink we first skated on. Our lips touch for the first time under a singular, bright light and fallen snow. The first time she let me inside her body, but more importantly, the first time she let me inside her mind. One of the scariest places on planet Earth for her, but one of the most beautiful for me.

Nights with our friends and Talon giving us a rotating list of nicknames that got stupider and stupider, winning all these championships and trophies and setting all these records, but nothing really mattered as long as we got to keep each other.

Learning with her as she worked so hard against an unkind brain, her smile growing wider and wider as the years went on.

But then we get to the painful parts.

Her eyes shutter closed, and she gives a little shake of her head like she's trying to get rid of a thought. But she takes a measured exhale, looks away, and closes the door.

"I don't study every culture in the world, Talon," Sloan offers dryly.

He waves a hand, like it's all the same to him, and really, it probably is, before he taps his finger against his palm. "We've got a wine tasting tomorrow in Provence, followed by dinner and free time."

"How gracious of you to extend us free time." Tia smiles tightly.

Talon points at her. "You're welcome, sis." He clears his throat, flourishing the paper unnecessarily, and keeps talking. "Day four: Walking tour in Florence, followed by disco night." He pauses, another dramatic point in Sloan's direction. "These next two are for you, Sloany. Day five: Rome, the Colosseum. We're going to learn about gladiators and then we're hitting the casino. Day six: At sea, and I'm personally planning on taking in some of the water aerobics offerings. Day seven: We're going to Pompeii."

I chance another look at her. She lights up. Brighter than the moon.

"Pompeii will be followed by a five-course dinner, during which I expect you will all be shedding more than one tear that this is almost over. Day eight—heading back to the port in Barcelona."

"And we can all go home?" Jay tosses his schedule onto the lounge chair beside him.

Talon frowns, a look of feigned hurt that might actually be real carving across his features. "It's almost like you don't want to be here."

I clear my throat, giving Jay a flat look, before forcing a smile towards Talon. "Of course we want to be here."

He points at me, but he's grinning again. "Now I know you're fucking lying."

"Can I go to bed?" Sloan asks, standing up suddenly.

It's nothing anyone else would notice—but I see her give another tiny shake of her head, and she looks at Talon with hard blinks.

Talon sketches a bow, smiling when he stands up straight again. "You're dismissed, Sloany."

I give her a tight smile, and I don't bother saying good night. It's not the kind she'd be interested in hearing from me anyway, but it might be the kind she needs—I can see her brain whirring from here.

We had a good-night ritual that worked for her. It worked for me, too. But not for the same reasons. I didn't need anything in my mind to go quiet. I just needed her. And I can't imagine she'd be interested in me counting the three things I loved about her most that day before kissing her three times across her freckles, three times on her mouth, and letting her take whatever she needed from me.

Tia reaches up, hand wrapping around Sloan's wrist when she goes to walk past. "Good night, I love you."

Sloan blinks down at her, offering her nothing but a strained smile, and not even a real word, just a general noise of agreement. "Mm."

I wait until long after the door to the balcony shuts, until I can see her retreating figure round the hallway of the suite, before turning to Tia. "She didn't say I love you back."

Tia looks away from the door, where she might have been watching her best friend, too. She angles her head, slicked back curls starting to escape from her ponytail. "Observant, Novotnak."

"Since when?"

"You know when," Tia answers simply. She pats Jay on the shoulder before she stands, offering her brother nothing more than a wave.

She stops beside me, her words just a whisper in the dark. "How lonely that must be. For her—thinking only bad things happen when she loves someone because her brain was wired to be cruel, and for you, living without her. I opened the dictionary the other day. Flipped to the page with the word *masochist*, and wouldn't you know? It was just your picture."

Tia's mouth lifts at the corner, all wry. She pats my shoulder, too, and she's about to walk by, but I lay my hand on hers with a shake of my head. It's the closest anyone's ever come to guessing why I actually left.

"I didn't want to cause her pain. I was trying to . . ." I can't really bring myself to finish that sentence.

It was easier to pretend she was better off without me. Because who would want to be with the shell of the man they loved? Who had promised them all these big dreams, promised the whole world, and used to stay up telling them stories so they could be safe from their own brain and sleep the way they deserved? But that man got dizzy and tired, and he couldn't keep up with any of his promises, and she deserved someone who could.

"I'm sure you had your reasons, Bohdan." She exhales sadly, shaking her head. "But at the end of the day, while you were ever-so valiantly trying to save her from you, you forgot that you helped Sloan save herself. That brain has been running rampant with no outside checks since you left."

She pats my shoulder a final time and follows Sloan into the suite.

I drop my head against the wall of the ship. Feel a bit like banging it and causing another bleed.

Jay clears his throat. "You okay? You want to talk about it?"

I jerk my chin and grab one of the bottles of beer Talon brought out in a cooler. Nothing really matters anymore, so I twist it open with my teeth.

"Don't tell me the great, big secret reason you left was because, what?" Talon looks exasperated, the lines of his face serious for once. "You thought she was better off without you? What kind of self-sacrificing bullshit is that?" He pulls a weird face, makes fists with his hands, and moves them in some sort of imitation of a robotic march. "I'm Bohdan, and I guess I've internalized so much toxic masculinity, I think there's only one way to be a man!"

"I couldn't stay up anymore!" I shout, arms splaying wide enough to hold my biggest failure out for everyone to see. Beer foams over the neck of the bottle, and I hold my hand up, try to shake it off, and fail, so I drop back against the wall again, pinch my nose, and sound more pathetic than I ever have. "She needed someone who could."

Talon's lip curls up, and he pushes off the railing, pointing at me. "Couldn't stay up? Do not fucking tell me you left her because you were, what, tired? Your brain was scrambled on national television. You had one of the worst cases of post-concussion syndrome ever seen in sports. And you ruin the one good thing in your life because you were tired? No shit you were tired."

I clench down hard enough on my jaw that it starts to radiate down my neck, telling me all I need to know about how my head's going to feel tomorrow. "I couldn't stay awake. I couldn't be what she needed. We used—before she went to sleep—I'd help her count and her fucking brain, man. She needs—" I cut myself off, it was a simple thing that broke it all down at the end of the day. "I couldn't stay awake for her."

Jay scrubs his face, grabbing a bottle but not opening it, just sitting there twirling it in his hands. "We know she has . . . worries. She's been open about it with both of us. You can say it out loud."

I close my eyes, and I try to remember what it was like when we were happy. Sloan smiling softly under the moonlight reflecting through those windows, lips parted at the Cupid's bow, my thumb tracing her cheek before my mouth met hers.

But all I can see is her face crumbling into nothing, all of her shrinking when I left.

Shaking my head, I drain the bottle. "Do you know what it was like? To see her turn inward every day? To see her brain eat her alive? To have the girl I loved when I was twenty and the woman I'd have fucking roped the moon for look at me every day and even when she didn't say it out loud, know she was wondering what she did wrong? To watch her start to believe it, when she spent so many years working so hard to try and unlearn the things the brain she was born with taught her? Because I couldn't stay up and tell her three things I loved about her before bed? And there was so much fucking noise in my brain I couldn't even remember to do it in the morning."

For the first time in his life, Talon looks disappointed in me. "That girl would have drowned for you."

"She was! She was fucking drowning and so was I! You two didn't live in that house. You didn't live in her head, and you certainly didn't live in mine." I punctuate each word with fingers to my temple. Pinching my eyes closed, I slide down the wall until I'm sitting against the ground, one leg propped up. I raise my hand, gesturing to each of them. "You can still fucking skate. You can still fucking play! You're retiring because you want to, Talon, not because you need to. And Jay—" I turn towards him with a resigned shake of my head. "You should have went first in the draft. Seattle wasted their pick, as it turned out."

Jay tugs at the chain around his neck with a shake of his head. "They didn't waste their pick, Bohdan." He exhales, comes to sit beside me, and drops a hand to my knee. "They gave you the C after one year. Most points in a season, more than once. You took them to a cup. You won them a cup. Still hold the record for most points in franchise history."

"They aren't an old franchise," I mutter.

"Brain might be broken, but he still remembers to self-deprecate." Talon's brows rise when he drops to my other side.

Jay rolls his eyes, but a smile fights at the corners of his mouth. Running a hand through his hair, he tugs at the ends, and one strand falls across his forehead. "What was it you said to Sloan before we boarded? Do those facts negate that she's still the most beautiful girl in the world?"

Talon leans forward, joining in with more exuberance than fits the situation, pointing at my hairline where the scar, starting to throb now, hides under a rogue wave. "Does the fact that you have that scar negate the facts of your career?"

I give them both a flat look. "I'm not answering that."

I know, logically, that even though it was cut short, my career was a good one. I've come to terms with that part of my life looking differently than I thought it would from the first time I set foot on the ice.

It's the carnage this stupid fucking scar left in its wake.

"And maybe . . ." Talon leans forward, eyes wide like he's eagerly waiting for our reaction to what he thinks is going to be an awe-inspiring, jaw-dropping statement. "Maybe you should have let Sloan tell you what she needed, instead of making a decision on her behalf."

Jay leans forward, bringing his hands together in a slow clap. "When did you get so wise, Talon?"

Talon grins. "Retirement's really opened my eyes."

"What's next? Talk show?" I ask dryly.

Before he can answer—I'm sure Talon has an extensive plan for a talk show he would host already written down somewhere, if not at least in his imagination—my phone vibrates in my pocket.

This stupid suite has Wi-Fi and it's the only place I can get service when we're at sea.

A text from Shay flashes.

> **Shay:** Have you thought any more about Zane's offer? They'd like to start talks when you're back.

Talon, who's never been able to mind his own business a day in his life, leans over my arm, eyes curious when they flick up to me. "What offer?"

I shove the phone back in my pocket in favour of the beer Jay hands me. "The network wants me to do some feature show next season . . . conversations with other athletes. Injuries, recovery, mental health. Bullshit like that."

"Like a podcast?" Talon asks. "Is that something you want to do?"

I shrug. "Maybe. I said I'd think about it."

"Maybe *we* should start a podcast." Talon twists the cap of his beer off, tossing it onto the ground beside him.

"We're not starting a podcast." Jay cuts him a sideways glance.

Talon nods. "We could. And we could call it 'The Only Podcast to Ever Exist.'"

"No. The only line to ever exist was bad enough." Jay rolls his eyes, bottle pressed to his mouth, hiding a smile.

"Well, has there been another line that's even come close?" Talon leans forward, raising his eyebrows.

"No."

Talon's arms go wide. "Then I rest my case. The only line to ever exist."

I smile in spite of myself, dropping my head back against the wall of the ship, where I hope the only girl to ever exist is sleeping peacefully on the other side.

Sloan

Then – College

I'm trying not to move around too much. It's not my bed, after all.

I usually like staying at Bohdan's. His bed feels just as much mine as my own.

But tonight—everything is so loud, the sheets aren't sitting right against my skin, and all I can think about are all the things I've done wrong.

I'd try to untangle myself, but he has one arm around my waist, his chin at home in the crook of my neck.

He's so exhausted. He crawled into bed right after his second practice of the day, barely bothering to take off his clothes.

I don't want to wake him, but my brain won't shut up—so I try counting.

I know the thoughts won't go away, I just don't want them to be so loud.

Tapping my fingers against my chest in time with the words, I mouth, *One, two, three.*

"Sloan," Bohdan mumbles, half asleep and voice rough. "What are you doing?"

"Nothing." My fingers still.

I swallow.

I blink.

I even try to shake it out of my head.

But it doesn't go anywhere.

It's a stupid mantra, but it's the one I've been singing to the tune of worries a child shouldn't have as far back as I remember.

Everyone hates you. No one loves you. You're not enough.

Do you remember when you were at lunch with Tia and her friends from her math class?

Your laugh was too loud.

Everyone found it grating.

"Sloan," he repeats, murmuring into my neck. "What's wrong?"

Pressing my eyes shut, I give another jerk of my head. "Nothing."

Bohdan's hand finds my chin, his fingers gentle. "Zlatíčko, don't lie."

"Your Czech is so much better when you're exhausted," I say through a wet laugh, and I reach one hand up to bat away the tears running down my cheek.

His grip tightens against my chin, his arm tensing around my waist, before he rolls me over to face him.

Bohdan isn't someone you'd describe as beautiful—he's too serious, all sharp lines and edges and dark eyes that only ever seem to lighten when he looks at me.

But he looks something like beautiful now, milky light streaming through the window of his bedroom, hitting the planes of his face and those grey eyes in a way that make him look like he should be on a billboard somewhere.

He blinks, thumb brushing across my mouth before his hand wraps around the back of my neck. "Baby."

He doesn't repeat himself. He doesn't ask again.

It's all he says.

An invitation.

I take it.

"What if . . ." I lean down, afraid to look him in the eye when I tell him in case he thinks it's true, too. "What if . . . what if everyone hates me?"

He doesn't even blink, but his fingers tighten against the nape of my neck. "No one could hate you." He says it like it's a simple fact.

"But they might."

"Did something happen today, Sloan? Or is your brain telling you something that isn't true?"

It's another thing that's so stupid, so embarrassing, and it's going to seem small to him, but it's not to me even though I wish so badly it was. "I laughed."

"You laughed," he repeats.

I wait for him to do the thing that's been plaguing me—to tip his head back, expose his neck with all those magnificent lines and cords in laughter that's not for me, but at me.

He doesn't.

"Then whoever heard you was lucky."

I roll my eyes with a wet scoff, slapping at my cheeks now. "But what if it was too loud? What if I was annoying? Do you think I'm annoying?"

"It wasn't, and no. I don't. I think you're fascinating." Bohdan takes a steady exhale. "What do you need me to do, Sloan? Do you need me to tell you that no one thinks you're too loud, that no one thinks you're annoying, that no one hates you? If you need reassurance, I'll give it. I'll stay up all night."

"My therapist says . . . reassurances aren't always good. Because they can just be temporary, and then the obsession is going to chase the reassurance I get from the compulsion of asking . . . and I don't know. It's stupid."

"It's not stupid." Bohdan moves his hand to my chin again, tipping it up. He looks at me in that way, stoic, serious about two things—and how lucky am I that one of them is me—and somehow, a man when he's surrounded by twenty-one-year-old boys. "And I'm not temporary."

I blink, and I tell him another fear. Maybe the biggest, scariest one I have. "You might be."

Bohdan closes his eyes with a slow shake of his head. "I'm not."

"You're twenty-one."

"You're nineteen."

"We aren't just reciting facts, Bohdan," I say softly.

Bohdan runs his thumb along my chin before moving it to my bottom lip. "Here's a fact for you. I've only really loved one thing in my life, and then I met you. Now I love you more."

"That's a reassurance," I whisper.

"No. It's a fact." Bohdan moves his thumb to my cheek. "Can I tell you three facts?"

I barely nod.

He presses his thumb to the first freckle. "Jedna. Your eyes go wider when you're talking about archeology more than anything else." He moves to the second. "Dvě. You snore when you're napping, but not when you're sleeping through the night." He smiles on the last one. "Tři. You've got terrible taste in television."

His mouth replaces his thumb, a brush across each freckle, before his lips find mine with a whisper. "And they're all things I love about you."

"You love those boring facts about me?" I smile against his mouth. The questions and the noises are all still there, they're just . . . quieter. At least for now.

Bohdan slides his hand across the back of my neck, cradling my head. He nods, mouth shifting into a smile, too. "Next time you think someone hates you, or that they don't love you, remember those three, boring facts about you that I love."

"Not a reassurance?" I murmur.

He shakes his head. "Not a reassurance."

"Can you tell me more tomorrow?"

"Every night before bed, for the rest of our lives. I'll tell you three facts before you go to sleep."

Sloan

Ropes of brown vine, weighed down by impossibly purple grapes weaving through stark green leaves in stepped rows, stretch across the shoreline, angling down towards the glittering ocean; the boats dotting the harbour look tiny from all the way up here.

I blink, watching the birds in the distance swoop low, close to the ocean and what might be fishing nets floating aimlessly behind all the boats, brightly coloured with peeling paint.

The sun warms my cheeks, down the sides of my neck, over my exposed shoulders, and a breeze lifts my hair, loose in an attempt to cover up the *B*, ink too stark now from the sun. I don't think I packed a single T-shirt for this entire trip, and it feels a bit like an open wound on display.

"What are you staring at?" Tia drops her chin to my shoulder, arms wrapping around me, squeezing briefly.

I don't tell her that I'm trying to take in as much of the view as I can. I stared at the headrest the entire drive from the port to the winery because I got stuck in the middle, and turning to look out the window would have meant looking at Bohdan.

I point towards the winery. To Talon doing push-ups off the edge of a wine barrel. "I think your brother's already drunk."

Tia cuts me a sideways look, adjusting the wide brim of her sun hat before she turns around to walk backward in front of me down the cobblestone path to the vineyard, the skirt of her floral-print dress dancing around her legs. "Well, four mimosas at breakfast will do that to a person."

"He's taking this retirement thing very seriously." I nod.

He pushes up a final time, clapping his hands before they make contact with the iron rung around the edge of the barrel again.

She smiles again, fondly. She pretends she doesn't, but she loves her brother more than anything. "He's having fun. He deserves it. It looks, sort of, like they all are. And that's hard to achieve. Bohdan takes everything too seriously to crack many smiles."

She points, but she doesn't need to.

I could feel his smile all the way from here, even if I couldn't see it.

The way the left corner of his mouth lifts higher, almost an infinitesimal amount, the slight crinkle at the corner of his grey eyes, lighter than usual and like the ocean under the early-morning sun, the angle of his head.

"You're sure about this?" Tia peers up at me from under the brim of her hat.

"Sure about what?"

"This ... truce." She gestures towards them again, Talon now crouched down, hands firmly on his knees, seemingly coaching Bohdan and Jay through the same push-up routine against the barrel.

I look away. I don't need to see the muscles of Bohdan's arms contract like that—the swell of his bicep against the cuffed sleeve of another loose, linen button-up. The flex of his shoulders as it stretches across his back.

I certainly don't need to remember what it felt like for those arms to cage me in alongside his legs: one on either side of my waist, him impossibly hard inside me, sweat-slicked ridges of abdominal muscle pressing against my chest, a wave of hair curling over his head, voice rough and every second word in Czech because he could never keep his head straight when we were together like that.

"I think you should fuck."

Whirling towards Tia, my palms find my cheeks, like I can cover up the flush. "Who?"

"You and my brother." She rolls her eyes, hand motioning back and forth between me and Bohdan. "You two, obviously."

"And why would we do that?" I straighten my shoulders and lift my chin, like I think the whole thing is improper, and I wasn't just fantasizing about him inside me.

Tia tips her head back with a bark of laughter. "Because you used to do it all the time. When was the last time you got laid?"

"None of your business."

"Since Bohdan?" She flips her hand over, studying her nails under the sun, like she wants to make sure her manicure stayed intact.

I narrow my eyes. "Of course not."

Tia nods, all sympathetic like she expected as much. "Him either, I bet."

"What?" I blink.

She gestures towards him again. I think Talon has them all doing tricep dips now. "Bohdan. I bet it's just been him and his hand for the last year and a half. With the memories of you to keep him company, of course."

"Don't." I widen my eyes, shifting on my feet.

I know what that looks like, too.

I've watched him. He's watched me. We've watched each other.

His palm gripping against the wet tile of the shower, hair plastered to his face, curling around his ears and at the nape of his neck, droplets of water running across his shoulders, down the planes of his chest while all his muscles contract—

"You're thinking about it right now, aren't you?" Tia's mouth curls into a catlike grin.

I feel a bit like shoving her, but I cross my arms instead. "No. I'm thinking about wine fortification. I hope they tell us about the process today."

She laughs again, linking our arms and tugging me down the path towards the winery. "Liar."

I try to concentrate on my sandals hitting the uneven cobblestones so I don't trip, fall, and have to explain to a French paramedic that I was too busy thinking about my ex touching himself while he watched me in the shower to notice where I was going.

But Tia's words, quiet and careful, interrupt all my other thoughts because they remind me of the thing I can't forget.

"You're sure?" she asks again, and I can feel her eyes on me.

"Yes. I need the Polaroid back. He can have his ring. And I'm finally going to know why."

I keep my eyes on the cobblestones now, one at a time, and I try to ignore the sounds I hear with each step.

———ele———

"What kind of rock is that?"

Bohdan looks over his shoulder, fingers stilling where they trail across the carved walls of the cellar.

"Provence is mostly limestone. The accumulation of marine sediments." He knocks a fist against an outcropping of rock, edges worn down by time.

I nod, folding my arms across my chest, covering my exposed shoulder with one hand so he can't see the tattoo, on display in this wine cellar we're supposed to be touring, because he looks so much like the boy I fell in love with, eyes rapt with fascination while he looks at the different lines, colours, and mineral deposits of rocks.

We're the only ones here. I went to the washroom when Tia, Talon, and Jay walked ahead to see the different types of barrels—mostly to tell myself I needed to stop thinking about Bohdan without clothes on—and when I came back, it was just him standing here: one hand in the pocket of his shorts, the other trailing across the walls, features lit by the swinging bulbs above him.

"Do you—" I start, a laugh catching in my throat. Tia was right. I don't know how to pretend not to know him. "Do you . . . study rocks for a living?"

His hand, wide with veins traipsing over the back, lies flat against the rock, and he gives me a sideways look. "No."

"What do you do?" The words sound so stupid, even to me, that I clap my hand over my mouth.

That makes him smile, and he pushes off the wall, shoving his hand in the pocket of his linen shorts. "I used to chase a rubber puck. Now I watch people chase that same rubber puck and talk about it on TV."

I blink. It's not really funny anymore.

"Maybe you could integrate your love of rocks," I say quietly, trying again.

"Yeah, well, rock facts don't play well on television." He gives me a wry shrug. "People are more interested in who's making plays, not the fact that the studio in Secaucus sits on sedimentary rocks. Shale, sandstone, siltstone. All part of the Newark Basin."

"I wouldn't know." I shrug.

A grin stretches across his face. "About the bedrock formation, or the kinds of things people like to hear during televised hockey broadcasts?"

"Either-or."

"You don't watch me on TV?" He angles his head.

"Sorry, no." I snort. I can't think of anything I'd rather do less than watch a pixelated version of a Bohdan I'd never get to have on my TV screen.

He cocks his head back, like he's affronted.

"You'd watch me?" I ask flatly.

Bohdan stops, the bulbs hanging from the wires mounted across the stone ceiling swaying above him, shadows dancing across his face. He nods. "Probably until my eyes bled."

I swallow, whispering, "That doesn't seem safe."

He shrugs, lips tugging to the side. "Can't imagine it would be. Not for the faint of heart, having you and losing you."

You didn't lose me, I think. You gave me up.

You had me and you let me go.

169

I close my eyes—I can't look at him anymore. Not when I still love him, even though I wish with my whole heart I didn't, not when he looks like that: impossibly stunning, impossibly out of reach, and more lovely than anything in the world, even here in a dank, centuries-old wine cellar.

He might've read my mind because his voice drops, a low, rough whisper just for me and him here in the dark. "Would be a fitting punishment, to have to watch you every day."

"Is that what it's supposed to be for me?" I blink, and he's just a silhouette while my eyes adjust. "Punishment?"

A fitting one, my brain whispers. It's what we deserved, at the end of the day.

To be left alone with our love. Not enough, never enough.

Bohdan surveys me, a muscle in his neck lengthens before tightening, and he lifts his brows before jerking his head. "No, Sloan. It was a last resort."

They're right on the tip of my tongue, so many questions I'd die to ask him, weighing it down enough that I can't really speak, and I wonder if they're the same things that sit heavy on his shoulders.

Why was it a last resort? Can he still not skate? Does his head still hurt him that much? Is it the noise? The lights? The glare from the ice?

Maybe it's my ghost chasing him the way his chases me.

He looks the way he did when he was still playing—all taut ridges of muscle. He's not old yet, and pre-concussion, he'd been planning to play until he was at least thirty-five, if his body let him.

I don't ask, and I wouldn't even if I could, because I'm not sure I can stomach the answer. I think, even after all these years, even after what he did, the idea of Bohdan carrying around baggage in the shape of that scar might be the worst thing that's ever happened to me.

Instead, I murmur, "This is violating the rules."

"You're right," he says simply.

"Strike one."

He smiles, soft and sad. "You want to implement a strike system?"

"It only seems fair. We each have something to gain, so . . . whoever has the least amount of strikes at the end of the week wins." My arms tighten across my chest, and I don't tell him that I can't pretend not to know him—I'll fail and lose, and I need the Polaroid.

I need to know why.

"Amended rules then?" He steps forward, one hand coming out of his pocket, extending towards me in the low light. "Just . . . whoever fucks up the least gets to win? Think I've already lost, but sure, I'll play."

I start to shake my head because I can hear it there—he didn't lose, I was the loser. He left me and I can only think of one reason why.

But Talon shouts for us, hands cupped around his mouth like we aren't in a contained cellar and the noise won't reverberate anyway. "Wine tasting time!"

Bohdan tips his chin towards the end of the cellar, and I don't need to look to know Tia smiles at me, vindicated, like she's won something. But I think Bohdan and I both might be losers no matter what, and he grips his jaw before holding up a finger. "Strike one for me, then."

Bohdan

Then – College

Talon and Jay love to party after a game—win or lose. Talon says it's good for morale. Jay's only serious about one thing—hockey—and he wants to spend the night either being lauded for his performance and celebrating his own superiority, or drinking his feelings away before he goes to the rink at six a.m. to start watching game tape and dissecting everything he did wrong.

I don't particularly care either way. I play well because I'm better than almost anyone, and when I don't, I usually take my frustration out on the ice. But I'm the captain, and Talon and Jay are the alternates, and our line is just generally the best in the entire country, so it's sort of expected.

The size and severity of the parties typically depends on how we played. And tonight, we played really, really well.

You can barely move through the throngs of people gathering in our hallways, standing littered on all levels of the staircase, blocking access to our rooms and all the quieter parts of our house.

Some of our teammates dragged a keg into the kitchen, and I think our goalie is upside down on it doing a keg stand right now.

Talon and Jay hold court where they usually do—in the centre of our living room, at either end of a beer pong table, already covered with cracked red plastic cups, puddles of foam dripping over the edges onto the scratched hardwood flooring, surrounded by their many admirers.

I play sometimes. Usually with Sloan. She makes an excellent teammate, and even though she doesn't have a competitive bone in her body, she likes winning games with me.

Tonight, though, she's on my lap, legs slung lazily over the arm of the chair, a red cup between her teeth, eyes glued to a Sudoku puzzle on her phone.

Nights like this work for us, when we're in our own little bubble. I don't always feel like talking, and Sloan doesn't always want to participate, but this way, she feels like she's still a part of things.

Talon says he can always tell if it's going to be a "bubble night" or a normal night if I sit down and play video games before the party starts.

"That's a six." I tip the bottom of my beer bottle towards her phone screen.

She frowns, taking the cup away from her mouth. Her lower lip sits in a pout and she cuts me a sideways look. "I wasn't working on sixes right now."

I knock my head against hers. "Well, I was."

"Alright, oh-so-wise Sudoku master. Let's see." She straightens her shoulders, making a big show of moving her finger in a circle to touch the right box before she taps the six at the bottom of the screen.

The number flashes green.

"Told you." I grin, biting down on her neck.

Sloan rolls her eyes, pushing my jaw away. Her hair shifts when she does, and for the first time I notice a small green loop sitting just inside her ear.

"What are these?" I tap at the pale green rubber.

Sloan's brow furrows, and her hand comes up like she forgot there was anything there, fingers tracing the circle before she smiles brightly at me. "Oh! They're new. Tia got them for me. They're for noise sensitivity."

"Do they work?"

"Yeah. I wore them to the game tonight." She nods, the seventeen still painted on her cheek creasing, her freckles visible just below the fading white paint. "They don't block any of the sounds, but they reduce them and I can still hear."

"Cool." I smile, pressing my mouth to her temple.

She swings her legs over the arm of the chair, setting her phone down. "I'm going to go get another drink. Do you want another beer?"

"Sure." I nod, watching her stand, tugging at the hem of her shirt before weaving through the crowd towards the kitchen. Talon pauses his throw to ruffle her hair, and when he sinks it, he immediately starts shouting for her to come back.

"Sloany!" He cranes his neck backward towards the kitchen. "Get back here! You're my good luck charm."

I don't hear it at first because Talon's voice carries, but when he realizes Sloan isn't going to do more than flick up her middle finger over her shoulder and he quiets down, it sounds a bit like someone just stabbed my brain.

Two girls sit on the couch beside me—probably Sloan's age, I think I've seen them around before, they might be friends with one of the rookies—huddled together, giggling and whispering, not all that quietly.

"She's so fucking weird. Why is she wearing earplugs?"

"Who knows. I've seen her cry at these parties like, seven times. He's so hot, he could do so much better."

"Maybe she's as weird in bed as she is everywhere else."

I bite down so hard I think I crack a tooth, my grip tightens on the bottle, and I don't know what I'm about to do but I turn with a jerk of my head. "What did you just fucking say?"

"You about done with your drink?" Jay interrupts, calling from across the table, arm suspended in midair, gripping the Ping-Pong ball so tightly the cords across his arms pop, drawing more attention to the array of tattoos spread across his bicep.

"Oh." One of the girls glances sideways at me before looking at Jay like he's just saved her, sitting straighter with this smile that's probably supposed to be flirty but just looks fucking demonic to me. "Almost."

Jay nods, a tight smile stretching across his face. "Great. Now you can get the fuck out."

"Pardon me?" She pulls her head back, blinking, a bit stunned.

"Couldn't hear me? I'll repeat myself before Bohdan beats the shit out of whatever loser boyfriend you came here with." Jay hikes a thumb over his shoulder before pointing back and forth between them. "Both of you can get the fuck out."

Her face pales, eyes cutting to me. I clench my jaw, jerking it towards the door. She swings her gaze to Talon, like she might find an ally there. But he claps his hands together and points towards the door, too, grinning when he says, "Don't bother coming back, either."

"Because we said she was weird for wearing earplugs?" the other one finally sputters.

"Because I just don't fucking like you." Jay flashes her a smile that's mostly teeth before he narrows his eyes. "Don't make me repeat myself."

Talon clicks his tongue, clapping again. "Chop-chop."

I bite down on a fist, breath ragged, eyes narrowed on them as they gather their ugly coats, tugging down on the hems of their dresses, and practically sprint out the door.

"Breathe, Novo." Talon shoves a cup of foamy beer in front of me, clapping me on the shoulder.

I drain the rest of my bottle, dropping it unceremoniously to the ground beside my chair, and grab the cup from Talon when I stand.

Rolling my shoulders back, I drain the mostly foam beer and drop that to the ground, too. I crane my neck, hoping for the only time since I've met her that Sloan is far, far away. Hearing something like that would fucking destroy her, and she spends enough time destroying herself.

I catch sight of her in the kitchen talking to Tia, propped up on the counter, head tipped back in laughter.

"Who did they come with?" I jerk my head towards the door.

"Forget them. They sucked." Talon's lips pull back and he waves a hand like it's of no consequence.

"Fucking losers." Jay nods, bringing his arm back to ready another throw.

"If Sloan had heard—"

"She didn't." Talon shakes my shoulders. "We've got her back, too, you know."

Talon and Jay ended up on the same team as me by chance, really. We all had plenty of interest from other schools. And we ended up playing on the same line because there was something there, innate chemistry, during training camp.

I'm not a big believer in fate or the universe or anything like that. But something, somewhere brought them to me, and dropped Sloan off in the same first-year dorm as Talon's sister.

Feels a bit like fate, maybe, if there's such a thing. That we're all supposed to be together.

I grin at them. "Thank you. She can stand up for herself, you know. It's just—"

"Yeah, we know." Jay cuts me off with wide eyes. "Quite frankly, I find her almost as terrifying as the other one."

"Are you talking about me?" Tia tips her chin up, arms crossing over her chest when she shoves her way towards the table.

Sloan follows behind her, clutching her cup, almost full to the brim with a new vodka soda, holding out a new beer for me.

"Not really." Jay rolls his eyes, tossing the Ping-Pong ball into an open cup. "I was talking about Sloan. But you are 'the other one,' so I guess I was, so to speak."

Sloan arches a brow. "The other one has a name, you know. Unless you've taken one too many hits to the boards and forgotten?"

"Don't pretend to forget my sister's name." Talon hits Jay in the back of the head with his palm before slinging an arm around Sloan's shoulders, gesturing with his cup towards me and Jay. "You want to play them, Sloany? We need to bring them down a few pegs—each scored two goals tonight, and now they think they're better than the rest of us."

"What about me?" Tia's hand comes off her arm, held up expectantly.

"You can referee," Jay deadpans.

Tia rolls her eyes. "Fine. No cheating on my watch. That means you, Talon."

Sloan looks over to me, tipping her head. "Do you want to play?"

"Yeah, why not?" I ignore Talon's arm around her and grip the back of her head, bringing my mouth roughly to her forehead. "You weren't going to win at Sudoku anyway. Might as well not win at this, too."

"Sudoku isn't a competition." I can hear the eye roll in her voice.

I shrug, pulling back. "Everything's a competition when I'm playing."

She shoves at me, brushing off her shirt and pursing her lips, before looking at Talon. "I think you're right. They're both a bit full of themselves tonight."

"Finally!" Talon raises a fist, triumphant, before steering Sloan towards the opposite end of the table. "Someone understands my brilliance. Hey—what are those things in your ears?"

"Oh. They're like earplugs. They help with the noise." She tucks her hair behind her ear, and Talon leans forward, inspecting, like he's getting a degree in otolaryngology, not economics.

"Can you get me a pair?" Jay glances up at her as he moves the cups back into a triangle.

"Why?" Sloan wrinkles her nose. "Do you think they're going to be a good accessory for your game day outfits?"

"No, so I don't have to hear Talon speak."

Tia nods along empathetically. "Don't worry, Choi, I have extras."

Talon throws his hands in the air. "Can we just play?"

Sloan laughs, and I think all the windchimes in the universe start moving together, swaying in a phantom breeze caused by a beautiful girl who somehow ended up here with me.

She rolls her eyes when I wink at her, and picks up her ball.

Maybe fate's not such a bad thing to believe in after all.

Bohdan

"I mean"—Jay leans forward, the chain around his neck lifting in the bubbles of the Jacuzzi, flush visible on his cheeks, eyes glossy and a smile tilting across his face—"it's really about the tannins, isn't it?"

It's a sorry imitation of Talon carrying on during the wine tasting.

But it's enough that we're all laughing. Probably too loudly to be drowned out by the noises of the Jacuzzi and interrupting whatever sleep the neighbours on either side of our suite thought they'd be getting.

Talon makes a carry-on gesture, leaning back against the headrest. "Look, you can all laugh all you want. But I listened today. I learned."

"I learned something, too." Sloan sits up, straightening her shoulders. Wisps of hair fall out of her ponytail, framing her face and sticking to her damp collarbone, the tie of her bathing suit doing nothing to cover her tattoo, on display like she doesn't care who sees. But that might have more to do with the wine than her sudden apathy towards the faded ink on her shoulder.

I think it might have been on purpose, actually.

I definitely think the blue string bikini—the exact same shade as her eyes—was on purpose. I did my best to look away when she and Tia came out to join us because the idea of seeing that much of Sloan again, sitting so close to her, and being unable to touch her, made me simultaneously feel like jumping from the railings of this balcony into the depths of the ocean and dropping to my knees in front of all our friends and begging her to forgive me.

But Talon insisted on a soak after all that wine, saying it would help clear our heads, even though I'm pretty sure that's scientifically proven not to be true.

"What's that, Sloany?" Talon smiles encouragingly.

She raises her glass. "That you're a douche."

We all laugh again. But it's not loud—everyone's so quiet in their laughter because they can hardly breathe, and it should be a sound that echoes across the ship to annoy our neighbours and out onto the ocean to let the world know we're all still here, and we can all still laugh.

Jay leans forward, ends of his hair falling into the water, clutching his side, practically wheezing. Tia can't stop fanning her face, and Talon drops his head back before thumping a fist to his own chest when he chokes on a sip of wine.

Sloan smiles quietly, shoulders shaking, eyes scrunched up against the tears.

I'm not really making any noise, and I'm not really laughing either. I should be—it was a funny, too-stupid thing she said that reminded me of being in college. But she's smiling in this real way I haven't seen in over a year and a half, and I can't really look away.

She looks at me, her lips turn down and her cheeks soften, and I can see it in her eyes—she's looking for approval, waiting for me to laugh the way everyone else is. She thinks I don't love her and she's looking for something, anything to tell her brain to shut up, that I still see value in her. That she's enough, even in some tiny, infinitesimal way.

There's nothing about Sloan that's infinitesimal to me.

Before I can think better of it, I wink at her.

Blue eyes go wide, her lips pillow and part before she blinks, swallowing slowly. I can see the flush on her cheeks from here, on her chest, curves just visible above the water, and I hate myself for that a bit, but she bites down on her lip, wrinkling her nose with a smile no one else would ever see.

Talon claps a palm against his chest again, finally swallowing, pointing towards Sloan before he practically parkours out of the Jacuzzi, and pushes to stand. "You're funny. I'll give you that." He makes a show of checking his watch. "Free time is officially over. Thank you all for your participation in day two of my Retirement River Cruise."

"I don't think you can classify this as free time. You made us get into the Jacuzzi." Tia fiddles with the yellow tie of her bathing suit before pointing at her brother.

"Not a river cruise." Jay nods, emptying his wine and hopping over the edge of the Jacuzzi to get out.

Talon starts, "What is an ocean if not a—"

"It's not a really big river, I'll tell you that for free," I offer, cutting him off.

I think Sloan smiles again, and I feel bigger than I have any right to be.

He makes a yapping gesture with his hands before stretching each arm out with an unnecessary swing. "I'm going to bed. I might be retired, but I'm not going to get sloppy. I'm going to the gym tomorrow morning if anyone wants to join me. Big leg day."

"I don't think that's on the itinerary," Sloan says quietly, mouth tipping into a smile behind her wineglass.

Talon narrows his eyes, studying her, before he cracks another grin. "I'm watching you this week."

He reaches out to ruffle her hair when he walks past the Jacuzzi, tracking water all over the balcony and back into the suite. It's not the first time he's done it, and it probably won't be the last, but I clench my jaw at the sight—the idea that he still gets to touch her like it's nothing, without thinking and without consequence.

Jay reaches out, tapping her forehead, grinning at her. "Keep the jokes coming, Sloany. His ego needs deflating."

A muscle in my cheek twitches.

"And what purpose do I serve then? I'm almost certain our parents only birthed me as a countermeasure for Talon." Tia straightens her shoulders against the headrest, twirling the stem of her wineglass.

"You"—Jay pauses, elbows resting against the edge of the Jacuzzi before he takes her wineglass, bringing his mouth to the exact same spot as hers was and taking a sip—"are here to look good. And you're doing a great job."

I press a fist to my mouth, cringing.

He's angled away from me, but judging by the way Tia starts giggling, slapping a hand to cover her mouth, and Sloan widens her eyes, he might try his hand at winking.

He's terrible at winking.

But he doesn't seem to care. Jay doesn't care about much other than making sure his game day outfits are more interesting than anyone else's and playing better than everyone else on the ice. Maybe that's the kind of grace I used to carry myself with, too.

He catches himself right as he steps through the sliding door, fingers tapping against the frame. "Think I'll work out tomorrow morning, too. You in?"

"What, the push-ups and dips off a hundred-year-old wine barrel this morning weren't enough for you?" I deflect, grinning. Doing things with my best friends just like we used to probably ranks third on the list of things I want more than anything on the planet.

It goes: Sloan, hockey, mundane things like being stupid in the gym with your stupid best friends.

Jay rolls his eyes, and I don't have the heart to tell him that sometimes working out is fine, but sometimes it leads to so much pressure in my head I think my eyes might explode.

He looks at me for a minute like he might want to ask, but he gives a jerk of his chin. "Let me know in the morning."

I nod, emptying the rest of my wine even though I shouldn't. I've had too much, and I was in the sun all day. My temple aches, and my neck feels tense.

Sloan waits, craning her neck to make sure he's gone before turning to Tia. "Why is he flirting with you?"

"I have no idea." Tia raises her palms, shaking her head. "I'm going to bed. Love you."

I watch the whole thing. It's like an exact repeat of the other night: Sloan smiling tightly, making a faint noise of agreement in the back of her throat instead of throwing out words she used to say all the time, Tia's face collapsing before she shoots me a look to make sure I know it's all my fault. She even whispers about the dictionary again when she passes me.

She leaves us out here, alone in a Jacuzzi, like it isn't a horrible idea.

I rub at my chest—it aches there, too, it always does.

"Why don't you—" I start, but Sloan beats me to it.

Her words come out all rushed, in one big breath like she's been sitting on them all night. "Have you been with anyone else?"

I don't tell her that counts as a strike. I don't tell her no, that the thought of someone else makes me physically ill, that I doubt I'd even be able to get hard for another woman, and that I'll be ruined with her for the rest of my life.

My lips curl back. "Jesus Christ, Sloan. I'm going to pretend you didn't ask me that."

I debate asking her if she thinks that little of me. I wouldn't blame her. But her shoulders sag, she slumps just a bit lower into the water with an exhale of a breath I think she was holding so tightly it hurt, relief all over her face, lips parting and eyes slowly closing while her cheeks go pillowy.

And then she blinks at me, and even though I know she's lying through her fucking teeth, I still hate the words that come out of her mouth more than I think I've hated anything in my entire life.

"Well, *I* date."

Leaning across the expanse of water, I cock my head. "Oh yeah? And what are the boys like that you date?"

Her chest flushes, and not from the temperature of the water, when she catalogues how much closer I am to her. She tries to give me a hard look, but the apples of her cheeks go pink. "They're not boys."

"Oh, I think they are." I nod, pushing off the edge of the seat and dropping to my knees in the centre of the tub. I can think of a million and one things I could do to her from here. She blinks up at me. I grin down at her. "Are they what you think about?"

"Inappropriate," she mutters, pursing her lips.

I shift forward, the outside of my thighs brushing her under the water.

Sloan squeezes her legs together, like she's trying not to touch me, but the tiny breaths she's taking tell me something different.

I've been reading her mind and her body since I was twenty—it's my favourite book, I've read it cover to cover.

I shouldn't do it. I shouldn't say it. But I'll live under her skin for the rest of my life because it's better than nowhere.

"Because I know what I think about," I start, voice low and rough, and I lean forward, mouth moving over her ear while I whisper the rest. "Only ever you."

She pulls back, eyes wide, heat creeping across her cheeks, fingers tightening around the stem of her wineglass, and her teeth coming down on her bottom lip.

I let myself look at her mouth for longer than I should, how she sits, so straight and all tied up in knots I'd love to untangle. I know how.

She knows I know how.

But I stand, her eyes rove over my chest, tracking the droplets of water, and the way I can feel all my muscles contract when I hop out of the tub. My eyes never leave her, heart still with her where she sits, and I walk backward towards the door. "Night, Zlatíčko."

—⁓—

She's what I think about when I get in the shower later.

I wasn't lying.

Always her.

Only ever her.

186

It's not even the way her lips part, the way her teeth come down on the centre of the full bottom one and I wish they were mine, how she blinks those blue eyes at me, the way her eyelashes flutter and her hair tumbles around her shoulders, showing me glimpses of me there, on her skin.

How when she breathes the curves of her chest expand and I know exactly what she feels like under my hands.

What her skin feels like when I scrape my teeth over her collarbone, that I know what it's like to take her in my mouth, tongue swirling over beautiful, perfect peaked nipples.

The noises she makes, head tipped back with impossibly loud, breathy moans, fingers digging into my shoulders, my name on her lips asking for more when I'd move to bury my head between her thighs.

What it's like to slide inside her afterwards, tongue tangling with hers so she can see how good she tastes.

How it feels when she comes, tightening around me.

It's none of those things—even though they're all enough to make me see fucking stars and forget my own name.

It's her laugh that has me wrapping my hand around my cock, one palm gripping the tile wall of the shower, jaw clenched and all the muscles of my neck tense down to my shoulders until I come with her name on my lips.

I can't open my fucking eyes.

I think there's an ice pick digging into my temple.

Or maybe it's the weight of loving her so much and breaking her heart that sits right on the crown of my head and crushes my brain.

It could be the fact that I have no right to think about her anymore at all, but especially not like I did last night.

I hate myself with every leaden fucking step I take to the bathroom to throw up.

Dawn inches across the carpeted floor through the windows, the curtains pulled open, swaying in a phantom breeze.

I know I should close them—that the sun's going to crack my skull in two when it finally rises in the sky.

But I left them open last night because I was thinking about Sloan, looking up at the stars, trying to see all the way to one of those universes out there where I still have her.

I leave them like that—it'd be a fitting punishment—press a triptan nasal spray to my nose, swallow a different pill with a sedative, and hope I fall asleep again even though I don't deserve it.

Sloan

I don't sleep.

In fact, my brain decides to replay the worst mistakes I've ever made.

There are a lot of things about my brain I hate, but I think the rumination might be the worst.

I think about things from years and years ago.

I think about times I laughed too loudly or talked too much, and maybe it's my imagination now after all this time—our brains can't be trusted, not really—but I think about everyone falling silent afterwards, and staring at me with forced smiles and abject pity, because really, who was I to think I had a right to take up space?

I think about all the conversations about me and echoes of laughter that took place behind closed doors.

I think about the time Bohdan caught me counting in the library and laughed, because what was that, if not laughable? Who takes comfort in numbers?

I think about the times I've made him late because I had to change outfits because the clothes didn't sit right on my skin, and even though he said it was okay, I don't think it was okay after all.

I think about the times I threw tantrums almost like a child, crying because things were too loud and too big and too much and he had to hold me against his chest. He said that was okay too, but it couldn't have been, not really.

I think about how he said he loved every single part of me and that he wouldn't change my brain even though that was my number one wish and still is after all these years, because my brain made me the person he loved more than anything. But he couldn't have loved me all that much.

I think about how the last time I said I love you, something very bad happened and I can never say it again, because the next time, it might be worse.

I beg it to stop, but nothing helps.

I try counting. I try to reassure myself even though that solves nothing. I try to shake the thoughts out of my head. I try cold water. I try ice from the freezer.

I give up and take an Ativan when the sky turns the same colour as Bohdan's eyes.

Sloan

Livorno—not Florence, because Talon really doesn't know geography—looks like it's probably quite beautiful from the balcony of the ship. A crumbling fort sits to the left, stretching out from the city, almost touching the quays of the harbour, and beyond the modern port terminal, all glass panels and shining windows, it looks like there's a cobblestone street leading right into the central piazza.

According to Talon, who was most definitely fed the information by the suite concierge, the port can accommodate up to eleven ships.

And today, ours is the only one docked.

Apparently, it's a nice city with enough to see when you're walking around. So much so that he made an executive decision to skip the ninety-kilometre drive to Florence, saying it would be hipper, cooler around here. Less touristy.

I didn't have the heart to tell him that probably wasn't something he could achieve in one of the main port cities of the Tuscan coast, but as it turned out, I didn't have the heart to get out of bed on time today, either.

Blinking behind my sunglasses, my brain feels foggier than it should, in this dull post-Ativan haze.

Maybe not really post at all because it's barely nine a.m., and I didn't look at the clock when I took it, but it couldn't have been later than five.

It's quiet though, my thoughts and all those mean horrible things moving along so sluggishly that they're in the distance, and I can't really touch them.

But the balcony door slides open, and I start forward at the same time Bohdan walks out—shirtless—shoving a tiny bottle to his left nostril and pressing down on the right side before inhaling.

"Sloan," he says at the same time I push my sunglasses up, worry bleeding into my voice when I ask, "Are you okay?"

His brow furrows, but I point uselessly to the spray bottle in his hand, and realization dawns across his features, beautiful and sleepy in the morning sunlight, every muscle in his body tensing and rippling unfairly.

"Zolmitriptan." He holds it up, and the obliques stacked along his side tighten.

"Oh." I blink. That's not what I meant—I could name all of his medications without even having to think about it, and I certainly know which one he needs to shove up his nose. "Is your head okay?"

Bohdan nods, pocketing the bottle in a pair of black athletic shorts that sit two inches above his knees.

Those aren't fair either.

He scrubs his face before answering. "Yeah. It's coming down . . . I just took it to take the edge off. Feels almost like a regular headache now."

"Do you even remember what one of those is like?" I tip my head, chewing on the inside of my cheek.

He snorts, lips tugging in a rueful smile. "No."

I nod softly, and he does the same. We don't look away, even though this awful silence permeates every inch of distance of the trench he dug between us that doesn't really belong.

Bohdan clears his throat and hikes a thumb over his shoulder. "I can go. I didn't realize you stayed onboard today."

"Onboard," I repeat, rolling my eyes, and he smiles. It makes my lungs fuller than it should. But I whisper, pointing towards the lounge chair beside me anyway, "No. Stay."

I hate the thought of him being in pain alone more than I hate the thought of being alone here with him.

He tips his chin towards the porcelain mug with the cruise emblem stamped on it. "Can I get you another coffee?"

"Oh." I blink. "Sure. Just—"

"Three small splashes of milk, and the tiniest bit of sugar." He arches a brow, voice incredulous. "I didn't forget your coffee order, Sloan."

I'm careful not to brush my fingers against his when I hand him the mug. I don't look at him at all, I watch the passengers file off the ship and become tiny dots when they move through the port terminal.

I don't want to see him reach out with those hands that I thought would hold me for the rest of my life, how they'll wrap around a mug of coffee so he can get me another because he didn't forget how I like it.

It's a simple thing that shouldn't be sad at all, but the first tear splashes on my thigh, right beside the frays of denim from my shorts brushing my skin.

I wipe a finger across my lash line with a shaky inhale when the mug reappears.

"Sloan . . . why are you crying?"

I hear the scrape of the chair, Bohdan dragging his closer to mine, and he leans in, a wave of amber hair tumbling onto his forehead.

"It's sad," I whisper, hands wrapping around the mug of coffee and my finger tapping against the porcelain rim.

He looks like he might want to reach forward, to stop me before I can start counting, but he exhales, palming his jaw. "What's sad?"

"Nothing." I sniff, taking a small sip. "You're just a stranger getting me coffee."

Bohdan says nothing, silent again, and I wonder if he sees it between us—that yawning trench full of awful things, casualties of the war between his brain and mine.

He must, because he gives his head a slow shake and whispers roughly, "I'm sorry."

More tears roll down my cheeks, splashing against my legs, and I think a few even make their way into my coffee. "No, I'm sorry. I set these stupid rules and I can't even follow them. Strike one for me. I guess we're even."

He's not sorry for the same things I am, but I'm sorry all the same.

I try to smile when I hold up a finger, but I start crying harder. Bohdan looks like he's in physical pain, scrubbing his face instead of touching me the way I know he wants to.

"I shouldn't have spoken to you like that." He closes his eyes, shaking his head. "I don't—I don't want you to think—" He drags his chair closer, his legs almost brushing mine. "No matter what, you need to remember that I respect you more than anyone in the entire world. Okay, Sloan?"

I swallow, frowning. I don't see how that could be true. But Bohdan touches me, his hands wide and strong across my exposed knees.

I feel a bit like I've been electrocuted. The kind that could either save a life or end a life, I'm not really sure.

"Not a reassurance, Sloan. That's a fact, okay?"

I nod quietly because Bohdan doesn't lie. Not about facts.

"Zlatíčko," he murmurs, one hand coming up, thumb ready to wipe the tears away, but he hesitates, hand hovering right there, and when I don't pull back, he cups the side of my face. "Why are you crying?"

My eyes close, I lean into his palm and pretend for a moment we're back there in the life we used to have, with all those simple things I took for granted because I thought they were mine forever.

His thumb brushes across my cheek, and my fingers scramble up his forearm, traversing old pathways and finding old friends in the cords of muscle, and I cup his hand with mine.

The sob sneaks up on me, and I let it out, so it doesn't threaten to choke me the way all the horrible things I think do.

Blinking, I inhale, shuddering and lips quivering. A mess, really. But I think he might be looking at me like I'm still beautiful to him.

"I can't pretend not to know you," I tell him, pressing his hand into my cheek even harder.

Bohdan shrugs, thumb stroking my freckles. "I wasn't trying that hard."

I choke on a laugh, and he smiles quietly, the lines of his face still all sharp edges.

His hand leaves my face, his fingers wrap around my wrist, gently, reverently, and he carefully pulls my hand away from my temple. He tips my chin up and I have to look at him now: bronzed from the sun, harsh ridges and lines of his body that were never hard on me, and a face that looks like it could make a statue weep.

"Let's change the rules," he says, like it's simple. "Spend the day with me. Spend the rest of the days with me. No pretending. Just me and you."

"And what, you'll give me the picture and I'll give you the ring back at the end of the week in exchange for my time?" I murmur.

Bohdan shrugs one shoulder again. "I don't care about the ring, Sloan. Keep it. Don't. Throw it overboard Titanic style. Just—don't pretend not to know me. Know me for the next few days, even if that means hating me, and I promise you, before we get back to Barcelona, I'll give you everything you want."

I nod softly.

His hand stays wrapped around my wrist.

I don't look away. Neither does he.

Our eyes stay on each other, and neither of us look down because we had everything we wanted, and it lies ruined at our feet.

Bohdan

Then – College

"You're sure?"

It's a stupid question, and it's met with the belated, stretching silence it deserves.

Shay clears her throat on the other end of the phone. "Am I sure? Yes, Bohdan, given that I've been doing this for quite a while, I'm intimately familiar with the rules of the draft. And seeing as you're the first-ranked player in the nation, and Seattle won the lottery—I'm fairly confident in my assessment. And you can tell Jay Choi, unless he overtakes you in points for the rest of the season, he's probably going to Philadelphia. But I'm sure he's on the phone with his agent as we speak, getting the exact same news you are, though I do hope he's receiving it better."

"I'm not receiving it poorly," I say flatly, pressing my head against my doorframe and banging it there once.

I can hear her eyes roll. "Really? The last time I got to deliver this kind of news to a generational talent kind of player—which isn't a lot, by the way—that they were going to go first overall, and a team won the lottery that didn't even have the worst record, he was elated."

Pressing my fist to my mouth, I knock my head against the frame again. "Kurva. Zkurve—"

She cuts me off before I can keep going. "Please don't swear at me in Czech."

"I'm not swearing at you."

"Really?" she deadpans. I can picture her, pressing her palms together and blinking at me from behind her mahogany desk in her office that sits way too high in a skyscraper in Manhattan. "Should I call Seattle and tell them you'll pass? Maybe call the league and say you want to be removed from the draft entirely? You can go to Europe like your other little friend, what a waste of talent that was."

"I don't want to go to Europe." I push off the frame, scrubbing my face. "I wanted to play in Canada."

"Ah." She sounds like she's nodding along. "So the girlfriend could go to grad school at home and you maybe wouldn't be apart for even longer. You know, Bohdan—"

"If you tell me Sloan's just lucky to be along for the ride, I swear to God, Shay—"

"I wouldn't say that," she interjects softly. "I like Sloan, quite a lot. I was going to say that I want you to remember what you want. That we probably couldn't have handpicked a better team for you. They structure their offense in a way that complements your playing style. You're going to respond well to their coaching, it's exactly what a player like you needs to bring out the best."

"I'm already the best."

She laughs. "There he is. This is a good thing. You have a record-breaking career ahead of you, Bohdan. And I can't wait to say I knew you when."

I nod, even though she can't see me.

Shay clears her throat again. "I have other calls to make. Not all my clients are going to fare as well in this draft as you. But I can try to negotiate something for her. Flying her out? God knows I've had to ask for stranger things, and God knows teams have given players stranger things."

"I'll have the money to fly her to Seattle."

"That you will. I'll make sure of it." I can hear the smile in her voice.

I tell her the truth, even though I'm not sure why. She's my agent, not my mother. She's barely a decade older than me. "I'm not disappointed. I don't want to disappoint Sloan. There's a difference."

"Can I give you some unsolicited advice? I won't even charge you for it." Her words turn sharp. "Life is full of disappointments. I promise you, in the grand scheme of things, this won't be one. Celebrate. Enjoy. Make headlines with Choi about drinking too much and causing a scene at a bar, waving around money you don't have yet. I don't care, I'll clean up after you. Just don't listen to anything Valdez says, or you'll end up in a frozen wasteland. My other line's ringing."

She hangs up, leaving me standing alone in the middle of the hallway.

I hear the low murmur of Talon's voice from downstairs, followed by the echo of the best sound in the world.

Sloan's laughter.

I take each step down the stairs, hating that she might stop laughing when I get down there, turn the corner into the living room, and she sees it all over my face.

It's not what I'm met with when I round the corner.

Talon sits in the middle of the couch, leaning forward, elbows on his knees and eyes glued to his video game, fingers moving with rapid speed across the controller. Tia sits beside him, watching and looking like she wants to grab the controller because whatever her brother's doing seems wrong, judging by the sounds of rapid gunfire and seemingly dying characters coming from the television.

Sloan's got her legs tucked under her at the end of the couch, an old sweater of mine with my number stitched along the hood hanging off her shoulders, and a textbook from her favourite archaeology seminar open on her lap.

"Well?" She closes the book, looks up, wrinkling her nose, and there's all this excitement etched in the curves of her cheeks.

Talon's phone vibrates against the coffee table. He chucks the controller to Tia and leans forward, eyes tracking the screen.

He looks back up at me, grin splitting across his face. "Seattle? No shit."

I nod, a bit afraid to look over at Sloan, but she's out of her seat, textbook clattering to the floor and her arms winding around my neck, head buried in my shoulders before I can start fumbling over some semblance of apology.

"I'm so proud of you," she whispers, small hands pushing into my back.

I wrap my arms around her and press my mouth to the crown of her head because I'm a coward and I do want to enjoy it, just for a minute, before she looks at me and I see the wheels turning.

"And you!" Talon bounds off the couch, practically pushing us over to get to Jay when he steps off the stairs. He claps his hands to his shoulders, shaking him. "Philadelphia. They've had the worst fucking record the last three seasons, but—"

Jay shrugs. "Not anymore."

Talon gives him another shake before he turns to me. "You'll get the mountains, Jay gets the 'passionate' fans, and I'll get the chocolate."

"You're thinking of Switzerland." Tia doesn't look away from the TV.

"Really?" Talon blinks.

"Yes." She finally breaks away, smiling widely at us. "Congratulations, boys."

"Huh." Talon considers, stepping back from Jay and shoving my shoulder harder than necessary. "This calls for celebration."

I feel Sloan nod against my shoulder before she pulls back, looking up at me so brightly, with this adorable wrinkle to her nose that doesn't seem like it is, but maybe it's hiding disappointment.

Talon's version of celebrating hasn't changed since the day I met him, so the night goes the way it always does: He invites our entire team over, fills our house with more people than the fire code allows, and plays music so loud you can't hear yourself think.

I'm pretty good at reading Sloan—I've learned a lot over the last two years, and I try to notice cues before maybe even she does, and I spend a disproportionate amount of the night watching her grip a red plastic cup, waiting for her fingers to tell me something.

But she speaks before they can.

Her hand finds mine; she pulls me up the stairs into the quieter hallway, pushes back against the doorframe where I was banging my head earlier, and takes the little noise cancelling loop earplugs out that Tia bought her. "Why do you keep looking at my hands?"

"I'm sorry." I scrub my face.

"You're sorry?" Sloan furrows her brow, tapping her cup to the Cupid's bow of her lip. "Bohdan, your dreams are coming true."

"Yours aren't."

She pulls her head back, and I see it then—the sharp inhale and the way her eyes go wide, fingers tightening against the red plastic.

"You wanted to go home," I clarify, words slow and measured, and I take the cup from her, emptying it before tossing it on the ground with all the others that Talon won't bother to clean up, even though the mess is his fault. "Go to grad school in Toronto or Vancouver."

Sloan blinks with a slow breath, a tiny nod of understanding. "Anthropology programs don't only exist in Canadian universities, you know. I can apply to UW, I can apply—"

"It's not what you wanted." I sound pathetic, voice all hoarse. I am pathetic, as far as she's concerned. In all the best ways and all the worst ways and I have been since she walked down those steps from her dorm two years ago.

She considers, scrunching her nose, and her voice cracks. "I didn't always . . . I've never felt like enough there. My head's always worse and it's all too loud but it's always quieter and . . . I feel like enough with you."

The idea that she feels quiet with me, enough with me, to want this so badly—that'll become the only thing I ever really remember about this day when I look back years later.

The best day of my life, but not for the reason anyone else would think.

"You'd follow a boy?" I ask dryly.

Sloan gives a shrug of one shoulder with a roll of her eyes. "You're not a boy. I don't think you ever were. Did you come out of the womb all sharp lines and seriousness?"

"Okay." I give her a flat look, but there's a stupid grin fighting at the corners of my mouth. "You'd follow a man, then? That might be even worse."

Sloan angles her head, all of her going soft and beautiful and not at all disappointed in me when she whispers, "Only ever you."

Sloan

Knowing Bohdan again feels a bit like waking up in your own bed after a long, long trip. Sunlight you haven't seen in months streaming through the window, sheets freshly washed, crisp and soft against your skin, head on a pillow that's meant to hold all the worries of the brain that lives in it.

Trying to forget him was like wearing around a second skin—one that was never touched by him, and never really fit right.

I spend a lot of time not liking the skin I'm in—metaphorically, and literally.

Metaphorically, because I have this brain that worries all the time about things I've only ever been brave enough to speak out loud to Bohdan, that wants to tear me down so I never escape its cycle, that thrives on its obsession with hating me.

Literally, because sometimes my brain tricks me and I feel like my skin's crawling.

Nothing sits right against it.

But right now, it feels just fine.

Warm from the sun baking down, and okay with being exposed and on display, my shoulders out under my tank top, legs only covered by loose denim shorts, and maybe, remembering what it was like to be loved by the man beside me whose arm brushes against mine from time to time.

"This ship is fucking huge. What a nightmare." Bohdan grips his jaw with a terse shake of his head.

He put a shirt on, fortunately for me, and everyone around him who stares when he walks by.

A statue, hewed from marble and stone and wonderful things, brought to life and walking around their ship.

I nod, cringing behind my sunglasses. "I really think I would have preferred the riverboat."

He holds his arms wide, muscles tensing. "We haven't even made one full loop around."

"Are you sure?" I point to a bar with fake palm trees on either side, casting shade down on the throngs of cruise goers lined up, some already holding giant, towering frozen drinks with curling plastic straws and umbrellas dotting the rims of their glasses. "I'm almost positive we passed that same bar."

Bohdan shakes his head again, and I can practically see his eyes rolling from behind the dark lenses of his prescription sunglasses. "They have them spread out all over the ship. I don't even know where we are."

"I bet there's a map included with our itinerary," I offer dryly.

He cracks a sideways grin just as we pass the bar, stepping under the awning of the ship and back into the shade. Shops and restaurants line the path, and passengers spill out onto the deck in no particular order, with no real care.

At one point, Bohdan sidesteps two teenagers sprinting past us, knocking into me. He reaches out, hands gripping my shoulders to stop me from tripping. We stay like that, immobilized until he clears his throat, and his hands find their way to his pockets.

We don't really have a destination—but I didn't think it was wise for us to sit still anywhere. My brain gets louder, crueler, when I sit still, and I can't imagine the horrible things it would have to say if I was alone with him.

We haven't said much either. It's not an awkward silence—those disappeared between us a long, long time ago. I don't think it's possible to feel awkward around someone who's as much yourself as you are.

But I try to break the silence anyway, because I'm not sure it's something that belongs between us.

"Is your—" I glance at him, pointing towards his sunglasses.

Bohdan speaks at the same time, hand scrubbing across a lightly stubbled jaw. "So you're—sorry," he says, a sort of sheepish grin playing across those sharp features in a way that makes my heart perk up, awake but still drowsy, and my lungs take this deep inhale I don't think I have any control of.

I blink, staring at the planes of his face before resting my eyes on his lips. Full, lovely.

Sensuous.

The word pops into my head, and I remember our first date, thinking it's how Tia would describe his mouth if given the chance.

She wouldn't have been wrong, but it's an absurd descriptor for Bohdan, and I snort, trying not to laugh.

"What?" Bohdan asks, and I can tell his eyes narrow behind his sunglasses by the way his brows come together.

"Nothing."

"Sloan," he says flatly. "You're a terrible liar."

I roll my eyes, holding a hand in the air. "Tia's always said you have a sensuous mouth."

He stills, and one hand comes out of a pocket, slowly taking his sunglasses off, folding them in the neck of his shirt where they tug down, revealing another sliver of bronzed skin, and he blinks grey eyes at me.

"That sounds like something she would say. But I know you're lying." He tips his chin to my fingers, feathering over my bicep.

I glance down. I didn't even realize I was doing it. I narrow my eyes at him, a bit annoyed he can still see right through me. It's something we used to share. I could have told you everything there was to know about Bohdan Novotnak.

The good: that this steadfast, patient, endlessly compassionate man lives behind all those features that look like they were made from stone and could cut it, too; that he's got this dry sense of humour, and even though he doesn't speak often, you're so, so lucky when he does. That he swears in this funny mix of English and Czech when he's angry. That you'll never beat him at chess because he's more patient than you. That he always holds the door open for others, and he always waits to make sure you've gotten inside safely when he drops you off somewhere. That he learned to count to six in five languages. That he loves his grandmother more than anyone on the planet—except for, maybe, the time he spent loving me.

The bad—there's really not much, and it's only bad because I wish he could see himself the way I do: He holds himself to impossibly high standards, and I've seen him break more hockey sticks than I think his equipment manager liked when he didn't perform to those standards.

But when he cut open his head, I think all those things bled out onto the ice and he faded away, something a bit like a ghost.

And I don't know anything about ghosts.

But when he grins at me, under the sunlight and just one person in a sea of people, he doesn't look like a ghost. He looks more corporeal than I've seen him in the last three years. "Do you think I have a sensuous mouth, Sloan?"

"I don't think there's anything sensuous about you." I angle my head. "Everything was always quite . . . hard."

His grin shifts to a smirk. "It's a good thing we scrapped the strike system. You'd be losing."

"Shut up." I smile softly, and I wonder if he can see the way the corners furl downward, a bit wilted, a bit sad.

Because I did lose.

So did he.

Another teenager knocks into me, sprinting by with a pool floatie around their waist. Bohdan's hands find my shoulders again, his jaw tenses, and he looks like he's about to tell them off, but they're already gone.

"You okay?" His thumb presses into my shoulder, and I feel it—the electricity that might live in him, maybe his eyes, because they're the colour of a storm, after all, going through all my limbs.

"Fine." I nod, offering him a tight smile and stepping back from his grip a bit later than I should. "We should move. It's growing hazardous just standing here."

Bohdan's fingers flex against the empty space I used to occupy, and he nods, shoving his hands in his pockets again.

But when we round the corner, we come to the end of this section of the deck.

And there's a giant neon sign flashing above the thoroughfare.

Below Zero
Ice Skating

It's just a skating rink on a cruise ship. Something for children, probably.

Nothing like the arenas we spent time in.

But my eyes find Bohdan, and it hurts all the same.

He rolls his shoulders back, eyes flashing with something that looks a lot like pain, and he stands, stoic and still, wonderful and lovely, but horrible all the same, looking back at something he used to have.

"Do you want to go in?" I whisper.

He nods, muscles in his neck taut, and one hand hovers above his sunglasses still hanging on the collar of his shirt, like he's debating putting them back on. He runs it through his hair instead, sending the golden-brown waves everywhere, one curling over his ear and another dropping down on his forehead right along the scar.

It's a practiced move. Intentional, and I know he must do it a lot—know just how to hide it in plain sight whenever he needs to.

The cool air and distinct smell of ice permeates everything when Bohdan pushes the door open. One palm against the glass, his arm angled upwards and all the muscles tense.

I smile gently at him, and duck under his arm, careful not to breathe. The last thing I need is to smell him, too.

It's a small rink in comparison to what Bohdan was used to, just a pad of circular ice with surrounding stands and banners hanging down from the ceiling, advertising the different events and shows they host. Enough room to move, but I can't imagine how crowded it gets.

And somehow, maybe because we're at a popular port destination or there's a talent show happening on board somewhere—right now, it's empty.

There's a skate rental stand to our left, with an employee in the standard black polo, the cruise line embroidered on the left breast in gold stitching.

He's got his feet kicked up, one hand behind his head, the other scrolling aimlessly on his phone. His eyes flick to us when the door shuts quietly, and he has to do a double take, practically falling when he hurries to sit up, straightening papers on his desk.

"Sorry—sorry. We haven't been busy today." He flushes, sitting up straight and folding his hands demurely. He can't be more than eighteen.

"It's okay." I smile softly. "We just wanted out of the sun for a bit. Can we—is the rink open?"

I glance away from the attendant when I say it. Bohdan hasn't said anything, and I'm a bit scared to look.

It's just a sheet of ice—but it's not, not really.

One hand grips his jaw before he presses his fingers to his temple. He gives a jerk of his head before he looks at me, just a strained smile and sad eyes.

"You can skate, if you want," the attendant says, scrambling out of his chair, the flash of his name tag finally visible. Enrique. "Won't you be cold?"

"We're fine," we both say quietly and in unison.

"Oh. Sure. Yeah. Whatever you want." He nods, holding up a clipboard. "You just need to sign the waiver and I'll get you fitted for—"

Bohdan cuts in. "I can fit the skates."

Enrique blinks before tugging on the end of his curls. He nods again. "Sure, yeah. Okay. I mean, that's not strictly allowed but . . . if you sign the waiver and promise not to tell."

"We won't tell." I smile again, trying to go for encouraging, but I can't really take my eyes off Bohdan.

If this was a movie—it might cut to a sad, tragic montage of what Bohdan sees.

I don't need the visual.

I know what he's looking at when he stares out onto the empty ice.

His whole life. His first dream. His first love, and maybe his greatest love as it turned out.

Blood.

Crimson, pooling along the ice and suffocating all those beautiful sparkles that reflect off the surface of a clean sheet.

The two of us drowning in it.

Bohdan's eyes pinch closed, and I can't help it—I walk behind him, dropping my chin to his shoulder, wrapping my arms around his chest. His hands find my forearms, and he drops his cheek to the crown of my head.

It's a gesture worth more than one strike, certainly.

But everything gets so quiet—the arena, my heart, my brain.

I can't hear anything.

Just Bohdan's breathing. It turns ragged for a second, and I have to squeeze my eyes shut.

But it feels a bit like, maybe nothing could hurt either of us again while we're standing there together.

Certainly not more than we've hurt ourselves.

I don't know how long we stand there, but Enrique clears his throat and awkwardly asks if we still want to skate.

Leaving Bohdan staring out at the ice, I sign the waiver for both of us, and Enrique cranes his neck, like he's looking down at my feet before he starts piling pairs of skates haphazardly onto the desk.

"Can I see them?" Bohdan asks quietly, coming to stand beside me, running a hand over the back of his neck.

"Oh, uh—yeah, sure, why not?" Enrique blinks, holding his palms out like he's presenting Bohdan the skates.

It's one of those surreal moments in your life—where it really does feel possible to be two places at once.

I'm here, on this cruise ship docked in the Mediterranean, skin pebbling against the cool air of the rink, watching a thirty-year-old Bohdan run his thumb along skate blade after skate blade, pushing down on the spurs, moving the tongues back and forth, and tugging on the laces.

I sit down, kicking off my sandals and extending my feet. Bohdan's sliding socks with the cruise emblem up my feet, followed by skates with laces he ties and tugs, rotates every which way until he decides they're perfect and sits beside me to do the same with his.

Our thighs just touch, the muscles in his tensing and stretching as he tightens the laces.

My hands lie flat against my thighs, somehow too warm for the temperature of the rink.

But I'm there, too.

Eighteen and watching a twenty-year-old boy make all these same movements, not at all clumsy like most boys are.

Tying up my skates and telling me I'm beautiful. Trying to impress me.

Falling in love and staring down the barrel of the rest of my life.

In both places, he stands first, holding a hand out to me.

In that old, forgotten, lovely place of youth—he keeps his hand in mine.

In this one, he drops it, making a fist, and tips his chin towards the empty ice before asking, words all hesitant and rough, "Sloan . . . can I—do you mind?"

I shake my head, voice soft. "Go ahead. Please."

Bohdan exhales, maybe a bit relieved, and he stares at me, grey eyes unblinking, before a muscle feathers in his cheek.

He turns, hopping over the boards with the grace of someone who's spent years doing this thing—who could have been doing it just yesterday—and then he's gone.

He's just a blur. A beautiful one. But a blur.

"Holy shit. He's fucking fast," Enrique mutters before whistling.

"He is." I smile, so wide I think my cheeks might split open and every good thing that's ever happened to me might spill over the jagged edges and find its way to the ice to be with that man who might also be in two places at once.

I lose count of how many times he skates by.

I lose count of the tears, too. But I can taste the salt of them on my smile.

It's this funny thing that's haunted me—a question I never really got an answer to, even back then. Whether he could still skate the same, could still do this thing he loved so much.

And right now, he looks like nothing's ever hurt him.

He stops, abrupt and with more precision than I've ever managed to do anything, sending a spray of ice over the boards just as I'm wiping my cheeks.

Bohdan inhales, not because he's winded. He hardly looks like he's worked up a sweat.

He looks impossibly happy.

Impossibly relieved, actually.

He steps towards the boards just as I do. His arms wrap around me when mine find his neck, one tangling in the waves curling there.

Bohdan takes another rough inhale, and everything around me blurs, I forget really, how badly he hurt me, and I bury my face in the crook of his shoulder.

"I never thought I'd get to see you do that again," I whisper into his skin. Warm, and already damp with my tears.

His lips find my temple, pressing roughly. "I never thought I'd get to do it again, either."

Bohdan's hands tighten against my skin, before one moves up and down my spine.

I count each sweep of his palm.

One. Two. Three.

His palm stills, pressing down against the base of my neck before he starts again.

I hear a lot of things when he does—not just the numbers.

I hear all the ways I've never been enough, but I hear these other quiet, tiny things, too.

Facts and truth he's given me over the years when I've struggled to fall asleep.

The way he loved my brain enough for the both of us.

But I can't stay here, listening to them. I know that much.

"You haven't ... skated?" I pull back, looking up at him. Beautiful, illuminated under the rink lights.

He gives a slow shake of his head. "Sometimes. . . but not like that. When I was . . . trying to rehab and recondition, I couldn't go fast enough for long enough before I got dizzy."

It's more than he's ever said to me about it.

It was like pulling teeth, trying to get him to tell me anything, and it turned out my hands weren't enough for those extractions, so somewhere along the way, I gave up.

"Are you dizzy now?" I ask quietly, a bit scared he might shut down again and I'll never know.

"No." He gives another slow shake of his head. "Not at all."

I nod, scrunching my nose against the tears. "Why don't you go again? I'll watch."

He might have hurt me impossibly, but as much as I don't have it in me to pretend not to know him, I can't pretend not to want every dream he's ever had to come true.

But Bohdan stares, and I think his eyes trace the freckles on my cheek, before he murmurs, "I'd rather see if I could skate with you again."

"Okay." I sniff, finally taking a step back from the boards and untangling my hands from where they were gripped around his neck.

He holds a hand up, and before I can think better of it, I interlace my fingers with his, and he skates slowly beside the boards as I walk to the entrance, a bit unsteady on the blades, like I was all those years ago.

His fingers tense against mine when I step onto the ice. "I can pull you."

"Okay," I say again, and he lifts my other hand, palms pressed together for just a minute, and then my fingers are in his and he's skating.

I'm in two places at once again—then and here.

I don't try to stop the tears, I let them fall, sniffing occasionally, never taking my eyes off Bohdan.

He doesn't take his off me, either. He skates backward, legs crossing over one another, blades slicing across the ice that's only ever belonged to him.

"You said you haven't skated like that . . . do you not skate?" I'm as afraid to ask as I am of the answer.

"I go out sometimes. But not like that. I've never tried to push my body again." Bohdan shrugs, rounding the corner with ease. "If I can't have the real thing, I don't want it."

"Is that why you're still alone?" I ask, a half attempt at humour, but it's a real question.

His eyes narrow on me, cheekbones sharpening. "It's why I'll be alone forever, Sloan."

He'd rather be alone than be with you, my brain whispers.

I snort to try and cover the sob.

I squeeze my eyes shut with a sharp jerk of my head. *Go away*, I want to whisper back.

The way I used to when I was little and didn't understand why or how my brain could be so cruel.

I focus on the feeling of the ice beneath my skates. Bohdan pulling me along, and I'm so sure he won't let me fall that I keep my eyes closed and I breathe in and out.

He doesn't say anything, but his thumb draws small circles across the back of my hand.

I open my eyes after I think we've done one lap of the rink.

And I must be back in time—or maybe I'm being slowly torn in two by the way Bohdan looks at me—just like he used to, before he became someone who could hurt me.

"Why'd you try today?"

He shrugs again, indifferent. "You've already seen me at my worst. I did the worst thing to you that you can do to a person. Why would you care if I couldn't?"

"I'd care." I say it so, so quietly, I don't even know if he heard me, or if I even wanted him to—but his eyes shutter, and his grip tightens on me before he swallows, blinking them back open.

Bohdan glances over his shoulder when we round the corner, blades of his skates slicing the surface in movements that still look practiced. "You're finally moving home."

"Yes."

He looks back at me, a faint smile, and my heart stutters when the left side kicks up just a bit more. "What are you teaching? Researching?"

"Teaching. A course on the intersection of archaeology and medicine." It all sort of tumbles out before my brain even has the chance to tell me that it's not the type of thing regular people care about. It would be right—maybe most people wouldn't care. But I know Bohdan will, and he's not regular. "There's so much we don't know about how medical practices were developed, how they were used . . . how they were influenced by the power structures of past societies. You know, recently, we've found medical instruments that were used by Roman surgeons. There are some really cool field study opportunities, and who's to say there isn't evidence for old psychiatric practices just waiting to be dug up?"

His fingers flinch, like he might want to let go. He doesn't—he sort of rolls his right shoulder back, angling his head, and I wonder if he wants to touch the scar. If that's become the type of habit for him counting is for me—one you do when you're in so much pain, you'll do anything to try and make it stop.

But he smiles, sad and resigned. "You never did get to go on one of your digs."

"No," I say quietly.

I don't want to wake my brain up. I don't want the past and the rules and the way he broke my heart to hear. I don't want them to stomp all over the highlight reel—the reasons I never did.

I could have gone for a semester, in the summer, anytime really. But I wanted to be with Bohdan more.

I didn't want to miss a single game with Tia. I didn't want to miss the nights in their house afterwards, crushed red cups and sticky floors, laughter—so much laughter that even though it was so, so loud and Tia had to get me earplugs, everything was quiet.

I didn't want a whole semester even further away from Seattle.

I didn't want to miss a single whisper, a single smile, a single laugh—I didn't want to miss any of it with him.

And it never occurred to me until much, much later that I was giving something up for something else—something I wouldn't get to keep.

"I'm happy for you, Sloan," Bohdan says, voice rough. "I'm sorry that you followed me and that . . . that it didn't work out."

He stumbles a bit over the last few words, and I do, too, but his grip doesn't.

I pull my head back, blinking. I've tried to reorganize and remap the whole thing in my brain—that it's better to have loved and lost than to have not loved at all. But those words tip the bookcase over, the one where I keep all those memories of him and me, shiny, sparkling trophies of this world-ending, heart-stopping love I was so lucky to have, and all of the new directions on my map twist and turn, and they lead me back to the place I try to avoid—the one that tells me it all must be true, that it was never enough.

That I made it all up.

That he doesn't think it was worth it and it never was, and maybe he never loved me anyway, because how could he love someone like me? Someone bad and awful and horrible and entirely lacking.

"You think it didn't work out?" I whisper the words, stumbling over them and blinking too much because I can feel my heart rate pickup.

Bohdan just shakes his head, and I think there's a point, but I must be missing it. I can't really see anything, the edges of my vision go fuzzy, and he asks, "When was the last time you said I love you?"

I don't want to think about that. I squeeze my eyes shut again, whispering, "Before something very, very bad happened."

"Something very, very bad did happen. You're right. But it wasn't—" He's saying it in this maddeningly patient way, how he used to, when he was trying to help me. But he can't possibly be trying to help me. I'm not worth loving, and I'm certainly not worth helping.

He swallows, finally letting go of one of my hands to scrub his jaw, but he doesn't slow down our speed. We loop past Enrique at the desk, back on his phone again, when Bohdan says, "It wasn't what you think. The worst thing that happened to me wasn't losing my career, Sloan. It was losing you." He jerks his head, grabbing my hand again. "If I had one wish, it wouldn't be to skate again. It wouldn't be for hockey. It wouldn't be for a stupid fucking game. It would be for you."

I can't breathe.

Or maybe I just don't.

But I do manage to say, "I'm sorry—sorry, I'm just—no."

And then I run.

Sloan

At least, I try in the skates.

He's always been quicker than me—an above-average muscle composition will do that to a person—and he's on me in a second, beside me with a hand suspended in midair just above my lower back so he can catch me if I fall, and I might, the way I'm stumbling around, just trying to get back to the bench.

"Breathe," he instructs when I take a shaky inhale.

I don't want to listen to him, but I do because my body has only ever been able to respond to two things: whatever vitriol my brain likes to spew, and Bohdan Novotnak's voice.

The tip of my skate catches as I step off the ice, and before I can even brace myself against the boards, he's got an arm around my stomach, the other hand pressing against my low back when I stumble towards the bench.

"Breathe, Zlatíčko," he whispers, and he's much too close. I can feel the ghost of his mouth kiss my ear.

"Don't." I push away, hands scrambling at his arms and trying to get so far away from him but it hurts so much, and the only place I can really go is the bench.

I sit down, fingers wrapping around the edge of the wood instead of trying to untie my skates. It's cool against my palms, and I try to focus on that, but it's impossible when he's right here and every bad thing I've ever thought about myself sits so heavy on my chest it might as well be a piano.

Instead, it's the words *I love you*, followed by *I'm leaving* over and over and over again.

"Okay." He nods, dropping into a crouch in front of the bench and getting to work on my skates.

I love you.

I'm leaving.

I love you.

I'm leaving.

I love you.

I'm leaving.

"Woah—is she—are you alright? Do you need an incident form?" I think Enrique stands to attention again, legs swinging off his desk and scrambling through stacks of paper on his desk.

"We're fine." Bohdan doesn't look away from me.

He unties my laces in movements of three—a tug in the middle, and one more on either end, right by the eye.

I don't think he realizes he's doing it—it becomes unconscious when you know someone the way we know each other, to mirror them the way he mirrors my breathing. Three seconds in, three seconds out.

He's gentle when he pulls my skates off, careful like he always was with me except for that one time, and his rough hands feel soft when he rolls the socks off, they're reverent almost, when he slides my sandals back on.

I go to stand when he's done—but he sits beside me, stretching his own legs out, and he places a hand over mine, still white-knuckling the edge of the bench. "Wait, please."

I nod, blinking.

I should go—I shouldn't wait for him. I should run, leave him behind the way he did me.

But my palms tingle, and the thoughts start.

They follow me the whole way back to our suite.

So does Bohdan.

Right behind me, hand hovering between my shoulder blades.

The thoughts hover, too.

All over me, and they puncture my skin with each step, each movement he takes to mirror mine.

Vile.

A brush of his thumb across the neck of my tank top to let me know he's there.

Pathetic.

A whisper of his voice, telling me to keep breathing.

Really fucking wretched, actually.

His hand pushing open the door to the suite.

So easy to leave.

Just us, alone here in this stupid, giant room with those giant windows that look a bit too much like the ones back in our old home.

"Keep breathing, and tell me what I said." Bohdan leans against the back of the couch, kicking a leg up, lines of his face set, somehow still endlessly patient with me.

"You lied," I whisper, hands clenching in and out of fists.

"I lied?"

"You lied. You said that if you had one wish—it wouldn't be for hockey again. It wouldn't be to skate, it wouldn't be for your career." I sniff with a tiny shake of my head, tears spilling down over my cheeks. "You said it would be for me."

"That's not a lie, Sloan. That's a fact." He shakes his head slowly.

"Don't you dare." I point at him and try to clench my teeth so my sob doesn't escape but it does. Loud and ugly and awful and taking up too much space, just like me. He's never lied to me before, not about a fact. But there's no way this one can possibly be true. "Don't you dare throw *a fact* in my face. It can't be a fact, Bohdan, because you left. You left when I was trying, so, so hard to help you. I did everything I could—I learned so much and I spent so much time on the internet and I brought home acupressure mats and I rearranged our furniture and I—"

His nostrils flare, and he bites down on the inside of his cheek with a slow shake of his head. "You were drowning in your own goddamn brain, Sloan."

I narrow my eyes, still pointing at him. "So what, you decided to shove my fucking head under the water for good measure?"

"It's not that simple!" Bohdan throws his hands wide before scrubbing his face and bringing two fingers to his temple, right at the precipice of the scar. He slams them there, punctuating each word. "My fucking brain wasn't working, Sloan! I couldn't—I was useless! I couldn't fucking do anything, except hurt you."

I'm not a resentful person.

At least, not actively.

And it's not an emotion I'd have ever thought I'd associate with Bohdan, but it's what bubbles up right now, just there, right under the surface, and it's horribly ugly, uglier than most of my own thoughts.

I give him a tight smile, and I wish my words were biting, but they aren't. They're just quiet and sad. "Well, you were certainly good at that."

Bohdan's eyes pinch closed, and he scrubs his face. "Don't I know it."

We're not very far apart—maybe a few feet. Him, propped up against the couch in this way that seemed like he was trying to be patient with me, but now I wonder if he's just trying to keep himself upright.

Me, standing here staring at him with the ocean visible just beyond him through those giant floor-to-ceiling windows, sparkling in this way that looks like possibility but actually might be cruelty.

"Why?" I whisper.

He presses a fist to his mouth.

He's not going to answer. But I'm resentful and sad and maybe a bit spiteful and I need to know, I need to know whether it really was me at the end of the day, that everything I tried wasn't enough and that it never would be.

"You said—you promised this morning. You said before we got back, you'd tell me why. That you'd give me everything I wanted."

I don't tell him everything I've ever wanted stands in front me with wide grey eyes, full lips parted with his rough breathing, a living thief hidden under tumbling golden waves on his forehead.

"Before we go back," he says, matter-of-fact. "I'll tell you before we go back."

"Now." I try to stand up taller, stand my ground, demand this thing I think I'm owed. But one of my proverbial feet slips on the edge of that awful hole of ugly things between us, and I add, practically begging, "Please."

"Just give me these next few days, Sloan. I promise I'll tell you, I just, please—these next few days of you . . . it's—" He pushes off the couch, whatever words he was going to say tumbling into nothing, and he closes those few feet between us, tucking my hair behind my ears before he cups my cheek, thumb curving over the smattering of freckles and pressing in on each one. "I wasn't lying, Sloan. In any life, in any world, in any universe—it'd be you."

I let my eyes flutter closed, and I lean into his hand. I shouldn't—because as good and lovely as it feels, it's maybe one of the most painful things that I've ever experienced.

But then he says his next words, and I think I've fallen down the hill and broken every bone in my body along the way.

"I might have left, but I never stopped loving you." His hand moves to grip my chin, and he tips my face up to his. "That's a fact."

"You're lying." My words sound like I've fallen, too, maybe caused quite a bit of irreparable internal damage along the way—cracking and sad and like I'm in so, so much pain.

"I'm not." He gives another resigned shake of his head. "Lie to me, then. The way you think I lied to you."

I say the only thing I can think of. The biggest lie I could ever tell. "I don't love you anymore."

The blow lands, and so does the duality of it.

His eyes flash, his jaw tenses before he swallows, and I can see it all over him—the way those words hurt and heal him all at the same time.

"I'd like to be alone now." I inhale, taking a small step back.

Another lie, and I think he knows, and I think this one hurts him, too, but he bites down on his lip, nodding, before he presses a rough kiss to my forehead and listens to me.

Sloan

Then – Seattle

My life changes forever on a Monday night.

Bohdan's does, too, in a different, but all-encompassing, giant way just the same.

It's a normal, regular game early on in the season. A team they've played before. I wasn't even planning on coming to this one because I'm teaching a seminar this week, but he asked—all formality and beautiful eyes and a smile I'd crawl for. One brush of his mouth against mine, this promise of all the time we'd get to spend together later before he leaves for a road trip, wrapped up in those navy sheets that make Bohdan look more otherworldly than usual, and I was done for.

But he packed my textbooks in my bag for me and left them by the door.

I've seen Bohdan get hit before—all kinds of hits really, cross-checking, bodychecking, legal and illegal contact.

I've even seen him get a concussion before. More than once.

It's not even the first time I've seen him hit the boards.

228

But nothing ever quite like this.

It happens too fast for me to even really notice. I'm more focused on the textbook in front of me, propped up on my knees, trying to concentrate on my proposal instead of the ambient chatter and noise of all the other partners sitting around in the lounge with me.

They're up 3–1, and he's already scored. He looks great, he always does, and I think it's safe to be something other than ever present, ever vigilant.

I see it out of the corner of my eye, and I flinch when he's smashed into the boards from behind. There's a collective intake of breath around the room when his helmet smashes into the glass at this weird angle—right at the precipice of his visor and the plastic.

The whistle blows, and a fight starts somewhere on the ice.

But he doesn't skate away. It looks sort of like the player who hit him was holding him upright—Bohdan staggers, and he looks a bit like he's trying to brace himself against the glass before his knees buckle.

It's when he hits the ice that I see the blood.

A small rivulet smeared across the inside of his visor that I can't even be sure is there, until it's joined by the rest—this crimson pool that somehow looks stark and beautiful against the ice, sparkling away on that giant television screen in the lounge, while Bohdan doesn't move.

I think I start bleeding with him.

Bohdan

Then – Seattle

It was just a bad hit.

An unlucky angle, the doctor said.

The way I couldn't brace myself or turn properly because I didn't see it coming. The way my temple smashed against the corner of my helmet. The way it ricocheted off the boards, and the way my brain got knocked around again for good measure when I hit the ice.

It wasn't the first time it got knocked around out there, but unfortunately for me, it was the last.

A million tiny things that happened in exactly the right way at exactly the wrong time.

Someone who works for me sues the equipment company, because there was a tiny flaw in the helmet that shouldn't have existed. Something about the polypropylene foam.

But I can't really bring myself to care about anything.

Because I can't fucking skate without getting dizzy.

I can't concentrate long enough to track a play, let alone try to make one.

The impossibly bright lights that once did me a kindness and shone a spotlight down on a beautiful girl with ebony hair and blue eyes decide they're done being nice. I can't even get on the ice under them anymore.

They're too bright, and it's too loud.

I try a lot of things to get it back.

I sprint on treadmills with oxygen masks strapped to my face to try and build my endurance again. I see all the specialists that money can buy. I try shorter shifts on the ice. Alternating games.

But it's never the same, and neither am I, so with the girl that stupid fucking hockey gave me sitting beside me at a press conference table with lights that make my skull feel like I'm bleeding, I say goodbye.

Because if I can't be great—I don't want it.

And it turns out, I can't be great at anything anymore.

What's that saying? You don't know what you've got till it's gone.

Sloan

Then – Seattle

Bohdan becomes a ghost right in front of me.

I watch him fade away each day, and I do my very best to hold on.

I hold on for dear life, actually.

Not even for my life—for his. For his life that could still be beautiful if he'd just let it.

For the apartment we have together and the beautiful views of the Sound stretching out, sparkling and endless, like all the plans we had he doesn't seem to want anymore.

Things we could still have: minutes and hours and days and years together.

He's here, living and breathing and still the love of my life even if he never gets to lace up another pair of skates.

But it's not enough.

I try not to blame him. Maybe that's what happens when a cut makes you bleed, and it takes your dreams with it.

Bohdan

I'm on my seventeenth lap around the ice—the same number I wore my entire life until I wasn't in the business of wearing numbers anymore—when I hear the banging of a hand on a plexiglass board.

It's not a sound most people could recognize instantly, but it's as intimately familiar to me as Sloan's voice is.

Talon whistles loudly, a smile painting his face, popping both his dimples, and he bangs on the boards again when I stop, sending a spray of ice towards them.

Jay gives a jerk of his head before holding out both his arms to me. "Jesus Christ, you're still so fucking fast, man."

A brow lifts on my forehead. "Doesn't really do me any good anymore, though."

I hug him anyway, Talon joins in, and the same way it did with Sloan out on this ice earlier—it feels a bit like I'm back in time.

"Once-in-a-generation kind of talent," Talon offers, pulling back in consideration. "Could skate away from a serial killer pretty fucking quick, if you needed."

"When would he need?" Jay presses his tongue to his cheek.

Talon doesn't answer and glances towards the desk, hooking a thumb towards me and the somehow still empty ice. "Can we join him?"

"Knock yourselves out." Enrique waves a hand, eyes glued to his phone and feet propped back up on the desk again, before his gaze snaps to us. "Not literally. That's a lot of paperwork."

Talon claps both his hands around my shoulders, giving me a small shake. "Don't worry, he's pretty familiar with that concept, don't think he'll be giving a repeat performance."

"Rough," I tell him flatly.

"Brutal." Jay nods.

Enrique doesn't bother asking if they need help with the skates.

Talon takes way too long deciding on his, weighing the merits of a pair of CCMs that look like they've seen better days and a pair of Bauer's that look like they haven't been broken in.

Jay grabs a pair at random, even though out of the three of us, he should take the most care, and we've done two lazy laps around the ice by the time Talon hops over the boards and takes off like it's a race.

It does turn into one.

It turns into multiple.

It turns into stupid drills and jumping over pylons on the ice and generally more dicking around than Jay should probably be doing. His legs are still worth something, after all.

Some families come in, looking at the rink like they might want to use it or test it out for their kids, take one look at us—three grown men behaving like the eighteen-year-olds we were once upon a time—and they change their minds.

I don't really have it in me to feel bad.

It's one of the only times I've felt free in over three years.

It's not possible for me to forget what happened with Sloan earlier—every single interaction I've ever had with her is categorized neatly in my brain. The absolutely fucking mind-blowing, the wonderful, the good, the mundane, the painful, and the outright bad.

I'd somehow file what happened earlier under two categories, diametrically opposed in their definitions: wonderful and painful.

It both makes me smile and makes me feel like I'm being fucking stabbed to think about it while I'm out here again.

I came straight here when she lied for the second time in as many seconds and said she wanted to be alone, when really I felt like dropping to my knees and telling her every truth I've ever known to get her to believe me again.

But that's in no one's best interest.

I can't give her what she wants, at least not in a way that's going to make sense to a brain like hers—as wonderful as I think it is, it does a pretty great job of hurting her—and I was a selfish piece of shit when I asked for more days of her time when she's already wasted so many on me.

Jay pulls up to a quick stop beside me, runs a hand through his hair, the shadows of all his tattoos stark from the sun. The gold on his rings glints, and he tugs absentmindedly on the chain that's slipped out from underneath his shirt.

"How do you feel?" he asks quietly, staring and thoughtful.

I nod slowly, considering. "A bit great, a bit pretty shit."

He tips his chin and his eyes find the scar, hidden behind damp hair, matted to my forehead. "Head alright? That's a lot of exertion."

"Nah. Head's fine." I'm still operating under the good graces of a triptan. I run a hand through my hair out of habit. "Has more to do with the first time I was out here today."

Jay cocks his head, and he looks like he's about to ask when Talon coats us with a spray of ice.

"I'm telling you, we should really do a podcast. We could do YouTube and have some of our episodes on the ice!" Talon pants, slightly out of breath with damp hair curling around his ears, before he blinks, asking, "You skated without us?"

"With Sloan," I clarify.

And it might seem dumb, but it's a necessary clarification, because I can see why they'd want to do it together.

She's the only exception.

Talon nods, slowly, looking for once in his life like he's chewing over his words, when Jay exhales, asking with a shrug, "And how'd the re-creation of your first date go?"

I give him a flat look. "Well, I was out here alone, wasn't I?"

"Not good, then." Jay nods thoughtfully, bottom lip extending.

But Talon shakes his head, pointing at me. "Quit fucking her around."

"I'm not fucking her around," I say, irritated. "I might be a piece of shit, Talon, but I wouldn't do that to her."

"You're not a piece of shit," Jay mutters, but he scrubs his face like he's exasperated.

Talon raises one hand, shrugging. "Bringing her skating isn't fucking her around?"

"It wasn't my idea!" My voice raises with my hands, and I catch Enrique looking up from his phone over at the desk, but one sideways glance from Talon and he's back to pretending to be busy again. "We

236

were walking around the ship because we made this stupid deal to pretend we were, I don't know, practically strangers, and neither of us could keep up with our end—"

"Wonder why." Jay raises a brow.

I feel a bit like flipping him off, but I cut him a look instead. "And we said we'd just . . . *not* pretend not to know each other. I asked her for the next few days, and I told her I'd give her everything she wanted before we got off the fucking ship—"

"Things you won't even explain to us, good thinking!" Talon flashes me a sarcastic thumbs-up.

I do flip Talon off before continuing, "And she saw the rink. It was her idea to come in. It was all going fine until I said I was sorry things didn't work out."

Talon's lips pull back, and Jay looks towards the ceiling, groaning.

"Didn't work out?" Talon's eyes sharpen before he exhales a scoff. "What the fuck is wrong with you?"

"Aside from the obvious?" I push my hair back with one hand and point at the scar with the other.

He waves a hand, like he's swatting the whole thing away. "Nah, that was like three years ago. I'm fucking sick of that. Quit using it as an excuse not to find happiness. You're not fucking up just your life, Bohdan. It's hers, too."

"Maybe I don't deserve happiness." I tug on the ends of my hair. I don't, not for the way I treated her and the person I became. "Maybe I don't deserve her."

Jay sighs. "No one, and I repeat no one, has ever loved someone the way you loved her."

Jay's only ever had one real love: hockey. He loves us, and he loves his dads, but it's not the same and I don't expect him to understand what it's like to love someone and to watch them be torn apart at your hands.

I shake my head. "I've said it once, I'll say it again, and that'll be the last time. Neither of you lived in that house. You sure as shit didn't live in my brain. I was not good to her. I couldn't take care of her. I couldn't take care of myself."

The lines of Talon's face change when he shakes his head, all contempt. "My sister said she found your name by the word *masochist*, but I'd bet my last endorsement deal you'd find it beside the word *martyr*, too."

In a weird turn of events, Jay takes the final shot, and it's a stupidly simple way of putting it, but I'm not sure it matters, the damage is done.

He's got this weird air of maddening patience about him, and he claps my shoulder. "What would you say to Sloan if she told you she felt like she was an unfit partner because her brain worked a bit differently from everyone else's?"

I don't say anything, and he widens his eyes, angling his head forward in wait.

"That I wouldn't want her to have a different brain. That it's what makes her exactly the way I love her."

I'm sure it's what she would have said to me, if I'd ever given her the chance.

Talon taps the centre of my forehead. "You've got a different brain now. But it's still yours, at the end of the day."

Pulling back—he's going to give me another migraine if he keeps tapping like that—I mutter, "Jesus, maybe you really should think about that talk show."

"It's the retirement, I'm telling you." Talon smiles, running a hand through sweat-damp hair. "Maybe some of it can rub off on you."

"Uh—are you guys almost done?"

We glance over to the boards. Enrique's hanging over them before he points towards the end of the rink where another attendant waits with a small ice resurfacer. "The performers need to warm up for the show tonight and you carved up their ice."

"Fuck yeah, we did." Talon claps both of our shoulders. "Let's go grab a drink, it's disco night."

"I actually have just the outfit." Jay smiles when he skates off, dropping to the bench to undo his laces.

"I'll bet you do." Talon's eyes find the chain hanging around Jay's neck before he glances at me, a bit of remorse living in the sad bend of his smile. "We okay?"

I tug on my laces, look at him, and nod. "Yeah, we're okay."

And we are—okay. I'd categorize the time skating with my best friends, something I never thought I'd have again, the same way I do almost everything related to hockey, skating, and Sloan now.

Maybe that's just my life now.

Wonderful, but fucking painful.

Sloan

Then – Seattle

It's cruel how quickly a home can become just a house.

How one of your favourite things about it can become this suffocating thing that traps you.

I used to love the big floor-to-ceiling windows in our apartment.

I loved the view of the Sound, of the pier, of the mountains stretching in the distance.

I loved the way our love made the whole apartment feel.

Jay doesn't like to visit because he says he feels like a bird in a glass cage up here. Trapped.

But I've never felt like that.

I've always felt free up here. Not like I was in this bizarre glass box, with everyone looking in. I've always felt like I was looking out at possibility.

Like we could go anywhere and be anything and nothing really mattered because Bohdan and I live here together with all our love.

It turns out, though, that things do matter. And there were things waiting out there to hurt us.

In this case, they were a weird hit into the boards, a malfunctioning helmet, and a fall to the ice.

Those things did turn this place into a cage or a box or a maze or something else awful and horrible, and they locked us in.

Just Bohdan's brain and mine, and I'm starting to wonder if those are two things that should ever be alone together anymore.

I'm trapped now—sitting straight up on the couch, eyes not where they should be, on my comps papers, but flicking back and forth between the front door and the clock on the microwave.

He's late.

He was supposed to skate again today. For the first time in weeks.

If I was a different person who didn't have a brain predisposed to cruelty, I might be able to pay attention to the tiny bits of starlight winking to life in me, saying that maybe, maybe he's late because it went so well and he's still skating and skating and skating, setting new speed records and carving up fresh ice. Smiling the way he used to.

That maybe he's the Bohdan I used to know. Whose head didn't hurt and who liked sunshine and bright things and didn't mind loud noises and got to spend his nights doing the thing he was born to do. Who didn't seem so horribly broken and sad all the time.

But I know by the way the door opens—a slow, sad, resigned creak that echoes across the apartment and stomps all over hope I didn't really believe in—it didn't go well.

I ask anyway. "How did it go?"

He drops his bag, and I think if it wasn't weighed down with so much equipment and unmet expectations, he might kick it clear across the apartment.

He slams the door instead, wincing when he does.

"Not good." He doesn't look at me when he says it.

Bohdan used to look at me all the time—like I was the only thing worth looking at really, and now, his eyes never land on one thing for very long, least of all me.

I've started to wonder if maybe I'm somehow this ugly reminder of the big, bad thing that happened to him.

But one of his neurologists said that sometimes, after head trauma, your ocular responses can shift.

I don't think she quite understood the question. I wasn't asking about his vision, the refraction of light, his pupils, or his eye movements.

I was asking why the man I love so much, who I think still loves me, can't look at me anymore.

"Do you want—" I try to ask if he wants to talk, even though I already know the answer.

"No, Sloan. I don't want." He walks right by me when he says it, like I'm not here at all—and maybe I'm not. He goes to our bedroom, and he slams that door, too.

I think another lock clicks somewhere out there in the hall, and I wonder how long it takes to suffocate on stale air that used to feel like love.

Bohdan

Turns out Jay does have the perfect outfit for disco night.

Some sort of short-sleeve button-up with brown stripes and jarring slashes of orange and yellow.

It's definitely psychosomatic, but the colours make my head start to hurt.

He pulls it off though, somehow.

Talon kicks back in his chair, curls of his hair lifting in the breeze coming off the ocean. He angles his glass towards Jay. "Dress code was optional."

"Never met a theme night I didn't like." Jay shrugs, the ice in his gin and tonic hitting the crystal when he takes a sip.

"You didn't even read the itinerary." I point towards the shirt. "You just willingly pack shit like that in your suitcase?"

He swipes a hand through his hair, rings glinting under the setting sun. "Vintage is in. Wouldn't expect either of you to know a thing about fashion."

Talon takes offence to that because he's contradictory and ornery about almost anything, even though Jay's right—he doesn't really care about fashion or trends.

I'm not listening—I've been tuning them out for years.

I'm busy craning my neck in a way that's pulling funny and I should probably stop, but we've been sitting on one of the decks at a bar for the last thirty minutes, waiting for Sloan and Tia so we can start Talon's stupid disco night.

The impending threat of a night spent in a loud club with flashing lights and grating music had me taking a pre-emptive propranolol. Not exactly psychiatrist recommended, but neither is a lot of my behaviour—including watching like a fucking hawk so I can see her first when she arrives.

She was in her room with Tia when we got back to the suite, and Talon said I was being weird, lingering around, so he dragged me here.

"What's taking them so long?"

Talon stops whatever tirade he was on about Swedish fashion and glances down at his phone. "Tia texted, says they'll be here in a few minutes."

I nod absentmindedly, still craning my neck.

He eyes me, lip pulling up. "Can you relax? You're going to fucking hurt yourself if you keep doing that."

"I don't like how we left things earlier," I mutter, finally looking back at Talon and Jay.

Jay snorts. "Probably should have thought of that a year and a half ago."

I give him a flat look. "Ha-ha. Thanks for that."

"Is he wrong?" Talon asks, leaning forward, and I think he's about to deliver another sermon I didn't ask for when Tia drops into one of the empty chairs.

She reaches forward, the silver sequins on her dress glinting under the fading sun, grabbing Jay's gin and tonic, taking a sip, and pretending not to notice when he tosses his hands up in exasperation.

"Where's Sloan?" I ask, impatient, hands tightening around my own glass.

Tia arches a brow, thinly veiled displeasure all over her face. "She's still getting ready. She said she needed . . . a bit more time to decide what to wear."

Her eyes flash when she pauses, and mine pinch closed.

"Fuck," I mutter, pressing my fingers to my temple.

"Indeed," Tia says flatly.

"So? People take a long time to decide on their outfits." Talon tips his chin towards Jay. "Look at him. The selection can really carry on."

"Not Sloan." I push to stand. "I'll be right back."

Tia purses her lips. "Haven't you done enough?"

I don't bother to answer—even though it's pretty evident that I have.

All kinds of irreparable damage.

"Bohdan." Tia grabs my arm when I go to walk by, and I glance down at her fingers, pressing down on my wrist, before my eyes flick to her face. Lips turned down, features soft, and all that ire gone from her eyes. She looks impossibly sad. "Don't. Not unless you're going to give her what she wants and really try to fix things. She can't go through it again . . . she doesn't deserve it."

"I know," I tell her, words rough.

It's the understatement of the century.

I'm not really sure what my plan is. Nothing's changed, I can't give her what she wants because the truth won't cut it, it's just going to hurt her more and I don't think she's going to understand.

I don't even understand.

I just know I can't sit here on this stupid ship, so close to her suffering.

It wasn't easy after I left—but for a few months, I was on an entirely different continent, and then the other side of the country, so it's not like I could sprint across the stupid decks of this ship, tempted to push children and families and annoying tourists out of the way to get to her the way I do now.

I sprint the entire way back to the stupid suite, and I shout her name the second I open the door.

She doesn't answer.

"Sloan?" I call again, kicking the door shut behind me.

Nothing.

There are too many rooms for five people in this stupid place, and a staircase in the centre of the living room leading to too many more.

But whatever magnet in me that attached to the one that lives in her when I was twenty still works, and I find her right away.

Standing in front of the bathroom mirror, twisting and tugging on an iridescent sequin dress not unlike the one Tia wore, the skin across her chest red.

My hands find the doorway, fingers turning white against the ridges.

I hate seeing her like this.

I always have—but it's worse now, because I made her this way and I can't kiss anything better.

Sloan takes a shaky inhale, batting at the tears on her cheeks before she starts pulling on the dress again.

It pulls on my restraint, too, because I cross the room, wrap a hand around her wrist, gently tugging it back before I roll my fingers off. "What's wrong?"

"I feel—it all feels so big and so loud and so out of control." She stretches her fingers uselessly in space, shifting back and forth on the balls of her feet, her words catching on a sob. "I feel it on my skin. These stupid sequins, they—"

I flash my palms at her in the mirror, hovering above her exposed shoulders, her collarbone and the curve of her chest reflected, scratched and irritated from her constant tugging on the dress.

"May I?" I point towards her shoulders. She blinks at me in the mirror, eyes shining with tears, and she gives me a small nod.

Sloan takes a shuddering inhale when my hands press against her skin, both of my thumbs sweeping in soothing strokes up the side of her neck.

"Do you feel my hands?"

She nods again, but something that looks like an involuntary shake of her head interrupts it. "Yes, but the sequins, this stupid dress—"

"Okay." I press my thumbs down, rubbing my other fingers along the jut of her collarbone. "You don't have to wear it. I'm going to unzip it for you."

She says nothing, but she watches me in the mirror when I lift one hand and I find the top of the zipper, nestled between her shoulder blades.

"Is this alright?"

Sloan swallows, nodding, biting down on her bottom lip.

I focus on the zipper, watching as I tug it down and the teeth separate one by one, revealing more and more slivers of her skin, smooth and glowing from the sun. I'm still standing, but she's brought me to my knees anyway.

I ignore the lace of her bra, the arch of her spine and swell of her hips, the intricate flowers stitched into underwear I have no business looking at, and I clench my jaw when I tug the dress down into a pool around her feet.

"Left foot, Zlatíčko," I instruct, and she lifts it so I can move the dress out of the way. "Right one now."

Closing my eyes, I breathe in and out, pressing a fist to my mouth before I stand, eyes meeting hers again in the mirror before I find a point somewhere over her shoulder and try to focus on the curved rim of the tub in the reflection.

"You can look at me," she whispers, voice laced with tears, but steady and sure.

I do look—and I wish I hadn't.

She's so beautiful I think it might fucking kill me.

I swallow, pinching my eyes closed before I ask, "Do you feel better?"

Sloan tips her head, considering, teeth grazing her bottom lip, and her voice so fucking sad I want to smash the mirror. "It's still—it's all over me, all the time, and I can't get it off."

"What?"

She blinks at me, one tear slipping past her lash line and falling over the pillow of her cheek. "All the ways I wasn't enough for you."

"Sloan—" I think the weight of the whole thing chokes me. It all sits right against my chest, and I don't think I'm going to be able to keep breathing if I don't fix this for her. "You're enough. You always were and you always have been."

"Then why can I feel it? Sitting right here, all over me, all the time, on my skin?" she asks, like it's a literal thing and she's really wondering.

"This skin?" I skate my thumb across her shoulder blade, back up across the lines leading to her neck. "Can I take it off for you?"

"I'm not sure how you'd do that." She chews on the inside of her cheek. "I think it's a part of me now."

"Let me rephrase. Can I show you just how fucking enough you are?"

Sloan inhales, blue eyes going wide. I watch her in the mirror, weighing the merits of me and the way I hurt her against the lie she told me earlier. But she swallows, lips parting, and she nods.

I don't have a plan. I haven't had one since I stood up and ran here.

But I've never really needed one, not when it came to her.

My body somehow knew what to do with hers when I was twenty, and I always knew how to hold her heart properly.

It's pretty easy to pick back up right where we left off.

Not those months where my brain stopped working, but the day I got hurt and all the years before that.

My hands find her waist, fingers digging in before I spin her around.

A tiny gasp in her throat, eyes still wide and her hands suspended above my chest, like she doesn't know where to put them.

I trace the constellation of freckles before dragging my thumb across her lips, pulling on the bottom one and gripping her chin. "Are these new? All weighed down with all those thoughts of not being enough?"

"My lips?" she breathes, blinking at me, one hand coming to rest tentatively right over my heart.

I hope she can feel it beat.

"Yeah, your lips, Zlatíčko. They new, too?"

"Yes," she whispers. "I hate them the most, because they've never touched you."

"I'm going to change that. How does a new first kiss sound to you?"

Those lips part—they're still fucking perfect and I hate that she thinks they're anything less than that because of me—the bottom one bowing in the middle, weighed down with all her perceived failures, but I think it used to be weighed down by how much she loved me.

She gives a little nod, and my mouth is on hers before I can listen to that broken part of my brain, sharp and stabbing, that tries to remind me I'm not good enough for her anymore.

It doesn't feel like I'm not good enough.

I think for the first time since I cracked my stupid head three years ago, I feel a bit like me.

My lips on hers, tongue sweeping across the seam, looking for permission before she meets it. Hands tangling and tugging in the hair at the nape of her neck.

Sloan, perfect the way she's always been perfect, every single swell and angle exactly the right shape and size to fit against me.

Her fingers, curling into the cotton of my T-shirt before her hands scramble across my back, nails digging into my shoulders.

A tiny moan into my mouth, and I'm done for.

She doesn't feel like this person carrying around all this heavy baggage I saddled her with when I pick her up. Her legs wrap around my waist instinctually, and she might as well be weightless, actually.

We're probably floating above this boat. In the stars, where we were definitely written for each other.

My hands leave bruises on her thighs, and hers tug sharply at my hair.

I kick the bathroom door closed behind us, and I kick the door to her room open, too.

I think the view of the ocean looks beautiful, but it's not really anything compared to her.

Not when I lay her down on the bed, unmade sheets swirling around her, and the last inches of sunlight drenching her skin.

"I'm going to talk, and you're going to listen," I tell her, lips still against hers.

Sloan says nothing, but I think her mouth shifts, maybe into a smile, right when I start to move mine along her jaw.

My teeth find the lobe of her ear, tugging gently three times, my cock throbbing against my shorts with each one. "These ears? The ones that you use to listen and learn and take in so much about the world around you? That find something interesting and something wonderful in everything? So fucking perfect. So fucking enough."

Her hands find my shoulders, her breath catches in her throat.

I move down her jaw again, over the lines of her neck, to the crook of her shoulders, dragging my tongue across her skin. "Flawless skin on flawless shoulders that might be the strongest part of you because they carry so much more than they have to. But they never collapse, even when you feel like they do."

Her back arches, chest straining against the lace of her bra, and I press my lips across the whirling edges, all the way to the curve of her left breast, teeth grazing her. "Your heart? Don't even get me fucking started."

I spend some time up there—thumb stroking her through the lace, brushing over each perfect, peaked nipple until she starts with the breathy moans, her hips shifting under me.

She gets a bit impatient when my hands grip her waist, thumbs stroking upwards across her skin in these tiny, gentle sweeps I know she likes.

I could spend all day—the rest of my days, actually—just like this, mapping her body with my tongue, but there's a lot I need to tell her.

"Here? Where all these things that keep you alive live?" I move down her stomach, resting my chin right above the lace of her underwear, tongue swirling across the band before I flick my eyes up. She's propped up on her elbows, hair tumbling across her shoulders, a flush on her cheeks. She blinks at me, and I say quietly, "Where I hoped a piece of me would live one day? This body? The home you'd give a baby? Perfect. Dokonalá. Very, very, very much enough."

A sharp inhale. Her eyes shift to cerulean, and I know she's trying not to cry.

"Ty jsi dokonalá," I whisper, brushing my mouth along the edges of the lace again before, very regrettably, leaving the spot so close to between her legs and propping myself up on the pillow beside her.

"I don't know that one," Sloan says softly.

"I won't make you guess." I give her a smile, half rueful, half sad. "You're perfect."

A furrow puckers her brow and she shakes her head. "It's weird because I don't feel . . . perfect or anything close to it, really, most days. And that's by and large because of my brain, but it's also—"

"Because of me." I don't let her finish, partly because I'm selfish and I don't think I could take hearing it from her. Not right now, not when I'm this close to her for the first time in over a year.

But mostly because I want her to know—I'm keenly aware every second of every minute of every hour of every day what I did.

"Yes." She sniffs, but then her face softens. "But right now, with you touching me, I feel about as close to it as a human being could possibly be."

It's a bad idea for so many reasons—and I am as horrible as everyone thinks I am, because I say the next words before I even give my brain a chance to remember that I'm setting her up for disappointment and failure again.

"Then I guess I shouldn't stop."

I don't.

She looks at me, a bit imploring and a bit hopeful, before I'm kissing her again.

It's like it used to be—I've got no idea how much time does or doesn't pass.

I just know it's *her* I'm kissing.

The love of my entire sorry fucking life.

Her tongue sweeping against mine.

Her moans I get to swallow because my hands wander—I can't help it, I've got a lot of lost time to make up for.

Gripping her jaw, just this side of rough, across her chest, over her bare skin because we lose the bra as soon as she arches up in permission, skating across her ribs, flared and open to me because of her ragged breath, but I'll pretend it's so I have access to her heart again. I trail my mouth along the whirls of lace at the top of her underwear.

Her teeth bite down on my bottom lip, and I groan, cock twitching in my shorts—I'll probably fucking die soon—and she whispers into my mouth, a tiny plea, "Bohdan, please, I need you to—I need—"

"Whatever you want, Sloan." I pull back, one hand gripping her chin. "Same rules apply. Whatever you want, whenever you want. You say stop, I stop."

I've thought a lot of things might kill me in the last few years, but none has come as close as her next few words. "Please don't stop, ever."

I groan again, mouth back on hers, devouring every small noise she makes when I slide my hand down her underwear, pausing right where she likes, moving my fingers in small circles—the way she writhes under me, how her fingers dig into my shoulders, the others clawing at my back, tells me at least that hasn't changed.

My luck might have drastically shifted—someone different was rolling the dice out there in the universe, because the other thing that seems like it might be the same is how her body responds to mine.

Sliding my fingers down the centre of her, I moan, pleading with her really. "Sloan, you're fucking soaked. I'll die if I can't eat you out."

She inhales, half a barely audible moan, half a laugh, and I pull away, my own breathing heavy, trying to get a look at her.

Flushed cheeks, swollen lips, and the constellation of freckles sparkling under her left eye.

"Sure," she says, like she's conceding something.

"Sure?" I repeat, voice strangled.

"I mean, sure. If you have to." Sloan nods, but I see the corners of her lips tilt upwards, fighting a smile.

It makes me smile, too. Forget for a second that I'm so hard and so gone for her I might explode.

But it's a bit like I'm looking at the person she was before I trampled all over her: soft, funny, but wildly stubborn.

"There's my girl." I grin, kissing her, roughly, before moving down her body again—hands tight against her waist, teeth scraping skin and tugging the lace down her legs so she's bare, right in front of me.

I inhale, eyes roving back up to Sloan's—she's propped up again, watching me, deep breaths heaving across her chest. So beautiful. Too beautiful, probably.

"Relax, Zlatíčko. I remember what you like."

"You didn't forget?" She tips her head to the side.

"I couldn't forget anything about you, even if I tried," I tell her, never mind the fact that I wouldn't try, and if memories were something you could hold, they'd be prying the ones of her from my hands when I died.

She smiles, soft and sure.

I don't wait any longer, I can tell by the way her shoulders roll back, how her fingers grip the sheets and her legs tense, that she's impatient.

I inhale again before sliding my tongue up her centre, stopping where she likes and making slow, almost lazy circles.

There's nothing lazy about it. Everything I do with her is intentional, right down to the slightest shift.

Her hands tangle in my hair when a moan catches in her throat.

"Perfect—" I groan, tongue flicking against her. "Fucking—"Her back arches and I bury my face deeper. "Pussy."

"Bohdan." She says my name, over and over again, her fingers tugging tighter on my hair with each stroke of my tongue.

I can feel when she's about to come—I know the way she moves, shoulders rolling back into the bed, bowing against it, how her moans get breathier, how she tastes right before—and I take two fingers, teasing, sliding them inside her, slowly, and start to move them in time with my tongue.

She does shatter, tightening, coming all over me.

I pull back, even though I could stay between her legs forever, but her hands tug gently on my hair, and when I look up at her, she's watching me, flushed and curious.

"You didn't forget," she says, words quiet when I lie down beside her, propping my head up on a hand.

"No." I shake my head, tracing her lips with my thumb. "I didn't forget."

Her shoulders rise, and she looks at me, resolute. "I want to do something for you."

"That was something for me," I reassure, throwing her a wry grin. "Trust me."

"I'd like . . . you inside me. All of you. Together, the way we were." She pauses, considering with a thoughtful blink. "I haven't been with anyone since you and I still have my IUD so—"

"I wasn't lying. I haven't been with anyone else either," I interrupt, and I think my heart might beat out of my chest. The idea of being inside her like that again—I shake my head. "Why would I ever want to be with anyone else when I've been with you?"

Sloan gives me a flat look—another flash of that funny, obstinate person. "You don't want me to answer that. Trust me."

"Sloan . . ." I start, but she cuts me off with a press of her mouth to mine.

"Please. I don't want to talk about any of it right now. The Polaroid, the ring, the night you . . ." she trails off, and it hangs heavy in the air between us. The night I left. But she blinks, and I think she closes the door on wherever she keeps that chapter of us in her brain. "I just want to be with you," she whispers, her lips traversing mine slowly, her palms sweeping across my shoulders, down my chest, and to the hem of my shirt.

I just want to be with you.

"I want to be with you, too." I groan when her hand slides down the front of my shorts, over my impossibly aching cock.

She's all I think about all the time—being with her like this, sure—but mostly just being with *her*.

When her hands rove across my back, guiding me back home, suspended over her in this bed, I imagine it's just another morning.

When I reach behind my head and tug my shirt off, and our skin touches, chests pressing together, I imagine we're back in Seattle.

Her hands, undoing the buttons of my shorts, gripping me and moving up and down, guiding me between her legs.

When I angle my hips, pushing inside her, inch by inch, and she gasps, nails digging into my shoulders, lips crashing against mine—maybe we're in Michigan.

Still together, just somewhere else.

With her—always with her—but maybe in a different world and in the body of the different me, and when her hips move up to meet mine, I bite down where that one piece of me still lives in the form of an old tattoo and try to swallow back the words he'd get to say.

I love you.

Sloan

Knowing Bohdan again is easy, but knowing his body again might be easier.

Maybe it's because we grew together and I think my body would know his anywhere—even if we were tumbling through the dark, somewhere out there in the universe.

The curves of my waist have swelled and shrunk and swelled again under his hands, and he's held and loved them all the same.

He went from a boy that already looked like a man to something even more otherworldly as the planes of his chest broadened, the valleys of muscle spanning his back dug in and deepened, and the topography of veins over his hands drew sharper lines.

I know it's wrong, but who could blame me?

It's like coming home and finally getting into your own bed after the longest trip away. Fresh sheets and sunlight and a morning breeze.

There's this part of my brain—the tiny logical part that never gets to rule over the obsessive parts—and it's telling me I'm forging pathways

I shouldn't be forging right now, because this isn't a fact, it can't be, he left—it's just a reassurance and this is going to do more harm than good.

But he whispers, a rough groan where his mouth traces my ear, and I can't hear anything else, "Lie to me again."

My nails dig into his shoulders, his palm grips my waist, trailing down my thigh where his fingers tense, hiking my leg up just as he pulls his head back in time with the roll of his hips.

Hair falling forward, waves askew from my hands raking through them, muscles taut and tense, and his full lips parted with another groan.

He's so beautiful, so lovely, so wonderful, and I think that tiny part of my brain tries telling me horrible things, too, but it's so far away when he's all over me and inside me like this.

"Zlatíčko. Lie to me." He says it again when my hips rise to meet his.

I can't really think of anything at all. I'm not sure what lie I'm supposed to tell, because I can really only think of one thing.

I love you, I love you, I love you.

A moan tumbles from my mouth instead, and I think there's some truth in it.

He's the only person who's ever made me feel so many things, and certainly the only person who's ever made me feel like this—that I'll explode from the pressure, from all the ways he makes my body tighten around him.

"Fuck," Bohdan groans, hand tensing against my thigh when his pace picks up. The muscles in his neck strain when he tips his head back. But when his eyes find mine, they darken impossibly, and his words are rough. "Sloan—fuck—krásná."

It's a word I'm intimately familiar with.

One of his favourites when it came to me, actually.

Beautiful.

And when we were together, it was one of the loudest.

It's loud right now—so loud, in fact, that it's the only thing I hear.

Three times over in my brain. In his voice, the loveliest sound in the world.

I don't even hear my own moans grow louder, my breathing getting sharper when Bohdan angles my hips, hands bruising me now.

But I do hear his voice when he speaks again. "You're so close, I can feel—fuck, fuck, fuck—come for me, please, Sloan."

He didn't even have to ask.

Not when he looks like this, sweat-slicked muscles tense, golden-brown hair tumbling over his forehead, dark eyes and teeth biting down on full lips.

Not when he feels like this inside me, either.

And not when he's him and I'm me.

I do come—louder than I should when it's not just our suite—but I don't think I'd be able to be quiet if I tried.

He buries his face in my neck, saying my name a bit like a mantra or a prayer. Over and over and over again when the muscles in his back tighten under my hands, and he follows me into the dark or wherever it is we are.

Bohdan stills, teeth grazing my skin, followed by a soft press of his lips, before he rolls his shoulders and pulls back, off me and out of me, to prop himself up beside me on the pillow.

It's a terribly empty feeling, being without him again after all this time.

"Hey," he says quietly.

I brush a wave off his forehead, making sure I run my fingers along the scar—his eyes shutter closed—and I wish, not for the first time, I had some sort of magic healing touch. I don't, so I smile gently instead. "Hi."

"You okay?" He grabs my hand, pressing his mouth across the tips of my fingers.

I'm not sure how to answer that because I am—as okay as I've been since the night he got hurt, but that's not right and it's not really okay because it's this sense of comfort and security based in reassurances and obsessions and compulsions, not facts.

But I don't have to answer, because something that sounds distinctly like a hand smacking against the door comes from just outside the room.

"Sloan?" Tia calls, voice muffled. "Are you in there? Are you okay?"

Bohdan shifts, the lines of his face softening with a slow grin that reminds me of who he was when we first met.

I wrinkle my nose, smiling. It is a bit like being back in college—all the times we'd sneak away from a party because we couldn't wait to be alone, and our friends would inevitably come looking for us.

"I'm fine," I answer, and Bohdan starts to trace my freckles with his thumb.

"Sloany?" Talon shouts this time, before trying to open the door. "Why the fuck is this door locked?"

An exasperated groan. Jay. "Because it's her room, man."

"So?" I can't see them, but I imagine Talon throwing his hands up in the air before he tries the door handle again. "We really need to talk to you. It's an emergency."

"It's not really," Tia yells back.

"No, I really think it is. Sloany!" Talon smacks the door again.

Bohdan exhales, a muscle in his jaw twitching, and he presses his thumb to my cheek, cupping the side of my face before his eyes cut to the door. "This ship better be fucking burning down, Talon."

Silence.

I feel a bit like laughing, and I bite down on my lip. Bohdan smiles, the left side of his mouth kicking up.

"Oh. You're not ... alone, then?" Talon asks, and the door handle gives a resigned, half-hearted shake.

"I think the sound of Bohdan's voice answers that for you." Jay sounds like he's rolling his eyes.

Another smack on the door, but it's lighter this time. Tia. "Sloan? Are you sure you're okay in there?"

The muscle in Bohdan's jaw feathers again, his hand tightens against my cheek before he pushes to stand.

I sit up, gathering the blankets around me, and watch Bohdan rake a hand through already dishevelled hair, all the muscles in his back contracting, and the ones running along his legs and quads popping when he tugs his shorts back on and hands me his shirt.

"We were alone, until you three decided to come along and ruin it." He waits until I'm safely covered up before he starts towards the door. He pulls it open, just a crack, positioning his body between me, here in this bed, and them on the other side. "And she's fine."

More silence.

I see the top of Talon's expertly styled curls popping over Bohdan's head like he's trying to peek inside the room, but Bohdan shifts and closes the door more. "I don't smell any smoke, Talon. What's so fucking urgent?"

"Sloan—this seems ill-advised." Tia tries to duck around Bohdan.

"This seems like it's starting to get a bit inappropriate. You guys can just meet us at the bar," Jay starts to interject.

But Talon talks over him. "Inappropriate? Oh yeah, like these two have ever cared about propriety. Making us watch for years while they hung off each other, and subjecting us to whatever torment is going on this week? I think we deserve to know what's going on. To see the fruits of our labour, so to speak."

"Just let them in." I roll my eyes.

Bohdan glances back over his shoulder, eyes tracing where his shirt drapes over my chest and the sheets swirl over my legs, like he's checking to make sure I'm covered up, comfortable enough.

I give him another nod, and it's stupid really, because I am comfortable, content, happy, and quiet for the first time in years.

He yanks back the door, throwing it open much harder than necessary. Turning his back to them, he comes back to the bed, one hand resting on my shoulder in this funny protective way like he's somehow still responsible for me.

It's comical, the way they tumble in through the now-open doorway, like they were all children with ears pressed there trying to hear what was on the other side. Tia, all shining silver sequins and hair curling around her face. Talon, in some sort of matching blue striped linen shirt-and-short combo, and Jay, in an outfit that really does sort of belong back in the '70s.

"Oh. Shit." Talon catches himself on the doorway at the last minute when he spots me, eyes flashing and immediately finding the ceiling. "Bad time?"

Jay cringes, rubbing a hand across the bridge of his nose. "Told you this was inappropriate."

"Sloan?" Tia asks, taking a small, cautious step into the room, her heels sinking into the plush carpet.

"Yes?" I widen my eyes, tugging at the sheet before Bohdan drops onto the bed beside me, one arm wrapping around so he can bring me flush to his chest.

"Oh." Tia blinks, mouth forming a small circle.

Talon finally glances away from the ceiling, a grin cracking across his face. He raises a fist in the air. "So this is on, then?"

Bohdan's hand tenses against my shoulder, fingers splayed out protectively across my skin. He's not going to answer.

It seems like a complicated, loaded question. And in theory, it is.

But the answer is simple.

Bohdan and I have always been on—by whatever juvenile definition Talon's using now, and by every single sense of the word you'd never be able to explain to someone who's never been in love the way we have.

"What do you want, Talon?" I ask flatly. "I'd like to get dressed."

"Would you really?" Jay deadpans, shaking his head and glancing up at the ceiling.

Talon knocks his shoulder with his fist. "Maybe they want to go for round two—"

"Maybe you should get the fuck out," Bohdan interjects, and I can practically hear his jaw grinding.

A smug grin inches across Talon's face, and he swipes a hand through his hair, sending the curls askew before he starts walking backward. "Sure thing. But don't take too long. I needn't want to remind you that this is my retirement river cruise—"

"Not a river cruise," Jay mutters before he glances backdown at us, face fighting the fracture of a smile and the corners of his eyes crinkling.

"—*my* retirement river cruise," Talon continues, cutting Jay a look. "And it's disco night. A mandatory event."

"Got it." I raise my eyebrows at him, pointing towards the still-open door. "I want to get changed."

Talon points a finger towards Bohdan. "You're welcome, buddy. See you at the disco."

He turns, jumping to smack his hand against the top of the door-frame, and disappears into the suite.

"Sorry, Bohdan." Jay's eyes find Bohdan's arm, wrapped around me, and he grins before following Talon.

Tia lingers—arms crossed, eyes narrowed and assessing, full lips pursed. Her fingers drum against the golden skin of her bicep. She looks like she's chewing on the inside of her cheek, but her eyes find mine, and the worry in her features smooths into nothing. "We'll talk at the disco?"

"Sure." I nod. "As much as one can talk at a disco."

She smiles fondly. "Remember your earplugs." She turns to follow her brother and Jay, but she turns back right before she closes the door. "I'm watching you, Novotnak."

The door closes with a tiny, resounding click, and it's just us in here again.

"Hey, again," he whispers, mouth pressed up against my ear.

"Hi." I lean back against him, letting my eyes close.

"You okay?" He strokes his thumb across my shoulder, sweeping it down over the jut of my collarbone.

I do feel okay. Soothed and quiet even, and the tiny logical part of my brain that rarely gets to win screams, trying to tell me how wrong this is. It's not real, and it's fake, and it's going to hurt me more in the long run.

But my heart so desperately wants this one thing now that I've had him again, even though I think it might be colossally bad for both of us. "Earlier you said you'd give me everything I wanted in exchange for the next few days with me. I know we keep changing the rules but what if . . . what if it's like this? Us?"

As soon as I say it, I know it won't be enough. I could die and be reincarnated a thousand times over and live every single life with him, and that still wouldn't be enough.

But I ask anyway, because once upon a time, there was a version of Bohdan who would never say no to me.

His thumb stills against my shoulder. "That doesn't seem . . . well advised."

I pull back, turning to face him. Lines of his jaw sharp, muscles in his shoulders and neck tense, and eyes looking like he might actually say no to me for the first time.

"It'll be like exposure therapy," I joke, even though it's sort of the exact opposite of how that's supposed to work.

It doesn't land. Bohdan's jaw ticks, and his nostrils flare.

"Please," I whisper before he can change his mind and sacrifice these two days of us on the altar of what he thinks is best for me.

His eyes shutter, and when they open, I know I've won. He shakes his head, pressing his forehead against mine. "You say stop—"

"We stop."

"And at the end of the week—"

"You give me the Polaroid. I'll give you the ring. And you'll tell me everything I want to know."

Something flashes behind his eyes, a storm readying lightning to strike and burn whatever this is down, but I press my lips to his and don't let it catch.

Our lips move, his against mine, slotting in like the missing piece of a puzzle you found tucked away somewhere in your childhood home—a bit like we did all those years ago, sitting up in his bed in that old college room of his when we collided in the best ways before the worst came years later.

There might be something poetic about it—us, back together on a ship floating somewhere in the ocean. I wonder about all the nautical disasters that came before us, and whether any two ships on a crash course for each other have ever actually gone down. I think that maybe, when someone finds the wreckage of this one, they'll be able to see it painted there across the hull.

The *Sloan Joseph* and the *Bohdan Novotnak*—they couldn't stop, even when they should have.

Sloan

Bohdan takes his time, even though Talon comes back to pound on the door and try to impress upon us the importance of disco night.

He waits until I pick out a new dress, a black tube one that seems like it'll be significantly easier on my skin than the sequins.

He asks if he can help me, and he drops into a crouch when I bend to step into it.

He pulls it up my legs, fingers skimming reverently over my body, eyes watchful and on mine the whole time.

He tucks his thumbs just under the material when he adjusts the top.

The left side of his mouth lifts when I shiver.

He doesn't bother with my underwear, but picks them up from the floor instead.

"Can I keep these?" He holds the black lace between his fingers.

I give a small shrug. "For the next few days, sure."

He smirks, eyebrows rising before he tucks them into the back pocket of his shorts. "You might have to fight me for these, Zlatíčko."

"What would you possibly do with a pair of my underwear?"

Bohdan pushes his tongue to his cheek, eyes dark. "I'm not sure you want the answer to that."

"How improper." I tip my chin up.

"Why don't you slide that dress back off and I'll show you improper?" Bohdan's gaze tracks across my chest, his eyes feel a bit like a caress where my waist meets my hips, and they land on the hem.

I reach down, maybe ready to pull the whole thing off again, or cover up more of my legs to try and drive him crazy, when a hand crashes against the door again.

"We can fucking hear you, you know." Talon sounds like he's cringing.

Bohdan's eyes stay on me. "Then leave."

"And to think I'd forgotten it could get like this," Talon mutters and the door handle shakes. "Guys, the disco waits for no one."

Jay groans, before he starts smacking the door in rapid succession. "As happy as I am for you both, could you please, please hurry up so Tia and I don't have to listen to him say things like 'the disco waits for no one' all night?"

I roll my eyes, but a tiny, fond smile blooms on my face and I scrunch my nose at Bohdan, whispering, "Later?"

He nods, tucking a wisp of hair behind my ears. "Later."

He whispers it—voice low, gravelly, rough—all the ways I've liked him sounding the best, and all full of promise.

His lips brush mine, and that kiss is full of promise, too.

I'm not sure how many promises he can keep in two days, and I should really only care about that one waiting for me at the end—the chance to finally move on—but promises shaped like his mouth and his body against mine seem far more important.

There's another smack on the door and Bohdan groans, tipping his head back before gripping his jaw. "I'm coming."

He throws the door open again, and they don't all tumble in this time, but they stand side by side, each wearing their emotions and assessments clearly. Jay, quietly happy, with eyes brighter than usual, the ghost of a grin while he tugs on the chain around his neck aimlessly.

Tia, head tipped to the side, blinking in assessment.

Talon, a wide, childlike smile. He gestures between us before rubbing his hands together. "So . . . you two? The river cruise worked its magic?"

Jay bites down on his cheek, looking like he's in physical pain trying to restrain himself from pointing out that we aren't on a river.

Bohdan shifts beside me, carved angles of his face sharp, and a muscle jumps in his jaw. He cuts me a sideways glance, waiting.

I bounce back and forth on the balls of my feet, folding my arms across my chest. "Not that it's anyone's business, but we've expanded the terms of our agreement for the next few days."

"A few days?" Tia gives me a dubious look.

I give her a tight smile, shifting again on my feet when Bohdan's thumb sweeps across my shoulder. "Yes. A few days. The remainder of this cruise that's definitely not on a river."

They all wear these emotions, too.

Jay's eyes go wide, flashing with the tiniest bit of doubt, before they find Bohdan, and whatever worry lines his face softens and his smile grows.

Tia's nostrils flare with an inhale, her eyes flick back and forth between us before they land on Bohdan's thumb, still tracing patterns across my skin. They cut down to my body, to the new dress and noticeable absence of sequins. She squeezes her eyes shut, cheeks pinching, like the idea that maybe I'm putting myself at risk hurts her. But she opens her eyes again, the amber in them melts just a bit, and she looks at us the way she used to.

Talon tips his head back and howls like a fucking wolf.

Bohdan cringes, hand leaving my shoulder to press over my ear, but there aren't enough hands or earplugs in the world to block out that sound.

Talon has the sense to look apologetic for all of two seconds when I wince.

"This was so worth the delay to disco night." He claps his palms together, a hollow sound echoes, and he throws a thumb towards the living room of the suite. "But the delay has gone on long enough, so you know, chop-chop."

Jay knocks my shoulder affectionately, brows quirking up before he scrubs his face and turns back to Talon. "Alright, let's get this over with."

Bohdan's hand cups the side of my face, and he studies me with all these unsaid things in his eyes and I think more promises than he should be making in the swirls of his fingertips against my cheek, but I don't have any time to decode them before Talon's waving a finger in the air and pushing them down the hall.

I adjust the top of my dress, about to follow, when Tia grabs my arm.

"Sloan . . ." She runs her tongue over her teeth before chewing on the inside of her cheek. "Are you sure about this? You said you were starting a new life back home, and the whole purpose of this agreement was to get what you needed to do that, not to sleep with him. This doesn't seem like starting over . . . it seems a bit like going back in time."

I roll my shoulder back, a sort of involuntary movement to try and separate myself from her touch and the truth written in the lines of her face.

It's something I don't want to hear right now. Not when everything's still so quiet and he's still all over me.

I narrow my eyes. "You were the one who said we should fuck at the winery!"

"I didn't think you'd actually do it!" Tia presses her fingers to the bridge of her nose, voice dropping to a hiss. "And you gave him your underwear?"

"He took those, actually," I say, petulant.

Tia gives me a flat look.

I hold my palms up. "What would you have me do? What did I say at the start of this godforsaken cruise? He's got an unfair advantage, look at him!"

I gesture down the hall to Bohdan, standing with Talon and Jay in front of the bar while Talon pours shots of tequila that look far too full, Bohdan's eyes cutting back to me every few seconds. Hair all mussed from my hands, a real smile carving the lines of his face differently than the usual stoic set, but just as breathtaking, with one hand shoved in the pocket of his shorts.

"He is very beautiful, you're right." Tia exhales softly, squeezing my arm before finally letting go. "But he's not more beautiful than you are important."

"Trust me," I whisper, pleading with her, really. I need her to understand, because if she's casting doubts, every bad thing I've been thinking is going to wake back up, and I desperately, desperately need a break from my own mind. "Please? I asked him for this. I say stop, we stop."

She studies me, head tipping from side to side and one curl tumbling down her forehead. She gives me a tiny nod, and an even tinier smile. "I hope you know what you're doing."

My eyes travel back down the hall, and they find him.

His find me, too.

If this hallway were the horrible, awful trench between us—I think there's this rickety, ancient ladder stretching from my end to his now, and I step onto the first rung, and I pray and pray and pray that I won't fall off and get swallowed whole.

Sloan

Then – Seattle

Our bed has navy sheets.

But I ordered a seafoam-green set today and bought a plant because I read online that calming colours have a soothing effect, and houseplants don't just purify your air, they're supposed to promote a sense of vitality.

All things that, according to this one blog I found, promote a positive and harmonious environment in accordance with feng shui principles, and might help to reduce migraine frequency and severity.

I'm not a stranger to an internet rabbit hole—I've spent a lot of my life researching things that someone else might find irrelevant.

But today, I might be the deepest I've ever been in one.

No one's come to my office hours, and usually that would bother me. But I can't imagine someone would stay if they did try to walk in and see me—hunched over my laptop, eyes bloodshot from the screen and the tiny text.

I might buy an acupressure mat, too. Or, a gift card to this traditional Chinese medicine practice not too far from our house. There's this one study from the *Journal of Naturopathic Medicine* I found that had some promising figures.

And that entire text I read last night about ancient remedies and practices dating back to 100 BC.

Maybe I'll buy both.

I'm about to click through my cart—a consultation and three sessions should be enough to get started—when there's a gentle knock on the door.

My supervisor stands there, dark hair pulled back, tiny threads of grey interspersed and visible in her ponytail. She has her arms crossed, casual, and a kind smile on her face. "Sloan."

"Dr. Amore." I slam the laptop shut, sitting up straight and blinking a bit too much. "I was just doing a bit of research. It's been quiet today."

"For your proposal?"

It's what I should be researching.

But I haven't picked up my proposal for my dissertation since the day Bohdan got injured. If it were real and on paper, not stuffed in a folder on my computer, it'd be covered in three months' worth of dust.

"Oh. No. Sorry—I know I'm late on it, I just—"

She shakes her head softly, her smile moving from kind to a sort of patient understanding that makes me feel like shrinking down beneath my desk.

"It's okay, Sloan. You can take as long as you need. You've got a lot going on."

Sympathy flashes in her eyes.

I swallow, nodding, and start tapping my fingers on the desk. "I'll be back on top of it soon. Bohdan just needs—"

"How's he feeling?" she interrupts, but it's not unkind. It's laced with the same pity living in her eyes. "I saw he retired."

He did. Sort of.

He announced he wouldn't be playing the rest of the season at a press conference a few weeks ago.

Those were the words his publicist gave him, anyway. That he'd be focused on conditioning and his health so he could try to come back next season.

The words weren't written like a death sentence. But when he said them out loud, wincing under all those bright lights and against the flashing cameras, and when he stumbled over the word *try*—they sounded like one.

Like someone was ringing a bell in an old town square, welcoming the world to his execution.

"He's just taking a break. For the rest of the season." I force a smile, my throat burns, and the tapping of my fingers increases.

Dr. Amore's eyes cut down to my hands, a crease sketches between her brow, and she nods. "I'm sorry, I misspoke. And how are you doing?"

"Me?" I blink. There's a funny sort of irony to her question.

I've spent my whole life thinking about myself—how rotten, how bad, how maybe secretly evil I must be—and the only thing that's ever rewritten the story was Bohdan's injury.

His headaches are my intrusive thoughts.

The blood in his brain that cleared up on its own is what haunts me when I look in the mirror.

Bohdan. Bohdan. Bohdan.

And everything I can do to make him feel better.

To fix him the way he fixed me when he picked me out of a crowd of thousands of people and made me feel like I was worthy for the first time in my life.

I blink again with a shake of my head. "I'm okay. I've learned a lot about alternative therapies for migraines. Acupuncture. Feng shui—I just bought some new sheets. They're a light green. It's supposed to be soothing. I thought it might help."

She looks at me like she feels a bit sorry for me.

But she shouldn't, he's going to love them.

—⁂—

And it's not that he doesn't.

He might, I can't be sure.

Bohdan never talked much before, but he certainly doesn't talk much now.

I sit, propped up in our bed, the new seafoam-green sheets pooling around my legs—the navy ones are buried in the closet—a text on herbal remedies open against my knees instead of anything else I should be reading.

I have a perfect view from here of Bohdan stepping out of the shower in the en suite. He dries his hair, wincing only a little when the towel touches his head, and he moves through the prescription bottles on the counter in the order they sit.

The first antidepressant.

The extra-strength ibuprofen prescribed to him.

He skips over the triptans—a good sign his head might not be bothering him too much—but he does take a sleeping pill.

His eyes used to find me first in any room, but he sort of looks right through me—probably through everything, actually—and he drops to his side of the bed.

"Do you like them?" I ask, tugging on the sheets.

Bohdan blinks, scrubbing his face and wincing slightly when his fingertips graze the cut along his forehead, still raised and pink against usually golden skin. "Like what?"

"The sheets." I tug the sheet up again, trying to smile.

His eyes skip over those, too, and he shrugs, dropping his head against the pillow. "Didn't even notice them."

"They sort of match the new plant in the windowsill." I point half-heartedly towards the pothos draped across the ledge, leaves curled outwards, waiting for the morning sun.

He presses his eyes shut, fingers finding the bridge of his nose. "What plant?"

He's not being rude, and even though he falls asleep right beside me, even though I watch his breathing, the way his eyes flick under his closed eyelids, tracking something that I hope might be a good dream, he's just . . . not really there anymore.

Bohdan

It's like college in the best ways. Like any time *before*, really.

There's no way we're floating on the ocean somewhere between Livorno and Rome.

We're somewhere else.

At least, I am.

Maybe I'm dreaming. It has to be a dream—because I'm in this stupid disco with my best friends, Sloan looking up at me, face soft underneath flashing lights that on any other day would send me to my knees, but I hardly see them tonight.

The only bright thing here is her. And despite everything I've done to her—everything I'm still capable of doing because I've got the truth she wants so desperately in my hands—there's nothing about her that hurts me.

She's the flash of blinding light, the smattering of colour across the walls and the floor and the entire world. The vibration of a too-loud bass in my chest, making my heart beat and keeping me alive.

That has to be psychosomatic—the power of whatever's left of my brain coming in handy for once, so I can stare at her, see those freckles thrown into contrast and painted with vibrant, white light, and nothing about it can hurt me.

She holds up another pair of grey rubber loops that match the ones nestled in her ears. She smiles—it stretches wider across her face than anything I've seen in years when she reaches up to place them in mine, fingers whispering over my skin.

They trace my jawline, her thumb running over my bottom lip, pulling down slightly before she places her hand on my chest, right above my heart.

A blanket settles over everything. All that noise I couldn't really hear anyway.

She rests her hand there, fingers tapping in time with the beat of my heart—one, two, one, two, one, two—before she slides it down, interlacing her fingers with mine. Back where they belong. The same hands that still hold my heart the way I used to hold hers, and I know I should let go, that I never should have gone along with it. But I don't think my head's ever felt clearer, and I follow the woman I've loved since she was an eighteen-year-old girl, and I let her drag me towards our best friends at the bar.

We do too many shots. We dance. We laugh too much and too loudly and for too long. I push her up against the wall in a random hallway just off the bar and kiss her with too many wandering hands and too much tongue and too many teeth coming down on her bottom lip.

And when they kick us out, our friends booing loudly and Talon proclaiming we ruined disco night with a smile bigger than any goal or championship ever produced—we go back to the suite, and I trace letters on her skin with my mouth that she'll never be able to read to tell her how sorry I am and how much I still love her and always will.

The sun rises at some point, rays stretching across the gentle, rolling waves of the ocean, and the milky sky tries to tell me I stayed up too long and drank too much and I should know better, because I'm only going to cause myself pain.

But it's Sloan under me and on me and beside me in my bed, and my head doesn't hurt at all.

Sloan

Then – Seattle

No one ever talks about just how loud silence can be.

It's deafening.

The loudest sound ever recorded was the eruption of a volcano on the Indonesian island Krakatoa in 1883. It was estimated to be around 310 decibels. It erupted on August 27, and collapsed the majority of the island, producing a tsunami felt in South Africa.

But I think silence is louder, and I think it might do more damage.

At least—Bohdan's silence.

That might be something more like an implosion, because it really feels like this apartment is turning inward on us.

I blink up at the ceiling and the shadows painted there from the light streaming in from the bedroom window.

He shifts in bed beside me, tugging on those seafoam-green sheets I was so certain might help, but it's not to get closer to me.

He's so far away.

He's Krakatoa and I'm South Africa.

I don't even remember the last time he touched me. And maybe it's that, the absence of him around me—this person that grew with me and moulded me and shaped me—that has me whispering quietly, not really to him but up towards the ceiling and anyone who might be listening, "Please just talk to me."

He stops moving beside me, the collapse of his island momentarily paused. I don't look, but I think he might pinch the bridge of his nose before palming his jaw. His voice is worn, rough around the edges in all the worst ways. "What do you want me to say, Sloan?"

"Anything," I whisper with this tiny kernel of hope.

He definitely shakes his head, and I feel those waves all the way over on my continent before the eruption comes.

It wasn't an implosion. It wasn't quick and quiet, barely a blip on the radar.

He's louder than he's been in months. "That I lost my fucking career? That I was supposed to be the best? Supposed to wipe away every fucking record ever and now I can't even go outside without my brain feeling like it's bleeding?"

Part of me collapses, but he keeps going, and takes the rest of me with him down, down, down into the ocean underneath us.

Bohdan

"You should wear your sunglasses."

Sloan taps my shoulder, and her skin only touches mine through the linen of my shirt, but it feels like lightning. She shrugs the tote off her arm, and the strap of her tank top slides down her skin, revealing the *B*, prominent from the sun. She starts to dig through her bag for my prescription glasses, moving past the myriad of pills and medication she threw in there this morning before we got off the boat.

I wrap my hand around her wrist, her pulse skittering beneath my fingers. I try to smile reassuringly before planting a rough kiss to the side of her head, because for the next few days, I can. "I'm okay, Zlatíčko. Promise."

"Are you sure?" She frowns, glancing down at the open tote again. "It's really bright."

It *is* really bright.

It's the type of day that has the potential to send me into hiding. The sun beating down mercilessly on the cracked streets of Rome where we wait in this impossibly long, snaking line to get inside the Colosseum for some sort of exclusive tour Talon organized. All of us dehydrated because we drank too much at the disco, and Sloan and I certainly stayed up way too late.

Jay groans every time he has to shuffle forward in the line, a ridiculous pair of thick white sunglasses that somehow look good on him hiding his eyes, and his usually immaculately swept-back hair falling askew over his forehead.

Tia's features contort into a frown whenever Talon shouts—which is a lot. He's glued to his phone, spouting out random facts about ancient Rome. She tugs the wide brim of her hat down with a whimper to cover her ears.

The corner of my mouth twitches.

It's bright out here, and it's bright inside my brain for the first time in a long time.

But Sloan's not wrong—I should wear them.

I just don't want to miss a single second. I don't want to see it in shades of grey.

I want the whole thing in loud, screaming Technicolor.

Sloan's lower lip pouts and she looks a bit insolent, but I grin at her, throwing an arm around her shoulder and pressing my thumb into her skin. "I'll be okay. I promise. And I know where to find the sunglasses if I need them. You've got the whole arsenal in there."

She rolls her eyes, tips her chin up when she closes the bag, and slides it back on her shoulder, covering up the tattoo, but she doesn't move away from my grip. She leans in, resting her head against my chest when we shuffle forward in the line.

"Being a gladiator would have been so fucking cool." Talon waves his phone around, a wide smile stretching on his face.

"No. It wouldn't have," Sloan offers flatly.

Talon stops, ignoring the throngs of waiting people behind us. He cocks his head, flashing his phone so quickly no one has a chance to see what he was reading. "And why is that, Sloany?"

She folds her arms over her chest. "Contrary to whatever film and television have made you believe, they were prisoners of war, criminals, and sometimes slaves. They fought to the death for the entertainment of a corrupt empire, and they had very few rights."

Talon blinks.

I don't need to see her to know she's rolling her eyes. My smile stretches.

"And archaeological evidence and forensic examination of their skeletons show just how brutal it was. Multiple, repeated fractures. They've even found evidence of bite marks that belonged to a lion on a man's pelvis."

"A lion?" Talon leans forward, ignoring everything else, before he turns and shakes Jay's shoulders, repeating himself. "A lion!"

"Why?" Jay moans, shoving Talon away and clamping his hands over his ears.

Talon stretches his arms wide and starts walking backward again when someone somewhere in the back of the line shouts for us to hurry up. "Why am I the only one who thinks that's cool?"

"You're the only one who isn't horribly hungover." Tia flips the brim of her hat up.

Talon points at me. "Bohds looks fine. Not even wearing his sunglasses."

"I am." I nod, grip tightening against Sloan's shoulder.

"I think we all know why." Talon gestures between me and Sloan, raising his eyebrows. "And I had like, four mimosas at breakfast. The only way out is through, my friends."

Jay stops, pushing his sunglasses up to hold his hair back. He frowns, this wild look of utter dismay on his face. "Wait—did that sort of make sense?"

"No." Tia flicks Jay's shoulder at the same time Talon lifts his palm for a high five.

Jay shakes his head, hands coming to grip the sides of his hair. "It did. It did make sense. Someone send fucking help."

The front of the line clears, and Talon sprints up to the ticket booth. "Sorry, Jay. No can do. It's gladiator time."

"It's not gladiator time. If it was, you'd be sprinting towards an arena full of armed men or maybe, if we were lucky, a bear." Sloan fishes her sunglasses out of her tote and tries to get me to wear mine in one last half-hearted attempt.

I shake my head.

Talon leans against the ticket counter, propping himself upon his elbows, pointing his chin towards Jay. "If you thought the life of a gladiator was bad, Sloany, you should hear this guy's knees when he tries to stand up."

Jay holds his palms wide in indignation, looking to me for support.

But I shrug, cringing. "They are creaky. I've heard them."

An entire lifetime of skating and playing and getting hit will do that to you.

Talon knocks a fist against the wooden counter, eyes alight with excitement and realization. "Maybe playing hockey is like the twenty-first-century version of being a gladiator—horribly toxic culture, my back is fucked, Jay can barely stand, and we all saw Bohdan break his head open!"

Sloan tenses under my palm, but before I can say anything, Jay clutches the side of his head again. "No—seriously. Someone help me. Because that sort of made sense, too."

Tia lays her hand on his arm, all feigned sympathy and understanding. "We really should get you inside."

Sloan angles her head, blue eyes soft when they land on mine. She's got this quiet smile, cheeks soft and pillowy, one freckle visible beyond the frame of her sunglasses.

I think the whole thing might be in Technicolor for her, too.

Her eyes find my mouth, and I still know everything there is to know about her, so I know she wants to kiss me.

I meet her half way.

Just a brush of my mouth against hers. Gentle. Nothing like last night—two people scraping for stolen, fleeting moments.

This kiss feels a bit like forever.

But it's not forever, and for once, it's not Talon interrupting us. It's my phone ringing in my pocket.

Sloan pulls back, her smile shifting to this funny, little line of mischief, and she reaches into my pocket, fingers scraping against my upper thigh through the thinner material, and she pulls out my phone, triumphant, looking like she's about to hang up on whoever it is when her eyes land on the screen.

She hands it to me wordlessly, blinking a bit too much and chewing on the inside of her cheek.

Shay.

"I'll be right there. I've gotta take this." I jerk my chin towards Talon, Jay, and Tia, where they wait with a guide just beyond the ticket counter.

I run my thumb over Sloan's cheek, and she smiles before walking over to join them, a bit braver than I think she actually feels when this giant reminder of my failed career and the thing that drove us apart waits on the other side of the phone.

Shay wastes no time when I pick up.

"Have you been ignoring my calls?"

I close my eyes, pressing my fingers to my temple out of habit. "No. I told you, I didn't buy the Wi-Fi package on the ship. Service has been in and out."

"I understand you aren't playing anymore, but for the love of God, Bohdan, if you tell me you squandered away millions and can't afford a Wi-Fi package on a cruise ship—"

"Maybe I just didn't want to talk to you," I cut in.

"Maybe I don't want to talk to you either, but we don't always get what we want—evidently. Zane is on my ass, Bohdan. I need to know if you're interested or not so I can start negotiating. Are you done soul-searching with Valdez and Choi?" Her tone takes a noticeable dip when she says Talon's name. She never got over the fact that he absconded to Sweden.

"Two more days. And it's not just Talon and Jay here. Tia's here too . . . with Sloan." I'm not entirely sure why I tell her, but I hear the small intake of breath and her voice changes to understanding.

"Ah. I'd imagine you haven't given it much thought, then?"

I haven't, not really. The entire idea of it had seemed preposterous when AJ floated it to me. It was only a few weeks ago—but it feels like forever.

Shay waits.

I watch Sloan—standing far away but so much closer than she's been since I got hurt. Palm flat against her chest, nodding along with something Tia says before her lips part in laughter, the whole thing reverberating the column of her throat and causing her shoulders to shake.

Mine again for two whole days.

The thought of saying yes—taking what arguably would be a good opportunity, and a chance to do something unique and different and maybe help someone the way I wish someone had helped me—makes me wish I was walking into the Colosseum to face all the bears and lions and predators of the Roman Empire.

It's what I'd deserve if I said yes.

My inability to talk and be vulnerable cost me more than any hit to the ice ever did.

I swallow. "Can you find me something back home?"

"In Brno?" Shay starts, incredulous. "I mean, there's probably some European league teams we could see about—"

"No. In Canada. Preferably Toronto."

She's silent again. The options aren't endless.

"I honestly don't really care what it is, Shay." I don't.

She waits again, seemingly weighing her next words, like she's trying to squash any bit of hope she might have for me in case it's not really real. "Does this mean—are you two back together?"

"No."

And we probably never will be. Sloan deserves more.

But I'm selfish and stupid and I feel like sacrificing something the way she always sacrificed for me so that she knows, without a doubt, when she steps off the ship, that she was always enough.

It was me who wasn't.

"I'll see what I can do," Shay says softly before she hangs up.

I watch Sloan for a minute longer, and the sunlight crests over the rough, crumbling rooftop of the Colosseum entrance, shining down on her.

A bright spotlight, painting pictures across her beautiful, perfect skin. But I can see it—marks I left and the way I littered her whole being with the ruins of our relationship. All over her, just like she said.

I don't know if I'll ever be able to erase them, but I'll see what I can do over the next few days, too.

Sloan

Then – Seattle

"You gave me a note on herbal remedies for headaches commonly used in traditional Middle Eastern medicine instead of your proposal brief."

It takes me a second—I look up from my computer, frowning with a slow blink.

Dr. Amore slides into the chair across from me, resting her elbows on top of her canvas tote. She folds her hands, interlaced fingers propping up her chin as she smiles patiently at me.

"Pardon me?" I blink again, eyes tracking across the busy campus café, unable to focus on one thing because I've been reading about the efficacy of minimally invasive neurology procedures to treat migraines.

"You gave me a note on herbal remedies for headaches commonly used in traditional Middle Eastern medicine instead of your proposal brief," she repeats, words calm and soft.

She'd be great at telling bedtime stories—it's exactly the kind of voice that would lull a child to sleep.

But it sends a warning signal to my nervous system, and my heart speeds up in my chest. I blink again, too much now, and my lungs do this funny thing where they expand, but I don't think any air comes in.

"I didn't mean to." My voice cracks, and my hands fumble to close my computer as quickly as possible so she can't see more evidence written across my screen—all the ways I'm failing at being a graduate student.

She sighs, features pinching before she purses her lips. Not in a harsh way, but like she's chewing something over. "How's Bohdan, Sloan?"

"Fine," I lie, sitting up and folding my own hands across my laptop in a sorry imitation of Dr. Amore. My fingers don't lie still like hers. They start tapping out counts of three before I can stop them.

One brow rises, breaking right through the falsehood. "And how are you?"

"I have my proposal right here." I dodge the question like it's a bullet, and it is—at least a metaphorical one. My tapping draws attention to the laptop. My proposal *is* in there, a dusty virtual folder that hardly gets touched anymore. It's not very good—probably the worst thing I've ever produced in my entire academic career—because I can't be bothered to do anything other than search for something that might fix Bohdan.

"That's not what I asked." She tilts her head, wisps of hair framing her face. "I asked how you're doing."

"I'm just tired," I whisper, scrunching my nose. "Bohdan's been having trouble sleeping."

It's another lie, but a half one. He either sleeps too much or not at all.

She nods, slow and thoughtful, and her hand finds mine, stilling my tapping fingers. "What's that saying? You have to put your own oxygen mask on first?"

She doesn't understand. Bohdan took care of me. He carried burdens and worries and horrible, ugly thoughts on his back with the promise of me returning the favour one day.

It's my turn.

"I am. It's on, I mean. My mask." I make a vague gesture to my face. "I'm getting enough oxygen." I force a smile. I think I feel the corners of my mouth crack, and if she'd just lean a little closer, she'd see what lives inside me—an entirely oxygen-deprived shell of someone who used to be loved.

Her palm flattens against the back of my hand with a reassuring pat, but I can feel what it's really saying—*I don't believe you.*

But she grabs her bag and pushes to stand. "I'll give you another week's extension. But it needs to be in by then, Sloan. Otherwise, you won't be on track to finish on time." She holds up her hands when my face falls, giving me away. "And that would be okay, you know. I don't think a single PhD in the history of PhDs has been completed on time."

I start to shake my head, fingers extending into space and desperate for something new to cling to—I certainly can't count to three on my relationship, and not on this laptop holding the only thing I'm supposed to be good at—but she presses a hand to my shoulder with a reassuring squeeze.

"Take your time. Think about it. You can take a leave or a break if you need. You're caregiving, after all."

Dr. Amore leaves me in this crowded café with my shut laptop and those words that really just sound like failure.

You're caregiving.

Not really. Not the way I think it should look.

I can't be taking care of Bohdan—at least, not the way he took care of me.

He hardly speaks and when he does, it's not really *to* me, it's just sort of these strung-together words that fall from the mouth I've loved since I was eighteen, not the person who used to live inside the body that's become a shell.

I can't be very good at it, if that's what I'm doing.

It's another thing I wasn't enough for.

That new worry slides into my backpack, sitting haphazardly on the ground by my feet, and it nestles right in beside the ones I've carried since I was a child.

I feel the weight of them when I slide the straps onto my shoulders.

It makes my steps home slower.

My legs seem heavier when I get on the bus.

I'm thankful for the elevator in our building that takes me all the way to the top—to that glass-walled apartment that's become a cage.

Maybe Jay was right all along.

Bohdan's in our bedroom when I get home. All the curtains are drawn, and the last bits of sun peak out from underneath them when they flutter in the breeze.

There's old game tape playing on the TV in the living room, and there's an exercise mat on the floor.

None of those things are good signs.

His brain is horribly cruel on days his body doesn't cooperate.

I gave up trying to tell him that I love him and the capabilities of his body don't really factor in for me. I don't think he was really listening, anyway.

I wouldn't listen to me. I'm clearly not very good at much.

My backpack hits the floor by our door with this impossibly dull thud. It's all those extra worries. All that baggage. All that not-enoughness that echoes through the empty apartment.

Before Bohdan got hurt, it's not an echo you'd ever have been able to hear.

But you can hear it loud and clear now.

Not enough. Not enough. Not enough.

I'm a bit quicker getting to our bedroom than I've been walking around since I talked to Dr. Amore—I dropped those failures with the bag, but I feel them, nipping and grabbing at my heels, dragging me back with each step I take.

I try to kick them off when I get to the door. I grab the frame and shake out each foot before I sprint on quiet feet towards our bed, swinging my legs up so no monsters can grab me, even though they're already in the room with us.

It wakes Bohdan, even though I tried hard to be quiet.

He cringes, eyes blinking slowly before he scrubs his face and rolls over to look at me. The navy sheets shift, falling just below the curved muscles of his arm.

I changed the sheets back.

The seafoam-green wasn't doing anything but hurting me.

He gives me a rare smile. Lazy. *Lovely.*

I don't think he's really awake yet. And as horrible as it is, this is my favourite him now.

The him like the one he used to be—before he wakes up and realizes the world stole from him and he's so, so sad.

"Hey," he whispers, words rough, but I feel like they're smoothing out all the worry lines stretching across my face, and pushing away the frown of my bottom lip.

"Hi. Can we—can we talk? I had—I had a bad day." I sniff, reaching out to touch him, but I think better of it at the last minute and flatten myself down on my side of the bed, staring up at the ceiling.

"Of course we can talk, Zlatíčko," he murmurs, and his thumb swipes across my left cheek.

I inhale sharply. I don't remember the last time he called me that, and I certainly don't remember the last time he touched me the way he used to—with reverence and love and lust and starlight.

It makes me brave.

"I feel like I can't do anything right . . . and I'm trying so, so hard. It's just not enough. It's never enough. I know it's silly but I bought you this new plant, these new sheets, I've looked up all these things you can try . . . and I know I'm not the team doctor, and I know I'm not in your brain or your body, but I'm trying so hard, Bohdan. I want you to have whatever you want—it's what I've always wanted. I can't fix anything. I can't fix this for you the way you fixed things for me. I can't even remember to submit the right papers for school and I'm behind on my grading. I don't think my students really like me anymore. I don't think you really like me anymore. But I'm still here, and I came all this way . . . I came here for you. The only thing I've ever really wanted is you. The only thing I've ever really been sure of is you, and will you please, please just let me in? Please just talk to me. Whatever horrible, depraved things you're thinking. I promise I'll treat them with care. All your thoughts. You . . . the way you are now. I just . . . need you. Please?"

He says nothing. I don't even feel him shift in the bed.

I hope I didn't hurt his feelings. I know it's not his fault. I know his brain is wreaking havoc and waging a war he can't win.

I squeeze my eyes shut. I breathe in and out before rolling over to face him.

He's still here.

Physically, at least.

But he's not here, not really.

He's asleep.

Sloan

"Hibachi."

"Hibachi wasn't on the itinerary."

"Well, it's my cruise, and I'd like to go to the hibachi." Talon grips the edges of the table, leaning forward, and the breeze rolling off the ocean sends curls tumbling over his ears.

Jay presses a palm to his forehead, lines digging in around the corners of his eyes. "Weren't we supposed to go to the casino? Why hibachi? Because you think they're going to let you throw one of the little flippers in the air?"

"I love hibachi." Tia nods, pushing the umbrella sitting in her drink out of the way to clear a path to the straw. Her eyes cut to me, the amber flecks coming alive against the setting sun.

"It's okay." It's not. I don't usually like the texture. But I pucker my lips, shrugging. Bohdan's hand, spread across my shoulder, where his fingers trace the edges of the tattoo, moves with me. I tip my head, glancing at him. "Do you like hibachi?"

He's behind his prescription sunglasses now—I think I saw him take a propranolol earlier, he really was out in the sun too long while Talon played gladiator—but he just jerks his chin. "No."

"He doesn't like anything!" Talon exclaims, tossing his hands in the air before throwing his whole body back in his chair and sending it screeching across the deck, two feet away from the bar table where we were watching the sunset until the word *hibachi* popped into his brain.

"Incorrect," Tia states simply behind her straw.

Jay starts gesturing towards us, saying, "Wrong."

At the same time, Bohdan's thumb presses down into my tattoo and his words, rough around the edges but not on me, slide down the exposed skin between my shoulder blades. "I like Sloan."

Talon tosses us all an exasperated look, but it shifts into one of pleading when he brings his hands together in some sort of mock prayer and taps them against his chest. "Please. Pretty please. I'm not above begging."

I try to laugh, but it dies when I hear my brain perk back up.

Bohdan can't like you that much—can't like you at all really—or he wouldn't have left.

I can't tell it to shut up, at least not out loud, and at least not here. I learned at a young age talking to yourself was generally frowned upon. So I squeeze my eyes shut and jerk my chin, and I hope the thought might finally fall out of my head, maybe through my ear canal, where it can tumble out on the ship deck and I can finally stamp it to death under my sandals.

I don't think anyone notices when I blink my eyes open again—Talon's arguing with Jay about whether shrimp or steak is better—but Tia's mouth sits in a shrewd line, one finger taps against the side of her glass, and I feel Bohdan tense beside me.

Neither of them have time to say anything—Talon wins a game of rock, paper, scissors against Jay that started and finished before anyone could intervene, and he's dragging us down the deck of the ship towards the hibachi restaurant.

It seems like the type of thing you'd need a reservation for on a ship this large with this many families, but Talon can be charming when he wants to be, and he somehow secures us a grill right in the centre of the room.

He points to the metal spatulas held by the chef when he slides into his seat. "Can I have one of those?"

"Knew it," Jay mutters under his breath, pulling out his own chair beside Talon.

The chef slashes the spatulas through the air. "No."

But nothing deters Talon Valdez, and he points his chin to the chef's hat. "What about one of those?"

They do give him one of those, and unfortunately for the rest of us, they have extras.

I think they're for children, because they don't fit right on any of our heads. Not that Bohdan's ever made contact. He grabbed it before it could get anywhere close.

Tia and Jay take selfies, and Jay must have had too much wine because he even goes on Instagram Live, panning the camera everywhere and zooming in on Talon, who somehow convinced the chef to let him come behind the grill, until fans started telling him how much Philadelphia sucked this season and he abruptly ended it.

Our friends laugh, and we do, too. Bohdan's fingers skate along my thighs under the table, and while Talon throws shrimp in the air and jumps backward when the heat of the flames gets to be too much, Bohdan and I talk.

We talk more than we did in the last year we were together. And I don't know if it's the ticking clock that hangs above our heads, or if we're existing in some other dimension since we scrapped the rules.

He tells me about his parents—retired now and so happy, spending most of their time back in Brno with his grandparents, who still ask about me every time they call.

He asks me about Lu, and a muscle jumps in his jaw when I say I'm on a hiatus from therapy, but he doesn't press.

I tell him about my new job, how I can't wait to finally get my hands dirty somewhere in the world, and I make this giant deal about the fresh start I'm getting, how I'm finally, finally moving home.

His features harden at that—eyes turning to slate, the muscles in his jaw tense, and he takes a heavy swallow. But he forces a smile and his fingers press into my thighs.

He shares stories about broadcasting. We laugh because it's not something either of us ever would have considered for him, but he says he likes it—sort of. He dodges my questions about Shay and whether he's getting a permanent spot at the desk next season, and he considers, taking a too-long swallow of water, when I ask him if it's hard to be around the thing he loved more than anything and not be able to have it.

His eyes find mine when he nods, voice somehow rough and soft and something I feel all the way down to my bones. "Yeah, it is."

I wrinkle my nose and listen to my brain when it says not to read too much into it, he's only talking about broadcasting. "Did you ever think we'd be . . . here?"

"On a floating mall in the middle of the Tyrrhenian Sea heading towards Naples while Talon plays chef?" Bohdan glances up at Talon, who's trying his hand at flipping one of the metal spatulas.

I smile, but it's not what I meant. I wave my hands around, and my chef's hat slides to the left, but Bohdan reaches out to straighten it. He tucks errant hair behind my ear, his eyes stay on me a bit too long, and I forget to breathe.

Swallowing, I gesture vaguely again. "No . . . here. Wearing chef hats made for children and catching up over hibachi like we're . . . strangers. Asking questions once upon a time we'd have been able to answer for the other."

"Only one of us is wearing the hat, Sloan," he deflects.

I glance at his hair, almost amber from the sun, messy from all the times he's run his hands through it and the too-high heat of the grill. I lean forward, and maybe I've had a bit too much wine like Jay, but I tug on the end of a wave curling over Bohdan's ear and whisper, "Do you want to pretend we're on the Titanic?"

"Not really." He gives me a flat look, but I think there's laughter hiding somewhere around the corner in his eyes.

"But . . . aren't we?" I ask softly. "Doomed to not make it to shore?"

He grips his jaw with one hand, and the other splays against my leg. I think his fingers might start tapping out counts of three against my skin, in time with each of his next words. "Two more days."

"Two more days," I repeat, tipping my chin up to brush my mouth against his. My fingers brush along his jawline, over the sharp planes of his cheeks, and tentatively, I reach up to touch the precipice of the scar hidden along his temple.

He tenses, but then his lips move against mine more urgently, and I forget it's April 12, 1912, and soon we're going to sink.

Sloan

Then – Seattle

It's a beautiful day—not a single cloud. A bright, vibrant sun.

The kind of day people would run outside for, lift their chin skywards, strip down to tank tops and shorts, and stretch their limbs out on blankets nestled in grass, sitting beside their best friends and people they love.

Unless you're me, and you lay there as the colours changed in the sky and became brighter and brighter but nothing in your world did, while you listened to the love of your life breathe in and out mechanically all night because he fell asleep when you were trying to talk to him.

Unless you're Bohdan, and you take one look at the sky through the window and physically recoil.

I watch him move around the apartment, grabbing things at random and shoving them into his hockey bag. He has an appointment with the team doctor. I'm not sure for what. He stopped answering a while ago, and eventually, I stopped asking.

I wait to see if he might notice me, standing there behind the kitchen island, mug of coffee in my hands. Eyes and cheeks puffy from lack of sleep.

He used to say he liked my face in the mornings after I couldn't sleep—just this tiny, little bit extra—because he said my freckles looked more beautiful.

But he must have been lying because he didn't notice me today.

"You fell asleep early last night," I try, this sad attempt at acknowledgement. My fingers tighten against my mug.

Pathetic, my brain whispers, peeking over my shoulder, watching as this person who used to orbit around me careens off into space without a care.

"Yeah." He doesn't look up; he just keeps tossing things into his bag.

"Oh, I just thought—when I came to bed—never mind, it's stupid." I wave my mug around, and coffee spills over the rounded edge. I don't even bother jumping backward. I just let it stain my shirt—some old one with a raccoon Tia gave me years ago.

I try again. I'm not sure why. "I'm attending a lecture on mummification processes today and how they influenced modern-day embalming."

He might nod, he might raise his eyebrows in acknowledgement, but his eyes pinch closed in pain when he shoulders his bag, and he doesn't say anything else.

You really are a loser, my brain giggles before splaying on its back to stretch out under the sun.

Sloan

"I don't think it's been this bright the entire week." Tia pushes her sunglasses up her nose to cover her eyes.

I tilt my head back, craning my neck up towards the sky. "You're right. There isn't a single cloud."

One of her manicured nails taps the porcelain of her coffee mug. "What do you want to do today? When my brother was drafting up his itinerary, I don't think he realized that 'Day at Sea' wasn't actually an activity."

"We can see what everyone wants to do when they get back from the gym." I move the rest of my fruit around my plate, watching all the other passengers spread out across the deck, enjoying their breakfasts out under the morning sun, trying not to imagine Bohdan laid out on the floor because maybe he pushed himself too hard and his brain started to bleed again.

Tia slides her sunglasses down her nose, eyes sharpening on me. "I don't think we should leave it up to them. I heard rumours about a . . .

belly flop contest in one of the pools. That has my brother written all over it."

"It doesn't have Bohdan written all over it."

Tia lets out a bark of laughter. "No, it absolutely does not."

"What doesn't have Bohdan written all over it?" Talon bounds towards our table, pausing to ruffle my hair before he swings out the chair at the head of the table, turning it backward so he can drop into it, arms slung across it lazily.

"A retirement river cruise," Jay deadpans, dropping into the seat across from Tia.

Hands settle on my shoulders, heavy and light and perfect and every wonderful feeling in this world. I tip my head back, smiling up at Bohdan. Hair askew, tumbling every which way, and grey eyes brighter than the sky.

"Hi. Was your workout okay?" I can't help it, but I glance at his scar, hidden under a wave cresting across his forehead.

"All good." He nods, but the corners of his eyes crease with something that looks a bit like worry when he pulls out the chair beside me.

Talon pulls a sheet of paper that looks like it's seen better days out of the pockets of his shorts, along with a black marker. "Seeing as tomorrow's our last official day, and even though you've both changed the rules of your little contest more times than I can count, I thought we could start our day at sea by tallying up the strikes between you two and declare a winner."

"We weren't actually keeping score." Bohdan presses his fingers to his temple, exasperated.

"I was." Talon shrugs, making a show of flattening out the crumpled piece of paper and uncapping the marker with a loud pop.

"You haven't even been around us the whole week. Wait—why do I have the most strikes?" I open a palm, incredulous, before aggressively tapping my finger against the edge of the sheet.

"Sloan." Talon gives me a look like he feels a bit sorry for me, mouth tugging to the side before he expertly slides the paper across the table and out of the line of fire for my finger. "Sloany. Come on." He blinks at me a bit too much before widening his eyes and gesturing at me. "Look at you. Ten strikes just for looking like that. Bohdan's dream girl walking around on the boat?"

I cross my arms and straighten my shoulders. "Well, that doesn't seem fair."

"Yeah, Talon, it's not her fault she looks like that." Tia holds a hand open towards me.

"Be that as it may . . ." He gives his sister a pointed look before the marker hits another line. "Yellow revenge dress. Great choice, but come on."

"Dress was brutal." Jay nods.

"I liked the dress." Bohdan presses his mouth to the side of my head, but I feel it bowing with a smile. "Yellow's my favourite colour."

It's not. It's cerulean because it reminds him of my eyes.

"Case in point." Talon clicks his tongue, eyes crinkling in sympathy. "Poor fucker didn't stand a chance."

"Never did." Bohdan's mouth moves against the edge of my ear in a whisper.

Talon waves the marker in an exaggerated circle before he hits the paper again. "As I was saying, ten points to Sloan for the dress. But before that, Bohdan, you had at least three points for that whole 'most beautiful girl in the world' speech you gave before boarding." He glances at Bohdan with a slow shake of his head. "And then that whole scene you caused at dinner, talking about what she looks when she—"

"Talon," Bohdan cuts in, words weighed down with warning.

"Well, am I wrong? You said it." He enunciates each word with a tap against the lines scratched on the paper, but Jay cuts him off with a groan.

"This can't be what you planned for the day at sea, man." Jay runs a hand through his hair before reaching forward and helping himself to the rest of Tia's coffee.

A line sketches between Talon's brow. "The plan was . . . day at sea."

"Day at sea?" Tia echoes before throwing me a knowing look. "That's not a plan, Talon. You—somehow—planned this entire cruise, but you couldn't pick a single activity for us to do on this giant ship all full of them?"

"Water aerobics." Talon doesn't miss a beat.

"There's no aerobics today. They're hosting that . . ." The words catch on her disdain, evident in the downturn of her lips. Tia swallows, like the words cause her physical pain. "Belly flop contest."

Talon slumps back in his chair, palming his forehead before his eyes go wide, a bit like a lost puppy.

Jay exhales, tossing a sympathetic cringe towards Talon. He drums his fingers along the table. "Remember when we used to play hide-and-seek in college?"

"We're thirty," Bohdan says flatly.

"Thirty years young." Talon nods enthusiastically, before his gaze swings back and forth between the rest of us, expectant.

Tia gives Jay a look. "Yeah, we played hide-and-seek in your shitty house that—"

Jay scoffs, interrupting, "It wasn't shitty."

Tia purses her lips before continuing, "You just had the biggest room. As I was saying, those were very contained games. We only had *your shitty house* with its sticky floors to contend with. This is a giant ship."

Talon looks around, lower lip extending thoughtfully before his eyes brighten from chocolate to amber, and he points the marker to the top deck of the ship. "What about if we just play on the top deck? It's smaller and less crowded up there."

Tia nods, tapping her finger against her nose. "That's not a bad idea. Everyone's probably going to be watching that highly sophisticated . . . contest."

"I always liked hide-and-seek." I offer Talon an encouraging smile.

"Yeah, because you and Bohdan would 'hide' in his room," Jay mutters with a roll of his eyes.

"Do you want to play?" I blink up at Bohdan.

His fingers drum against my shoulder and he looks down at me, sharp lines of his face too serious for the fact that we're discussing a children's game, but he softens when he winks down at me. "If you do."

I do, actually.

It's a beautiful, bright day. My heart and my brain feel beautiful and bright, too, and tomorrow isn't here yet.

Maybe if I hide well enough, it'll never come.

"Not it," I say, scrunching my nose before looking back at everyone else.

Talon says it last, too busy angling his head so he could study the top deck of the ship with a shrewd expression that tells me he was trying to scope out possible hiding spots.

"Fuck." He groans, scrubbing his face before he swings his finger between all of us. "Ten minutes to hide, or you're all disqualified and I win by default."

———◦◦◦———

My hiding spot leaves a lot to be desired. I picked the place anyone would be most likely to find me—the library—found a book about the excavation of Pompeii, slid down against the shelf in the furthest corner of the room near a supply closet that might have made a better refuge, and tried to stay out of sight. It's also the place Talon would be least likely to look. He's never been a good seeker—he takes it too seriously and never thinks to look in the obvious places.

But someone else looks for me.

"Thought I might find you here. What are you reading?" Bohdan's words skitter across my skin, my heart skips in my chest, too loud and too awake, and I glance up, away from my book.

He looks more beautiful than usual, features shadowed from the low lights, hair almost bronze against the reflection off the rows of mahogany shelves, imposing and taking up all this space with the stretch of his shoulders in this quiet corner of the library.

"Excuse me." I push to stand, shoving at his chest with my book. He doesn't move. "This is my hiding space."

"So?" He grins, dropping his head against the bookcase. "I like the library as much as you do."

I point my book at him before sliding it back into its rightful place on the shelf. "You're supposed to be hiding, too."

"I am," he says, voice a bit rough.

"Hiding alone, Bohdan," I emphasize, pressing back against the stacks of books when he moves to cage me in, ropes and cords of muscle in his arms popping when his palms lie flat on either side of my head.

His eyes strike matches over my cheeks, little fires starting to burn everywhere they touch. "Where's the fun in that?"

"Bohdan," I warn, pursing my lips to hide my smile, about to make a show of ducking under his arm, but he shifts with me, one thigh coming between my legs, trapping me between him and the shelf.

A sharp inhale catches in my throat, and I try to swallow down the pulse of pressure, the way he feels, angled right up against the centre of me.

But he sees it all over, tracking the way my eyelashes flutter, my teeth dig into my lip, how I shift against him without realizing it before my brain whirs to life—wide-awake and telling me it's bad and wrong to feel like this, to want him, in public.

Told you, you're rotten. My brain shakes its head, the slow cadence of disappointment.

"Sloan." He cocks his head back, appraising with measured words. "Does that feel good?"

"No," I try to say, breath caught on my ribs or maybe those old pieces of me we both broke, but the only thing I can really think about is what he feels like between my legs, and how horrible that makes me.

"Sloan," he repeats.

"What?" I whisper, blinking a bit too much, staring over his shoulder at the wall sconce mounted next to a shelf dedicated to books about the French Riviera.

He angles his head, lips hovering above mine. "It's okay if it does. It doesn't make you bad."

313

My eyes pinch closed with a jerky shake of my head, and I wish all the thoughts would fall out, but they sink their claws in and hold on for dear life. "But we're in public. Anyone could find us . . . it's not . . . appropriate."

His thumb finds my chin, tipping my face up before he gently brushes it across each of my eyelids, inviting them back open. Bohdan's voice drops, this hoarse call against a raging sea, and he throws me these buoys I don't think I deserve to catch. "You're compassionate. You're funnier than you have any right to be when you're being the most stubborn woman on the planet. And you're allowed to feel good things."

"What?" I murmur.

"Three facts, Sloan. You're not bad." He shakes his head, slow, a bit sad and a bit soft for the way his cheekbones look like they could flay me open. "Far from it."

"But—"

"No buts," he says with a firm press of his thumb to my chin, before he looks over his shoulder and tips his head towards the closet door. "Come here."

"Anyone could find us." I still, but it feels a bit quieter in my mind because how could I be bad when someone like him thinks I'm wonderful? He's right there, all hard edges, pressure builds in my core, and when my palms find his shoulders, fingers digging into the muscle, I roll my hips forward.

The left side of his mouth tugs into a sideways grin. He guides me, purposeful and insistent, all the way into the empty closet. He looks down at me, words full of promise when he turns the lock and says, "They won't. I've got you, Zlatíčko."

He does have me, even after all these years.

Even in an empty supply closet. My back against the door while he props me up against the ridges of muscle in his thigh.

His mouth brushes mine, soft and careful, before he drags his tongue along the pout of my bottom lip, all the way across my jaw, where it swirls against my earlobe.

"Use me," he whispers, gravelly, teeth scraping against my skin, hands finding my hips, fingers bruising when he catches a low moan with a swallow.

He has me the way he always did. Heart in his chest, best friend to the one that lives in mine, hands on me, rough and gentle and then rough again when he grinds me against the muscles of his thigh.

"Come," he instructs; words like his teeth where they scrape against my jaw.

I roll forward, against the hardness of his leg, golden skin soaked with me through my own clothes, and I bury my face in his neck, nails digging down into his shoulders, trying to quiet all the noise caught in my throat when I combust from the inside out.

"*Kurva.* Fuck, fuck, fuck." Bohdan shifts against me, straining against the linen of his shorts, hands digging into my hips, just this side of pain, and the muscles in his jaw tense, carving a line down his neck when he groans.

"Did you—" I breathe, lifting my head from the crook of his shoulder.

"Come in my pants?" He lifts a brow wryly, swiping a thumb across his mouth. "Not yet, but we need to get back to the stupid suite before I ruin my fucking shorts."

"I'm sorry?" I blink, before sniffing a laugh.

"I'm not." He jerks his chin, grinning at me, before his fingers tap softly against my hips. "Trust me."

I do trust him, even after all this time and after all this hurt. And there are these words I'm dying to say, they're all over me, written on all this new skin he crafted with those rough hands, and I think they're what my heart says when it beats, still erratic and too fast in my chest.

I love you, I love you, I love you.

But I don't trust those words again, not yet.

"Found you." Bohdan breathes, dropping his forehead to mine.

He did find me, I think. Then and now, and I wish he'd find me forever.

Bohdan

I don't think Talon was thinking about anyone but himself when he picked the cruise itinerary.

He certainly wasn't thinking about me and Sloan.

Or, if he was, it was probably something like, "Bohdan liked rocks in college and Sloan loves ancient shit—they'll love Pompeii."

He wasn't thinking about the fact that we were already an eruption the size of Mount Vesuvius that left nothing but ash and dust in our wake.

He wasn't thinking about the fact that we're Pompeii, wrecked and dead and frozen in time.

He wasn't thinking about the fact that somehow, we'd find each other again here, and against all my better judgement, because I love her more than anyone has ever loved anything in the history of the universe, I'd let her convince me to crawl up out of the rubble and go back in time for two days before everything erupts again.

It's not lost on me when I watch the early-morning sun inch across her skin and her eyelashes flutter in her sleep, study her hands and her fingers where they're curled into the pillow, and try to memorize the way her hair falls across her collarbone and how her nose twitches with these tiny snores I'd listen to on repeat from now into eternity.

It's not lost on me when she blinks her eyes open, sleepy and slow. Or when her lips shift into a pout, when they open for mine, and my tongue meets hers, her legs wrapping around my waist and inviting me inside her, and we move together under the morning sun, languid and unhurried like we've got all the time in the world.

We don't have any, not at all.

It's the last day and tomorrow, she's going to trade me the cup ring for a Polaroid I'd have died to keep and the answer to her question I'd have rather taken to my grave.

We're the volcano, not dormant at all, and I feel the pressure building inside her when she starts to tighten around me, her moans into my neck are the shifting of tectonic plates, and I come when she does, but it's her whisper against my ear that causes the eruption.

"I wish this didn't have to end."

Bohdan

Then – Seattle

You fell asleep early last night.

Yeah.

Oh. I just thought—when I came to bed—never mind, it's stupid.

It's not stupid, but I am.

Really fucking brutal and terrible actually.

Can't skate.

Can't see the sunlight without it causing me blinding pain like some sort of fucking vampire.

Can't even hold a conversation with the person who has my heart in their palms.

Can't do fucking anything.

My fingers tense against the porcelain rim of the sink, and I glance up at the mirror. I can't see myself—it's covered in steam from the shower, and usually that'd be for the best. I'm not a big fan of looking at my own reflection anymore, but I wipe the steam off and force myself to look today.

Hair matted to my forehead, but the angry red scar peeks out from underneath. Grey circles under my eyes because my sleep is all over the place. Hollow cheeks covered in unkempt stubble because I forget to shave most days.

I try to forget most things. That I should be playing. That I had a dream and it got stolen by a stupid accident. That I was the best. That I'm supposed to be closing in on records. That I should have almost a decade left of playing in me. That at the end of the day, it's unfair because guys get hit all the time and this doesn't happen to them.

But it happened to me.

I'm not sure if that's whatever's left of my scrambled-up brain trying to protect me—my psychiatrist says forgetting can be a powerful thing, but it's not always the best.

Forgetting was working, sort of.

Until I started to forget things about Sloan.

A muscle in my jaw ticks, and I clench the sink before making a fist and knocking it against the countertop, right beside my little pharmacy of pain meds and too many antidepressants to count.

I don't think they're really working, either. They make me foggy and sluggish and slower than the stupid accident made me on the ice.

I feel a bit like swiping them all off the counter. I don't—I open them up one by one and swallow them with water from the tap instead.

I tried skipping them, but the nausea and the brain zaps were almost worse than what it feels like to be on them.

My eyes find the mirror again, but it's not my reflection I see.

It's Sloan.

Standing in the kitchen this morning, sunlight streaming in and doing things to her eyes that I would usually notice but my brain just skipped right over. Hands gripping a mug and I can see now that her finger was tapping against the handle in quick counts of three.

Cheeks red, her usual soft smile strained.

You fell asleep early last night.

She needed me, and I was supposed to tell her three things I loved about her. Three facts to help her, and I couldn't.

Truthfully, I probably couldn't have strung three facts about anything together even if I tried.

I blink, and it's just me in the mirror again.

Some pathetic shell of a man.

"Fucking useless." I smack my hand against the side of my head. "You don't deserve her."

Maybe a different me did.

But this stranger? Whoever he is?

He doesn't deserve shit.

Bohdan

Then – Seattle

It takes me longer than it should to work up the courage to do it.

I didn't do it the day I should have—when I looked in the mirror and realized I was worthless and the only thing I could do right was hurt her.

I'm not sure why I pick that day—a random Wednesday.

I grab the singular sorry duffel bag I packed earlier and sit down on her side of the bed by her feet, not close enough to reach her even if I was tempted. And I would be. Always with her.

Maybe it's something to do with the fact that I can feel how beautiful she is with each beat of my heart. It's not just blood pumping through my veins.

It's her laugh.

It's the stars living in the freckles on her cheeks.

It's the way she has the covers tugged right up to her chin.

How her hair fans out across her pillow and it might as well be the silk they used to weave into tapestries to tell love stories in all those ancient worlds she finds so fascinating.

But each time my heart does what it's supposed to do, beating to keep me alive and keep me here with her, I feel all those things, and I feel the pulse of blood that makes my scar throb and it reminds me I don't deserve any of them anymore.

I stare at her, gilded by the moonlight shining through the windows, before I open my mouth and stomp on the already ruined wreckage of our lives.

I should talk to her—finally—tell her that I'm dizzy all the time, and at this point, I want to die just about every minute of every day because I'm living in a body I don't think belongs to me.

I know what she's going to hear and what kind of brutal web of lies her brain is going to weave—that she isn't, wasn't, won't ever be enough.

But that's not true. She's gravity, the planet, the solar system, the universe, the whole galaxy.

I swallow, and I do it anyway.

"I love you." She says it like it's a "but," a sort of qualifier that's going to make me stay.

It won't. It can't.

"I'm leaving," I tell her, running my thumb across her cheek one last time.

I think she says I love you again, but I can't hear anything over the pounding of blood in my ears and the pulse of fucking pain lancing across my head that buckles my knees by our front door.

She doesn't follow. She's trapped, and I don't think it's her brain keeping her in our bed.

It's mine. She's stuck up here, in a cage I built for us. When I open the front door, I hope it sets her free.

I don't remember doing it, but I leave.

I leave all the way to Brno to stay with my grandparents for three months.

I walk with my grandmother every day when she goes to Svoboďák. It's more time than I've spent outside in months. I tell her over Turek and sometimes Becherovka that I don't think I'll ever be the same, and that's why I had to go.

That I hope one day Sloan understands, and even though it fucking kills me, I hope she thanks me for it.

The thought of her moving on hurts.

The sunlight hurts. My head hurts. My heart hurts.

I hurt, because there's this piece of me missing.

Left behind with all these unsaid things.

That I love her.

That it wasn't her.

That she was always enough.

That she's the best thing that's ever happened to me.

That I'd fall on the sword every day if it meant she had a chance at being happier without me.

And when I do go home, I leave them the same way—unsaid—and I move across the country so she'll never have to see me again.

Sloan

It's my favourite day on the cruise.

It's not just because we spent it exploring this archaeological phenomenon I've wanted to see my entire life.

It's not just because everyone gets excited when I do and Bohdan looks at me instead of looking at all these other things he should love.

It's not just because we laugh more than we should when Talon asks the guide in all seriousness if the preserved food would still be edible underneath all that carbon.

I do feel young and invincible again, and it is quiet inside my brain. But it's not those things either.

It's because Bohdan pulls me aside, right before we walk up the gangway back onto the ship.

The air full of brine, stings when I inhale, and birds swoop low overhead, calling out loudly, occasionally diving into the water by the quay. But I just smell pine and snow and quiet nights. Him.

He wraps his fingers around my wrist, and it's his heartbeat I think I hear when he brings my palm to his chest.

He studies me, head angled to the side, eyes roving over my face thoughtfully, tracing the pillow of my cheek, the slope of my nose, and the set of my lips. So serious, like always, and I know whatever he's going to say next is horribly important.

I feel a bit like I did all those years ago, standing on those steps leading up to my dorm while he set me on fire, and I wonder if the flames ever really went out.

"This morning in bed . . . you said you didn't want this to end." Bohdan takes a measured swallow.

"I don't," I whisper truthfully.

"I don't either." He shakes his head, and the way his hair falls, I can't see the scar. It's like it was never there. He presses one hand over top of mine, and I feel his heart rate change under the cotton of his shirt when he keeps talking. "What if it didn't? What if we left together?"

"I'm moving home," I say, words a bit like fragile glass that could crack any moment. If he asked me not to, I'm not sure what my answer would be.

He smiles, slow and sure. "I know. I'll follow you. The way you followed me."

"Why?" I ask, because I still can't imagine being someone worth following.

"I won't survive not knowing you again."

A cloud tumbles across the sky, and when it does, a ray of sunlight stretches across his face.

His eyes don't pinch closed. He doesn't squint. He doesn't look like he's in pain at all, actually.

"The ring. The Polaroid," I start, and I might be scrambling for excuses, because as much as the idea of Bohdan fills my lungs up with more oxygen than they've had in months, it scares me, too.

I don't say it, but those other words—that other thing I asked for—hang there, too.

The why.

He taps his thumb against the back of my hand. "Don't give it back. I told you. I don't care. But I'll bring the Polaroid, we'll talk and—" He cuts himself off with another swallow and a jerk of his chin. "And whatever happens . . . we'll get through it this time. I promise."

It's my favourite day, because for a few hours, I believe him—and I almost believe in myself.

Bohdan

What happened all the way back in 79 AD when Mount Vesuvius erupted and destroyed Pompeii was bad.

What happened a year and a half ago when I destroyed us was bad.

What happened when my head cracked against the ice and destroyed my career was bad.

And I thought what happened this morning was bad. When Sloan stirred up all that magma still there because I'll burn for her forever and forced it up through all that rubble and all those fissures in the earth when she told me she didn't want it to end.

She smiled more today than I think she has in a long, long time, and maybe it was a trick my brain played on me when I caught her wiping away tears of laughter that made her eyes bluer than they had any right to be—and I thought I could be a good thing for her again.

How could anything to do with loving someone this much ever be bad?

It's what made me pull her aside and swear we'd get through anything, because it would take something more than an eruption or an implosion to keep me from her again.

I meant what I said—we'll get through anything and everything—and I promised myself when she blinked up at me, standing there under the sunlight, that I'd tell her anything and everything she needs to know tomorrow like she asked, and I'll never leave again.

I memorized numbers in too many languages for her, and I'll memorize the words *I'm sorry*, too.

Talon taps his foot impatiently at the top of the gangway. He widens his eyes when we step back onto the ship and I put my arm around Sloan, tugging her closer. "What took so long? You two decide you need to run back to Pompeii to collect dust samples from the rocks and take a look at that fossilized bread again?"

"Carbonized," I correct.

Jay gives him a flat look. "The bread you thought you could eat?"

Talon throws his hands in the air. "I didn't think you could actually eat it, I thought maybe it was partially—you know what? Never mind. Can we get a picture? It's our last night."

He hikes a thumb over his shoulder to the studio photography backdrop, displayed by one of the information desks, and the photographer waiting there, currently aimlessly clicking through as families line up one by one.

"Is that one of those ones where they superimpose you onto some obviously fake background?" Jay looks more disgusted than he probably should be by the prospect, but straightens the sleeves of his striped linen shirt.

"Talon," Tia whines, tipping her head back before gesturing to her hair and the curls escaping what was once a ponytail. "I look like shit from the heat."

"You could never look like shit." Jay throws her a grin that only has her rolling her eyes.

I press my hand into Sloan's shoulder. "Do you want a photo?"

She looks up at me, thoughtful. "Why not? Commemorate the occasion."

Her voice drops a bit, but Tia's eyes sharpen momentarily, a shrewd, assessing sort of look passing over her face before she cocks her head, studying the way my palm rests against Sloan's shoulder.

She's been looking at me like that all week—lying in wait to see if whatever new, inventive way she thinks I'm planning on hurting Sloan might somehow reveal itself in the set of my jaw or the way I roll out my neck.

But Tia doesn't understand that the only thing I want as much as I want Sloan is to prove to her that even though a very bad thing did happen the last time she said I love you, it doesn't mean it will again.

It won't.

Tia doesn't say anything, but she does smile a bit before rolling her eyes when her brother makes us stand in some sort of horrible, awkward prom pose, Sloan in front of me with my arms around her waist, positioning Tia and Jay similarly so he can stretch out across the floor between us.

He makes us wait until it's developed and pinned to the board alongside all the other photos of smiling families. Jay was right—it is superimposed onto a very obviously fake photo of a beach, but Talon practically sprints to tear it down anyway, holding it up in something like triumph.

"I don't think you're supposed to do that." Jay points to the ripped edges of the photo, jagged where Talon tore it from the board.

He waves him off. "Whatever, man, I'll pay for it."

"When you do, make sure you ask for more than one copy. I'm sure we all want to remember this week." Tia flashes her brother a tight smile.

"I'll put it on our next fridge," I murmur, pressing my mouth to the top of Sloan's ear.

They were words just for her, but three sets of eyes snap to us, each one our friends' attention rapt, a bit like it was when they found me in her room the other night.

"Did you just say *our*?" Tia's mouth parts and her amber eyes go wide.

"What fridge?" Talon blinks, confused.

"No shit." Jay's gaze darts back and forth between us, and maybe he senses the sort of cataclysmic shift that happened this morning when I heard her whisper what she wanted—that it was still me after all this time—because understanding dawns and he raises his brows, smiling fondly when he swipes a hand through his hair.

I feel Sloan fidget under my arm, the way she rolls her shoulders so they're straight. "Bohdan's going to come home with me."

"No fucking way." Talon glances back and forth between us, still holding the picture up. "For real?"

That same look crosses over Tia's face, but it disappears into a smile when Jay starts shaking her shoulders, his face fracturing with a grin when he asks, "What should we do to celebrate?"

Sloan shrugs again, but I can feel the more relaxed slump of her shoulders, and I can hear the smile in her voice when she waves a hand in the air and says, "Let Talon pick, it's his cruise."

He doesn't hesitate. "Water aerobics."

There's a collective groan—but no one argues with him.

It's how we end up in a too-crowded pool with people trying to wrap their heads around the synchronized movements, and a too-loud thump of a bass from a nearby speaker that should hurt my head but doesn't because it's Sloan's hand in mine, tugging me to the corner of the pool.

Jay takes it too seriously, claiming he hasn't had a good workout the entire trip.

Tia gives up halfway through and stretches out a nearby deck chair, sun hat pulled low over her face so she doesn't have to watch the spectacle.

Talon almost gets into a fight with a thirteen-year-old who accidentally knocks him over the head with a pool noodle.

Sloan doesn't like organized group activities like this because she hates that people might be watching her, so we whisper about our friends and plan out our fictional new apartment. I think of all the ways I can prove to her I'm worthy again, and occasionally pretend to look interested in the instructions when Talon throws a pointed glance over his shoulder.

He abandons the class eventually, making us move to a smaller pool where he swears up and down that he can swim a faster lap than any of us and successfully goads Jay into a race.

They tie, actually, but they each think they won, and they make me join so someone can actually come in first.

"Good luck." Sloan's mouth tilts into a soft, quiet smile. "You were always faster on ice than them. Water can't be very different. I think you'll win."

I press my thumb to her bottom lip. "Already did."

Sloan

"You look beautiful." Tia squeezes my fingers. "Grey is a great colour for you."

I glance down, tugging at the silk dress clinging to my thighs. "Oh. Thanks. It seems kind of like a waste to dress up like this. I didn't realize the five-course dinner to cap off the cruise would be on our balcony."

She nods thoughtfully, tapping her index finger to her pouted lower lip, somehow avoiding smudging the pink lipstick she spent ten minutes in the mirror expertly painting. "It is a bit odd, Talon usually likes to make a spectacle. But you heard him going on and on today when we were in the shuttle—how this is one of the only ships in the world equipped with a suite like this."

I give her a look. "It was quite the soliloquy."

"He really should consider public speaking as a future career now that this cruise is over." Tia wrinkles her nose before straightening the front of her own dress. When she's decided it all lies exactly as it should, she peers up at me, all furtive. "Or . . . matchmaking. He's going home with you? That's not walking away from him tomorrow morning, Sloan."

Her eyes cut to the glass doors of the balcony, to Talon, Jay, and Bohdan standing out there beside a table set with decorations that border on ostentatious, ornate crystal glasses and gold-rimmed charger plates keeping the white tablecloth from catching on the ocean breeze.

"Because I don't want to walk away. I don't want it to end." I shift back and forth on my feet, and I try to smile at my best friend, but it catches on something.

"Sloan." She breathes, her fingers feathering in space before they brush across my shoulder. She pauses at the tattoo, like she's afraid to touch it, before she makes a show of straightening the straps of my dress. "Is that . . . is it the best idea for you two to just jump right back into things? I've watched you these last few days, and I get it, I do. There's never been a love for you like his, and there'll never be a love for him like yours. But—"

I don't get to hear what she's going to say next because Talon knocks on the balcony door, eyes wide and expectant. He doesn't say anything, but he taps an invisible watch on his wrist.

Tia makes a waving motion before she rolls her eyes, muttering, "I have no idea why he's in such a hurry. It's not like we're going to miss a reservation. The whole dinner was already catered!"

"You don't think it's a good idea?" I whisper, but she's wise to my tricks and she knows it's a sad plea for reassurance.

She exhales, smoothing back imaginary escaped curls from her bun. Her words say one thing, but her eyes say another. "I just want *you* to be happy."

My lips part, another plea ready, but Talon throws open the door. He leans forward, hands gripping the frame, causing the shoulders of his tux to buckle. "Guys, come on. You only have to play along for one more night."

He blinks pleading eyes at us, and I force a smile, gathering the skirt of my dress to follow Tia out onto the balcony into the night air.

Tia pats her brother's chest as she walks past. "We've had a blast, don't worry. Maybe we should make it an annual thing?"

"Really?" Talon perks up, standing taller on the balls of his feet.

"No," Jay answers, shrugging off his white dinner jacket and tossing it onto the back of one of the chairs before he sits down.

"It's been fun, Talon." I try to smile at him, but my eyes wander right on by everything else and land on Bohdan.

One leg kicked up against the glass railing surrounding the balcony, hands shoved into the pockets of his suit pants. Black jacket stretching across perfect shoulders, the top three buttons of his white dress shirt undone, one wave of hair curling down and hiding the scar. He angles his head. "Zlatíčko. You look beautiful."

"Thank you," I murmur, brushing out invisible wrinkles in the front of my dress when Bohdan kicks off the railing to hold my chair out for me.

"You're welcome, Sloany." Talon grins, tapping my shoulder affectionately before pulling out his chair.

"She wasn't thanking you." Jay runs a hand through his hair, sending the ebony strands falling every which way.

Talon shrugs one shoulder, reaching across the table and pouring a too-full glass of scotch from a crystal decanter. "She should be. No retirement river cruise, no getting absolutely dicked—"

"Do not finish that fucking sentence." Bohdan cuts a glare at Talon, brushing his fingers along the stretch of my shoulder before he tucks my chair in and takes the seat beside me, a hand resting across my thigh.

"Well." Talon waves him off before knocking his fist against the table and raising his glass of scotch, the amber liquid sparkling beyond the intricate crystal detailing. "The retirement river cruise is officially coming to an end."

"Not a river," Tia mutters, ripping a bread roll in half and attacking it with a butter knife.

"What a shame." Jay raises his brows before emptying his wine and grabbing the bottle on the table to refill it.

"I personally think it's been very enjoyable." Talon bothers to look affronted for two seconds before he turns to Bohdan, grin catlike. "Bohdan, did you have a good time? Maybe you'd like to give a toast. Anything you want to thank me for?"

Bohdan shrugs, the corners of his lips turning down, but I can tell by the way his left cheek twitches that he's fighting a smile. "No, I'm good."

Talon scoffs, leaning back in his chair, waving the glass of scotch around again. "Shay might want to rethink that whole mental health sports thing. Like pulling fucking teeth trying to get you to talk."

I blink.

Bohdan stills, hand suspended midair as he reaches halfway across the table for his glass of water. The other tightens against my thigh.

I shift, turning to face him, almost preternaturally slow and still.

I think I'm back in the horror movie we stumbled into when I saw Bohdan for the first time on the gangway.

There *is* something in the room with us, and it never left.

A breeze lifts off the ocean. Stars wink in the sky above us. But I don't notice them. I blink again. "What mental health sports thing?"

Talon doesn't notice anything either. He gestures to Bohdan, the cuff links on his tux catching under the moonlight. "Network wants to make

Bohdan the face of athletes' mental health. Imagine him, on TV? Talking about his feelings?"

"No," I say quietly. "I can't."

Bohdan runs a hand down his face before palming his jaw with a slow shake of his head.

"You're going to what? Host an entire show?" I push back from the table with shaky hands and an even shakier heart. "When you couldn't even talk to me?"

"Sloan—" he starts, grabbing the edges of my chair like he's going to try to drag me closer to him.

I dig my heels into the ground, childlike. "Don't."

He presses his eyes closed and flashes his palms in the air before pushing his own chair back.

"Oh ... no." Talon cringes, tugging on the ends of his hair before straightening his bow tie.

Jay groans into his fist. "Jesus Christ, Talon. You can't keep your mouth shut to save your fucking life."

"What did you do?" Tia asks, but she's not looking at her brother, she's looking at Bohdan.

Told you, my brain exhales, sympathetic and scornful all at once. *What have you ever mattered?*

I inhale, the air sharp and stabbing and painful. My voice cracks. "I begged for you to talk to me. I *begged*."

"I wasn't going to take the job, Sloan. Why would I want to do that? When that's what fucking cost me you?" Bohdan holds his arms open, eyes sharp and on me before he tugs at his hair, wincing when his fingers graze his scar. "I asked Shay to find me something back home—"

"That's not the point, Bohdan!" I raise my voice at him for the first time since before he got hurt.

We fought sometimes, in the way that all couples do.

When he turned into a shadow in front of me, things got so, so quiet. And not the good kind of quiet I used to beg for. It wasn't a reprieve for my brain. Sometimes, I thought about screaming or yelling or begging him to hear me. But the idea that my voice might scare away whatever parts of him were left, as silent and lifeless as they were—the idea that he might realize all those things I'd been telling him about myself for years were true—had me whispering.

But I don't feel like whispering now. "You still can't talk to me. Can you?"

"I didn't want to hurt you." He presses his fingers to his temple.

"Sloany—" Talon starts, leaning across the table with an open hand, like he's expecting me to take it. "I'm sorry, I shouldn't have said anything. It's not a big deal, I swear. I—"

"Let her yell, Talon," Bohdan says, words firm, eyes never leaving me.

Tia reaches forward, grabbing her brother's hand where it stays outstretched on the table. Talon Valdez is so many things—facetious, absurd, ridiculous—but he loves his friends so, so much. It's painted all over his face, how much it hurts him that he hurt us.

She interlaces her fingers with her brother's and gives his hand a reassuring squeeze before glancing to Jay, who's already halfway out of his seat. "We'll go back inside. You guys can meet us later."

"No. Stay." Bohdan gives a sharp jerk of his chin. "I deserve it."

Jay cringes, drops back into his seat and stares pointedly at the ocean.

"Sloan?" Tia looks at me, imploring, like she's waiting for direction, and I think if I asked her, she'd do her very best to throw Bohdan overboard even though she's half his size.

"Why'd you leave?" I tip my chin up, wrap my arms around my chest, try to inhale and prepare for the thing I've been dreading for so long. That he'll tell me how horrible and vile I am. That I was right all along. But his eyes close, resigned, his fingers find the bridge of his nose, and it's then I realize. I shake my head, words hardly a whisper. "You don't even have a good reason, do you?"

You're not even worth having a legitimate reason. I imagine my brain doing something mundane—a horrible, evil girl from middle school who barely spares you a glance while she's filing her nails.

The set of his jaw sharpens. Grey eyes turn to stone and he stares, assessing, before he tells me the truth. "Because I couldn't love you without hurting you."

A laugh catches in my throat. It cuts me open, I think.

It's horribly painful. Not quite ironic—but it's something. That he could look so beautiful out here under the moonlight, silhouette framed by the ocean, and give me this simple answer to this question I tried to make into this giant thing that would finally, finally free me.

It doesn't free me.

Not at all.

It shackles me.

My worst fear—my biggest worry—wasn't that all the bad, evil, horrible things I've thought about myself were true.

It was this. That I was so worthless, so *nothing*, that there wasn't even a good reason to explain it all away.

I watch as my brain turns new keys in new locks and whispers cruel new things, and I think I'm right back where I started.

"It wasn't just your choice though, was it?" I try not to cry, but I feel the tears sting my cheeks when the breeze hits my face, and this dam inside me I've spent so, so long keeping closed bursts. "You said we were a team—you said that when we were practically just kids. And when it was my turn to take care of you—it just wasn't good enough. You what, got bored of waiting for me to figure out how to do it properly? You left me. You gave up on me."

"It was me who wasn't enough, Sloan." He says it so quietly, my brain tramples right over it. "I gave up on me. Not you. Never you."

I point at him with a shaking finger and push to stand. "I gave up so much for you. I gave and I gave and I gave because that stupid game was your dream."

"It wasn't my dream."

"How is it possible that it wasn't? When it was gone, so were you!"

He stands, and he's so much taller than me. I forget about our friends, he takes up so much space out here on this balcony and in me still. There's this part of me, and it's not as small as I wish it was—I don't think there's anything in the world I want more than to bury my face in his chest and cry. The way I did my whole life because he's always been a safe space and he always made me feel better.

Bohdan gives a final, resigned shake of his head. "I was going to tell you, Sloan . . . I swear. But this . . . this is why I waited, why I didn't want . . . how was I supposed to tell you that? That you gave up so much for me and it all turned into nothing?"

"Nothing?" I choke. "There you go with that word again. *Nothing.* You know you told me that once, right? The one time you fucking deigned to talk to me? You said you had nothing left. But there I was. A living, breathing person, lying beside you in bed every night and begging you to let me love you and take care of you the way you took care of me." Tears blur my vision, and I think they slice me open when they slide down my face. The way my heart stumbles, it does feel a bit like I'm bleeding out. I press a palm to my chest. "That almost breaks my heart, Bohdan. Almost makes me feel sorry for you. That you think you were nothing. I gave things up for *you*. And I did it happily, because you were enough for me, but apparently, I wasn't enough for you."

I dig my palms into my eyes, a sob sneaks up my spine, but his voice, unrestrained and wavering and wild, rings out, fighting for me, the way I wish he would have back then.

"What do I need to do to show you? You want me on my knees?" He takes a step closer to me, not measured, hardly steady at all, and he does drop to his knees. His hands find my waist, his thumbs press into my hips, and I feel them through the silk of my dress—firm, warm. Much steadier than he looks. His voice cracks when he keeps talking. "There. I'm on my knees, Sloan. You want me to crawl? I'll fucking crawl for you. In front of our friends. In front of every single person on this fucking ship, if that's what it takes for you to realize you're enough. That it was always about me, and it was never about you."

Tia snaps her fingers, her voice a bit like the lighthouse sounding out in the night, trying to warn us that we're getting too close to shore and we're going to crash. "Bohdan, you've done enough."

"I love you, and I never fucking stopped." Bohdan shakes his head, and if I believed enough about myself to believe I was someone worth crying over, I'd say that there might be tears pooling along the bottom of his lash line.

"Bohdan," Jay cuts in, voice laced with something like warning.

"Let's take a minute." Talon raises his hands, and tries to give us all a strained smile.

Bohdan doesn't seem to hear them.

But he hears me.

"Stop," I whisper softly. It's quite the sight, and once upon a time I would have said this was all I wanted. Bohdan finally cracking open his chest, giving me a glimpse of what was going on inside him. But this isn't how I wanted it to happen, it's dark and cavernous and sad in there, and I think there's still something horribly, horribly wrong inside me that nothing can fix right now. I reach out and brush his hair off his face. His eyes shutter closed and he leans into my palm at my next words. "I'm saying stop now, Bohdan."

He does. Right away.

He doesn't get off his knees, but he exhales and presses a fist to his mouth.

He stays there when I take a measured step back, when Tia's hand slides into mine. When her arm wraps around my shoulders and she guides me back towards the suite.

I look back when I hear him say, "I love you."

I leave anyway.

Just like he did.

Sloan

You'd think it'd be one of the worst nights of my life.

Ranked third of all time, maybe. Or that it would be a toss-up between the night Bohdan got hurt, the night he left, and this one. The night I realized the only person I need to love right now is myself.

But it's not. Not really.

Because there are other people here that love me, and the prospect doesn't feel as scary as it has my entire life.

Tia crawls into bed with me and braids my hair. Talon brings me a glass of ice water. Jay hugs me longer than I think he ever has.

And Bohdan stays away because I asked him to stop.

My worst fear came true—served on a silver platter to the cruelest parts of my brain.

I sit with that, all flayed open and exposed, and there's no Bohdan here to tell me facts that suggest otherwise.

I sleep, exhausted but undisturbed and dreamless, until the morning light spills across the floor.

Tia shifts, her curls just peeking up from underneath the duvet when I get up. It's early, but I feel a bit like watching the ship get closer and closer to the port.

The door creaks, but it doesn't disturb her.

It disturbs Bohdan, still in his suit, sitting against the wall across from my door, one knee raised with his elbow resting there, turning a worn paperback over in his hands, when he jerks his head up at the sound.

"Have you been out here all night?" I ask softly, sliding along the brocade wall to sit beside him.

"Yeah. I didn't want—" He pauses with a sharp flinch. "Had visions of you somehow sneaking out in the middle of the night and taking one of the lifeboats to shore so you could get to the port earlier than the rest of us." He gives me a dry grin and tosses the paperback down onto the floor beside him.

I poke at the corner of the book. "*American Psycho*?"

"It's Talon's." Bohdan's brows lift with the left corner of his mouth.

I snort. "Has he even read this?"

"I don't think so." Bohdan gives me a strained smile and drops his head against the wall. He swallows and rolls his neck, blinking bleary eyes at me, the lines tugging around them grooved deeper from a lack of sleep. "Are you okay?"

I give him a sad, tired smile. "No. Are you?"

His nostrils flare with an exhale and he shakes his head. "No."

I reach out and try to smooth away the worry line etched between his brow.

It's instinct, woven into the fabric of us, right alongside the running stitches that spell out the way we love each other, to want to take care of him. My worst fear came true last night, and that still didn't change.

He stills at the contact, features softening before he speaks, voice low and rough. "What do you want, Sloan? I meant what I said. I don't want to be without you."

"I don't either," I murmur.

He raises a hand, holding it up with all the possibilities of all the things I think he would do for me if I asked. "You want me to follow you? I will. You want me to chase you? I will. You want me to move to a remote cabin in Alaska and never speak to another soul again while you live out your life? I'll do that, too."

"I want"—I close my eyes, take a measured inhale and try so hard to be brave—"to get off this ship. I want to move home. I want to go back to therapy. And for once in my entire life, I want to feel like enough for myself."

"I want that for you, too. It's all I've ever wanted." He smiles, sad and quiet, knocking his head against the wall once before trying to toss me a grin. "I should probably increase my sessions with my psychiatrist. Add communication to the agenda."

I smile back, but my eyes start to burn. "Bohdan Novotnak, soon-to-be expert communicator."

"I'm sorry for what I did to us." There's a fissure in his voice like that trench between us, and he palms his jaw.

"It wasn't you." I reach out, fingers trailing gently across his forehead to rest against the raised edge of the scar. "Brains can be cruel."

He exhales, sharp lines of his face turning rueful. "I wish I could have talked to you back then."

"Me too." I half laugh, wiping away a stray tear.

"Can I call you? When you get home?" He tugs on the ends of his hair, and I blink. He looks a bit like a boy again—softer, somehow. Not stoic and steadfast. A bit adrift, like me.

I hope we drift back together one day.

"I think . . . I'd like you to wait. I'll send word when I'm ready to hear from you." I try to give him a prim nod.

"Send word, will you?" A grin cracks across his face, his eyes get lighter but all that does is show me that there are real tears, unshed and shining there. That maybe I am a person worth crying over.

"Expect a carrier pigeon," I say through a wet laugh.

"There's my girl." He exhales and reaches up to cup my cheek, thumb pressing into each freckle in turn. "Jedna. Dvě. Tři."

We're in two places at once again—then and now.

I'm eighteen and he's twenty and he's counting my freckles and telling me he loves me in a too-small dorm room.

I'm twenty-eight and he's thirty and he's counting my freckles on a cruise ship about to dock in Barcelona and I'm asking him to let me go.

"You'll wait for me?" The last word hitches on a sob and I close my eyes while he brushes away my tears now just like he did back then.

"Yeah, Zlatíčko. I think I will."

Bohdan

It might be more painful to say goodbye to Sloan on the gangway than it was to see her again—standing there, beautiful and brilliant, shining under the sun, waiting to board the ship.

My scar feels tighter than it should, pulling along my hairline, and the telltale throbbing starts the second I step down onto the dock. The corners of my vision are a bit fuzzy, and I know what science would say.

It's the sleepless night spent propped up against a wall. It's the dehydration from drinking more alcohol than I should have. It's the exposure to all that sunlight over the last seven days. It's the fact that I wasn't exactly keeping up with my medication regimen the way that I should have.

Those things are probably all true.

But they're not as true as what my heart says in my chest each time it beats.

It's the girl.

It's letting her go.

The wheels of her suitcase hit the worn wooden planks of the dock with a thud, and she looks up at me, the angles of her face soft, the freckles on her cheeks stark.

She blinks, shifting back and forth on her feet, and I don't think she realizes she's doing it, but she fiddles with the strap of her tank top, covering the tattoo. Uncovering it. She takes a shaky inhale, drops the strap—over the *B*—and reaches into her back pocket.

My cup ring sits in her outstretched palm.

"Sloan—" I start.

She scrunches her nose, shaking her head. "Take it. I definitely broke more rules than you."

I do take it. Not because she broke more rules than me—I broke the biggest ones of all—and not because I'm particularly interested in keeping it, but I'm selfish and I want to feel my skin touch hers one last time.

She shivers when my thumb scrapes along her palm.

I reach for my wallet, but she holds her hand up. "Keep the Polaroid. I hope one day I won't need it back."

I feel a bit like laughing—my prized possession I'd have died to keep, and now I'd trade it, willingly, for a time machine or one more chance to make things right.

She must see it in the lines of my face, because she tilts her head to the side, hair tumbling over her shoulder, and she winces, eyes darting around the dock like she's waiting for the bad thing to happen, and whispers, "I love you."

"I love you, too," I say, voice rough. I palm my jaw before grinning at her. "Never stopped. Never will. I'll be waiting for your pigeon, Zlatíčko."

She laughs—it catches on unshed tears, but she tips her head back, her eyes sparkle under the sun and her palm splays across the golden skin of her chest.

Time stops and I want to hold on to that sound for the rest of my life, but Tia steps down onto the dock beside her, nudging her shoulder. "Sloan, you ready?"

Sloan gives her a shallow nod, and she forces a bright smile when she hugs Talon and Jay goodbye.

Tia holds her arms outstretched, and she pops up onto her toes when she hugs me, whispering softly before she kisses my cheek, "Who knew your martyrdom could end up serving a purpose greater than your self-sacrifice?"

She pats the side of my face before she interlaces her fingers with Sloan's, and steers them both, luggage rolling along behind them, to the opposite end of the dock.

Sloan looks back once. She doesn't say anything, but she holds her hand up in a tiny wave.

I wait until she looks away before dropping my head back and staring up at the sun a bit too long.

"Sorry, Bohdan." Jay runs his thumb along the inside of his chain.

"No one to blame but myself for this one." I press my fingers to my forehead before scrubbing my face. "Sorry we ruined your cruise, Talon."

"You didn't. But, I am sorry your life got upended." Talon gives me a pinched smile, fiddling with fraying rope bracelets around his wrists. "Again."

I scoff, holding the ring up and spinning it around on my finger. The turquoise diamonds brighter when they catch in the sun. "Think I should pitch this into the water?"

"Jesus, Bohdan—no." Jay reaches out, snatching it off my finger and pocketing it. "You can have it back when you've regained your sanity."

"So, never then?" Talon taps his temple. "Head's scrambled on that one."

"Easy." I give him a flat look.

"Too soon?" Talon cringes before drumming his fingers against the hard shell of his giant suitcase. "What should we do tonight? Don't have to fly out until tomorrow. There's this boat you can have dinner on and watch the sunset—"

"No," Jay and I both speak, cutting him off.

Talon holds his hands up, exasperated. "Do you want me to see if I can get last-minute FC tickets? Friend of mine from Sweden plays for Barcelona."

They both turn to me, expectant.

"Yeah, alright." I nod. "That sounds okay."

Talon grins, knocking Jay on the shoulder. "Look at him, communicating his wants and needs already."

"He's got a long way to go if you count five words as communication," Jay murmurs, but he glances at me, a softer, rare, encouraging smile stretching across his face.

He's not wrong. I do have a long way to go.

"It's bright." Talon points up at the sun hanging in the sky before his thumbs start furiously moving across the screen of his phone. "Put your sunglasses on."

"Thanks, Dad," I mutter, and when I pull them from the neck of my shirt, I look back down the dock.

Tia and Sloan stopped about halfway down the cobblestone street. Sloan's crying—taking these giant, gasping inhales that Tia mirrors, hands planted firmly across each of Sloan's shoulders.

A line of lancing pain snakes down my scar. The muscles in my thighs twitch, ready to push past everyone still milling around as they exit the ship, ready to tear the world down to get to her—all those languages I learned to count to six in ready to roll off my tongue.

Tia turns her head, gaze catching mine, and even though she's too far away, she mouths something to me when she squeezes Sloan's shoulder.

It might be *I've got it* or *She's got it*, and either would be true.

Tia won't let anything happen to her.

I wish it was me walking away with Sloan.

But she's bigger and braver and better than she's ever believed and someday she won't need to count and she won't need facts and she won't need me—but I do hope when that day comes, she'll still want me.

Sloan

The first thing I do in my new apartment, tucked a few blocks away from the university—the converted main level of an old, creaky house with a front porch and features that add character at the cost of practicality—isn't have one of those nights you see in the movies.

The girl who realizes she needs to love herself first dances around her apartment, listening to music, and drinks cheap wine because she can't afford anything else.

I sit cross-legged on the floor, surrounded by stacks of boxes. I tug down the sleeves of an ancient sweater I'm wearing—it was one of Bohdan's in college, with a giant number seventeen painted on the back that started to peel over time—along with a pair of his socks that are almost worn through at the ankles, and I open my laptop to talk to my therapist for the first time in months.

"Hi." I lift my hand in a half-hearted wave when Lu blinks at me through the screen, chin propped up by her hand, fingers drumming along her skin. "Bet you thought you'd seen the last of me."

Lu arches a brow before giving me a look. "I actually wished I hadn't, Sloan."

"Well." I try to smile, but end up wiping away stray tears. "Here I am. Already crawling back to you."

She considers, black hair swinging across her shoulders. "You don't look like you're crawling. You look like you're in a beautiful apartment about to start a new job teaching something you used to dream about. You might be sitting on the floor, but I'd say you're actually standing quite tall, Sloan."

"I don't think I feel tall yet."

"You will." Her nose scrunches sympathetically, and when she leans forward in her chair, she feels so much closer even though she's miles away. "So, spill. What made you call? I gave you a list of therapists that practice in Toronto so you could do some of that important, in-person work you've been expertly avoiding."

I do laugh a bit this time, dragging a knuckle under each eye before straightening my shoulders. "I think I need someone who knows me. It was recently brought to my attention that you're my third-longest relationship. And seeing as one of those doesn't really exist anymore, at least, not the same way . . . I'd guess that makes you number two." I flash her two fingers in a sad attempt at deflection before blinking up at the intricate moulding carving along the ceiling and the slow, steady turn of the fan. "You remember Talon?"

Her smile pulls tight, but the tugging at the corners looks a bit like fondness. "How could I forget? He used to pick you up after sessions when you were in college and he'd ask to go through your file together because he thought he had some sage wisdom he could offer."

"I'd forgotten about that," I whisper. My smile *is* fond—and it doesn't hurt as much as it did before the cruise, to look back at the people we used to be.

"You have good friends, Sloan. People that love you." Lu nods before she sits back, picks up her clipboard and waits.

I tell her the whole thing in excruciating detail. And it is excruciating. It cuts me back open, my heart breaks and my ribs that used to be Bohdan's hands crack, and I think all of me spills onto the floor of this new apartment.

"What was that like?" Lu asks gently, blinking dark eyes at me. "Being with Bohdan again?"

"Wonderful." I don't bother to wipe away the tears. "But a bit like a reassurance, I think. When he left . . . it wasn't just about me as a person anymore." I gesture vaguely to my forehead, like Lu can see my brain sitting there on display. "It was all about my worthiness of being loved by him."

"Themes can switch." She nods thoughtfully, and she sees it on my face—the horror that he might become something I'll never, ever have again. "And they can switch back, and they can go away entirely. It's not forever, Sloan."

"Okay."

She keeps going. "What was that like, having your worst fear come true?"

"Horrible." I sniff a laugh.

"But you didn't run away. You didn't beg for reassurance or facts from Bohdan. Why?"

"I guess I just thought . . . wow, you've been right all along." I tap my forehead again. "For real this time, here's the evidence—he's on his knees on the balcony of this stupid suite and I just got so, so tired. I didn't really feel like fighting it anymore."

Lu nods, looking a bit proud. "That's not how I would describe it. It takes quite a bit of fortitude to sit with your discomfort. It sounds a bit like you practiced some ERP techniques all on your own. How'd that feel?"

"Awful, I don't want to do it again."

She laughs this time, head tipped back before she gives me a look that suggests I'll actually be sitting with my discomfort more often than not, and she asks me a question that seems obvious, but I've never really thought of it that way. "Before Bohdan loved you, did you love you?"

"Oh." I laugh, batting away the tears trailing down my cheeks. "No, not at all." Lu leans forward, dark hair obscuring her face when she scribbles along her clipboard, and my eyes go wide when this horrible new fear wakes up. "Do you think that means we can never be together again?"

Her nostrils flare and her lips purse. An expertly drawn brow rises on her forehead like she's not going to answer because she can see my brain, ready and waiting. But she does, and I know it's going to be the last time I hear her say it. "No. I don't think living with or experiencing any form of mental health challenges precludes two people from having a very happy—very healthy—relationship." Her pen hits the edge of her clipboard. "But I think we've got a lot of work to do before you can be, and so does he. Okay?"

I imagine a me gathering up all the contents of my chest spilled out there on the floor. I imagine that me kissing the broken hands that used to be ribs and whispering thank you. I imagine a me that leaves them there and gets to work repairing all the cartilage and things that live in her own chest.

I nod. "Okay."

Bohdan

When the doorbell rings and I notice it's 11:13 p.m., I have a fleeting, dumb—painful—thought that it might be Sloan.

That she flew here from Toronto and found herself outside the door of my apartment in Brooklyn.

That she's ready and still loves me and still wants me.

I'll have to explore that one in therapy tomorrow, because it's only been a few months since the cruise, and I just abandoned packing halfway through so I could look at old pictures of us.

Even if she was ready, I'm certainly fucking not, and she deserves the best version of me.

That thought lives with every single step I take down the hall though, because hope is a powerful thing, but it dies a quick death and I flatten my hair down over my scar to stop the phantom twinge when I open the door and see Tia Valdez standing there.

"What are you doing here? It's late." I glance over my shoulder as she follows me into the apartment, arms crossed and eyes wandering around, appraising everything.

"I just finished work." Tia gestures vaguely to the paned windows lining the loft, like I'd be able to see her office on Wall Street all the way from here. She studies the winking lights of Manhattan stretching out just across the river, angling her head back and forth. She whistles, tapping the edge of a box with the pointed toe of her heel. "Quite the view you've got, Novotnak. How come we never hung out here?"

"You wouldn't have crossed the Brooklyn Bridge."

"I happen to love Brooklyn. You just . . . disappeared for a little while." She gives me a knowing look that's a bit sad before gesturing to all the boxes scattered around the apartment. "What's all this?"

"Trying to figure out my next move."

Her eyebrows knit together. "I saw you on TV last week. It's always such a joy for me when you commentate on Jay's games, actually."

"Yeah. I turned down the whole network thing, but I'm doing the occasional guest spot. I don't hate it." I swallow before deciding to try opening up a bit. "I spend most of my time with my psychiatrist, though."

"How's that going for you?" she asks, head tipping thoughtfully.

"It's not the hardest thing I've ever done," I say honestly.

"I'd guess not." She smiles, but it doesn't quite meet her eyes.

"You can yell at me," I offer.

She blinks, confused. "Why would I do that?"

"Because you never have." I shrug, dropping down onto the couch.

"Bohds . . ." Her voice softens, she presses a hand to her cheek before she folds herself down beside me, grabbing one of mine and interlacing our fingers. "I *was* mad at you. I am still, a bit. But I don't . . . blame you. I just wish you'd talked to us. Told us how bad it really was. Talon would have flown home from Sweden in a heartbeat. Jay would have been there every day he could. I'd have transferred to a West Coast office without a second thought. We all love you, you know?" She squeezes my hand, and a single tear escapes down her cheek. "You're ours to protect, just like Sloan is."

I nod, gripping my jaw before I swallow heavy and ask, "How's she doing?"

"Good. I know you're not a big socials guy, but she posts sometimes. Look—she went with us, Suny, and Mateo when Jay was playing Toronto." Tia plucks her phone out of her purse, flashing a picture of Sloan, sitting in arena seats just like I've seen her a million times, smiling and happy between Jay's dads, Tia and Talon flanking either side.

There's a dull throb along my hairline, and I can feel my heart in my throat. "She looks beautiful."

"Always does." Tia nods, dropping her phone back into her purse. She looks around, lip curling back when she sees the mess I've made. "You want some help packing?"

"Yeah. Alright."

She points a manicured finger at me. "I charge though."

I give her a dry grin. "Think I can afford it."

"You answer one question about your feelings per box." She straightens her shoulders, throwing me a smile that's mostly teeth and makes her look like an exact replica of her brother.

"Oh, come on." I raise a hand, and I laugh for the first time in a long time. It feels a bit hoarse, and it sounds strange, echoing through the half-empty apartment. But it doesn't hurt.

She gives me a pointed look before snapping her fingers. "Let's get to work, Novotnak."

Sloan

Time passes in these funny little chunks when you're healing.

You go forward. You go backward. Sometimes, you stay still.

I sit with my discomfort. I mother it, the way my mother never really managed to mother me.

I start a new medication, and I don't hate it.

I let myself be sensitive. It might be a superpower like Bohdan said, after all.

I let things be too loud and too big and too much. I pop in my earplugs when they are.

Months go by and the seasons bleed.

The leaves on campus sprout—bright and green and beautiful. They fade under the autumn sun and they fall off, golden, but floating back down to the earth. They get covered in giant, fluffy snowflakes that make the world go quiet.

My students wish me a good winter break, and one of them gives me a book I haven't read on the earliest records of psychiatric practices across civilizations.

Jay flies up from Philadelphia to put up my Christmas tree with me before a road trip. His dads take me out for dinner when they come to see the Nutcracker on New Year's Eve.

Bohdan's grandparents send me a birthday card.

Tia watches reality TV with me over FaceTime. She gets more into it than me and we buy tickets too many live recap podcast shows.

Talon stays on my couch for what's supposed to be a month but turns into two when he meets a professional golfer named Gavin and falls in love. Talon Valdez in love is a really special thing to witness, and I don't tell him because it would go to his head—but I think it helps form new pathways in my brain and one of the ribs in my chest belongs to him now.

I practice saying I love you. I try it out on Gavin first when he brings me coffee cake from a new bakery down the street because I'm grading and couldn't meet him there. I say it casually, tossing the words out there, not even in a full sentence—just "love" and "you." He ruffles my hair and he smiles.

Nothing bad happens, so I practice more and more.

And one night while the snow melts and the world outside shifts to spring again, when missing him and loving him feels so much more like joy than it does pain, I send a text message.

> **Sloan:** Hi.

> **Bohdan:** Hey.

Sloan

"This guy has got to leave the villa," Tia moans, waving her wineglass around. Through the computer screen, I see some splash over the rim, falling down and seemingly landing on her keyboard. She tips her head back with a tiny shriek of frustration, batting at it.

"I like him." Talon shrugs, tossing one arm over the back of his couch.

"You would." Jay rolls his eyes, tugging up the thighs of his compression boots and stretching his legs out across his couch.

"I regret inviting you to join our weekly reality television FaceTimes." I try to glare at them all, but I think it gets lost because the quality of four-way video calls really declines when the screens are so much smaller than usual.

Talon pulls his head back, affronted. His eyes narrow before they go wide at something on his phone.

I'm not sure what he could possibly be looking at—it's not a very riveting episode.

I usually turn my phone on do not disturb when we do this. I did today, too, because I'm trying not to check for texts from Bohdan. We talk a bit each day, and it's an exercise for me not to answer right away.

Talon clears his throat. "Anything interesting happen today, Sloany? Like, anyone come to your door?"

"No?" I frown.

"Like . . . any solicitors? Nothing?" He shrugs again, bottom lip extending.

"The last solicitor I had was *you* and you wouldn't leave my house for two months."

"You get weird when Gavin's on the tour." Tia gives her brother an exasperated look before tugging on a loose curl.

Jay exhales, brow pinching together. "Check your texts, Tia."

She purses her lips and makes a big show of straightening her shoulders, finger poised and ready to flick through her phone. Her eyes go wide. "Oh. Sloan, we have to go."

They all hang up at the same time, leaving me staring at my own reflection on the screen alone. Bewildered and blinking.

It's my turn to be affronted when I text our group chat—it has a stupid name that doesn't even make sense, courtesy of Talon. *Reality TV Real Ones.*

Sloan: What the hell?

Jay: Sorry. Proud of you, though. Keep up the hard work.

Tia: I love you.

Talon: You're welcome.

He follows that up with a giant, exaggerated winking emoji.

My brain doesn't even have time to whir to life to start telling me they all obviously got sick of me—it's a bit slower with those types of thoughts these days—because there's a knock on my door.

Slow. Measured. Steadfast.

I know exactly who it belongs to before I even open the door.

Golden-brown hair, a bit darker than usual because the sun's only just started to shine again, pushed back off his forehead, the faded pink scar snaking across his temple on display for the world to see. A light dusting of stubble he doesn't usually have carving across the planes of his face. Grey eyes like an early-morning sky when the day hasn't started yet so it can be anything at all. Navy long-sleeved shirt pushed up his forearms, ropes and cords of muscles traipsing across them, and the *S* at the precipice of his left elbow, a bit faded from time but still there.

Permanent.

My heart stirs in my chest, very much awake. It sits, beating a bit too fast at the sight of him, protected by ribs and cartilage of my own making and gifts from the people who love me.

"Got your carrier pigeon." Bohdan cocks his head, tossing his phone in the air once and catching it.

"Oh." I breathe, running a palm across my chest. "They move a lot faster than they used to, what with modern technology and all."

"They do." He nods thoughtfully before tipping his chin over my shoulder to my kitchen, visible just down the hallway. "Fridge is looking pretty plain, Zlatíčko."

"I don't have any art worth hanging up yet."

His full lips slant into a frown. "Can I interest you in some?"

"Yes, please," I whisper.

He pulls it from his back pocket—I know what it is by the size and shape of it—but it's wrapped in something.

Paper that's been folded time and time again, frayed a bit around the edges just like the Polaroid.

My fingers tremble, and I'm not sure if it's from his eyes on me after months and months, or if it's this new, blooming feeling in my chest.

Happiness. Excitement. A bit of trepidation, but there's really nothing to be afraid of anymore.

The picture of me, smudged and blurred now, almost worn through, sits in the middle of a certificate.

Certificate of Qualification
This is to verify that Bohdan Novotnak has satisfactorily communicat-
ed about his thoughts, feelings, needs, and wants in accordance with the
Statutes of the Province of Ontario.

"Did you make this?" Laughter bubbles in my throat, I try to angle my shoulder to wipe the tears away. But Bohdan beats me to it, a singular thumb swiping across my cheek.

"No." He presses his thumb against each of my freckles before he reaches forward, tapping a stamp on the corner of the certificate. "My psychiatrist did. He wasn't super keen on the idea because he says it's lifelong work, but I won in the end."

"You always do," I murmur fondly, my eyes finding the stamp. It's from the university hospital. My heart plummets, but not into nothing.

Not into this pit of despair that used to live in my stomach. Into every good feeling I think there's ever been. "This says—"

"I moved here six months ago." He keeps his eyes on me when he says it.

"You came."

"I said I would. There are psychiatrists and neurologists all over the world. There's only one you." The left corner of his mouth lifts with his brows. "Been to your class a few times. No one's ever looked more beautiful holding up an ugly, misshapen pot that was used for bloodletting back in the day."

My chest constricts. "I never noticed you."

"It's a big lecture hall," he says with a hint of pride.

"It is." I nod softly.

Bohdan takes a measured step forward, across the trench between us we've both started to fill, and he lands safely on the other side, here in the doorway of this apartment with me. His eyes pinch, lines dig in around the corners like the years between us but neither of us fall in, and his voice cracks. "I'm all healed up now. Can I come home?"

"I think it's going to be a lot of work." I press the certificate and Polaroid right above my heart.

He nods again, thoughtful, but a real grin—corporeal, not a ghost, not a shadow—carves across his face. "Yeah. That's alright. Looking forward to it, actually."

"Me too," I whisper.

And I am. Very much so.

His thumb swipes across my cheek one more time before it travels across my jaw, whispering over my lips, and his fingers tangle in my hair at the nape of my neck.

He doesn't count my freckles. I don't need him to, and I don't want him to.

Bohdan angles his head down, his mouth hovering just over mine. He speaks, words low, vibrating with promise, and they breathe new air into my lungs. "You'd spend the rest of your life working on building a whole new home with some guy?"

My lips meet his and the words might get lost when our mouths slot together, a brand-new piece to a brand-new puzzle, but I think he hears them anyway. "Only ever you."

Bohdan

Three Months Later

"Gavin can't be our first guest."

"And why not, Jay?" Talon gives him a contemptuous look, getting a bit too close to his own computer.

Jay flicks his hand, like he can wave Talon off through his screen. "It feels a bit like . . . nepotism, I don't know."

I lean back in my chair. "That doesn't exactly fit the definition of nepotism."

"I said I didn't know!" Jay throws his hands in the air before giving me a sarcastic thumbs-up. "Hey, great guest spot covering the game last night, by the way. Real riveting television."

I arch a brow. "It was the most boring game I've ever seen in my life. I didn't have a lot to work with. What did you want me to do?"

He runs an absentminded hand through his hair. "I don't know—talk a bit more? Haven't you been working on that for like a year?"

"It was boring because I wasn't playing." Talon flashes us both a grin.

Jay opens his mouth like he's about to argue when the door to this makeshift office I've made in our apartment while the three of us try to sort this out creaks open.

"Hi." Sloan peeks her head around it, fingers curling against the edges of the wood.

My eyes skate over them—I see her thumb twitch, but she doesn't start tapping.

"Sloany!" Talon's grin grows, and he waves his hand in invitation. "Come settle a debate for us. We're trying to decide on our first guest. Jay says it should be our coach from MSU, but I think it should be Gavin."

She doesn't. She widens her eyes at Talon before folding herself down in my lap, hands interlacing around the back of my neck.

"Hey." I brush my mouth against hers.

"Hi," she whispers back.

I hear Talon. "Oh. They're ignoring us."

"It's just like college," Jay echoes.

I still love her in that giant way I did when I was twenty, but it's not really like college.

Not at all.

Sloan tips her head. "We have to leave for therapy in forty-five minutes."

My eyes cut to the time displayed across the corner of my computer screen. "Shit, okay. I didn't notice the time. I'll be out in a second."

She presses her mouth to mine again, fingers twirling in the hair at the nape of my neck before she pulls back, hops off my lap, and holds her hand up in goodbye.

Talon waves, a bit manically, craning his neck until he notices the door close. "Therapy? I thought you guys both just went? I keep tabs on your schedules, you know."

He does. They're taped to his fridge.

I shrug a shoulder. "Yeah. We did. But we're going to couples once a month."

"Everything okay?" Concern darkens Jay's eyes, visible even through the screen.

I nod. "All good."

"Seat belts are on, though?" Talon knocks his fist against his desk. "I can fly down at a moment's notice, you know. I miss your couch. It's comfortable."

"Seat belts are on." I resist rolling my eyes at the dumb phrase he coined to make sure Sloan and I were each taking care of our mental health—meds, therapy, communication. "Tia's coming up this weekend. Your services won't be needed, thanks though."

Talon nods in approval before holding his arms open. "If that's the case, this first meeting of *The Only Podcast to Ever Exist* is officially adjourned."

I think I hear Jay saying that can't possibly be the name when I hang up and follow after Sloan.

She sits, propped up on the kitchen counter, legs swinging so her feet bump against the cupboards. She raises her eyebrows at me, words catching on barely suppressed laughter. "I can't believe he convinced you to start a podcast."

"I think he's bored," I tell her, coming to stand between her legs, palms lying flat against her thighs.

"Why, because he's a kept man now that he's with someone who makes more money as a professional golfer than he ever did playing hockey in Sweden?" She rolls her eyes, looking a bit more beautiful than she should when she's being ornery.

I grin, gripping her chin and tilting her head up so I can get a better look at the freckles painted across her cheek. Still the brightest stars in any sky. "I don't think anyone can really *keep* Talon Valdez."

"You can keep me, if you want." She blinks up at me.

"Yeah?" I ask, and she nods with a tiny smile that I lean down to kiss. "I think I will."

Sloan

Six Months Later

I think my favourite thing about getting to spend four weeks watching students dig in the dirt—supervised by professionals, obviously—isn't even the fact that I got my own hands dirty.

It's not that it's this thing I got to do all for myself, and I got to spend hours and days learning and having interesting conversations about all sorts of anthropological theories.

It's not even that I worried significantly less than usual while I was gone.

It's coming home to a quiet house with a quiet brain. But it's not the kind of silence that used to scare me.

Bohdan's eyes flick up when I knock softly on the doorframe. A smile spreads across his face, and he tosses the folded paperback in his hands haphazardly onto the nightstand beside the bed where it skids to a stop, teetering on the edge. "How was it?"

I practically sprint across the floor so I can sit in bed beside him, bouncing onto my side with a childlike exuberance I don't think I possessed even back then. "Really good. I think the students had a lot of fun."

"Did anyone find anything?" He rests his head in one hand propped up against the headboard, arm stretching behind him, the muscles along his biceps and triceps tugging taut.

"No." I frown, crossing my arms.

"Chin up, baby. There's always next time. When do you supervise again?"

"I have the three-week session in British Columbia in the fall."

The lines of his mouth slip into a lazy grin. "Fingers crossed for an ugly mug or something then."

I roll my eyes, pushing at his shoulder even though he doesn't move an inch, before I brush his hair off his forehead, all mussed from sleep and hiding the scar he doesn't mind keeping on display anymore. "How was your head while I was gone? The new pills?"

His specialist put him on something new—a CGRP receptor blocker. It's supposed to help with migraine prevention. Bohdan leans into my hand, and I drag my thumb down the bridge of his nose before letting it rest in the centre of his lip. He bites at it before nodding. "Really fucking good, actually. I think I only had one episode the entire time you were gone."

"Did you skate at all?" I ask. It's been a big topic of conversation with his psychiatrist. How to reclaim pieces of the him he used to be without tumbling back in time.

He nods. There's a tiny twinge of something that used to be pain in his smile, but it looks a bit more like wistfulness now. "Yeah, when Jay was in town. During their practice. It was fun to be on a pro-level rink again."

"What else did you do?" I sit up straight, brushing a hand along the pop of muscle on his shoulder, down his carved chest.

He inhales sharply when my fingers graze his skin. "I went up to Uxbridge with Gavin to golf. Talon's not in town. There's a course up there where all the holes are mirrored after famous ones from around the world."

"The retired professional hockey player turned golfer? What a cliché you are." I paint my hand down the ridges of his stomach, fingers toying with the elastic stretching taught across the V of muscle dipping there. "No raccoon shirt?"

"Sorry. Fresh out of vermin clothes. I'll leave those to you." He grins but it quickly shifts when my hand skates across the length of him, straining against the fabric of his shorts.

"Did you miss me?" I whisper.

"Can't you tell?" He presses against my palm.

I blink, sliding my hand across him again. "You want to make love?"

"Make love?" He gives me a flat look, but he rolls his shoulders back, exhaling loudly.

"Sex, but make it romantic. Proper." I tip my chin up. "You know, the way we would when you'd get home from all those long road trips."

His fingers wrap around my wrist, stilling my hand. His eyes darken and his voice turns to gravel. "How about I just fuck you senseless?"

"Indecent." I purse my lips.

"Zlatíčko," he warns when I try to move my hand again.

My grip tightens, and he loses his restraint quickly.

He sits up, too fast for me to stop him, but I shriek, laughing, when he flips us over and pins me beneath him on our bed.

One of his knees knocks my thighs apart, and he swallows the sound I make when he angles his hips down, right against the centre of me.

His tongue slides against mine, his teeth dig into my bottom lip, his hands—rough and warm and *his*—strip off my clothes, and each messy, too-hurried moment says the same thing—*I missed you.*

He spends a bit of time trailing kisses down my neck, biting where it meets my shoulder, tongue swirling across my chest, tugging each nipple between his teeth and kissing away the hurt while his fingers make small circles between my legs that have me panting.

"I love you," he groans into my neck when his fingers, soaked with me, move to my leg, splaying against my thigh and lifting it when he angles his hips, moving so he's finally inside me.

"I love you, too." I say it back like a reflex, something you don't even think about. Certainly not something that hurts.

His forehead rests against mine, breathing ragged, and then his hands are on my hips, flipping us over again so I'm on top of him.

"Fuck." Bohdan drops his head against the pillow, eyes closing, lines of his neck tense. His thumbs dig into my hips, bruising, as he moves them in time with his.

I tip my head back, a moan catching in my throat, and my nails dig into his chest.

I hear these words he says: my name like something he's prayed for his entire life, krásná and dokonalá over and over again.

And for the first time, I think those things about me, too.

He comes when I do—it takes a bit longer sometimes because of the medication I'm on. He waits for me like he promised he would sitting in the hallway of that ship that changed the trajectory of our lives.

I nestle beside him, head angling into his neck where I can feel his pulse move in time with his heart.

"I can't imagine my life without you. Not getting to meet and know every single version of you." He presses his mouth roughly to my forehead, and his thumb travels across my shoulder in wide strokes. My fingers tap against the planes of his stomach.

But I don't count them.

"Me either." I angle my chin up to look at him, smiling softly.

And I do know him.

Him then and him now, the way he knows me then and me now.

It can be a bit tempting to go back in time, I think. Sometimes, when I look at him, it feels easy. I see him the way I did then—young and too serious for his age, full of dreams and life and promise. Or sometimes, I look and I see him as a shadow. Those feel like the most dangerous steps backward.

But I'm not particularly interested in taking them.

There's no one I'd rather be than someone loved by him, and there's no brain I'd rather have than the one that brought me here.

He looks a bit young right now, under the moonlight streaming in from the window, sweaty and spent and so in love, and I could pretend to be the us we were, and I feel the twitch of my feet, a bit tempted to be in two places at once.

But this is my favourite place we've ever been, here and now. And even though it's hard sometimes, I think I'll stay.

Acknowledgements

There are so many people to thank in the acknowledgements section of a book, and I can usually go on and on in mine—but I want to start with the two people who got me here.

Bohdan and Sloan, you might be fictional, but you aren't really, not to me. You sprouted in my brain and you poked through the soil, but then you (stubbornly) didn't want to come any further. I had to dig and dig and dig to get to you. It wasn't a pleasant experience, but you challenged me as an author and as an artist, and while I was digging, absolutely covered in dirt and holding tiny green fragments of you up in triumph when I'd finally unearth them—you helped me grow. And what a privilege that is, to be able to learn from the art you create. It was one of those things I didn't recognize as such at the time, but I think I'm a better writer for it, and I'll never be thankful enough.

To the people who quite literally pulled me along when I was kicking and screaming and trying to dig my feet into the ground of "I can't do this": Benjamin, Esther, Emma, Brooke, Amber, and my Spice

Girls—you didn't let me give up and you always believed in me when I didn't believe in myself.

To my alpha and beta readers: Esther, Becca, Christina, Mary, Natalie, Brooke, Emma, Madeleine, Sophie, and Amber—thank you so much. You helped me shape Bohdan and Sloan when I was struggling with them, and I'm forever grateful you gave me your minds, your time, your energy and your support.

Summer, thank you for turning my stick figures into this cover. I'm not sure how you do what you do, but you've got a beautiful and talented mind.

Briana, thank you for your skills and your attention to detail. I'm lucky to have you as an editor.

To anyone who has ever picked up one of my books and given them a chance, you keep me (and all the other authors you read) going.

And thank you to you, for sticking with Bohdan, Sloan, and me, until the very end.

xoxo,

Haley

More by Haley Warren

About the author

Haley is an almost-academic who traded peer-reviewed manuscripts for stories about flawed people falling in love.

A big fan of her dog, horror movies with a splash of comedy, and the millennial peace sign, Haley is usually researching her next travel destination, consuming urban fantasies (give her a magical school or a vampire with a cellphone any day of the week), and concocting the most gut-wrenching scenes she can drag a reader through on their way to a HEA while she does reformer Pilates.

Self-deprecating to a fault, Haley actually wants nothing more than for her readers to find a home for all their flaws, mistakes, and baggage in her characters so they realize that they, too, deserve a love the likes of which could only be found in a book.